SHADOW
OF A
SHADOW

SHADOW OF A SHADOW

A LYDIA TWOMEY THRILLER

CRISPIN KEITH

The Book Guild Ltd

First published in Great Britain in 2023 by
The Book Guild Ltd
Unit E2 Airfield Business Park,
Harrison Road, Market Harborough,
Leicestershire. LE16 7UL
Tel: 0116 2792299
www.bookguild.co.uk
Email: info@bookguild.co.uk
Twitter: @bookguild

Typeset in 11pt Minion Pro

Printed and bound in Great Britain by 4edge Limited

ISBN 978 1915603 883

British Library Cataloguing in Publication Data.
A catalogue record for this book is available from the British Library.

Many thanks to
Genevieve Pentelow, Jan Carr and Jo King

BY THE SAME AUTHOR

Cyan Blue: Lee Turner Thriller 1
Present Tense: Lee Turner Thriller 2
Bleak Down: Lee Turner Thriller 3
The Babel Switch: Lee Turner Thriller 4
Hydra: Lee Turner Thriller 5
Donalbain [Sequel to Macbeth]
The Last Lobster and other stories
A Change of Scene: The Adventures of Hilton Keith
Self: a biography of Claude Keith
A Teacher's Guide to Using Listed Buildings

MI5 CAST LIST

Name	AKA (nickname)	Role
Martin Froome	Luther	Shift Manager, H11
Lydia Twomey	Schizo	Investigating Officer, Internal Security
Peregrine Webb	Perry	Commander, Internal Security of MI5
Miss Parmenter		Personal Assistant, Internal Security
Adam Thornton	DG	Director-General, MI5
Gerard Bell	The Dong	Commander, H11
Maureen (Mo) Dennis	Farah	Admin Assistant, H11
Dennis Dunn	Double D, Piggy	Archivist, H11
Maggie Willis	Maybe	Admin Assistant, H11
Maddy King	George	Archivist, H11
Damian Curry	Vindi	Shift Manager, H11
Brian Powell	Nylon	Technician, H11
Ashar Chowdry		Investigating Officer, Internal Security
Jon Small		Investigating Officer, Internal Security
Miles Mason	Perma-tan Man	Commander, Special Operations, MI5
Ian Forrester	Marcus Forrest	Freelancer Agent, Special Operations
Mark Longford		Agent, Special Operations
Darren Holmes	The cabbie	Agent, Special Operations

1

MARTIN

Martin Froome paused before he switched on his hall light. He always paused at this juncture. It was part of the training: listen, smell, notice – even feel, if you could, any difference in your home. Reach out with your senses. If any aspect, however small, was even just a tiny bit off, step back through your front door, close it and contact your manager.

He switched on the hall light.

All that training: it was bollocks, of course. They told you it could save your life if some foreign agent or some opportunist burglar was waiting for you, but he'd been going through this routine for over twenty years now and all it had done for him was to make him thoroughly paranoid.

Well, he was over it now. In his early days in the service, he'd thought he was frightfully important and that the stuff he carried in his head was vital to every enemy of the state. But now… why was he thinking about all this? Because…

He turned right into his kitchenette and plonked the reusable plastic Waitrose bag on the black stone effect laminate work surface. It gave a satisfying clank. A jar of Loyd Grosman

Puttanesca sauce (half price), spinach and ricotta fresh tortelloni (half price), a ciabatta loaf (60% off in the rotting section), and a very nice bottle of Nero d'Avola (£3 off). All those savings had virtually paid for the bottle of vodka. Add the DVD box set of Sons of Anarchy and his evening was all set up.

He opened the fridge, then paused.

Why had he been thinking about the entrance routine?

Because… because something was different this time.

Not the sound – the humming of the fridge, *The One Show* on TV in the flat below (deaf bastards), the rumbling of traffic on the Kennington Road; they were all normal. Not the smell – the wine he'd spilt on the carpet last week and the cleaner he'd used to get rid of the stain, the iffy odour from the kitchen sink.

So the 'feel' – how was it different? No, it was the smell… a new smell… peppermint? Can't stand peppermint…

A shadow on the fridge door.

A sharp prick like a bee sting in the back of his neck.

He would have fallen face first into his fridge if he hadn't been caught gently round his armpits.

"Thanks, mate," he mumbled.

It was all very confusing: his legs had given way and he had no idea who had saved him from falling into his fridge and he wondered if it was a dream and he was afraid he was going to pee himself and his head was swimming and he was losing consciousness and whoever had saved him would think he was drunk and then word would get back to work and and and and…

A final devastating moment of clarity: I'm going to die, he thought.

He was correct.

2

LYDIA

"I've got a temporary posting for you, Lydia."

"Thank you, sir." She kept her tone neutral, but she didn't expect it to be good news. She told herself they don't send MI5 officers to Afghanistan.

"Yes, I thought it would be a good idea if you had a cooling-off period from Internal Security. This will be a good opportunity for you to develop new facets of your skills." Peregrine Webb kept his blue eyes firmly on the middle distance, somewhere over the Thames towards the office blocks of Lambeth.

"I see, sir." What she meant was: look at me when you're flushing my career down the toilet, you cowardly bastard. "Why?"

"Well…" Webb paused, weighing his words carefully. "You're thirty years old, you've proved yourself to be very bright and combative, you've been with us ever since you left university – which university was it?"

"Birmingham." Not Oxbridge.

"That's right, Birmingham. Splendid place – terrific clock-tower. Yes, well, you've shown signs of needing new challenges lately."

"What signs are those?" She sat up straight in the high-backed chair placed in front of Webb's desk. Even so, she had to look up at him – his swivel chair had been jacked up just enough to enable him to look down his nose at all those who had to sit before him, should he deign to look them in the face.

"I'm transferring you to H11." Webb's voice hardened. He wasn't going to be pushed. His aquiline features remained resolutely in profile.

"What signs, sir? It would be helpful for my career development..."

Webb used the political tactic – ignoring the question and repeating himself. "I'm transferring you to H11."

"Where's that, sir?" The Outer Hebrides? The maximum security wing at Rampton? Middlesborough? No, not Middlesborough, please!

"It's less than fifty yards as the crow flies from where we sit now." Webb gave a little laugh. "Except, of course, a crow can't fly under the ground."

"So it's in the basement of this building. What is H11, if I might ask?" A torture dungeon? The chapel? The cleaner's cupboard?

"Don't worry – I'm not seconding you to anything dangerous or unpleasant. H11 is essentially a filing department."

She was going to be punished by stultifying boredom, then – something even more mind-numbing than her present assignment scrolling through the social media accounts of the most recent batch of graduate recruits to MI5.

"That's a shame," she said. "So what does a filing department need with a highly trained special investigator like me? And how come I haven't heard of H11?" She was aware her voice was rising and her chin was jutting aggressively towards her boss, but as long as she stayed cool and professional, she didn't have to give him an easy ride.

"It's completely hush-hush. I needed someone with the Triple A security rating, and you have it. You'd be surprised at just how rare that rating is. You're a major asset to this department, Lydia, and I will always look after your interests." Webb tore his eyes from the view of the Thames, and fixed Lydia with one of the self-deprecating, lopsided smiles he used far too often for it to have any credibility.

Lydia failed to melt. "What does H11 stand for?"

"It doesn't stand for anything. In World War I, when they invented a new weapon they called it a tank – a deliberately anodyne but meaningless word to mislead German spies. H11 stands for nothing."

"What's the nature of these hush-hush files?"

"H11 houses documentary evidence of all the murkiest secrets our nation wants to keep safe."

"I thought that was done in Minus Two, with Section D holding the back-up."

"Aha!" Webb smiled broadly, as if he was being clever. "You're right: Section D shadows Minus Two, but H11 is the shadow of the shadow." He chuckled at his clever description. "You'll be working within the shadow of a shadow."

"We need that many layers, do we?" Lydia found herself getting interested, despite her determination to stay cool and detached.

"Well, H11 stores data in a different way from the others."

"How?"

"It has no digital access. It is disconnected from any computer anywhere in the world, including all computers in our own service. It's one hundred percent insulated from any would-be hackers; such insulation is known as an air gap. Most of the records in H11 are kept as physical artefacts – on paper, on analogue recording tape or reels of film. It houses the most sensitive data that cannot be trusted even to Minus Two or Section D. Even I have no idea what is down there. You can understand why anyone who goes down there has to have a Triple A clearance."

"What's the point of holding information that nobody, even top MI5 bods like you, knows exist?"

Webb bridled. He obviously didn't like being termed a 'bod'. "That's not for you to know or for me to say."

"And why do you need to send someone into this most inaccessible place, sir?"

"Oh, it's just routine – you know, protocol." He waved his hand. "Given the sensitivity of the department, if any staff members die whilst working for H11, we have to investigate it, both inside the department and outside it. Someone has died. You'll replace the dead man until they get a replacement, and at the same time you'll investigate his death – if there's anything to investigate." Webb sounded just a little too casual and airy.

"So just how did this man die on the job – savaged by a box file?"

"Good pun, Lydia. He died on the job – not at work, but at home. Auto-asphyxiation." Webb sat back, clasping his hands on the desk. Now he looked unbearably smug. "It seems our man Martin Froome was decidedly kinky."

"Go on."

"Well, I'm sure you know all about auto-eroticism, even though you don't practice it yourself."

"I assume you've checked."

"Of course, but it's not one for the ladies, really. It seems our Mr Froome was pleasuring himself by three quarterly throttling himself with a noose attached to his bedroom door, and unfortunately went the extra quarter. Sexual paraphernalia found adjacent to the body. No suspicious circumstances beyond that. No forensic evidence of anyone else having been in his flat for at least a fortnight."

"If you've got a file on my sexual habits, then you've got one on his, too. Yet he must have had a Triple A security rating to work in H11. Why wasn't this auto-eroticism picked up?"

Webb shrugged. "He had no known sex life at all. He was a loner. He drank alone. A bit weird, but then most H11 staff are a bit weird. Anyway, having sex with oneself is hardly a security risk, is it? Quite the opposite: it's seen as very positive in security vetting."

"CCTV on the night of his death?"

"We're chasing it up, but you needn't worry your head about the external stuff. Your job is to be inside H11, investigating from within. The less you know about the case the better, really. Keep an open mind. If they know you're investigating the death his colleagues may clam up."

"So how long do I have to stay buried in the bowels of the basement?"

"Not long – until Froome's successor is appointed. As I said, we're not treating the death as suspicious. It's just routine protocol, ticking boxes. Of course, if something comes up, then it will be a huge career opportunity for you. I mean, you've been spending a lot of time recently on routine vetting. This could be a breath of fresh air for you."

"In the basement. Thank you, sir. I really appreciate your interest in my career."

Webb had the decency to look sheepish, but shook it off quickly. "Now, you need to get on with things: there's a paper file in my PA's office. You need to read it under Miss Parmenter's supervision, internalise it, and then destroy it under her supervision as per regulations. It'll tell you all about your role while you're seconded to H11. Of course, you are not to breathe a word of this to anyone else. I'm afraid there's a fairly lengthy list of restrictions for anyone working in H11, but you'll only be there for a few days. Or so. Probably. You report to H11 at 9.30 tomorrow morning. Any questions?"

"No, sir."

"Chop chop, then."

Actually, she had a whole list of questions, a veritable burning raft of them, but now wasn't the moment. She looked up at the portrait of the Queen circa 1977 that hung behind Webb's head, got up from her chair, and left his office.

3

LYDIA

"So you found us, then, love?" The grey-haired woman behind the reinforced glass screen beamed at her.

Lydia had to bite back a retort; what kind of moron couldn't find her way to a department in a building she'd called her workplace for the last eight years? Admittedly, she'd had to ask her way once on the way down, and she'd already had to submit to an iris recognition scan, but she was a grown-up.

"Yes, thank you. No problems."

"Welcome to the House of Fun, Ms Twomey. You may not have been briefed on all our security arrangements. When I buzz you through the door you'll find a locker room, except there are no lockers, ha ha. You need to leave all your bags, electronic devices including mobile phone, your very nice leather jacket, your motorbike helmet – in fact, anything other than your basic clothes – on a bench in plain sight of the cameras. The briefing papers ought to have stated that you should not wear clothes with pockets while in H11." The lady looked at Lydia's jeans. "But we won't make you take them off today."

"Too right you won't."

"Unless you lose a game of forfeits, ha ha."

"You what?"

Lydia's outrage was cut off by the buzz and the security door sliding open. She stepped forward into a small room with benches round the walls. On the benches were three neat piles of personal effects – two male, one female.

She sat down on the bench and shut her eyes. She hadn't made a great start. The lady was obviously just joking, and Lydia had taken the bait. Ease your way in. Behave yourself. Enjoy meeting new people. Put on your imaginary Raspberry Beret and charm the socks off everyone.

She took her phone from her pocket, took off her beloved studded leather jacket, and placed them with her motorbike helmet beside her on the bench.

"Ready to come through, love?" The lady's voice came from a speaker on the wall.

With a sigh, Lydia got to her feet. "Yes."

The door at the far side of the room slid open and she stepped into an office unlike any that she had seen before. It was festooned with an amazing display, a riot of red, orange, purple and yellow silk flowers in bright blue vases along the filing shelves, sprouting from behind a large photocopier and arrayed across the desk at which the grey-haired lady sat. There was a cloying smell of lilacs, presumably from a spray; it was like a tart's boudoir, but impressive all the same.

It wouldn't do her any harm to show a bit of enthusiasm. "Wow! Is this Elton John's dressing room?"

"Helps make a windowless basement a bit brighter, eh? Against all regulations, of course." The lady got up and pushed back her swivel chair. She was wearing pink beach shorts and a summer blouse emblazoned with poppies. "Welcome, love. Come and sit down with me, if you can find a space. Can I get you a cup of something? I'm Farah, by the way."

"I didn't see a Farah on the personnel list. Farah, as in Fawcett-Majors?"

"No. As in Mo Farah. My name is Maureen Dennis on your list – Mo to my friends. Admin Assistant."

"Ah, yes. How do you do?"

"We all use nicknames here. Real names can be very confusing. I'm Maureen Dennis, and there's Dennis Dunn, one of our archivists – you'll meet him in a minute – and… do you want a cuppa?"

"No thank you."

"We've got five different varieties of tea and four different blends of real coffee. I can't tempt you with a Darjeeling Reserve or a Cuban Blue Mountain?"

"No, I'm fine, really. Thank you."

"Well, take that pew. We don't stand on ceremony here." Farah indicated a desk chair with a pile of box files on it then sat back down in her own chair. "Just sling those files on the side, next to those gladioli. You're not scheduled to see the Dong until ten, so I'll take you through some of the protocols while you're waiting."

"See the Dong?"

"Our commander. We call him the Dong. Don't worry, he hasn't got a luminous nose, ha ha. And it's nothing to do with the American word 'dong', either. We may be mad down here, but we're not smutty."

"I see. Perhaps you'll call me Alice, as in Wonderland."

"The Dong is from Edward Lear, not Lewis Carroll." Farah tutted. "But he's called the Dong because he's Mr. Bell. Not very clever, I know." Her broad smile returned. "It was originally Ding Dong, but that was a bit of a mouthful. Anyway, we'll have a nickname for you soon enough, love."

"I can't wait." Any name would be preferable to 'love'.

"The first thing I need to do is to get a photo of your face. For departmental security." She pulled open a drawer in her desk and extricated a camera from a jumble of rubber bands, pencils, pencil sharpeners and ribbons.

"Surely you've got one already if they've sent my file down."

"Yes, but you look miserable as sin in it. We need a picture of you smiling." She picked up a small camera on her desk.

"But no one uses smiling faces for security photos."

Farah beamed. "That's why we do down here. Anyone not smiling on their lanyard is immediately identified as the enemy." She aimed the camera at Lydia. "Smile."

Lydia struggled to raise a sick grimace. This is ridiculous, she thought.

Farah pressed the shutter and the flash went off. "I suppose that'll do," she said, looking at the LCD screen. "I'll print off copies for the rest of the department. We won't keep this picture on any shared computer system, of course, but it'll go on your H11 lanyard."

"Maybe I can have a better one done later."

"Oh, don't worry, love – you've got a beautiful face."

"No, what I meant was..."

Farah patted her ample pink shorts. "Now, I suppose you'll be interviewing us all about poor Luther?"

Lydia looked blank.

"Luther – Martin. Martin Luther. Martin Froome – the man you're replacing as Shift Manager."

"Oh yes, I see. What do you mean, interviewing you?"

"Well, we all presume that you're from upstairs, from Internal Security, sent down here to investigate his death."

"Ah." So much for Webb's idea of going undercover.

"We're not stupid, you know." Farah leant forward and adjusted a luridly yellow flower in the vase between them.

"Of course you're not stupid."

"But we are all down here for a reason." Farah smiled. "Including you."

"What do you mean?"

"What did you do wrong to get yourself posted here?"

"Sorry?" Lydia tried to look blank.

"Nobody gets posted down to H11 because they've requested it, and nobody gets posted here as a reward for good service. We've all been moved to the naughty step for something, love. Down here we find it helps to share the tales of our misfortunes."

"Well, Farah, give me a day or two to get my story straight. Perhaps I should talk to the Dong first."

"Suit yourself. There's plenty of time."

"I doubt it. I'm only here temporarily, just until a permanent replacement for Martin is appointed."

"That's what our other shift manager, Vindi, thought when he arrived." Farah paused. "Four years ago." She paused again.

Okay, Lydia thought, I get the picture, lady: I shouldn't expect any early release. I can take it. I can do stoicism. I didn't cry when I fell off my bike and broke my collarbone and chipped my elbow when I was six. I live alone now, in the loneliest city in the world, and I cope – sort of.

"Now," said Farah, "I'll show you your office and the toilet and all the important things. Come on." She levered herself out of her chair and beckoned to Lydia to follow her through the door at the far end of the office.

In the narrow grey corridor, Farah opened the door on the right. "This is the archive workroom. I'll get Double D to show you round, because I don't understand what goes on here. It's very technical, and I'm definitely not very technical. I can't even programme my own watch, ha ha."

She shut the door before Lydia could go in, and then tapped on the next door. "Here's the khazi, as we call it. There's just the one – no ladies and gents down here, I'm afraid, but everyone's civilized. You'll notice that bin, though." She indicated a large bright red bin next to the toilet. "All your sanitary towels, paper, wipes, anything solid, has to go in there. We're not allowed to flush away anything manufactured."

"Bad drains here?"

"No. It's security: so you can't flush any files or secrets down the tubes. There's a grille along the pipes somewhere to stop stuff getting out."

"What happens to the contents of the bin? Can't you smuggle stuff out in the waste bin?"

"Everything in the bin gets put through the grinder and then the incinerator. It's not one of my favourite jobs, I must say." Farah grimaced. "That mirror over the basin is the only one down here. I can see you're not wearing make-up, love. Just as well, because this place isn't set up for girls."

Farah shut the door. "Next door we've got the kitchen. It's on the small and basic side, but then we don't do much entertaining down here, ha ha." She opened the door to a pokey galley. "There's a cupboard up there on the right marked 'Luther' where you can keep your food. I'll change the name on his cupboard when we know your new name. There's the fridge, microwave, the kettle and the toaster. You can bring down whatever food you want, but you're not allowed to take any back. All wrapping and food waste goes in my grinder."

Lydia reached up and opened Luther's food cupboard. There wasn't much there: a jar of Marmite, half a packet of chocolate Hobnobs and a packet of grissini. No clues.

"He loved his Marmite, Luther did. Poor man. Can't stand it myself." Farah wiped a little tear away. "Makes you feel all funny to see a man's food when he's dead." She turned back. "I'll show you your office."

Across the corridor, Farah opened another grey door. Lydia followed her into a small office, into which four desks had been crammed. The walls were covered with pictures of flowers and jungles, making it seem even more cramped.

"That's your desk, love – the neat and tidy one. That one next to it is Vindi's, then the other two belong to our archivists, Double D and George. It's very cramped, but there's only ever two of you on duty at the same time."

"There are no computers."

"You've no need for one, love. There's one in the main office, and the Dong has one, but of course they're not connected to the outside world."

"So how do I do my work?"

"Paper and pen, love. All the inventories and all our work records are on paper. Security. It may take a bit longer, but no one can slip anything onto a memory stick down here, that's for sure."

"Farah, would you mind if I just had a little sit-down on my own at this desk – just to collect my thoughts and to get a feel for things down here?"

"'Course you can, love – good idea. I'll be back in my office. Don't leave it too long – the Dong will see you at ten."

After Farah had gone, Lydia sat back in her new chair. In Martin's chair. What was he thinking as he sat here on the day of his death? Was he terrified he knew something that was going to get him killed, or was he oblivious, thinking only of his sex games that night? What work had he been doing that day?

There was only one ring binder on the desktop. She opened it. It was a catalogue for office supplies. No clues.

She opened the top desk drawer: pencils, biros, a glue stick, a hole punch, a ruler, blu tack, scissors, a box of paper clips, a pack of playing cards, a calculator and a tin of peppermints, all laid out so neatly they looked like they'd been arrayed for an inspection. No clues.

She opened the lower desk drawer: it was empty, except for three paperback novels – two spy thrillers by John Le Carre and one by Robert Harris. She flipped through them, but nothing fell out. No clues. Martin Froome was turning out to be Mr. Dull.

She bent down to go through the wastepaper basket beside the desk. There were a few crumpled pieces of paper which she picked out and placed on the desktop. As she straightened, a white patch under the rim of the desk top caught her eye.

She felt for the patch. It was a piece of paper, stuck to the wood with blu tack. She carefully removed it and slid it into her jeans pocket, without looking at it or bringing it above the desk surface and into the view of the CCTV camera. Instead, she smoothed out the crumpled balls of paper she had retrieved from the wastepaper basket.

They were all blank. Again, no clues. She dropped them back into the wastepaper basket. Why would Martin put blank pieces of paper in the wastepaper basket?

She got up out of her seat, waved to the CCTV camera, and left the office.

Farah was waiting for her in the corridor. "Time to meet the Dong."

"I'm just popping to the loo," Lydia said, and turned into the toilet.

Inside, she carefully checked for a camera, but couldn't find one. Be thankful for small mercies, she thought – they don't actually perve on us when we're having a pee.

She took out the piece of paper from her pocket and unfolded it. It had a series of eight digit numbers in two columns, written in pencil, but no words. The numbers made no immediate sense to her. She refolded the paper, pulled up her jumper and stuffed the paper into her bra. It would be a good test of this famously tight security system when she left this evening.

She flushed the toilet, washed her hands in the basin, and took a long look at her face in the mirror.

Her short black hair looked a bit too severe. Her blue eyes looked too wide, her pupils just a little too dilated, as if she was on some chemical. The lines round her mouth looked taut. She could feel her heart pounding.

Get a grip, she told herself. You are an investigator with eight years' experience and a reputation for dishing out as good as you get. This is a routine assignment, dealing with an accidental death. What's the big deal if his desk has been searched and sanitised?

Be very careful, girl.

4

LYDIA

Farah ushered Lydia into the Dong's office. "Cuppa, Dong?"

"No thanks, Farah." Gerard Bell was already standing. He moved forward to shake Lydia's hand.

Farah left, shutting the door behind her, as Lydia shook Gerard's hand. His hand was firm, dry and warm.

"Take a seat, Ms Twomey." He indicated a colonial rattan armchair, and lowered himself into another, before crossing his long legs.

Any hopes Lydia might have had that the weirdness of H11 was confined to Farah and her office were already shredded. Bell was dressed in a tropical white linen suit, a bright Hawaiian shirt and open sandals – at least he wasn't committing the sartorial crime of wearing socks. His very unlovely toenails were a few inches from her jeans. On a coffee table in front of them was a magnificent display of silk orchids and on the wall beyond was a huge plasma screen which displayed an image of a pagoda rising behind a rice paddy.

Gerard saw her studying the image. "I took that in the Mekong delta on holiday a couple of years ago. I've got a large stock of images – the display changes automatically every half hour. It helps me to remember that there's a world up there."

"And what about that statuette?" Lydia gestured to the far wall of the office, which was taken up entirely by bookshelves, except for a recess with a terracotta figure of a man with an arm raised.

"He's Baal – the Lord. He's my protective spirit. Do you like him?"

"It's… unusual." Lydia found it rather creepy. "I haven't seen anything like it in any office I've been in. Baal gets a bad press in the Bible."

"Old Testament propaganda. I bought him from a tout outside a site in Tripoli, Libya, in 1978. I was a young man then, and it cost a fair whack. They sold lots of fakes, but I knew this was the genuine article. It's Carthaginian, over two thousand three hundred years old. Extraordinary. He's been with me ever since, protecting me. He's never let me down."

"I thought that buying from touts was frowned upon – it encourages the destructive robbing of archaeological sites."

"I've never been a great one for rules because nothing is ever straightforward, black or white, wrong or right. You learn that in this business. It's a free-for-all in Libya – there's never been any proper policing of sites. I'm a responsible custodian of this treasure, and when I retire, I will donate Baal to the British Museum."

Lydia found herself staring at Gerard's extraordinary face. He wasn't old, but his features were scored by a lattice of deep creases, folds and scars. Lydia thought he looked like the actor John Hurt, and not totally unlike the statuette of Baal.

"I like quizzes, Ms Twomey." The facial canyons moved in a mesmeric way when he spoke. "I see you studying my face. Answer me this: who described their own face as being like a wedding cake left out in the rain?"

"I'm sorry. I didn't mean to stare." She was off on the wrong foot again.

"Who was it?"

"W.H. Auden, I think."

Gerard clapped his hands in delight. "Well done! We've got a proper intellectual down here at last. Here's the supplementary question: what did David Hockney write when he drew Auden's face?"

If this man was trying to embarrass her, she wasn't going to give him satisfaction. She answered calmly. "If Auden's face was so wrinkled, Hockney wondered what his scrotum looked like."

Gerard threw back his head and laughed. "Ha! Brilliant! Not a suspicion of hesitation or deviation. I like it. You're going to fit in perfectly down here, Ms Twomey."

"Glad to hear it."

Gerard leaned forward, his face suddenly serious. The rattan chair creaked. "There is a point to all this tomfoolery, Ms Twomey: we're preserving our sanity. When you are entombed, year after long year, four floors below ground level, within impenetrable walls, cooped up with dangerous secrets and prohibited from communicating with the outside world, there's a risk of becoming… a trifle unhinged."

"I can believe it."

"Our most deadly enemy isn't some fiendish foreign agent or irritating investigative journalist – it's boredom. Boredom can kill here."

"Do you think that's what killed Martin Froome – what drove him to do what he did?" Lydia felt she had a chance to wrest control.

Gerard paused. "I am sure it was an accident. Who knows what drives someone to do such things?"

"So you know the circumstances?"

"Yes. I'd be grateful if you don't share them with the other staff immediately. They're upset enough as it is."

"I need to question them about it."

"All in good time, Ms Twomey. Morale, mental health, esprit de corps – they're fragile commodities down here and I have to manage them carefully, as will you, as my deputy. Martin was my deputy; that role passes to you now. Anything that rocks the boat has to be dealt with delicately. I will tell them when I deem it right."

"Oh." She would be referring this issue upstairs to Webb.

"I was telling you about boredom." Gerard was back in assured control. "Do you know how many information requests we get per month? Go on, have a guess."

"Twenty? Five?"

"On average, less than one per month. We guard information that most people don't know even exists, or if they do know about it, they wish it didn't exist. How would anyone request to use a piece of information when they don't know it exists? It's a definition of redundancy, but we're still here. There are seven of us employed in H11 with not enough work to go round."

"So wouldn't it be better to just seal this place up, and forget about the contents? The taxpayer isn't getting a great deal."

The lights flickered. There was a momentary blink of darkness.

Bell smiled. "That's quite unnerving when you're four floors below ground level, eh? We've got back-up generators that come on automatically in the event of a power failure."

Lydia didn't waver. "It's no problem. I was just saying: wouldn't it be better to seal this place up and save the money?"

"Most of the stuff we hold is useless crap: who wants to know which politician has buggered which little boy? Who cares what one of our royals said about a Saudi prince half a century ago? What is much more important is what people think we hold on them. It's all about perception, rather than reality. There are powerful people all over the world sweating on the possibility that we hold the dirt on them, and that if they do something our government doesn't like, they'll get exposed. Potential – that's why the taxpayer willingly stumps up."

"So this place is just a dirt-box, a blackmail repository?"

"Not entirely. There are a few genuine hum-dingers buried here. Things you'll wish you never knew." He eased back in his rattan chair, which creaked.

"Hence the madness."

"What you see is not madness – it's a conscious strategy. We keep the darkness back by dressing as if it's high summer and pretending that the oppressive heat down here is caused by tropical sun. I set quizzes. Farah brings in treats for everyone – she's a wonderful cook. Vindi trains for marathons between the filing stacks. We all bring strategies and we all support each other. As the new morning shift manager, you will be expected to contribute strategies and to support your team."

"I see, sir. I'll do my best."

"Your former boss, Perry, has had a chat with me about why he selected you for this transfer. Did he share his thoughts with you?"

"No, but I can guess what he said to you."

"Well, you need to put all that history behind you. Obviously MI5 never wipes the slate completely clean, but as far as H11 is concerned, you've got a totally new start."

"But I've never been…"

"I know – you've never been accused of a misdemeanour so you've never had a chance to defend yourself. It's a bugger, isn't it? But remember, down here we're all in that same boat: we've all been transferred, relegated, under some unspecified cloud. So we support each other."

"I understand, sir."

"And don't call me 'sir'. I'm the Dong." His smile set new creases running across his cheeks and up to his forehead. "Oh look." He pointed up to the plasma screen. "We've moved from the Mekong to the Danube. That's Budapest."

"Okay, Dong." She smiled back.

"What did you pick up from under Luther's desk?" The sudden change of tone was a jolt to Lydia. Bell was leaning forward, his eyes glittering, ready to analyse any hesitation on her part.

"Nothing." She lied smoothly, she hoped. No cheap interrogation trick was going to work on her. "I picked three pieces of paper out of the wastepaper basket. They had nothing on them, which I thought was very strange. If I was to have a wild guess, I'd say someone had got to Martin's desk before me and had gone through it, maybe removing or replacing certain items. It was extraordinarily tidy."

"Luther was a very tidy man." Bell said it carefully, never taking his eyes off her face. "You should have been briefed not to wear clothes with pockets. I'd be obliged if you reversed your pockets so everyone can see you have nothing in them."

"You don't believe me, do you?" Lydia stood up and pulled her pocket linings out of her jeans. She stood over Bell. "If you require a strip search then I need your Admin Assistant to be present."

Bell sat back, and smiled. "Of course I don't. You're rather overreacting, Ms Twomey. Sit down, please."

She sat. "Do you always spy on your colleagues via your CCTV? Do you watch it on your giant plasma screen? Does the old Mekong Delta get regularly switched over to the steamy passages of H11?"

"Security is our business down here. I reserve the right to oversee all operations." He sounded huffy.

"So instead of welcoming me as soon as I arrived, you spent your time spying on me through your cameras. Some people would call that controlling behaviour."

The smile hadn't left Bell's face, but he looked less urbane and relaxed. "Perry Webb warned me you would be feisty. He added that this department would be good for your personal development."

"What else did he say?"

"He said you were very bright, very beautiful and very serious. He's usually an acute judge of character."

Lydia had always thought of Webb as a stuffed shirt – someone who'd risen to power through his public school and Cambridge connections. "He's got at least half of that wrong. Speaking of pockets, how come you're wearing a suit with them? Is it one rule for you and another for minions?"

"We all adhere to it. Look." Gerard took off his jacket and handed it to her.

All the pockets were sewn up. Lydia handed it back.

Bell smiled like a kindly headmaster. "I was once given an excellent piece of advice from one of my bosses, over twenty years ago. He told me I should choose my issues carefully – you can't go to the cross for all of them."

"How come you ended up here, then?"

5

PERRY

"Sorry to keep you waiting, Perry: Minister needing reassurance. They gave you a coffee, I hope." The Director-General held open the door to his office.

"Yes, thank you. I even got a biscuit." Peregrine Webb knew that the word 'sir' should be inserted at the end of a sentence when addressing the Director-General at the start of a meeting, but they had been firm friends ever since Cambridge, so such formality seemed artificial.

"Splendid." The DG strode across the acre of carpet and sat down behind the range of screens on his desk, waving for Perry to take a seat. "Now, what can I do for you?"

"It's just a heads-up at this stage – almost certainly nothing. Gerard's deputy down in H11, a chap called Martin Froome, died two nights ago. Looks like an auto-erotic accident."

"Poor chap. Can we be sure he was on his own when he died?"

"Forensics say so."

"Good. Any dependants? Press get hold of it?"

"No, and no. Froome didn't turn up for work next morning

so Gerard called him, got no response and called me. My chaps found the body; they kept the lid on. Apart from the report to the police, no one else is in the loop. It's all remarkably clean."

"Jolly good. I presume you've put someone into H11."

"Yes – a girl called Lydia Twomey."

"Fine. Everything seems under control, so what's the issue, Perry?"

"There's an awkward gap. The CCTV at the foot of the stairs in the block wasn't working. The security firm are adamant that it had been in perfect working order just twenty-four hours previously, and they have the footage to prove it."

"Post-mortem results?"

"All clear: nothing to counter an auto-asphyxiation verdict."

"Well, thank you for keeping me informed, Perry. I'd advise a second enhanced post-mortem, but beyond that there's nothing much you can do."

"I've ordered it already."

"Of course you have. Let me know if anything emerges. Thank you for keeping me informed."

The Director-General's eyes were already fixed on his desk screens as Perry made his way over the carpet to the large heavy door.

6

LYDIA

The voice was strong and smooth, filling the dead air with sweetness. He was singing 'Oh What a Beautiful Morning'. Lydia, as she stood under the harsh strip lights between the subterranean file stacks, could almost visualise the mid-west corn prairies. He was standing with his back to her, a huge wide figure in a bizarre jazzy red shirt, checking labels on the spines of a row of metal box files.

"Hello." Lydia tried to interrupt as gently as she could. "What a beautiful voice!"

The figure jumped. His head swung round, and she saw a look of panic across his fleshy face. He had a small goatee beard, straight dark hair slightly too long – not exactly a style icon.

"Sorry – I didn't mean to surprise you. That's why I called out from back here." She was off on the wrong foot again. "I'm Lydia Twomey, your new Shift Manager. You must be Dennis Dunn."

His mouth worked like a fish's for a second, before he gained some sort of composure. "You gave me a start. I'm used to being on my own in here." Home Counties accent.

"Sorry." Christ, she thought, I've started off by apologising to Farah, then Bell, and now Dennis. "I just came to introduce myself."

"I'm called Double D here in H11. How do you do?"

"Double D – for Dennis Dunn." Stating the obvious seemed the safest bet to someone with wide eyes and a shaking left leg. He looked like he was ready to run away from her.

"No – they like to take the piss. It stands for Double D Cup you know, on a bra – on account of my figure." He put his hands to his jazzy red shirt – Lydia couldn't help but notice the ample man-boobs above a considerable paunch.

"That's outrageous!" She meant it – she was horrified. "Have you complained? That's workplace bullying, sexist, probably harassment. As your new line manager..."

He shook his head. "No, no – it's fine. Everyone is kind down here. I don't mind what I get called."

"Oh well, that's fine then. Double D it is." She moved towards him. "Tell me, Double D, what are you working on at the moment?"

He took a step back. "I'm... I'm checking that the contents of each file are still present." He held up a file to show Lydia the little window in the spine. "If one of these files is empty, then there's a world of trouble."

"Has any file ever gone missing?"

"Not in the three years I've been working here." She could hear the pride in his voice.

"Presumably you don't spend your entire working life checking that the files are all present, do you?"

"No, of course not. But each file needs a visual monthly check. My present major project is a programme of renovation. The analogue tapes don't last forever, so I'm rerecording them all onto digital disc. It's a lengthy business, as you can imagine."

"How many tapes have you got to do?"

"There's 26,325 hours of old analogue recordings at the last count. We've renovated 31% of it so far."

"That's a lot of bugging."

"The tip of the iceberg; did you know that GCHQ currently holds files on over 270,000 British citizens? That's truly a lot of bugging. A lot of our tapes down here are old – some are historic."

"I can imagine. It's going to take years to rerecord them."

He shrugged. "We've got years to do it."

"Do you listen to the tapes when you're recording them?"

"Only... only when there are problems. Normally they're on times 32 speed."

Double D had a face easily read: alarm, then pride, and now back to alarm. His eyes were darting to the CCTV cameras, then along the stacks, and back to Lydia.

"So sometimes you get to discover things you'd rather not know?"

"You're going to ask me about Luther, aren't you?"

She forced a smile. "Well, you've obviously sussed why I've been seconded down here. I'm not trying to hide it from you. Do you have any thoughts about Luther – about his death?"

"I hope they're not trying to sell it as suicide. Luther would never, ever top himself." As he shook his head, wisps of his black hair fell across his face.

"As far as I know, no one is trying to sell it in any way. Why do you say that?"

Double D was picking at his thumb with his index finger, and Lydia could see sweat start to darken his red shirt. "Because we haven't been told anything – not a single detail. We were his closest friends. Why are you keeping us in the dark?"

"The Dong makes those decisions. I'm sure he has your best interests at heart."

"At best, we're being treated like children."

"And at worst?"

"There's a cover-up of something very nasty. If he's been killed, it's vital all our team are informed – who knows who'll be next? We all need to review our personal security in the light of any threat." Double D shook his head, and then looked squarely at the CCTV camera, addressing it directly. "The deal down here is that there are no secrets between us."

"I understand your anxieties, but I really don't think you should worry. There's probably a delay over the post-mortem, and…" She wanted to put his mind at rest and was about to tell him it was an accidental death, but she was under orders.

"Yes?" Double D paused for an answer. "You obviously know the details."

"They will tell you if you're in danger. I promise, as your temporary line manager, I will inform you as soon as I hear of anything that suggests you're in danger."

"Thank you." He didn't sound convinced. He half turned, and fiddled with a file box on the shelf behind him.

"Why did you say Luther would never kill himself? Did you know him that well?"

"We all know each other well. We share a cell called H11. And… and I knew Luther better than anyone else down here."

"You were special friends?"

"He wasn't gay, if that's what you're angling at. Anyway, homosexuality is no longer regarded as a security risk." His nose went up in defiance. "I'm sure we're both glad about that."

She didn't bite. "Of course. Did he share confidences with you on his sexuality?"

"Is it relevant to the investigation?"

"It might be."

"Might be?" He was backed right up against the rows of grey files, his hand clutching hold of the nearest one.

"All right: it is."

"Luther was completely straight, as painfully straight and shy as a man could be. Believe me, I'd know if something wasn't right or if he was unhappy."

"Was he in a relationship?"

"No. It was difficult for him to meet anyone, and because of this job we're not allowed to go on internet dating sites. I tried introducing him to some of my straight friends, but he was shy, as I said."

"So how did he satisfy himself?"

"Now you're going too far, Miss Twomey." His voice shook with indignation. "How do you satisfy yourself? You see? It's not a question you want to answer. If you want to ask me questions like that about one of my best friends before he's even been laid to rest, you'll need to give me much more information to justify it, and you'll need my senior officer present in an interrogation room."

"I'm sorry. I really didn't mean to offend." Peregrine Webb would laugh if he got hold of the recording of this conversation: here was his feisty nightmare apologising yet again. "Look, I think I'd better get back to the office and read up a bit more about my new job. There's obviously a lot to learn. Bye for now." She turned away.

"Bye, Miss Twomey."

There was something in Double D's voice that made her turn back to him. He was standing, face away from the CCTV camera, fixing her with an intense stare that she couldn't ignore – it was almost a glare. As if in sympathy, the strip light above his head flickered and clicked for an instant.

She smiled back at him, then turned again and made her way along the row of filing shelves. Double D was clearly an Am-Dram Queen who could strike a pose and communicate with his body and eyes, but that sort of stare wasn't to be found in *Oklahoma* or *My Fair Lady*. It was more Ibsen or Miller.

A distress signal.

At five o'clock, Lydia clocked off, signing the log in Farah's office, going into the cloakroom to collect her helmet and rucksack, walking past the first security scanner and through the external door, into the long concrete-lined corridor. At the far end there was an iris recognition test, and then another scanner to walk through. She only realised when she got through the second scanner and was waiting for the lift in the dimly lit hallway that she had been holding her breath throughout the whole process – for nearly a full minute. She hadn't triggered the alarm, but she could feel the piece of paper with Martin Froome's numbers burning against her breast.

The lift bell rang, the door opened, she walked into the lift and pressed the button for the third floor above ground.

She had held it together. She had smuggled the piece of paper through the tightest security MI5 was able to provide.

It was only when the lift stopped at ground floor that her unruffled exterior started to crack. Two young women got into the lift and stood chatting, their backs turned, but Lydia didn't hear their words; blood was pounding in her ears and she could feel herself starting to shake. Although she had been expecting some stress symptom, the suddenness and severity took her by surprise. She could feel tears welling up; she turned to face the lift buttons: second floor, still going up.

A wave of anger flowed through her. Don't be such a weakling, you stupid cow! You're an experienced professional spook. Pull yourself together – that's what her mum would say.

The lift stopped, the door opened, and she stumbled out into the normal world, where no one wore tropical beachwear and there were no artificial flowers or rows of grey files – just comforting bland magnolia-painted walls, slightly grubby burgundy carpets and restrained lighting.

Two men she vaguely knew walked towards her down the corridor, and she wondered if they could see she was shaking.

They passed her with a 'hi' smile each, but no sign they'd noticed anything amiss.

Lydia pushed into the ladies toilets. Mercifully, they were empty. The avocado green of the walls and basins was comforting, but she made straight for a cubicle. She dropped her rucksack and helmet on the floor, slammed down the toilet lid, slumped down and put her face in her hands. She was still shaking.

After nearly five minutes of deep breathing, she took the piece of paper out of her bra, holding it like it was radioactive. A second viewing of the ten sets of eight digit numbers brought no enlightenment, except that the pencil used to write them was at different stages of sharpness for different numbers – Martin was obviously compiling the list over a period of time. She could only guess what the numbers represented – file numbers, maybe?

She had made it through all H11's security with the slip of paper in her bra. But why had she done it? Why didn't she hand it over to Bell? Why on earth had she broken security protocols, taken such a stupid risk? And what had she gained? Now she had possibly sensitive, even potentially dangerous, information which she couldn't share with either Webb or Bell – she couldn't admit she'd broken the security of the most secure archive in the service. Why, why, why?

Because… because her instincts had taken over. This was a supposedly routine assignment, but everything felt wrong. Maybe Martin's death was no accident. Somebody – perhaps the person who killed Martin Froome – had been looking for this piece of paper.

She felt totally alone.

7

PERRY

"Thank you for seeing me so promptly, DG. Sorry for bothering you, but you need to know there's been a development." Perry found he was sweating under his crisp white collar and he fought the urge to loosen his navy blue club tie.

"This is about the H11 death, I presume."

"That's right." Perry instinctively looked around the room before proceeding, even though he knew they were in the inner sanctum, completely screened from the outside world. The black blinds were down. Behind the absurdly expensive original Matisse prints on the pastel walls there would be a layer of electronic insulation. "I had the enhanced post-mortem carried out, and it seems as if the first one did indeed miss something of some significance." He paused.

The Director-General raised immaculately groomed eyebrows.

Perry continued. "There's no trace of anything untoward in the original toxicology report, but the enhanced inspection did find a needle puncture in Froome's neck. Of course, if the assassins were skilful with the dosage and the injection, the toxic traces would be gone by the time we found the body."

"So our man was nobbled?"

"Probably. Even now we can't be certain."

The DG fingered his chin. "Hmm. If he was nobbled, then it was a highly skilled job. How many people in this country are capable of something that would fool our initial post-mortem?"

"Impossible to be sure – less than twenty, I'd say. Some of our own chaps are technically capable of it, but of course..."

"Put the feelers out. This has the potential to turn very ugly."

"I'll do that. But we can't rule out a foreign agency."

"Thank you for that most lovely thought, Perry. This is sounding worse by the minute. Tell me, what is your most likely hypothesis for this killing?"

"Four years ago we had an unexplained death in H11 – you might remember it." The Director-General nodded. "We put one of our chaps into H11, Damian Curry, but he didn't come up with anything. As there were no unpleasant consequences out in the wider world, we concluded that the victim, a woman called Cariad Jones, had probably been using her access to the classified information held in H11 to blackmail someone powerful, and she was bumped off by said powerful person. Our best hope is that this is a similar scenario."

"Was there any evidence to back up your conclusion about Cariad Jones?"

Perry squirmed. "Not really. It was more the lack of evidence for anything else, despite exhaustive investigation. Because everything has remained quiet since, there hasn't been anything else to go on. Often with H11 matters it's best to let sleeping dogs lie, and your predecessor concurred."

The DG frowned. "How was this Cariad Jones killed?"

"Nudged off the platform at Embankment tube, under a train."

"Surely there were witnesses? CCTV footage from Embankment?"

"Ah." Perry felt his face burn. "The CCTV was malfunctioning at the time."

The DG's smile was glacial. "And the CCTV at Froome's block of flats was malfunctioning on the night of his death."

Perry nodded. "I agree: it may not be a happy coincidence." He studied the carpet – a red Persian design.

"Perry, are you recommending that I let sleeping dogs lie this time, like my predecessor did?"

"I'll make sure everything that can be done quietly, under the radar, is done. One feels that making a big noise, putting out feelers that are too intrusive, might stir up more trouble than it's worth."

"You're assuming that doing nothing solved the problem last time. It may have allowed something very bad to continue. If I go along with your recommendation I could be open to accusations from the Minister of complacency."

Perry was minded to reply that the Ministry of Complacency was an apt name, but instead he said nothing. He spread his hands, as if to say that it was the DG's call.

The DG shut his eyes for a full fifteen seconds. Perry waited for the words from on high.

The DG opened his eyes and fixed them on Perry. "Very well. It's your show – you do it your way for now. But we both know just how awkward this could be, so I want to be informed as soon as there's any development of any sort."

"Thank you, DG. I'll do all I can."

Perry got up out of his padded seat, and made for the door.

"Good luck, Perry. Oh, by the way, are you playing golf on Sunday morning?"

Perry turned back. "Hoping to. What about you? We haven't seen much of you lately."

"If I don't get summoned by the Minister – again." The DG pulled a face.

As he walked down the corridor away from the DG's suite, Perry could feel the thirty-year-old rugby injury in his left knee go into spasm. That was a very disagreeable interview, he thought. That's the trouble with hierarchical organisations: everyone above you is positioning themselves to shift the blame for fuck-ups onto you, and everyone below you is angling for your job. The DG might play a cosy round of golf with him from time to time, but if the Minister wanted a scapegoat then it would be yours truly who'd be in front of the firing squad; no Cambridge friendship would save him.

As he turned into his office anteroom he was met by Lydia Twomey sitting in the chair by his office door. She had been reading a book, which she now stuffed into the rucksack on the chair next to her.

Perry silently asked himself why the sight of this bright pretty girl should fill him with anxieties. He attempted joviality. "Ah, Lydia! What are you reading? I wish I had time to read."

"Reza Hamid." Lydia got up. "And it's half past seven in the evening. I've done a full day in my new place of employment before waiting here for the last half hour."

Why did Lydia always have to make everything into a casus belli?

"Reza, eh? Pretty woman – but very severe. The 'feminist razor', they call her. I've met her a few times at social gatherings. Your new boss, Gerard – his wife is Reza's literary agent." He was gratified to see that Lydia was impressed.

Perry submitted to iris recognition, unlocked his office door, and turned back to her. "Come on in."

For a full twenty minutes after Lydia had gone, Perry sat in his chair under the portrait of the Queen, staring out at the lights in the office blocks over the darkened Thames. A call had come through from his wife Glenys, but he'd ignored it. She was used to him being late, and he didn't feel like going to the charity cocktail party. He never felt like going to charity cocktail parties.

He reached into his inside jacket pocket and extricated a small packet. He opened it and popped out a small white pill, which he put in his mouth. That's better, or it would be in a few minutes.

In her own way, Lydia had been as awkward as the DG had been. Her main observation about H11 was that it was MI5 in microcosm: the entire staff is ethnic white British, the managers are men and the women make the cups of tea. Very helpful – thank you for that. She'd expressed the opinion that Froome hadn't died in an accident, but Perry judged he was right not to distract her with the details of the enhanced post-mortem. There was nothing she could do with such knowledge, except worry about it. There wasn't much he could do about it either: tomorrow he'd put together an investigative team but he didn't hold out much hope for positive results.

For a man used to being assured and in control, he was full of doubts. He'd sent Lydia down to H11 because he'd judged that she needed her abrasive edges sanded. He thought she'd be able to cope with the intellectual and personal challenges presented by that freak-show down there. After all, she was clever and resourceful, and no one could push her around. Now he wasn't so sure: she looked distracted, maybe shell-shocked. He got the impression she was holding something back from him – perhaps her pride was keeping her from letting on what a shitty day she'd had. She could be surprisingly vulnerable and insecure at odd moments.

He worried about whether Lydia would cope with Gerard. Could such an ingénue, despite her feistiness, deal with a man of infinite charm, charisma, and a very dangerous reputation? Many powerful people feared Gerard as if he was the Devil incarnate, stoking the fires in his subterranean lair.

Perry didn't really believe what he had told the DG. Martin Froome didn't fit the picture of a lone blackmailer: there were no signs of any ill-gotten gains, no evidence of gambling habits or secret vices beyond moderate drinking; his Triple A security assessment suggested how painfully conventional and honest he was.

The truth was almost certainly a lot darker.

8

DENNIS

"What is it, Piggy?" Paul's kind brown eyes anxiously scanned Dennis's face from beside him on the sofa.

"Oh, nothing. I'm fine." Dennis shook his head. He took another sip of his Hennessy brandy and swirled it round his mouth. The fumes warmed his nostrils, giving him a moment of bliss.

"Don't give me that." Paul tapped him lightly on his arm. "I watched you all through the rehearsal: you were off with the timing of your steps and your words were all over the place. When we went through them together last week you were perfect. You just weren't concentrating this evening. 'Shall We Dance'? It was more like 'Shall We Divorce?' Poor Davina – she must be wondering if she's got bad breath."

Dennis sighed. It was a hazard living with the director of your production, and he'd always found it hard to hide anything from Paul. "It's just work. You know, just a bit stressful since Martin died. We still don't know how he died or when the funeral is."

"You poor thing. You're grieving. I understand." Paul stroked the back of Dennis's neck. "But I still think you should give up that job."

"And do what? They're closing down libraries all over the country." Dennis looked round their living room. It was only a small flat in Willesden, but this room was exquisite: beautifully furnished, lovely carpets and rugs, fantastic home cinema and hi-fi, china Staffordshire spaniels on the mantelpiece, with this lovely man sitting next to him. He had so much to lose.

Paul didn't give up. "Get a transfer to another department – one that isn't so secret. I hate it that you can't tell me anything about what you do all day."

"I suppose I can try again." Dennis said it without hope. He'd tried before and got nowhere, but now… now he knew 'they' would stop him getting free. 'They' thought he knew something – he was sure of it. Martin had known too much and that was why he was dead.

This new girl, Lydia something, was asking awkward questions. 'They' would get alarmed; 'they' might think he was going to blab something to her. 'They' wouldn't allow that. He would be eliminated like Martin.

Paul's stroking of his neck was soothing him. He closed his eyes.

Paranoia – the Dong always said it was their greatest enemy. 'They' probably didn't exist, and there probably wasn't a dark secret – certainly not one Dennis knew of, anyway. Martin probably died of natural causes or in some stupid accident. Dennis had just allowed the death of his friend to churn up this silly hysteria that was completely messing with his sense of reality.

"You know, Pogo, I would willingly die for you." Dennis's voice was dreamy.

"Don't be so melodramatic, Piggy." Paul lightly cuffed the back of his head.

Dennis allowed Paul's fingers to smooth his blues away.

Next morning the paranoia was back with a vengeance. Dennis had always paid full attention in their personal security training sessions. He knew all the tricks to ascertain if he was being followed, and now he thought – knew – he was being tailed.

The guy was lean, white, stubbled chin, about thirty-five years old, skinny black jeans, baseball cap and tan jacket; he was chaining his bike to the railings outside the tube station. Except he wasn't chaining anything – he didn't even own the bike. Dennis had spotted him walking without a bike along St Paul's Avenue while he was on his way up Dean Road towards Willesden Green tube station.

Dennis knew that if he waited around here he'd be late for work, but this was too important. He bought a *Daily Telegraph* at the news kiosk, pretended to scan the front page, then opened up an inside page, peering over the rim.

The man with the baseball cap looked up from the bike, saw Dennis wasn't going anywhere in a hurry, hesitated for just a second or two, then walked calmly past Dennis to the barrier, put his Oystercard through the machine and disappeared from view.

Dennis folded his paper and followed through the barrier. Instead of descending the stairs to the southbound trains, he took a deep breath and rushed down the stairs to the northbound platform. As per training, he then waited on the stairs, just out of sight from southbound platform.

His luck was in: the first train to arrive in Willesden Green was northbound. Dennis timed his run perfectly, just making it onto the train as the doors closed. It was like a cliché in one of those films, he thought. As the train pulled out, he could see the man with the baseball cap standing in the April morning sun on the crowded southbound platform.

As the train pulled towards Dollis Hill, Dennis slumped down in a seat and allowed himself a sigh of relief. He had done pretty well and his stalker had been pretty amateurish. A southbound train clanked past as his northbound train slowed on the approach to Dollis Hill.

Dennis alighted at Dollis Hill and made his way over the bridge to the southbound platform, which was already crowded with a new batch of commuters. It was four minutes before the next train came in; when it arrived it had a fair number of people standing in all the carriages. Dennis chose the most rammed carriage – he was hardly a small man who could hide easily in a crowd, but hopefully the man in the baseball cap had caught the previous southbound train and would be in Swiss Cottage or Baker Street by now.

When the train pulled into Willesden Green, Dennis found he was sweating profusely and his brain was filled with ghastly scenarios: what if there were two people shadowing him, not just the man with the baseball cap, and the other had taken the northbound platform and followed him to Dollis Hill? What if they were an assassination squad rather than just following him?

Stop it, he told himself. He'd gone through all the procedures learned in training, and the danger was over. The train pulled into Willesden Green.

The man with the baseball cap stepped off the platform and into the carriage where Dennis hung from a strap.

9

LYDIA

"Welcome to our monthly full staff meeting, brought forward for a very sad reason." Gerard Bell's lined face looked suitably crushed, but Lydia thought it was a consummate performance. "Firstly, a big thank-you to Maybe, Vindi and to Nylon for being here out of their normal schedule. I'm sure Double D will join us once he's raised himself from his gorgeous perfumed bed." A few chuckles. "Also may I extend a very warm welcome to the new member of our team – Lydia Twomey, aka Schizo."

"Schizo?" It was like a boot in her solar plexus. Lydia could feel her face flame. "As in schizophrenic? Is that how you see me?"

She looked round at the others sitting in the confines of the Dong's office. She'd seen them sizing her up, probably frowning at her clothes; she'd declined to wear beach clothes and had put on a denim shirt over black jeans (with pockets inside out) this morning. They were all dressed for the Marbella seafront, but Lydia didn't have to play Bell's games; this was only a temporary posting, she reminded herself.

Farah beamed. "It's your name, not your character, love. Twomey – two me's. D'you see?"

This was so unfair! It was controlling – a way to bolt down the uppity newcomer into her place.

Bell pulled his devastating creased smile. "Of course, if you feel it's sexist, homophobic, discriminatory or against legal workplace practice, we can find another nickname."

Lydia looked again at the others. They were all looking at her intently, ready to size up her reaction. She wasn't going to blow her stack for their entertainment; she shook her head. "It's okay. Just as well my name isn't Flora Heckinbottom."

There were a few laughs – they sounded friendly. She'd passed the first test.

"That's settled, then," said Bell. "Welcome Schizo. Let's complete the introductions. You've already met Farah, but not the rest of the team. Start us off, Vindi."

"Hi, Schizo, I'm Damian Curry, or Vindi – Evening Manager." A sharply handsome man wearing a Haringey Harriers athletic vest that showed off his trim physique, he lounged beside the plasma screen. The current display was of an Icelandic snow-flecked mountainside; Vindi, ineffably cool, looked as if he'd just come in from a run along the fjord. She'd briefly met Damian before, but she hadn't taken any notice back then; he'd been seconded to GCHQ when she'd joined the MI5 Internal Security department.

"Hi there – I'm Maddy King, or rather, George – Archivist." The pretty blonde girl in her late twenties sitting next to Vindi smiled. "Welcome." A plum in her mouth, Sloane Ranger labels on her floral blouse and dinky blue shorts, tanned thighs – George was from another planet to Lydia.

"Hi, Schizo. I'm Maggie Willis, called Maybe down here and called Mum at home – Admin Assistant. We hope you're very happy here." The woman sitting with Mo, partly obscured by the fake orchids, looked to Lydia to be the quintessential secretary – neatly pressed yellow blouse, cropped mousey hair, restrained ear studs, ring on her marriage finger, mid forties, slight Thames estuary accent. Lydia wondered what on earth such a woman could have done wrong to get herself posted to H11.

Bell waved forward a man with a pale shaven head but a Rasputin-style beard. He was wearing a day-glo green set of overalls. "And now, Schizo, you must meet the most important person down here, though only once a week: our esteemed technician."

The man shuffled forward from the bookshelves, where he'd been trying very unsuccessfully to blend in. "I'm Nylon, but if you meet me upstairs I'm Bri – Brian Powell. I sort things out and clean things up."

"He's a genius," Bell said. "There's nothing he can't fix."

Brian shook his head and moved back to the bookcase.

She was glad she hadn't made a scene about her new name – on reflection it was no worse than the others: Maddy King – Mad King George – George, Damian Curry – Curry Vindaloo – Vindi, Maggie Willis – Maggie May – Maybe, or Bri – Nylon. Harmless fun, perhaps.

"Well, that's the introductions done." Bell clapped his hands. "Now, I need to give you the very sad news about Luther: he died of auto-asphyxiation in his flat. I'm sure you all know what that is, so I won't go into details. It was clearly a tragic accident, and no one else was involved. That's all the information I have. Full stop."

Lydia looked carefully at the reactions: a gasp from Maybe, who put her hand to her mouth and then started to shake her head. Farah patted Maybe's arm to comfort her, then seemed to sniff away a tear of her own. Nylon was shaking his head and fiddling with his beard, tutting. George screwed up her eyes and mouthed the word 'no'. No reaction at all from Vindi – he might as well have been playing poker.

Lydia tried to cement her observations into her memory – at this moment there seemed nothing untoward in the reactions, but she needed time to analyse them.

Bell continued. "I can't give a date for any funeral at present – they've got autopsies to do – but as soon as I have a date I'll arrange a schedule so all of us can attend, bar a skeleton crew to man the fort here – it will be Schizo and one other. Schizo will take over all Luther's duties in the meantime. We need to make it as seamless as possible. I expect you all to co-operate with any questions that Schizo may have for you, and I know you will all give her a traditional H11 welcome. We need to support each other at this bleak time. Any questions?"

Silence. Lydia could see that Farah appeared to be dabbing her eyes and Maybe's lip was quivering.

A sudden chill ran through Lydia. It took her totally by surprise – at first she had no idea why she was shivering in this crowded hot room. Then she collected her thoughts. It was fear, she realised, a horrid lurch towards a total conviction that… she hesitated, loath to give in to such thoughts. It was no good: she was sure she was sitting in this room with a murderer. Someone in this room had murdered Martin Froome, or had ordered his death. It was gut instinct, a feeling, but it was so powerful it was overwhelming her senses.

She looked round at her new colleagues. She had no feeling as to which of them was the guilty one, but the presence of a murderer was very strong.

No – this was paranoia, just like Bell had warned. There was no evidence. The security services worked on evidence, not on hunches. Control yourself, girl!

They all seemed to be looking at her, so she spoke. "Shouldn't we be checking what's happened to Double D?"

Bell attempted to suppress a look of intense annoyance. "I was just about to ask for a moment of silent reflection on the life of our very good friend and colleague, Luther." He closed his eyes.

The others followed suit, leaving Lydia with her eyes open, scanning the faces of her new colleagues, looking for any signs, clues that would identify the killer. It was a ridiculous task, and she knew it.

She found her eyes lingering on Vindi – he had a certain lithe animal grace about him. His beard was close cropped, his hair short and dark; he had long graceful fingers and long eyelashes. She was torn between attraction and fear; this man looked as if he could make killing into an art.

Bell opened his eyes. "That's the formal side of the meeting over. I thought we'd do a brief quiz in honour of Luther." Cue good-natured groans from Farah, Maybe and George. "So we'll have Vindi with George and Maybe in the evening team, and Schizo with Mo and Nylon in the morning one, with Double D to join them if he turns up."

There was more grumbling as Lydia swapped seats with Maybe to sit next to Farah, but she could see they were all smiling. Nylon stood behind them.

Nnnrrnnggg.

It was a sort of rumbling sound, like a burp going from Nylon's throat back down into his stomach, like some desperate repression of air deep inside him.

Farah didn't seem to notice it, but Lydia found it oddly threatening.

"We'll take a beating on this, without Double D," Lydia whispered to Farah.

Farah smiled back. "The Dong's too clever for that. It will be all square coming to the last question – you'll see."

Farah was right: Vindi pulled out a great answer connecting Luther to hornets (Luther Blissett played for Watford, nicknamed Hornets), Lydia knew how many theses Luther had pinned to the door of Wittenberg Cathedral (ninety-five), George knew that Martin Luther's portrait had been painted by Lucas Cranach the older, Nylon knew that Gene Hackman's role in the Superman film was Lex Luthor and Farah was handed a nice easy one (Idris

Elba in the TV series). Sure enough, after several rounds it all came down to the tie break.

Lydia watched Bell closely. He was clearly enjoying this; he read the last question as if he was Lawrence Olivier at Agincourt. "Who killed his or her friend driving a Mercedes on Laurel Canyon Boulevard?"

There was silence. Lydia looked at the faces – deadly serious, riveted on Bell's craggy features.

Nnnrrnnggg: again, that internal eruption from the man in the day-glo overalls standing directly behind her. Again, no one else seemed to notice.

"No takers? Okay, here's the second clue. This person was also involved in the films 'Mo Money' and 'Meteor Man', but not as an actor." Bell's tone was no longer light-hearted – there was something deadly serious…

"Luther Vandross." Lydia said it without thinking. It was a pure guess – he was the only Luther she knew not to have already featured in the quiz.

"Bravo, Schizo! You have led your team to victory. Most impressive." The tension dissolved instantly. Bell beamed at her, and Farah patted her on the back. Nylon stepped back to the bookshelf, allowing Lydia to breathe in. Maybe and George gave little whoops – they clearly didn't mind losing. Vindi didn't react.

Lydia made a mock bow from her seat and gave them all a big smile, but inside she was struggling to analyse what had just happened: was this a harmless game designed to keep their morale up? Was this Bell's exercise in control? Was there a message hidden in that last question, or was he merely dramatising, hamming it up?

Bell was speaking again. "Farah has brought in one of her legendary cakes, so we'll meet for coffee in the main office at 11.30. In the meantime, I am going to leave Schizo in here, so she can use my office to interview each of you individually about Luther. I will take up residence in the main office, where I'll go through your monthly targets and routines with each of you individually. Any questions?" A brief silence. "So, Schizo, who would you like to interview first?"

"What about Double D? Is it usual for him to be this late, especially when it's a full staff meeting?" Bell would have to learn that she didn't give up easily.

"No, he isn't in the habit of arriving late, but such things can happen when you use public transport in London. He's a grown-up, and I trust him to do his best to get here on time. If there's a problem, then it's already happened." Bell's voice was honeyed reason.

The others nodded along with him.

Lydia knew she had to retreat. "I'll see Vindi first." She got up and stood by Bell's desk.

The others filed out silently, leaving Vindi still lounging in his chair underneath the bookshelf, his long legs crossed and his long hands clasped behind his head. The statuette of Baal behind him seemed to stare blankly at Lydia as if in solidarity with Vindi.

She took the seat behind Bell's desk and motioned for Vindi to sit across from her.

Ten seconds. No movement from Vindi; no expression on his face. The book on the shelf above Vindi's head was a big heavy tome – the Ascent of Man; Lydia willed it to topple off its shelf onto Vindi's head but of course it wasn't going to move.

Lydia got up, rounded the desk and moved to the far end of the room. "I'm not playing these silly macho games. I'll come to you. You can say you won."

"Take a seat." Vindi indicated the chair next to him.

She sat in it. "What's the problem, Vindi? Or can I call you Damian?"

"Vindi's better, thank you, Schizo."

"Okay, Vindi. Just help me out here: why are you so hostile to me?"

"I'm not – I'm just puzzled."

"What's puzzling you?"

"Why are you interviewing me? I'm the same grade as you. I was sent down here from Internal Security, like you, but four years ago. I'm the one who knows what goes on down here. Why is this your investigation, not mine?"

Lydia kept her voice level. "A woman called Cariad Jones from H11 was killed four years ago and so far her killer has not been brought to justice. I'm told it's still your investigation. No doubt you're still busy with it."

Vindi kept the poker face.

She continued. "I've been given this second death to investigate. I'd like your help; we could work well together. I'm not here to interview you – I'm here to ask you for your help. Feel free to ask me my thoughts about the death of Cariad Jones."

"I see."

"Has our boss upstairs contacted you?"

Vindi gave a short, bitter laugh. "Ha! Peregrine Webb must hate you to have sent you down here, but believe me: he hates me a whole lot more. There's no way he's going to speak to me if he can possibly help it." Lydia saw his fists were clenched tightly on his lap. "And I'm not going to do anything to help him."

"What happened to stir up so much bad feeling? The story in the department was that you behaved inappropriately towards his daughter Kate."

"I believe the current term is 'fake news'. The victors always write the history. He can put out whatever story he likes while I'm filed away down here." Vindi's brown eyes stared at her with extraordinary intensity.

"So here's your opportunity: put the story straight."

He hesitated, but then shook his head. "What's the point?"

"The point is we need to find Martin Froome's killer, before he or she kills another of your – our – team."

"Luther killed himself." He looked away, as if asking the statuette Baal for confirmation.

Lydia clapped her hands in frustration. "Come on! You don't believe that, and neither does anyone else down here. I personally didn't know what to believe, but I made up my mind when I saw the way you all reacted when you got the news."

He turned back to her. His dark eyes flashed at her. "How did I react?"

"You showed no reaction at all. Good play-acting. If you cared at all for your comrade and if you believed he killed himself in an auto-erotic accident, you'd have shown some shock or some sadness. You know the story is bullshit."

Vindi nodded slowly. Lydia thought she detected the ghost of a smile. "You've discounted the possibility that Luther might have confided in me about his auto-erotic adventures; hence my lack of shock." He spread his hands, and this time he smiled openly. "Until Webb asks for my help, he's not getting it. And I'm not handing you your ticket to get straight out of here while he leaves me to moulder for another four years. If I identify Luther's killer, I'll do it on my terms, and I'll take the credit. I will do anything I can to get out of this hell-hole."

She nodded. "That's honest."

"Are we done now?"

Lydia fixed him with a stare of her own. "If someone else from H11 is killed in the meantime, think hard when you look at yourself in your mirror."

Vindi got up and walked out of Bell's office without a word or a backward glance.

Lydia called out as the door shut. "Please send Maddy – George – to me."

It wasn't Maddy who came through the doorway. It was Bell.

"So sorry, Schizo. I need my office back. It's Double D – a bit of an emergency."

10

LYDIA

Lydia leapt to her feet. "Is Dennis all right?"

"That's what I'm going to find out." Bell was impatient, testy, as he ushered her out of the office.

Dennis stood in the corridor, quaking, almost rippling under his sweat-soaked shirt. When he saw Lydia he looked away.

"What's happened, Dennis?" she asked.

He didn't answer, but squeezed past her and into Bell's office, slamming the door behind him, leaving a swirl of cologne and sweat in the air.

He's terrified, she thought. He was uneasy yesterday, but something has spooked him badly since then. She wanted to follow him into the office and listen to his story but she knew Bell would chuck her out, and Dennis obviously didn't want to talk to her.

She hurried down the corridor to the main office. George, Farah and Maybe were all there, talking in hushed whispers. They turned to Lydia as she entered.

"Do we know what happened to Double D?" Lydia asked. "Is he all right?"

"He didn't say anything." George seemed the calmest of the three. "He just came through the door from the cloakroom shaking and crying. The Dong whisked him off at once."

"Has he been like this before?"

They all shook their heads.

"At least he's safe down here. He's with friends," Farah said. "I'd like to put my arms around him and give him a big slice of cake."

"Yes, he's safe down here." Lydia nodded, but she didn't feel so sure.

"No cake for him: he's on a diet for his production." Maybe shook her head. "He's playing the King of Siam in 'The King and I'. He's always wanted that part. Perhaps that's what's stressed him – pushed him over the edge. He's very highly strung, you know."

They stood awkwardly for a moment.

Lydia broke the silence. "Well, I suppose we all need to just get on with our jobs. I'm sure the Dong will sort things out for Double D. In the meantime, could we talk somewhere private, George? Maybe in the archive stacks?"

"Sure." She smiled. After all the complicated men, George seemed sweet and easy.

They found a corner away from where Vindi was ranging along the files with a fierce look in his eyes. They sat cross-legged on the floor, underneath a CCTV camera, looking along the dimly lit row of grey files.

"It's jolly nice to get another woman of roughly my own age down here at last," George started. "I hope you like it here and decide to stay, at least until I can get my own career back on course."

"It's good to get a positive reaction from one of the team at last."

"Oh, don't mind them. They're all well meaning, really. They don't know how to relate to someone new and dynamic on the scene. They'll come round to you – you'll see." Her smile was warm and open, but Lydia wasn't totally convinced.

"You're very kind. Have they been under this stress for long?"

"We're always under pressure, but obviously Luther's death has hit us all very hard."

Lydia decided to go for it. "You don't actually believe he killed himself by auto-asphyxiation, do you?"

"Why do you say that?" She could feel George's warmth ebbing away.

"You repeated the word 'no' several times when you heard the news."

George shrugged. "It was probably 'oh no'. But yes, it does seem out of character. He was a genuinely nice chap."

"Don't nice chaps do things like that?"

"I wouldn't know." Now she sounded almost frosty. "I just know it wasn't what I'd expect him to do."

"What did you know about his home life?" Lydia ploughed on.

"Nothing much. You'd need to ask Double D – he socialised with Luther a bit. I mainly work with Vindi on the evening shift so we didn't see them that often."

"What was Luther working on down here when he died?"

"You could look it up in the log – it's in the main office. We have to enter all our contacts with the files in it."

"Do you think he could have discovered something dangerous or politically sensitive before he died?"

George shook her head, a blonde curl falling across her forehead. "Look, do you really think Luther could have been murdered?"

Lydia nodded. "I'm assuming it until I hear proof to the contrary."

"Gosh."

"Gosh what?"

"The Dong said it was an accident. I trust him. I've worked in the service for four years, and you're the first person I've met who assumes as a default position that her bosses are lying to her."

"I don't hold default positions – I'm just a natural sceptic, an empiricist who works things out from evidence. Working in Internal Security you have to question everything. What about you? You must have some anti-establishment bone in your body if you've been transferred here. What did you do?"

"Oh, it was an unfortunate case of sexual harassment. I dealt with it like a twenty-six-year-old: badly." She laughed.

"Of course you did! Any woman of your age has a right to deal with such a thing badly, and not get victimised for it. The bastards!" Lydia looked up at the white ceiling in exasperation. Why was it always the female victim who lost out, and why did they accept it so meekly?

George laughed. "No – it wasn't like that."

"What do you mean?"

"I wasn't the victim – I was the harasser. I like to get what I want, and on this occasion I got a bit carried away."

"Sorry. I jumped to..."

"It's fine. Maybe I look like a victim, but I've never been one. People often judge me by my looks. It's always a mistake." George gave Lydia a friendly but overlong stare. At close quarters, Lydia could detect steel in those green eyes. "We're going to get on well – I know it."

Was that a prediction or a threat?

Lydia smiled back. "I know it too. So tell me, George, what do you do to keep yourself sane while you're down here?"

"What do you mean?"

"Vindi works out, the Dong devises quizzes, Double D sings – what do you do?"

"I work hard. I'm very ambitious, and I'm going to get out of H11 with a glowing reference. In any lull, I plan my future career."

"That can't be all you do, even if you have very big plans. You get plenty of lulls down here."

George laughed. "You're right: it's one long lull usually. Actually, I'm writing a novel. Mind you, I don't write it at work – I wouldn't be so unprofessional, and anyway I wouldn't be allowed to take anything I wrote out of here, but I plan it in my head – obsessively."

"What sort of novel?" Lydia had already guessed the answer.

"It's a murder mystery – subtle yet gory."

"I'm sure there's some inspirational material in some of these files."

George gave her a long hard look. "I would never do anything like that. I want to live to a ripe old age."

"I didn't mean that…"

"Look, the contents of these files aren't at all nice. If you don't treat them with care and total respect, you'll find yourself in very deep waters."

"Very sage advice, George." It was Bell. He appeared from behind a stack, moving almost silently in his open sandals.

Lydia and George struggled to their feet. "Is Dennis all right?" Lydia asked.

"Yes, I think so."

"Can I speak to him?"

"I'm afraid that's not possible." Bell looked suitably serious.

"Why not? Has he said he won't talk to me?"

"I've come to find you to ask if you'd like to join me in my office, where I can update you on the situation." He gestured the way back through the stacks.

"Oh. Thank you."

She followed him along the corridor, past the kitchen and toilet, to his office. She sat below the plasma screen, which was now displaying a Germanic castle. Bell sat down opposite her.

"Where's Dennis? What happened to him?" she asked.

"Double D has had a breakdown. I sent him home. He was in no fit state to work. I've told him to take the next three days off as a minimum, and then to report to the medical office upstairs."

"What did he tell you had happened to him? Something must have spooked him badly."

"He's having paranoid delusions, I'm afraid. It's not uncommon down here."

"What, precisely, are his delusions?" Lydia leaned forward.

"He imagines he's being followed. It's obviously triggered by the death of his friend Luther. He fears an assassination team are out to get him because these people may believe that he knows something important."

"Does he know something important?"

Bell spread his hands. "We all know important, dangerous secrets – it's what H11 is about. It doesn't mean we're in imminent danger of being assassinated."

"Yet that's what's happened to Martin Froome."

"You and I have both been briefed: Luther's death was an accident."

"You really believe that?" She couldn't keep the scorn from her voice.

His face was immobile. "Until I'm told otherwise – yes. It's not something I'm prepared to discuss any further, because neither of us know any more than we've been told, and I, for one, do not indulge in unfounded speculation." He sounded stiff and wounded.

Lydia tried another tack. "Why does Dennis think he's being followed?"

"A man got on the same tube train as him."

Lydia continued to fix him with a stare.

He resumed. "Double D went through an elaborate procedure to shake this man off, but they still shared a carriage down to Baker Street. Then they both changed lines and also shared the same carriage down to Embankment."

"Did anything happen between them?"

"Nothing."

"Have you got a description of this man?"

"Yes." His face was set.

"Please share it with me." She was going to have to drag it out of him.

"Why?"

"Because I might want to follow it up."

He sighed. "About thirty, male, white, dark stubble, wearing a baseball cap and a tan jacket; that's all Double D said."

"Thank you."

Bell fixed her with a frown that creased his face alarmingly. "Schizo, I won't have you do anything that endangers Double D. His welfare is my priority right now. He's very fragile, and anything that threatens him may push him over the edge. He's terrified of talking to you."

"I understand." She said it with a level voice. Inside she was burning.

I understand more than you think, you controlling bastard.

11

BRIAN

Bri Powell had his feet up on the desk and a cup of tea in his hand. He'd closed his eyes and was breathing deeply, like they'd taught him in the service. He always savoured his breaks alone in the Techie Mess. It was a scruffy sort of place, full of bits of junk and stupid jokes stuck up on the wall, but it was where he felt most at home, especially when his colleagues weren't there. It wasn't that he disliked the other techies, but he found them wearing at times; in fact he found most people wearing most of the time.

"Hello."

He hadn't heard her enter. He swung his legs off the desk and jumped up out of his chair, all in one motion. His hot tea splattered his trousers.

Lydia Twomey stared wide-eyed at him. "God, I'm sorry," she said. "I didn't mean to startle you. I didn't even realise it was you without your day-glo overalls on."

"No, no, it's all right. I only wear them down in H11. I didn't hear you. I was miles away. I've always been jumpy, ever since…" He cut himself off.

"Ever since your service days in the Paras? I'm sorry."

"You've read my file." She would know the circumstances under which he'd been invalided out seven years before.

She nodded. "I've read the files on all the H11 team. It's routine procedure. Look, I'm really sorry. Can I make you another cup of tea?"

"No, I'm fine. Are you here to interview me about Martin Froome?" He moved so his wet crotch was hidden from her by his chair. "I won't be able to help you much."

"I thought I'd pop in and have a general chat. I've finished for the day down in H11 but now I've got to wait to report to my upstairs boss, so I thought I'd get to know you. May I sit down?"

Bri nodded at the chair at the opposite desk. She walked over and sat down. He sat, happy that his wet crotch was now hidden below the desktop. He looked across to her, but then averted his eyes. She was very pretty.

Nnnrrnnggg. He needed to manage his insides with this girl around. She mustn't think he was rattled.

"What should I call you up here? I seem to have got it consistently wrong down in H11."

"Like I told you down in H11, Bri is fine up here." He swallowed. His mouth was dry – he could have done with that tea.

"You have a unique view of H11 – you're the only person who sees the place regularly but isn't fully part of it. How do you find it?"

"It's all right. They're nice enough." Brian was trying to recall all his training in resisting interrogation. Present as small a target as you can – that was one of the key rules.

"What sort of work do you do down there?"

"Whatever I'm asked – mending shelves or desks. Shifting anything heavy. Cleaning – I sweep the floors, clean the toilet, clean the cooker, that sort of thing. There's a strict division of duties, as you know – they call it 'demarcation'. We can't have an officer grade doing those things." There, he hadn't given her anything to chew on.

"Do you think that we officers should clean up after ourselves? I think we should."

He shrugged. "It keeps me in a job."

"Do you mend the computers?"

"I've never had to. They're very basic ones down there – nothing much to go wrong." He didn't want to get sucked into this.

"But you're an expert, right? You could mend them, or access anything in the H11 computers, if you needed to?"

"You've read my file." She knew that he was one of the prime computer trouble-shooters in Thames House.

"Who do you mainly talk to when you're down in H11?"

"Whoever will talk to me: mainly Farah and Maybe."

"They're very friendly, aren't they? They make you feel at home."

"Yes." He wasn't going to play that game.

"Had you noticed any tension in the days leading up to Martin Froome's death?"

"None."

Nnnrrnnggg. He needed to stay cool.

"Not even Dennis? You've heard that he's off with stress now?"

"No I hadn't heard. I don't usually get told things. Poor him." Bri twirled a strand of his beard around his finger.

"Did you know of any reason why anyone might hold a grudge against Martin Froome?"

"Why? He killed himself. You were there when we were told."

"Do you find working in Thames House dull, humdrum, after the excitements of the Paras? You seemed to have led a very eventful life as a soldier."

"It was a different life – I've put it all behind me."

"Do you think that the H11 colleagues treat you as an outsider?"

That question took him by complete surprise. "Why do you say that?"

"The way they looked at you – it was the same as how they look at me. And Bell – he patronised you."

"Hey, wait a minute! I never said anything…" He was totally off balance now.

"But it's true, isn't it?"

She'd pushed his button. "Not all of them are like that."

"Who's nice to you, then?"

"Farah. She's like my mum. I call her 'Sweet' and I call Maybe 'Sour'. Sweet and Sour – that's how they are." He knew he'd slipped, but he didn't care. He'd waited a while to share this with someone. "And Bell – the Dong as he likes to call himself – he's so stuck up – thinks he's so superior, so clever."

"What about Dennis? No one could object to him, surely?"

"He's a faggot." Bri knew that he was way out of line now, but he was enjoying himself. He loved the way this girl's blue eyes widened every time he said something shocking. "And Martin – he smelt of booze most days."

"So what's your view on Vindi – Damian?"

"He thinks he's hard. Ha! I'd take him with one hand tied behind my back."

The girl Lydia smiled – nice teeth. "George seems a nice girl."

That was like a bucket of water thrown over him. How the hell had this girl got him going, blabbing like this? He could never ever say what he thought of the Goddess of the Stacks. They'd lock him up and give him electric shocks.

"Yes." There – he'd managed to step back from the edge of the precipice.

"Why do you like her?"

"You said it: she seems nice. I don't know her, really. I haven't got anything else to say about H11 colleagues."

Nnnrrnnggg.

"Oh." She looked at him closely. She knew he was hiding something.

So the interrogation went on, with this girl acting like she was ferreting out gossip from a barroom chat and Brian playing it all with a dead bat. He didn't give her anything more. He told her that he never talked about his time in the Paras – it was past and gone. He told her about his love for heavy metal bands like Iron Maiden and Motorhead; she tried to curry favour with him by saying that she liked Patti Smith and the Velvet Underground, but he wasn't impressed. He was amazed that she went on trying for so long before she gave up, stood up, shook his hand and left the Techie Mess.

Once she was gone he made himself another cup of tea and sat sipping it, letting the steam moisten his face. Brian found most women unsettling, but this one was uber-scary. She could creep up on you and she asked questions that his mum would have called 'impertinent'. Brian really didn't like anyone showing an interest in him, least of all a young woman with big blue eyes.

She'd got him all steamed up, and that was dangerous.

12

PERRY

It had already been a bad day for Peregrine Webb, and it was about to get worse. He'd consumed his self-allocated daily ration of 'little white helpers' but felt in need of just one more. He'd set up a team to look into the Froome death, but they'd started with no good ideas, and after a day of putting out feelers, shaking a few trees and generally moving the stationery around their desks, they'd come up with precisely nothing. He'd had an ominous enquiry from the DG asking how the investigation was going.

It was gone 6pm – the time he'd promised Glenys he'd be home – and he had Gerard Bell and Lydia Twomey waiting to see him. Neither of them looked happy; he wasn't ecstatic to see them, either.

He invited Gerard in first. "Glad you could make it up here, Gerard. We don't see enough of you these days. How's it all going?" He indicated the straight-backed chair in front of his desk and sat down in his swivel chair behind his desk, beneath the portrait of the Queen, as if she was his defender.

"It's not going well." Gerard sat down heavily, with a grunt. His white suit, bizarre shirt and lack of socks looked sorely out of place in Perry's office.

"How can I help?" Perry kept the tone optimistic and light.

"The girl out there."

"What's the problem?" Perry could guess, but it would be good to hear Gerard say it. Perry was Marlborough, Cambridge and Boodles, while Gerard was Winchester, Oxford and the Athenaeum, but they had joined the service in the same intake and had both been fast-tracked, tipped for the top. Perry felt Gerard had always regarded himself as quietly superior, an intellectual, while Perry had always regarded himself as a sounder, more reliable chap. Gerard's missteps had resulted in him falling from grace, all the way to the depths of H11, but Perry's career had subsequently stagnated, too; now they were both thinking about exit strategies and pensions.

"That girl you've sent me: I want you to take her back." Gerard was doing his best to look and sound casual, but Perry was gratified to notice signs of annoyance.

"That's rather radical, Gerard. I know she needs careful handling, but she's bright and dynamic. I thought she'd be a good match for H11." Perry had to admit he was already enjoying this conversation more than he had anticipated.

"She's disrupting my team and endangering my staff. I won't have it."

"How is she disruptive?" Perry tried hard to disguise his gloating.

"She's refusing to buy into our way of doing things. But much worse, she's caused one of my staff, Dennis Dunn, to go off with what might be a breakdown, and now she's insisting she interview him at his home."

"What do you want me to do, Gerard?"

"I've told you: pull her from the case. Take her back into your 'careful handling.'" Gerard lolled back in his chair, legs crossed, as if he were relaxing in front of the fire at his club, but Perry knew he was fuming.

"I'm sorry old chap, but no can do. The DG has taken a personal interest in the case, and in Lydia's involvement." Okay, it was a slight exaggeration, but one Gerard couldn't argue against.

Gerard uncrossed his legs and leaned forward. Suddenly he was on the attack. "Why on earth would the DG take an interest in a case of an accidental death of a comparatively junior officer?"

Ah. Gerard had him there.

"That's what I was about to brief you about." Perry shifted awkwardly in his seat. "We've had a second autopsy done, and I'm afraid to tell you that your man was probably assassinated – puncture mark in his neck – then posed to make it look like auto-asphyxiation. A skilled professional job. The DG has ordered a full investigation team."

Gerard leaned back and recrossed his legs. "So if I hadn't come to see you this evening, when were you going to tell me this very unwelcome news?"

"This evening." Perry knew it sounded pathetic, weak. "I was going to tell you as soon as possible. Obviously I needed to tell you before I told Lydia."

"Oh, she knows already. All day she's been trying to tell my team that Martin was murdered." Gerard smiled; his teeth were as eccentric as his face.

"How did she know?" Perry could feel himself blush. He looked away, over the Thames to Lambeth.

"She worked it out. Just like I did. It wasn't hard to do. And now she's winding up everyone she talks to down in H11."

"I'm sorry about that."

"So am I." Gerard stood up. "So am I, Perry. Just get her out of my department by tomorrow. Find an excuse, anything. Tell her now. I don't expect to see her down there again, and I expect prompt, full briefings on everything that you and your team come up with. Oh, and one other thing: please put an armed guard on

Dennis Dunn's home, starting now. Make sure his panic button is working. The poor man is terrified and he needs reassurance."

"Do you know how much an armed guard costs per day? I can't be paying indefinitely just to reassure an archivist with paranoid delusions." He paused. "They are paranoid delusions, aren't they?"

"Don't let that girl get near him – it could tip him over the edge." He marched over to the door and waited to be buzzed out.

"Look, Gerard, I'll keep her out of your hair for a couple of days, but I'm not going to be dictated to as to whom I appoint or withdraw. The DG will want to know how she's getting along so I can't permanently take her out of H11. I'll also give your man twenty-four hours of armed guard; after that you need to get him medical attention. How's that?" He pressed the button to release the door lock.

Gerard shook his head. "It's not good enough, but it's a start. If my man dies..." He turned and left Perry's office, leaving the door open.

Perry sat back and once more looked out over the Thames.

Well, well. He hadn't seen Gerard as rattled as that since the day he was sent in disgrace down to H11. Perry found Lydia difficult, but she'd really got under Gerard's skin like a rash. Good for her.

"Can I come in, sir?"

He swivelled in his chair. Lydia had put her head round the door.

"Yes, please do, Lydia. Shut the door behind you." She walked over and stood in front of him. "Please sit down." She obeyed. "It seems as if you've ruffled a few feathers down in H11. Gerard's not very happy with your performance. He wants me to withdraw you."

"I haven't got into the routine archiving yet, if that's his problem. I've been preoccupied with getting to the truth about Martin Froome's murder."

"Murder? What makes you think it was murder?"

"Confirmed inferences. I'm sure you have your reasons for withholding the truth from me, sir, but please don't ask me to stop working it out for myself."

"I was going to tell you this evening."

"I'm sure you were. Please don't let me stop you now."

Perry recounted all the facts of the case, and confessed that the outside team had made little progress. He looked over the Thames for most of the story – he found it hard to face her.

"So you've got no leads yet." Lydia was brisk. "I've got two. First, interview Double D – Dennis Dunn. I'd like to be in on it. He's hiding something."

"We can't do that. Gerard has told me he's terrified – especially of you."

"Who is terrified of me – Dennis Dunn or Gerard Bell?"

Perry actually laughed. "Dennis Dunn, but I think everyone is terrified of you. Anyway, you can't go near him. He could be suicidal."

"That isn't true, sir. Bell is just trying to control him, keeping him away from me. The whole set-up in H11 is designed by Bell for his total control – the nicknames, the fancy dress, the quizzes – they all dance to his tune."

"Are you saying Bell is deliberately hindering our inquiry? Think carefully before you answer, Lydia – this is a serious allegation."

She stopped. It was indeed a serious allegation. She spoke slowly. "I am not saying he is deliberately hindering the inquiry – yet. He's a paternalist who looks after his team by controlling them, and he thinks this inquiry will weaken his control and threaten his team."

"That's a mature assessment, Lydia. Let's keep it at that. Now, you said you had two leads – what's the second one?"

"The man on the tube train who spooked Dennis Dunn. Bell said it was Dennis's paranoid delusions, but we should check it out. This man allegedly waited for Dennis on the platform at Willesden Green, waited again when Dennis tried to shake him off, rode in the same carriage down to Baker Street, changed with Dennis to the Bakerloo Line, got on the same carriage again, and rode with him all the way to Embankment. If I was Dennis, I'd be freaked, too."

"It probably never happened – Gerard says it was a paranoid delusion."

"We could check whether it happened."

"Even if it did happen, it was probably just a coincidence, blown up into a conspiracy by Dunn. Plenty of people take that route to work. I mean, this man didn't communicate with Dunn, did he? He didn't threaten him."

"His very presence would be a threat. I have the man's description: about thirty, male, white, dark stubble, wearing a baseball cap and a tan jacket. You can get hold of the CCTV footage from the platforms and the carriage then we can check him out. We may be able to identify him, and then pull him in for questioning."

"Well…"

"Have you anything better to do with your team, sir?" Her nose tilted upward into combat mode.

"I suppose it's worth a punt." Again, he was talking to the Thames.

"It might save a life – possibly Dennis's, maybe mine."

Perry tapped his Montblanc fountain pen on his desk. "What on earth makes you say that? I hope Dunn's paranoid delusions aren't catching."

"We now know Martin Froome was killed. Why would someone want to kill him? It's very likely the reason was related to his work – he doesn't seem to have had a life outside work. So was he killed to shut him up? Because he knew something he shouldn't know?"

"What are you driving at, Lydia?"

"Unless Martin was a blackmailer, which seems out of character, no one outside H11 has a motive to order his assassination. The only people who know what Martin was working on and what he had in his head are his colleagues inside H11. That suggests that one or more of those seven or eight people in H11 conspired to murder him."

"Make up your mind. Which is it – seven or eight?"

"Seven colleagues plus the technician who goes down once a week; he does have access to H11 but he doesn't seem very involved with the rest of the team. If Dennis is killed like Martin was, it will be one of his six surviving colleagues who is trying to cover something up."

"This is just conjecture."

"Yes, but if I get any closer to the truth, he, she or they won't be asking for me to be withdrawn from H11 – they will be trying to murder me. I need your unconditional and honest support if we're going to get a result. I'd like to stay alive."

"You have my support." He omitted the adjectives. As he said it, Perry felt a wave of indigestion welling up through his guts. "But..."

"Yes?" Her blue eyes flashed a challenge.

"I don't want you going down to H11 tomorrow. Give Gerard and his team time to digest the news of Martin Froome's murder. They need some space. I'll get the external team chasing up the CCTV footage of the man on the tube trains – that was a good idea of yours. Take a day's leave."

"Oh. This is the deal you've made with Bell, is it? Keep me out of his way?"

"We all have to make compromises, Lydia, and the more responsibility we have, the more people we need to accommodate. Just enjoy your day off."

Long after she'd gone and he had arranged an armed guard team for Dennis Dunn then recorded Lydia's description of the man on the tube, Perry remained in his dark office, staring across the Thames, ignoring the calls from Glenys.

Just one more pill.

13

GERARD

"Good to see you, Gerard. Louisa's doing awfully well."

"Still batting for Britain, Gerard? Splendid. Keep up the good work."

"You're looking well, Gerard. Been on some exotic trip again, have you?"

Most encounters for Gerard Bell at his wife's book launches lasted about ten seconds: enough time for some politico, agent or publisher to clap him on the back, ask him an inane question, and then escape before Gerard could give an answer. The showbiz types obviously had no idea who he was but would look at his distinctive face and wonder if they knew him. The ambitious young things would try to engage him in conversation to find out who he was and whether he could further their career. Book launches were strictly duty for Gerard, and this one wasn't even for one of Louisa's own authors.

He'd returned home out of sorts after a trying day, and Louisa had insisted that he come out with her to the Reading and Writing Room of 1, Whitehall Place, for the launch of an ex-minister's memoirs. She'd said he needed a change of environment with something different to think about. He'd protested that the venue was just round the corner from his work so it was hardly going to take his mind off it, but to no avail. So here he was, stuck in an overheated room with over two hundred guests swilling the mediocre bubbly. Overhead the crystal chandeliers twinkled, their light absorbed by the thick rich Pugin wallpaper and heavy red curtains. His brogues sank into the spongy salmon and grey carpet.

It was purgatory.

Louisa networked relentlessly, at first with Gerard on her arm, but he soon made his excuses and drifted to the edge of the room. He stood under one of the patterned columns, viewing the guests, trying to count how many names he knew. Several people looked away when they saw him – he was always amazed at how many Westminster people seemed to know what his role in MI5 was, when it was supposed to be so secret. He was also surprised at how many of them imagined H11 held dirt on them personally.

One man reacted to Gerard in a different way: Lord Brooke fixed him with a momentary glare, before moving smoothly to chat with the Shadow Spokesman for Food, Fisheries and Farming. Gerard watched Brooke waffle a few words, pat the politician's arm, glance to check Gerard hadn't moved and then slide to the next group, his bald head like a pale egg bobbing above the other heads in the scrum under the chandeliers. Brooke was working away from him, but Gerard knew that he would turn – he was locked on to his target.

Lord Brooke: not the Tory ex-minister Lord Brooke of Sutton Mandeville, nor the ex-Trade Unionist Lord Brooke of Alverthorpe, but the third Lord Brooke, the ferocious litigator, the sleek alpha male of the libel courts. Gerard watched him homing in like a Cruise missile on Gerard's position under the column. He considered nipping off to the toilets, just to annoy

Brooke, but he didn't fancy an encounter at the urinals with the man.

Gerard was fending off some polite conversation from an earnest young historian (and aspiring author, of course), when Lord Brooke finally slid alongside him. The historian stammered an excuse and moved on, leaving Gerard alone with Brooke in a crowd of two hundred people talking about themselves. No one would ever hear the conversation that was about to start.

Gerard got his retaliation in first. "Good evening, Brooke. Here's a quiz question for you: how did Robert Greville, the second Baron Brooke, die?"

"I've got no time for your games, Bell." The hairless head, the steely grey eyes and the thin mouth showed no sign of humour or comfort. "I've heard there's a cock-up in your kingdom."

"Who told you that?"

"It doesn't matter. My clients want you to know that they're watching developments. Keep me informed."

"Official Secrets Act, old chap."

"Don't give me that!" Brooke's face betrayed no expression, but the low voice was heavy with the sort of suppressed rage often deployed by bullies. "Get it sorted. Quickly. Cleanly. Let me know when it's done."

"Before you go, what's your answer to the quiz question?"

"Don't try to threaten me." The tone was even, but deadly serious. Gerard was pretty sure a parvenu like Brooke would have researched the family history of the aristocratic Brookes, so he'd know that the second Baron had been the world's first sniper victim, back in the English Civil War.

Brooke turned his back on Gerard, put his champagne flute on a waitress's tray, took a canapé from another proffered tray, and moved off into the crowd like a circling barracuda.

Gerard leaned back against the column. All around the vacuous chatter and serious business continued unabated, as if nothing had happened. He closed his eyes and concentrated on restoring his heartbeat to an even rate.

"Are you all right, sir?" A strong Polish accent.

He opened his eyes. The waiter in front of him was looking concerned but also a little wary, as if he had to deal with drunks on a regular basis, even in a place this smart.

Gerard clicked back into gear. "Yup. Fine, thank you." He strode off into the crowd, looking for Louisa.

She was listening to a well-known publisher listing his triumphs.

Gerard touched her elbow. "I'm going home, darling. Not feeling great." He gave her a peck on the cheek, and made for the door.

Louisa shot him an anxious glance; the publisher didn't break stride with the fascinating tales of his cleverness.

Gerard had escaped just in time: they were testing the microphones, marshalling everyone for the presentations. He got his coat from the cloakroom attendants and made his way past security into the street. It was only a few yards to Embankment tube station, but he walked past it, turned left under the bridge where the homeless were settling down for the night, and on along the embankment, the Thames on his right.

The sky was as clear as it ever got in London and it was warm for April. He kept walking. The Thames glistened. The cars passed on his left, headlights picking up the exhaust fumes.

God, what a day! First that wretched girl upsetting his carefully constructed ecosystem down in H11 – his 'kingdom', as Brooke called it. Next the trouble with Double D, poor man. Then Perry getting all arsey. And finally this bombshell from that bastard, Brooke.

Who had leaked the shit to Brooke? It wouldn't be anyone in his H11 team, that was certain. It wouldn't be Lydia Twomey, either; no way would she be in with Brooke and his sort of clients.

Perry? Surely not: he'd know Brooke, but any leak would weaken Perry as much as it would hurt Gerard. The DG? Definitely not – this was political dynamite.

The damage was done. Now what?

He kept walking.

It was close to midnight by the time he'd got tired of walking by the Thames, caught the District Line tube back to Kensington, then walked to their elegant house in Phillimore Place. When he dragged himself up the stairs, Louisa was in her polka dot pyjamas, sitting up in bed with her laptop. She looked stunning – a Klimt model with her Art Noveau haircut. She saved her work and closed the laptop.

"Not still working, are you darling?" He slumped and lay face down on the bed. "Tell me you were trawling the fashion sites."

"We've received an extended avalanche of dross recently. A literary agent's life isn't one long party, as you well know. Besides, I didn't want to go to sleep before I had the chance to check you were all right. Where have you been? You had me worried."

"I'm fine. I just wanted a walk to clear my head." His voice was muffled by the duvet.

"You looked like you'd seen a ghost when you left."

"Just tired: a lot on my plate at work." He looked up.

Louisa leant forward and kissed him on the top of his head. "You're always working too hard, poor lamb." She laughed.

He laughed, too. "It's too late at night for sarcasm."

"I hope that beastly man Brooke wasn't horrid to you. I saw him hunting you down; he didn't look at all friendly."

"He's never friendly. Litigation is his vocation."

"You be nice to him, Gerry darling. He's got powerful friends." She ruffled his hair.

"So have I. Mostly the same ones, though." He sat back up. The blood rushed through his head, making him dizzy.

"Go and have a bath. I've left the water in and it should still be warm. A good sleep will put everything to rights."

"Thank you dear." He got to his feet and shuffled off to the bathroom. "I envy your optimism."

14

LYDIA

"You shouldn't have come all this way. I told you I was fine."

"Is that all the welcome I get?" Lydia gave her mum a kiss and a hug, noticing how much thinner she was. She stepped into the ground floor maisonette and across the tiny hall into the kitchen. "I'm frozen. Are you going to offer me a coffee? I'll make it."

Her mother followed her into the kitchen. "You'll do no such thing, my dear. I'm perfectly capable of making a couple of coffees." She nudged her daughter out of the way, and filled the kettle from the water filter jug. "It's so good to see you, Lyds. How are you? Why are you off work today?"

"I've got a day's leave so I thought I'd see how you were. I haven't been up for weeks."

"If you'd given me proper warning, I'd have made a cake."

"That's a good reason not to give you a warning."

Sarah Twomey stood back and looked carefully at her daughter. "You're looking thin. You're not eating enough."

"I could say the same for you, Mum."

"You always fuss. My specialist, Mr. Yates, says I'm doing very well, all things considered." Her smile was brave but tired.

Sarah busied herself getting out the mugs, milk and the biscuits, while Lydia dumped her helmet in the hall and took off her leathers. It had been a tedious wet ride up the M1 to Nuneaton and she had started out at dawn but she was glad she'd made the effort.

Her mother had been diagnosed with Multiple Sclerosis nearly ten years ago, when Lydia had been away at university. Then five years later, just when Lydia was starting to make progress in MI5, her father had died. Lydia had offered to give up work and move back to Nuneaton, but her mother had fiercely rejected the offer, maintaining that she was perfectly capable of living independently.

Lydia returned to the kitchen as Sarah was about to pour the boiling water over the Tesco's instant coffee granules in the Penguin books mugs – Sarah had Virginia Woolf's 'A Room of My Own' and Lydia had Jane Austen's 'Pride and Prejudice'.

"Let me do that, Mum."

Her mother shot her a look of anger. "I can do it perfectly well, thank you."

"Sorry." She watched as Sarah poured. At one point the boiling water did get directed onto the table, but Lydia kept still. They sat down on either side of the blue Formica-topped table, and Sarah dabbed the puddle of water with a Socialist Worker tea towel. Lydia took a chocolate digestive biscuit, and waited for the inevitable inquisition.

"So is there a new relationship on the horizon?"

"No, Mum."

"You've got to get over him, Lyds."

"I thought we agreed that we won't talk about him." Only yesterday, Lydia had congratulated herself for not thinking about James for a whole morning. He had decided to leave, putting his career above his relationship, and had left for New York. End of story.

Her mother didn't give up. "I'm not talking about him – I'm talking about you. You won't stay young and beautiful forever.

There are other pebbles on the beach, you know. Do you still do your yoga?"

"When I can. It's mainly middle-aged women."

"What about your friends from uni? Do you see much of them?"

"They're spread all over the world now. Jenny's got two kids and Megan's expecting. They're very busy."

"And you're still committed to living in that poky little flat in Hanwell, all on your own?"

"I like it. I can afford the rent and I've still got eight months on the contract. Hanwell is handy for getting to Nuneaton. I'm fine, honestly." Lydia took a bite of her biscuit.

"You look tired and stressed."

"Thanks for the encouragement."

"But lovely. Pale and interesting, they call it. What are your colleagues like? Surely there's a nice shy single man pining for you somewhere in a corner of your office. There always is."

Lydia laughed. "Ha! Chance would be a fine thing! The single ones are either kids, predators or prats. Anyway, they think I'm gay."

"You must have given them some cause to think that." Sarah frowned, but she was laughing too. "You're a very contrary girl."

"And what about you, Mum? Any man pining for you across the Community Centre counter? There always is one, you know."

"They're mostly very sweet and rather sad." Sarah looked away.

"What's wrong, Mum?"

"Nothing, dear."

"Yes, there is. Please tell me."

Sarah was silent for a full twenty seconds. Lydia waited. She looked away, trying to work out where the postcards stuck on her mother's kitchen unit were from. She dreaded the answer.

"I'm giving up my work in the Community Centre."

"Oh, I am sorry." Lydia reached out and took her mother's hand. "Has 'it' got worse?"

"No – I think I'm fine." Sarah withdrew her hand to her lap. "I'm holding my body together. You haven't seen me shake, have you?"

"So what's the problem?"

"Mr. Yates calls them 'cognitive problems'. They're not serious. I can look after myself perfectly well. But… well, I am getting a bit forgetful. Silly things, you know. My balance isn't great – I've had a couple of falls – nothing I can't deal with, but it's not a good look behind a community desk. I've got lots of very good friends but I shall miss my job horribly, I know."

Lydia stood up, and stretched out her arms. "Come here, Mum."

Sarah grumbled and said there was no need for drama, but she stood up, and was folded in her daughter's arms. A few tears were silently shed.

Lydia spent the rest of the day ferociously sorting things. She moved the heavy pieces of furniture and cleaned under and behind them. She went through her mother's bills and online bank account, cancelling some old standing orders. She obtained the names and telephone numbers of the social services office who should be providing support, but she wasn't able to get through to them without a prior appointment. She went round to the neighbours, the Kamkars, a nice old Kurdish couple, for a chat about her mother's situation, but they were more in need of support than her mother, and expressed their gratitude for all the help Sarah had given them.

Finally, Lydia went shopping with her mother on the bus. Lydia insisted on buying her mother a reclining garden chair for the coming summer. Sarah wanted to buy her daughter a respectable blouse, so they had a hilarious time inspecting a range of inappropriate tops. The rain had gone and the sun shone. They ate sticky buns in Riversley Park and made up silly stories about the passing walkers. They laughed a lot. Lydia got the new chair stuck in the bus door on the return journey and they laughed some more.

When it was time for Lydia to put on her motorbike leathers for the journey back to London, Sarah hugged her daughter and Lydia worked hard to hold back the tears.

"You look after yourself, my dear. Drive safely."

"Of course I will, Mum."

"I don't know if that man is going to follow you all the way back to London."

"What? What man?" Lydia frowned.

"The man who was following us around town today."

"There wasn't anyone following us, Mum."

"Yes there was. Didn't you see him in the park? I was going to make up a story about him. I thought maybe he was your security back-up, or something. I don't know what work it is you do down there, but it all sounds very cloak and dagger."

"What did this man look like? I didn't see anyone." I wasn't looking for anyone, she thought. I was too busy concentrating on giving my mother a nice day.

"Oh, I don't know. About your age, black stubble like most young men have these days. He had a cap on, so I couldn't see his face clearly. Maybe he's the young man pining for you from the corner of your office."

"Mum, are you absolutely positive you saw this man following us? Are you sure it wasn't one of your cognitive problems?"

Her mother looked hurt: the corners of her mouth turned down. "I'm sorry I told you about that. We had such a nice day."

Lydia shook her head. "I'm sorry, I'm sorry. I believe you. It's just a shock to learn that someone's been following me. You don't need to worry about it – I'm sure it's nothing – probably just some work training exercise."

"Hmm." Her mother didn't look convinced. "You look after yourself, Lyds."

"I'm just popping out the back for a minute, Mum."

Lydia slipped out of the back door, and through the tiny back garden. She pulled the bolt back on the garden gate and slipped into the alleyway.

The setting sun shone along the length of the alley, blinding her for a moment. She ducked down into shadow, but she was too late: she saw someone move fifty yards away at the end of the row of maisonettes, and then whoever it was had disappeared. She sprinted to the end of the alley, but there was no one there. She heard a car start up on the road beyond the privet hedge. She raced to the gap in the hedge, and was just in time to see a silver hatchback car, probably a Ford Fiesta, disappear round the corner.

Lydia stamped her foot. "Shit!"

She walked back to the alley, and then to her mother's garden. Why on earth would someone follow her on her day off? Why would they come all the way from London up to Nuneaton? What would anyone think she could possibly be doing in Nuneaton, for Christ's sakes? Was it the same guy who'd followed Dennis on the tube? She had no answers.

"Did you see him, then? Did you catch him?" Her mum was standing on the back doorstep. "I told you he was following us."

"Yes, Mum. Nothing to be worried about: just one of the trainees from our office. When I get to work tomorrow I shall have a big whinge about not being told I was being used as a guinea-pig today."

Her mother shook her head, but she went along with it. "Well, I'm glad it's all cleared up, anyway."

Lydia smiled and gave her mother a hug. "You were right, and I never spotted him. It looks like there's not much wrong with your cognitive faculties after all."

"You just look after yourself, Lyds."

"You keep saying that. I'm a big girl now."

"I worry about you."

"And I worry about you. We've got worry in our DNA."

Lydia rode her Kawasaki back to London, constantly checking her mirror for a silver hatchback.

Next morning Lydia arrived early for work and went straight to Peregrine Webb's office. Webb's PA, Miss Parmenter, was already in, and asked her to wait in the outer office.

At 9.10am Webb arrived, but he rushed past Lydia. "Sorry – very busy. Make an appointment with Miss Parmenter, please. Don't go down to H11 until I've seen you."

The door closed, and he was gone.

Lydia was granted a slot with Webb at 10.30, so she went off to find the H11 investigation external team. She found them down the corridor – two operatives in a cramped office. She knew both of them well: Jon Small was the same age and grade as her, while Ashar Chowdry was a grade below. Lydia had assessed both as capable and conformist.

Ashar looked over her thick-rimmed glasses. "Hi Lydia. Webb told us that you'd be with us all day. But…"

Lydia pulled a face. "All day? I was supposed to be back with H11 today."

"It must be a change of plan."

"Is that because you've got some stunning progress to share with me?"

Ashar smiled. "Not exactly, but we've got one breakthrough. It's your man on the tube: we've got the CCTV coverage of him, but it's unclear as to whether he's definitely shadowing Dennis Dunn. As Webb says, it could just be coincidence that they've travelled the same route in the same carriage."

"Can I see the coverage?"

"Sure."

Dennis had described the man correctly: in his thirties, lean, black stubble, baseball cap. Lydia watched the CCTV clips from two stations and two tube carriages, and at no time did this man look directly at a camera. His face remained shielded by the baseball cap's peak. Lydia was in no doubt: he was a professional. Dennis was right to be freaked.

Was this the man who had trailed her mother and her in Nuneaton? Who was he working for? What was he trying to achieve – surveillance, a warning or something worse? Whatever it was, Lydia was now part of it.

"Do we have anything to identify this man?" she asked.

Ashar shook her head. "As you can see, there's not enough to give our face recognition software. Jon's going through any possible matches with known agents, but we're not optimistic."

"What about results from putting out the feelers? Any foreign agency activity? Have Six, SO15 or GCHQ been contacted?"

"They have, but nothing has come up."

"Can I see your case file on Dennis Dunn?"

"It's on 'Restricted', so I'll have to log you in."

Lydia scanned down the details, most of which came from the file she'd already studied. As expected for a man with Triple A security rating, there were no juicy details, no psychiatric history – just the story of a good professional. The only blip had occurred shortly before his transfer to H11, when he had accused his line manager of a homophobic remark. His line manager had denied it and the section boss had sided with the line manager.

Lydia found what she was looking for in the case file: Dennis's address and phone number. She picked up the desk phone and dialled.

The phone rang for a full twenty seconds before going to voicemail.

She left a message. "Hello Dennis. This is Lydia Twomey, or Schizo if you prefer. I need to talk to you urgently. Yesterday I was followed by the same man who followed you on the tube. I think we can help each other. If you can tell me all you know, we can share the burden. Call me on my mobile – 07729448115. Please."

Ashar was looking across the desk at her, mouth open. "Have you just phoned Dennis Dunn?"

Lydia stared back. "Yes."

"We were told on no account to contact him. Were you given permission?" Ashar's eyes were magnified by her glasses.

Lydia weighed up gently reminding Ashar that officers of a junior grade don't question their superiors, but she opted for another route. "Don't worry. I'm going to report to Webb now."

She got up and left the office.

In Webb's outer office, Miss Parmenter met her with thin pursed lips. "I made you an appointment with Mr Webb at 10.30. If you'd like to return at that time, then…"

"I'll wait, if that's all right. If you can tell him it's extremely urgent, that would be helpful. I've done something that he needs to know about, and I can't email it to him." She sat down outside Webb's door, arms folded.

Miss Parmenter adjusted her Paisley scarf, looked down at her screen, appeared to scan it for a few seconds, scrolled down, tutted to herself then looked up at Lydia. Lydia smiled at her. Miss Parmenter looked down at her screen, scrolled down a bit further, sighed, and gave up her pretence.

She pressed a button. "Sir, Lydia Twomey is waiting to see you. She says it's urgent… yes, I told her… she says she's done something you need to know about… yes, sir." She looked up at Lydia. "He'll see you when he's free." She smiled frostily and looked back to her screen.

Three minutes passed in silence.

The door of Webb's office erupted open. Webb glared through. "Come in, Miss Twomey."

Lydia followed him in and sat in front of his desk.

"Ashar's just phoned to tell me what you've done." He was barely containing his simmering fury.

"I would have told you myself, but I was denied access to you."

"You knew Gerard Bell said that any attempt to contact Dunn could push him over the edge, yet you've done just that."

"I left a message on his answerphone. He can ignore it if he wishes. It's hardly pushing him over any edge. He's in danger, and speaking to me may actually save his life."

Webb sat back. "So what's changed to make this so urgent?"

"That's what I was going to tell you first thing this morning, but you were too busy to see me." She told Webb about the man following her in Nuneaton.

Webb nodded. "But you never saw this man yourself, right?"

"Only in the distance, but my mother's description of the man was almost identical to Dennis Dunn's."

"With the greatest respect to your mother, it doesn't sound like she's the most reliable witness, given her condition. She saw someone whom you, trained as you are, failed to see. It's highly possible she erred."

Stay calm, Lydia told herself. Don't let this man's ignorance provoke you. "Sir, I think it's highly probable that Dennis knows something vital about Martin Froome's death, and I'm sure that someone is trying to stop him talking to us, by isolating him in his home and by scaring him with this shadow they've put on him."

"This allegedly dangerous agent took yesterday off to go shopping in Nuneaton with you." Webb was like a defence lawyer who knows he's got a watertight case. "Your implication is that Gerard Bell is deliberately trying to cover up the details of Martin Froome's death. Where's the evidence?"

Lydia paused. This was the time to confess about the slip of paper she had carried in her bra, but which was hidden in her flat now. No – she was in enough trouble already. Such a confession would get her suspended.

"I haven't got any evidence. But if Dennis can be persuaded to tell us all he knows, he will have nothing to fear from any agent who might kill him to silence him, because it will be too late. If it is paranoid delusion, then unburdening himself will cure him."

Webb shook his head vigorously. "You're presupposing a lurid conspiracy when there is no evidence for one. As a result, you risk pushing a vulnerable man with paranoid delusions over the edge to possible suicide."

"I've been through his file again this morning. He has no record of paranoia or of suicidal tendencies."

"You've contacted him against the wishes of superior officers."

"I have a very good recollection of our last meeting. At no point did you expressly forbid me to contact Dennis Dunn."

"On your head be it, Lydia." He looked at her solemnly. "Let's hope you've called it right."

"Was it you who put the tail on me to Nuneaton yesterday?" She shot the dart at him suddenly to catch him off guard. She watched for his reaction.

Webb laughed. "With my budget? Now that really is a paranoid delusion. I can't afford more than one day's guard on Dunn's flat. Why on earth would I – or anyone else for that matter – want to tail you?"

"To make sure I stay away from Dennis."

"I can do that by just ordering you."

"If Dennis Dunn says he wants to talk to me, I'll talk to him. I presume I have your permission to do so."

They looked squarely at one another, their wills locked.

Webb looked away first. He swivelled in his chair to study the Thames. "Yes. Yes, you have my permission. I just hope you know what you're doing. Now leave me to catch up the backlog of my work in peace before I change my mind."

As she walked back down the corridor to have an awkward conversation with Ashar, she felt the phone in her jeans pocket vibrate. It was a text message.

Come to my flat at 5. DD

"Yes!"

15

DENNIS

Dennis was standing by the phone when the voicemail from Lydia came through. His immediate reaction was to move away, shut himself in the bathroom, and not listen to whatever she said. But he lingered and heard the full message.

She sounded sincere. Of course you never can tell, but you can feel sincerity, even on an answerphone message.

The problem was, he had nothing to tell her. He'd had nothing to tell the Dong two days ago. If the guy in the baseball cap on the tube had abducted him and tortured him, he still wouldn't have given anything away. There was no secret lurking in some remote corner of his brain. Well, nothing beyond a few hair-raising political sticks of dynamite that were locked in the files of H11, but everyone in H11 carried those in their head. There was no reason why he had been singled out for this treatment.

So was Lydia truthful when she said that she'd been followed by the same man? Dennis had spent several hours the previous day scanning the street for a glimpse of a baseball cap, but the only people he'd spotted were his guard detail, in three different shifts. So it was possible that baseball cap man had taken the day off to go after Lydia. But why would he do that? What was the connection?

The connection was obvious, if it existed: the death of Martin. The death had seriously freaked Dennis. They – whoever 'they' were – thought that he knew something incriminating about Martin's death. But he didn't! That was what was so frustrating. Maybe if he daubed on a sheet the words 'I know nothing', then hung it out of his window, they'd leave him alone.

But why would they think he knew something? What if he knew something but hadn't yet realised it? It was true that things had got a bit stretched and a bit irregular at work. There were bad vibes creeping into the place; Dennis had felt pressured lately. There had been certain irregularities. What if…

That's when he realised he did indeed know something – something very bad.

"Oh. My. God."

He felt his legs shaking – his knees quite literally knocking. He lowered himself to the carpet, and crawled into the lounge. He told himself he needed to stay away from the windows, to stay out of a sniper's field of fire. Jesus, there could be snipers out to get him!

He crawled behind the sofa, and lay there panting. He needed time to think. The guards who had protected him yesterday were gone, but there were good locks on a very solid apartment door, so as long as he opened it to no one, and as long as he stayed away from the windows, they couldn't kill him. Now what?

His first instinct was to call Paul at work and get him to come back to the flat. But that would put his lover in peril. Lydia had said that if he spilled the beans to her, they would share the burden. He now realised it was a mortally dangerous burden; he didn't want Paul to share it.

He pulled his mobile phone from his pocket and crawled back to the landline phone. He reached up to the table, pressed the button to replay Lydia's message. He entered her number into his phone, and then drafted a message.

Come to my flat at 5. DD

He delayed pressing 'send'. His finger was shaking and he was sweating. Was this the right thing to do? Would 'they' intercept the message and kill both of them? He'd given her plenty of time to get out of work and to journey here before Paul returned from work – was 5 the best time?

He pressed 'send'. It was done – he was committed.

He went down the stairs to check that the bolts and the chain on the flat door were securely fastened, then climbed the stairs and crawled across the lounge floor to draw the curtains, before returning to his place behind the sofa.

Now he needed time to think. He had to tell Lydia the exact truth before things got covered up. He had to present precise demands for his and Paul's security because once the balloon went up 'they' would definitely be coming after him. He crawled across the floor to the table, took a notepad and pencil off the table, and took them back behind the sofa.

Why did he stay behind the sofa, now his door was locked and the curtains drawn? Because he was sure 'they' would be coming to kill him. He started writing – at first furious scribbling, but gradually the whole horrible story became clear in his mind; he slowed down, and set it all out. How could he not have seen what was going on?

An hour later, Dennis was regretting not asking Lydia to come to his flat as soon as possible. He'd climbed out from behind the sofa, finished his notes, folded them and put them under one of the Staffordshire china dogs on the mantelpiece. Now he was sitting on the sofa with nothing to do except worry. He thought about texting Lydia to ask her to come sooner, but every text would be an extra risk.

He realised he had tears running down his face. He felt a wave of overwhelming sadness wash through him. This wasn't how it was all meant to pan out. He'd joined MI5 straight from university, envisaging a life of glamorous intrigue but also safety. His parents had always been supportive, and they'd said that this would be the making of him. He'd worked really hard, yet he'd been shunted off to H11. He'd been well supported by his colleagues in H11 – they'd been good friends – but now there had been this massive betrayal.

Things could never be the same again. He'd ask Lydia to get him to a safe house, and that would mean no more rehearsals for 'The King And I'. God, he'd really wanted that part all his life! But that was nothing compared to…

The doorbell rang.

He struggled up from the sofa, wiping the tears from his cheeks. Had Lydia sensed his desperation and arrived early? Was this the killers come to get him?

He tiptoed down the steps to his door. If 'they' could hear him from the other side of the door, they might be able to shoot him through even this thick wood. He peered through the spy-hole.

It wasn't Lydia standing by the bins in the little front garden. It wasn't the man in the baseball cap or any other hard-eyed assassin. It was a friend, a colleague. Christ, what a relief.

"Hello, Double D. I've just called round to offer you some support. I thought you might want some company if you were coming in to work later to see the Medics."

Shit! He'd forgotten he was due to see the medical team this afternoon.

Of course, he couldn't go in now, but this friend could at least keep him company until Lydia arrived. 'They' wouldn't dare storm this flat with a witness inside.

He unhooked the chain, shot the two bolts back, and unlocked the door.

"Come in," he said. He stood aside as the friend walked through the door, and then he carefully clicked the catch-switch, shot the bolts and hooked up the chain. "Sorry about these precautions," he said. "I've had a few worries over the last few days."

He followed his friend up the stairs and into the lounge.

His friend no longer had hands in pockets. The friend wore gloves and held a small gun, levelled at Dennis. "I've come to tell you we're holding your Paul."

Dennis shook his head, as if to clear it of this nightmare. He let out a brief hysterical giggle. "What do you mean, holding Paul? Who are 'we'?"

"We hold your partner, Paul Green, captive. We're sorry that we had to do it. We don't want to harm him, but if you don't co-operate we will be forced to kill him."

"Wait a minute. You're not... not the person I..." Dennis couldn't get his head round this.

Too late, the penny dropped.

16

LYDIA

Lydia arrived at Dennis's door at five on the dot. She didn't believe in taking informants by surprise. She rang the doorbell and stood by the bins where Dennis would be able to see her clearly through the spy-hole.

No reply. She rang the doorbell again, this time with anxiety welling up inside her. She'd checked out the flat from the road and noted that the curtains were drawn and that no lights were on, but it was consistent with Dennis feeling under pressure.

No reply. She rapped on the door with her knuckles and called his name – not too loudly as she didn't want to alert the occupants of the ground floor flat, if they were in.

Still no reply. Maybe he was inside, panicking. It was worth calling out to reassure him, even if the occupants of the downstairs flat heard her.

She lifted the letter box flap. "Dennis, it's me, Lydia. Let me in – everything is fine." She paused. "Look, even if you don't want to talk to me, just let me know that you're okay."

She didn't need to shout – he was probably a few inches from her on the other side of the door.

No reply. Maybe he'd panicked and done a bunk.

She rang the doorbell of the ground floor flat. She'd ask them if they had seen Dennis leave.

No reply.

She was trained to pick a door lock and she carried the equipment, but if he'd bolted the door she was still locked out. Anyway, she had no authorisation to break in.

She took out her mobile and called Webb.

"Hello. Who's speaking, please?" It was Miss Parmenter.

"It's Lydia Twomey. This is supposed to be Mr Webb's personal number. I need him urgently."

"He's in a meeting. I'll get him to call you back when he's free."

"This is an emergency. I'm on active service and I need to speak to him right now."

"I'm sorry, but…"

"Just fucking get him on! Now! This is a matter of national security!"

A blast of Purcell's Trumpet Voluntary replaced Miss Parmenter, before being abruptly cut off mid-peal.

"Hello, Lydia, this is Webb. It had better be good. Miss Parmenter tells me you've just sworn at her."

"I'm at Dennis Dunn's flat in Willesden. He said he'd speak to me at five. He's not answering his doorbell."

"This is hardly an emergency, a matter of national security. He probably doesn't want to talk to you, after all. Does that surprise you?"

"He'd tell me if that was the case. I think he may have been assassinated."

"Any evidence?"

"No, sir. Do I have your permission to break into his flat?"

There was a pause. "No. Wait there. I'll send back-up. Wait for them to arrive – I'll give them instructions. Make sure that the scene isn't disturbed in the meantime. We want no local fuss, and definitely no reporters."

"Right, sir."

"Keep up the good work." He hung up.

Lydia sat down on the doorstep. It would be at least forty-five minutes before any back-up arrived, so she had time to think.

If Dennis had done a runner, where would he go? If he'd been assassinated, who were the killers working for? How had the killers gained access to the flat? There was no sign of a forced entry. And why kill him at this time? Because they knew that he was about to talk to her? How could they know this?

The only people who knew about the text message were herself and Webb plus anyone Webb had notified; and GCHQ, if they were monitoring either her or Dennis's phone. What if Gerard Bell had called it right and Dennis was indeed suicidal? That one was too shitty to contemplate.

"Hello. Can I help you? What are you doing here?" The tone was friendly, but he made Lydia start. She jumped to her feet.

It was an elegant man in stylish blue suit with a well-groomed beard. He carried a bunch of lilies.

"Who are you, sir?"

"You answer first. You're in my garden."

"I'm a colleague of Dennis Dunn's. He invited me to come and talk to him. Are you his partner?"

"I need proof of identity." Though he was dressed like an entrepreneur, the man had the grace of a dancer. He was on the balls of his feet, perfectly balanced, poised for flight.

She held up her lanyard.

"Are you the new girl – the one called Schizo?" He moved past the bins to the door.

"I am." Dennis should not have divulged such details, but now wasn't the moment.

"I'm Paul." He held out a slim hand for her to shake. "Come on in. I don't know where Dennis has got to, but you can wait for him in the warm. It's nice you've come round to see him – he's been under the weather lately. Actually I've come back early because I'm worried about him."

He took out his latch key.

"I'm sorry, Paul, but you can't go in yet." She tried to get between him and the door, but he stood his ground.

"What do you mean – I can't go in? This is my flat."

"I've been ordered not to allow anyone inside. I'm sorry."

He took a step towards her. "You can't do that. You have no right. It's my property."

"We think something might have happened to Dennis."

"Exactly what?" His eyes widened. Outrage was giving way to alarm.

"We don't know. I've called for back-up, and I've been told not to let anyone in until they arrive."

Paul rang the doorbell and called out. "Dennis! Dennis! It's me! Paul! Let us in."

"Please don't shout, Paul. We mustn't attract attention. For Dennis's sake."

"What are you talking about? Who are you to tell me what I can and can't do in my own property?" He put his key in the latch.

Lydia had to act. She moved to take the key. Paul tried to bat her hand away, but his hands were like butterfly's wings, and Lydia took the key out of the door.

"Look, I'm really sorry, but you can't go in. It may be a false alarm, but we think your flat may be a crime scene which must not be contaminated. We'll set your mind at rest as soon as we can, but we can't allow you to go in before we've checked the place out."

Paul stumbled back against a dustbin. "What do you think might have happened?"

"We don't know, and I don't want to alarm you."

"He's probably popped out to the shops." Paul didn't sound convinced, and Lydia couldn't bring herself to nod. "If you think he's killed himself, then you're wrong. I know he wouldn't do that. I know him too well."

"No, I don't think he's killed himself."

"You said it might be a crime scene. What crime are you talking about, then?"

"Let's just wait for my back-up, shall we?"

"Do you think he's been murdered?"

"Let's not alarm ourselves with…"

"I'm going in. Give me my key." Paul stepped forward, hand outstretched. "Dennis might be lying up there in the flat, needing urgent assistance. I'm not waiting down here a minute longer."

"I can't let you in, Paul." She kept her voice firm.

He stepped back. Paul's voice was quavering, but he didn't shout. "You lot – you spooks – you need to hush everything up, don't you? That's all you're interested in – sweeping everything under the carpet. If you don't let me in right now, I'm going to walk off down this street, and I'm going to call every newspaper and tell them to get here pronto. Now, you wouldn't want that, would you?"

"Nor would you."

"Try me. I've got over a thousand followers on Twitter. One tweet from me and there's all hell to pay. If Dennis is up there in some sort of trouble, I'll do anything." He turned to walk away. "That includes shouting to anyone who'll listen that the spooks won't let me in my own home."

It was time for Lydia to surrender. She got out her leather gloves and put them on. She put Paul's key in the door. "I'm going in. You wait down here until I give you the all-clear."

He nodded.

Climbing the stairs, she knew something was very wrong.

"Dennis?"

No reply. She hadn't expected one.

Upstairs, the living room was empty, but the note on the table was placed so that she couldn't miss it. It took a few seconds to read and no longer to digest: Dennis was dead and she was getting the blame. To her, it had all the hallmarks of something Dennis had been forced to write by a murderer – the shaky scrawl, the final message of love to Paul, and the absence of anything spontaneous or unexpected. To any neutral it was patent evidence that she had driven this man to suicide.

"Shit!" She had only seconds to take the decision: if she left the note where it was for the team to find, she'd get the blame for the suicide, she'd be suspended and removed from the case, probably disciplined and maybe more. That's what the murderer – if there was one – wanted. If she picked it up, she was digging herself deeper into the hole.

She picked up the note, pulled up her sweater, and stuffed the note in her bra. This was getting to be a habit.

Steeling herself, she went in search of the body.

She found him in the bath. His body had slumped a bit, so that his face was half submerged while his knees were pushed up above the dark crimson. She was glad that she couldn't see any expression on his face – she was already feeling enough guilt as it was. His arms were hidden by the dark water, but she was sure that the forensic team would find slashed wrists.

She didn't risk removing a glove to test the temperature of the water, but the bathroom was still warm. He wasn't long dead. Shit, she thought – maybe I could have saved him if I'd arrived earlier. Shit, shit, shit.

"Dennis – are you there?" It was Paul's voice, from the living room.

She rushed out of the bathroom and barred his way.

"Paul, you can't go any further. Please turn back around and wait outside."

"Why? Tell me what's happened." His eyes were wide.

There was no way of sugar-coating it. "Dennis is dead. I'm so very sorry. He's in the bath. There's blood in the bath water. We mustn't contaminate the scene. Please, turn around."

"Let me see him. Please. I beg you. I promise not to touch anything. I need to see him. I need to understand."

Lydia hesitated, then stepped aside.

"Thank you."

Paul looked into the bathroom, his face creasing with anguish. He shook his head vigorously. "No! There's no way he'd… he'd slash his wrists with that razor." He indicated the cut-throat razor in the soap dish. "I gave it to him." He turned to Lydia. "He never would have killed himself. I know that, in my deepest heart. He loved me too much." His face started to crumple.

Lydia led him back to the living room.

Paul stopped and looked round the room. "Someone's been in here and killed him – I can feel it. This place is different. Look." He pointed to the Staffordshire dog on the mantelpiece. "That's Benny. He's wrong!"

"What do you mean?"

"He's looking outward, at us, like his twin, Bjorn." He pointed at the other china dog. "That's wrong! Benny always looked at Bjorn and Bjorn looked outward at us – it was our private joke. Someone has moved Benny, tidied him. Dennis would never, ever do that. Someone has been in here."

"Do you have a cleaning lady?"

"No. I'm certain Dennis would never kill himself without leaving a message to me. We loved each other far too much for him not to have done that. He would have told me why. He was always leaving me little notes – that's what that pad on the table is for. I'd be heartbroken for the rest of my life if I thought he'd killed himself without telling me why."

The note burned in Lydia's bra. Paul would be heartbroken for the rest of his life. She couldn't leave him like this.

"Just a minute, Paul. I've something to show you." She reached up her sweater and pulled the note from her bra. She gave it to the astonished Paul.

She expected blazing fury from him. She flinched as he looked up from the note.

He shook his head sadly. "Thank you. I can see why you wanted to hide such a note." His voice was gentle, resigned. "I don't blame you for Dennis's death, and nor did he."

"What do you mean?"

"This note is fake. Obviously he was forced to write it." Paul smiled in triumphant vindication.

"How do you know?"

"He would have called me by my pet name – Pogo. He'd never have addressed it 'Dear Paul'. And he'd never have put kisses at the bottom. We had our own symbol for the foot of our notes to each other – I'm not going to tell you what it was. This note," he held it up, "is absolute proof that he was forced to do whatever he did."

"Can I have it back, Paul?" she held out her hand.

"Don't worry; I won't share it with your bosses. You're safe. But I want to keep it within me. It's his last message to me." He crumpled it up and put it in his mouth.

"Oh Christ! You've just destroyed vital evidence in a murder case."

"You were going to destroy it yourself."

Touché.

"We need to go and wait outside now, Paul."

This time Paul obeyed. They walked down the stairs and stood by the dustbins.

"You do believe me, don't you? You don't think Dennis committed suicide?" Paul was still shaking his head.

"I believe you. I think he was murdered." It was out of her mouth before she realised she had broken protocol once again.

"Who killed him?"

"I don't know. Did he say anything about threats to you?"

"He was terrified. That man who followed him on the tube – he thought he was going to kill him."

"Who did he think the man on the tube was?"

"He didn't know. He said that some dark forces thought that he knew something dangerous, but he didn't know anything. I don't know exactly what you people do at work, but I know it's sometimes bad. Dennis was totally innocent, that's all I know."

"Was there anything at work that was worrying…?"

Paul lurched forward, and Lydia braced herself to push him back from the door. But his head came to rest on her breast and his shoulders shook as violent sobs shuddered through him. He was still holding the bunch of lilies, and now they were crushed against her.

"I loved that boy so much."

Lydia could feel the warm tears soaking through her blouse. She put her arms around him, and cradled his head.

17

LYDIA

"I'm afraid you're in rather hot water, Lydia. Let's take the charges in their chronological order. First off, Miss Parmenter says that you swore at her over the phone."

Webb was looking at her with one of his 'sad father' looks. It infuriated her. She resisted the impulse to tell Webb that his 'hot water' metaphor was inappropriate given the horror she'd witnessed just three hours before.

She took a breath. "I admit it: I did swear at her. I'd called your emergency hotline – I needed to speak to you immediately, not be put on hold. I was outside that flat not knowing what had happened to a colleague of ours who may have been bleeding to death while I listened to Purcell's Trumpet Voluntary. The bathwater was still warm when I eventually discovered the body."

"Let's move on to the second, more serious, charge. Gerard is calling for your head. He's pointed out that he warned me you were pushing Dennis Dunn towards suicide, yet low and behold, you find Dunn in his bath with his wrists slashed, immediately after you make an appointment to see him."

"You gave me explicit permission to visit him, sir. You were sitting in that chair, about nine hours ago. I recognise there's no formal record of you doing so, so it would be possible for you to deny it, but I'm confident that you wouldn't do such a thing."

That hit home; Webb turned in his chair and looked out over the Thames for his next salvo. "But that's not all, is it? I explicitly told you over the phone not to break into the flat until the back-up team arrived, and yet not only did you disobey me by going into the flat, but you allowed a member of the public to enter, thus allowing the crime scene to be contaminated."

"I contest your interpretation, sir. Firstly, if you really believe it was a suicide, then it's not a crime scene." She paused, but Webb stayed silent. "Secondly, it wasn't just a member of the public – it was Paul Green, Dennis Dunn's partner. And thirdly, we didn't break in; we used Paul's latchkey."

"When you contacted me to say no one was answering the doorbell, I told you not to let anyone in. You disobeyed my orders. Fact."

"Paul threatened to run down the street shouting that the spooks were barring him from his own flat. He said if I didn't allow him in he was going to tweet the scandal from his phone immediately. He pointed out that Dennis might be lying upstairs, bleeding to death, and that we needed to get in immediately to potentially save his life. If I'd refused, and Dennis had died while we were arguing downstairs, how would that have looked in the media?"

"You know we can stop the press printing that sort of story." Webb said it stiffly, face still averted.

"We can't immediately control social media, though. The story would have gone viral before we got on the case." Lydia pressed home her advantage. "I'm sure you'd agree that I called it correctly."

"Hmm." Webb turned to face her once more, as if he was on firmer ground. His blue eyes fixed hers. "Ashar has interviewed Paul Green: apparently you told him you believed Dunn hadn't committed suicide, that he had been murdered. Is this true?"

Lydia nodded. She was disappointed in Paul that he'd disclosed that detail, but she'd been foolish in letting it slip. She was even more disappointed that Ashar had passed the disclosure on to Webb. "Yes. I'm sorry. It just slipped out when I was trying to calm him down. I was agreeing with his conviction that Dennis was murdered."

"But you knew that it's strictly against protocol, a disciplinary matter, to give your personal opinion on such a matter to a member of the public, especially when that person is so emotional and all the facts suggest you're wrong."

"I am truly sorry for my mistake, sir, and I'll take the rap for it. But I do believe Dennis Dunn was murdered." Webb put his hand up to stop her, but she disregarded it. "No way would he slash his wrists just hours after contacting me to set up a meeting. I have his text – it's proof he wasn't scared of me. Paul Green told me that Dennis wasn't scared of me and he wasn't going to kill himself, but that he was terrified of being assassinated by persons unknown."

"Why would Dunn think that? He sounds like someone with mental health issues."

"He has no record of mental health issues. The man following him on the tube had freaked him out. Martin Froome's death was a shock and a warning to everyone in H11, even though they still haven't been told the truth about it. Somebody in H11 is covering up something very important."

"You need to have evidence for that sort of allegation, and you have none. I have to tell you, Lydia, all the preliminary findings point unambiguously to a suicide. Of course we'll be doing a detailed forensic sweep of the flat, but we don't expect to find anything."

"Just like you didn't find anything in Martin Froome's flat. These assassins are highly skilled – we probably trained them."

"Now you're being ridiculous." He didn't sound convincing, but he managed to dredge up some menace for a threat. "Talk like that can only harm your prospects."

Lydia ignored his threat. She was on a roll. "You probably don't want to find anything – it's much more convenient to believe that poor Dennis Dunn committed suicide and there's no security lapse in the service."

Perry Webb shook his head in sorrow. "Lydia, do you really want to destroy your very promising career? Look, you've had an upsetting day. Go home now, have a nice hot bath and a big whiskey. Try to get a good night's sleep, and come in tomorrow with a clear head. I will contact your professional representative and invite him or her along to a meeting tomorrow."

"Am I to be suspended, sir?"

"That will be decided tomorrow. Go home now." Lydia took his gentle tone as good manners rather than reassurance.

"Thank you, sir." She stood up, glanced at the Queen above Webb's head, and walked out of his office. Have a bath! She didn't even have a bath in her flat.

She breezed past Miss Parmenter's desk without glancing at the crone, and pushed into the corridor. This wasn't the time to stand and fight. The important thing was that Webb hadn't yet suspended her.

She turned right and made her way down the corridor to the case room. As she walked in, Ashar looked up from her desk.

"Hello, Lydia. Have you been suspended?" She stood, ready to shepherd Lydia out of the office.

"Why on earth would you think that, Ashar? No, I haven't. You'll be glad to know I'm still right there with you and Jon on this case." She sat down at the desk opposite Ashar.

Ashar swallowed. "Yes, of course. What did Webb say about what happened at Dennis Dunn's flat?"

Bitch, Lydia thought. You're the one who's tried to get me suspended. "He told me to carry on the good work. I think I've persuaded him that this is probably a murder case."

Ashar regarded her sharply through her thick glasses. "Really?"

"Have you put your interview with Paul Green on the system yet? I'd like to view it."

"Um, yes – it should be available."

Lydia logged on, found the interview file, put headphones on and zoned Ashar out of her head.

Paul interviewed well: he refused to be led by Ashar's questions and kept to his insistence that Dennis had been murdered. He explained the significance of the moved china dog, but Ashar wasn't impressed. Ashar then asked a few questions that implied Paul himself might be a suspect if he kept up this insistence, but Paul was not intimidated. Ashar terminated the interview once she had gone through the formal procedures and the arrangements for Paul to spend the night away from his flat.

As Lydia took off the headphones, Ashar was putting on her coat. "Well, I'm off home, now. It's been a long day. See you tomorrow."

"Yeah, see you." It was as if there was an invisible iceberg in the room.

Lydia waited until she was alone in the office, before starting a new search in the case files.

She opened the file on 'baseball cap man'. There was his partially hidden face captured on the CCTV footage, there was the list of searches Jon had made – and where there had been nothing this morning, there was now a possible name: Ian Forrester, thirty-two years of age, discharged from the army aged twenty-five, served eighteen months for inflicting grievous bodily harm five years ago. Present address unknown, but thought to be moving around squats in the Tottenham area – several addresses listed.

The door to the office opened. It was Jon.

"Oh hi, Lydia. I didn't expect you to still be here." He smiled.

"Why? Had you heard I was suspended?" She looked down at her screen, and exited the file on Forrester.

"No! You haven't, have you?" He sounded genuinely shocked.

"No, but the report Ashar and you submitted to Webb has dumped me in it."

Jon ran his hand through his thinning hair. "I'm really sorry about that. It was really awkward. If you want me to speak up for you, I'll…"

"Don't worry about it. I'm going home now." She closed down the computer. "You look like you could get some rest, too."

"It's been a long old day."

"Sure has," Lydia said, thinking poor Dennis hadn't got through it.

When Lydia arrived back in Hanwell, she took a full five minutes to check there was no one on surveillance outside her flat. She took an age to scout out her motorbike garage, before locking her bike in. Entering her cramped attic flat, she went through every security routine twice, yet her heart was still hammering when she finally bolted the door behind her, closed the blinds and turned on the light. She meticulously checked the bathroom, checked under the bed and even in the broom cupboard.

Everything was in order.

She sat down in her only armchair, facing the Frieda Kahlo reproduction. She needed to think. Why was she blamed in the faked suicide note? Why would the killer of Dennis want her to be blamed? That was obvious: so that she would be removed from the case, silenced. Why would they want that? She knew nothing of any worth. The only thing she had was…

The list of numbers! Someone must have suspected that this list existed, and had guessed that she'd smuggled it out of H11. She'd brought it back to the flat and had studied it, but it meant no sense to her, so she'd hidden it. Perhaps it would make more sense this time.

She reached across to her bookshelf, and pulled out her copy of *Penguin Modern Poets, 10: The Mersey Sound*. She opened up the book. She'd slipped the list between Brian Patten and Roger McGough.

It wasn't there.

She flipped through the rest of the book: nothing. She checked the floor, and then the shelf, in case it had fallen out: nothing. With rising alarm, she took out the other books along the shelf and checked each one: nothing. She took a deep breath and thought really carefully about whether she had moved the list, whether she'd hidden it somewhere else: no.

The list had been found and removed. Someone had broken into her flat.

18

PERRY

The DG sat in silence, his fingers on his chin.

Perry had recounted the facts, laid out the alternative hypotheses and then had given his own personal judgement. A strategic little white helper taken beforehand had kept him calm and measured. He thought he'd given an impressive performance, cogent and persuasive; he was disappointed that the DG couldn't dredge up a compliment.

"Hmm." The DG had an antique grandfather clock in his office – Perry found the sonorous ticking of its pendulum intensely irritating. Such furniture had no place in a tech-savvy modern office – it was an anachronistic affectation.

Perry knew better than to try to hurry the DG, but every second of delay was screwing his guts ever tighter.

At last, the DG condescended to speak. "So do you really think that this was a suicide?"

"As I said, everything points to it. They've been very thorough with the forensics, I can assure you. They assure me the wounds were self-inflicted. There's no forensic evidence of anyone else being in the flat at the time. Dunn took strong painkillers before slashing his wrists."

"With the greatest respect, Perry, not everything points to suicide. The man's partner insisted it was murder, and pointed out how the china dog had been moved. The first officer on the scene, Lydia Twomey, who you've assured me is very bright, is similarly certain. There's no suicide note. The front door chain wasn't bolted. Is there any CCTV evidence? It's been lost in the previous cases."

Perry shook his head. "There was no CCTV in his flat – he's not a high enough grade to warrant it. And there's none in his road, I'm afraid."

"What a shame."

"Gerard Bell is confident his man committed suicide after harassment from Lydia Twomey. He had interviewed Dunn, assessed that he was highly vulnerable and had sent him home. The death took place after Twomey had contacted Dunn."

"I presume that you had given her permission to contact him?"

Perry opened his mouth. No sound came out. He tried again. "Yes… yes."

"Yet you suspended her earlier this morning."

"Well, there were other irregularities in her conduct, which I've outlined to you. I went through her conduct formally with her and her union rep. They both accepted the suspension. And Gerard was incandescent last night." Perry saw the DG frown. "But… we can always reinstate her after a suitable inquiry."

"Hmm." The DG closed his eyes.

Perry knew judgement was nigh, and he was a lot less confident than he'd been a few minutes before. In the old days the boss would always side with the senior officer's stance, but recently things had begun to slide in the service.

"Right." The DG opened his eyes. "I want you to reinstate Lydia Twomey."

"Really, sir?" He couldn't keep the dismay from his voice.

"Yes. I want her to go back to work down in H11 tomorrow morning. Caving in to Gerard's demands makes you look weak, Perry; we can't have that. I know it would be very convenient if this was a suicide, but it would have been convenient, too, if Martin Froome had died accidentally. Two convenient deaths in one small department within a week is a coincidence too far for me. You're to treat it as murder until there's concrete evidence otherwise."

"Right-oh." Perry's heart sank. The two bases of his managerial policy had always been to smooth things over and to act only on solid evidence, and now he was being ordered to make a big fuss about a case with no evidence at all.

The DG leant forward, elbows on his desk. "You need to know, Perry – and this is strictly entre nous at present – that there's a piece of pretty serious political nastiness moving towards us, where evidence held by H11 is going to be crucial. The Minister has been seeking assurances from me. I have to be totally confident that Gerard Bell and his whole team are onside. If there's any shit down there in H11, I want Lydia Twomey to stir it up so it rises to the surface. She'll need your full support."

"She has it, of course."

"I know that. Make sure she knows it, and that Gerard Bell knows it, too."

As he walked back to his own department, Perry could taste the garlic chicken he'd had for lunch repeating on him. Throughout his career he'd enjoyed a consistently generous comfort zone, but now it had completely evaporated and he was left hideously exposed.

First Lydia: she'd looked terrible when he'd hauled her into his office to suspend her this morning. She'd admitted she hadn't slept well, and she looked stressed as hell. She didn't accuse him of betraying her, but he felt intense guilt all the same. He assured her he would tell the DG that he'd given her permission to talk to Dunn, but the suspension was for the other matters; Lydia had just nodded – Perry took it that this whole thing just confirmed her prejudice that male bosses couldn't be trusted. He himself found it hard to argue with that unstated view, but really, he wanted the best for her. She was so lovely, bright and idealistic – it would be such a waste if her career was destroyed by this unpleasantness. It would be hard facing her and explaining that the DG had overturned her suspension and that she was ordered back down to H11 immediately. He needed to think very carefully about how he explained it all to her or she'd be submitting a grievance procedure.

Then he had to deal with Gerard, that bastard: he'd made Perry look weak to the DG by forcing him to suspend Lydia, and now he was going to kick up an almighty storm when Perry told him Lydia was to be reinstated back down in H11. Perry feared and envied Gerard for his razor wit and his wide scholarship, for his glamorous wife and his well-connected arty friends. Last year his own wife, Glenys, had written a lovely novel set in Greece, where they'd been on holiday, but Gerard's wife Louisa had hardly concealed her contempt for the quality of the prose and had made no attempt to find a literary agent. This snobbery had shattered Glenys's confidence and had humiliated Perry. Then there was the other, long buried issue, the one he still couldn't bear to dig up.

The DG wasn't much better: he blithely set colleague against colleague if it suited his political ends. He was happy to use a young woman like Lydia to stir up Gerard; he wouldn't care if it destroyed a promising career – he hadn't even met the girl. And how dare the DG say that he, Perry, looked weak! If it wasn't for the consistently patient diplomacy of people like him, the service would have descended into permanent division and crisis many years ago.

Damn them all!

Perry reached into his pocket for another pill.

19

LORD BROOKE

"This was delivered by courier, sir. He said it was urgent." The office junior handed Lord Brooke a plain envelope.

Once the junior had left his room, Lord Brooke tore it open.

"ALL CLEARED UP"

"About bloody time."

Lord Brooke was not a gracious man.

20

LYDIA

The suspension had come as no surprise to Lydia. That spineless Peregrine Webb had probably told the so-called inquiry that she had approached Dennis Dunn without his authorisation, and she was being fitted up for the blame for the suicide. Probably the most sensible thing would have been to spend the morning with her union rep preparing a grievance procedure, then spend the afternoon getting drunk.

But the loss of the list of Martin Froome's numbers had changed everything. Somebody had known she possessed it and had broken into her flat, found it and taken it. They'd probably done it while she was being shadowed in Nuneaton. They'd left no signs of a forced entry and everything had been left perfectly in place; this was a professional job, possibly carried out by a MI5 colleague. Now they knew that Lydia knew about the numbers, she was as dangerous as Martin and Dennis had been. She couldn't go to Webb, so the only way to escape the fate of Martin and Dennis was to get to the truth before the assassins got to her.

Perhaps it was someone she knew who had been in her flat. She shuddered at the thought that it might be Bri Powell. That man was seriously creepy; he would have been through her knickers drawer as well as taking the piece of paper.

Setting out on the trail of the baseball cap man was liberating. At last she was being proactive, rather than dancing to the tune of her useless or manipulative bosses. She'd roared off from Thames House on her motorbike, checking she wasn't being followed, and had made her way to Edmonton, North London.

She'd been expecting dirty, dangerous streets when she arrived at the last known squat address of Ian Forrester, but Fore Street was outwardly respectable if scruffy and battered, rammed with traffic, dominated by the roar of the North Circular just half a block ahead. She chained her bike to a hospital sign and surveyed the street. Opposite there was a kebab shop (closed) and an optician's called 'The Angel', though the 'g' had fallen off. The address for Ian Forrester's squat was occupied by a gaming machine shop called Quicksilver. Posters on the windows promised 'fun' and the chance to win £500, but the doors and windows were guarded by heavy iron shutters. Above, the black window frames betrayed no signs of habitation: no lights, no curtains.

Lydia strolled down the street, past a nightclub, two pawnbrokers, a barber's, a bank, an off-license, a chicken takeaway, a Subway and finally a Pizza Express before turning up a side road to make her way to the back of the row. Behind was a walkway next to a Lidl car park. She counted her way along until she came to the address of Quicksilver; there she was met by a high wall and a very solid iron gate, securely padlocked.

She had limited experience of squats, but this didn't look right: it was all too neat and well fortified. There was no rubbish, no signs of occupation at all. She made her way back to the main street, and along to the front of Quicksilver. She tried to peer through the iron shutters, but there was nothing to be seen.

She pushed through the purple door of the Turkish solicitors next door. Warm air and perfumed carpet cleaner wafted into her face. A young dark-haired woman smiled up from behind a waxy green plant on a grey desk.

"Hello. How may I help you, please?" A north London accent, but Middle Eastern phrasing.

"I need to speak to someone who lives upstairs – next door." Lydia saw a momentary flash of panic cross the girl's face. "But I can't get in there. Where is the access?"

The girl regained her composure quickly. "Next door? We don't know anything about next door. Sorry." She quickly looked down at her computer screen.

"Who can I ask?" Lydia kept her tone casual.

"I don't know." Lydia could see the girl's hand hovering over an alarm button below the desktop. She was clearly nervous, unsure of how to handle this. "I just work here."

"No worries. Perhaps your boss could help."

"She's very busy. I can't disturb her. She's with a client right now."

"Have you seen this guy?" Lydia held a photo of Ian Forrester over the green plant. "He's a good friend of mine from the army. I promised to look him up."

The girl hardly looked up. "No. Doesn't ring any bells." She restarted tapping away at her keyboard.

"Oh well, thank you." Lydia turned and pushed the door open, out onto the street. She stood for a while, looking through the solicitor's windows at the young girl, who kept her head down. Eventually the girl cracked, looked up, saw Lydia looking in, and instantly resumed her word processing.

"Now what's spooked you, I wonder?" Lydia said out loud. "Why should a woman working for a solicitor give a monkey's about the squat next door?"

Lydia turned, and waited for a moment to cross the crowded street, sprinting between buses and vans. Two down from the An'el Opticians was a food store. She went in, past the stacks of bottled water, plastic shopping baskets and cellophane-wrapped watermelon sections. A middle-aged man was transferring oranges from a box into the fruit stand.

"Hiya. I wonder if you could help me." Lydia put on her most winsome smile.

The man straightened. She judged him to be Mediterranean, maybe Turkish or Lebanese. "How?" He didn't sound friendly.

She proffered the photo of Ian Forrester. "I'm looking for this guy. He's a friend of mine from the army. He's been living opposite you. Does he come in here?"

The man's dark eyes scanned her carefully. "Are you just starting out in the police? That's not the way you ask these things."

"I'm not in the police."

"Where's your back-up?" He raised his eyebrows, as if it was a threat.

"Have you seen this guy?" She kept the photo outstretched. The man hadn't even glanced at it.

The man looked her straight in the eyes. "No."

There was nothing for her to do but to leave. She walked off down the street then negotiated the traffic to cross back to an off-license on the opposite side. The paintwork was peeling, the windows were covered with advertisements for travel cards and mobile networks that enabled cheap contacts with the third world – Somalia for 6p.

She pushed through the door.

She was met by a smiling Sikh in a red turban behind a counter. The merchandise, mainly piles of cans and cases of bottles, was stacked up behind him. "Hello. What do you need?"

"I'm looking for a friend who lives in a squat round here, but I can't find him. He's called Ian Forrester." She put the photo down on the counter.

The Sikh kept up the smile. "You know, I am intrigued." He wagged his finger at Lydia. "You're not police. You're not in debt collection. You don't look like you're a lawyer's private investigator. Who are you working for?"

"No one. This guy was a friend of mine from the army, and he and I used to..."

The man nodded. "Army – maybe, maybe not. You and him together – I don't think so. I don't think so at all."

"So you know him?"

"I don't know him personally. But I am a good businessman. I need to know what is going down around here. How much will you pay me for information?"

"I'll give you twenty pounds for his address."

He laughed softly. "Twenty pounds? Now I know you are no professional. Twenty pounds is a joke. You know, it is dangerous for me to give you information. I take a risk."

"Why? Is Ian in some sort of trouble?"

"You give me one hundred pounds, and I will tell you the name he uses now, and his present address."

"I haven't got a hundred pounds on me. Will you take a card?"

He laughed again. "You are a real joker. There's a cashpoint at the Santander, along the street."

As she put her card into the cash machine, Lydia reflected that this transaction would be clocked up by GCHQ in Cheltenham – any suspended officer was closely monitored, at least electronically.

She returned to the off-licence and laid the bank notes on the counter.

The Sikh picked them up and counted them, before stuffing them into the back pocket of his trousers. "Your Ian Forrester – you don't really know him at all, do you?"

"Why do you say that?"

"No way would this man ever live in a squat. He may look scruffy, but he's sharp, man. Smells of expensive cologne. When he comes in here he buys only the best." He paused for effect. "You know why I am giving you this information? Because I hate the fucking Turks."

"I don't understand."

"Your Ian Forrester – Marcus Forest on his Mastercard – stays in the flat above the Turk's office, up the road." He smiled, pleased with himself.

"The solicitors?"

He nodded. "I don't know who you represent, but if you can put those Turks in a whole heap of shit, it's worth much more than the £100 you've just given me."

"Why do you hate the Turks?"

"Have you got another hundred pounds?" He smiled again.

"No, but if you hate them, any dirt you've got on them could help me stick it to them."

The Sikh hesitated, then shook his head. "It's not worth it. But if you're working for the good guys, your bosses might find these Turks very interesting. Check them out. That's all I'll say."

Lydia thanked the Sikh and walked back out onto the street, back to Quicksilver. Next to the solicitor's office was a door, painted in the same purple, with two keyholes and three buzzer buttons on the doorpost. There were no names next to the buzzers.

She walked on up the street debating her next move: confront the solicitor's assistant and demand entrance, or wait, and force an entrance after dark?

Her mobile vibrated against her breast. She stopped and took it out.

It was a text from Webb:

Suspension lifted. Return to Thames House for urgent meeting.

It made up her mind: she turned on her heel, walked back to the purple frontage, and pushed into the solicitor's office. A young couple were sitting at the desk with the solicitor's assistant, who looked up at Lydia with undisguised alarm.

"Get your boss out on the pavement immediately. This is an emergency, and the reputation of your company is at stake."

The young couple looked up at Lydia in bewilderment. The assistant pressed her alarm button. Lydia hoped she hadn't alerted the local police station.

It took less than five seconds for the door to the inner office to burst open, and a well-built, sharp-suited middle-aged woman with immaculately coiffed, dyed tawny hair was standing in front of Lydia. Her powerful musk perfume was at odds with the aggression in her eyes.

"What is it, Bercu?"

Lydia held up her MI5 ID card. "I need immediate access to your premises."

"What is this?" The woman spat out the words. "This is not a warrant card. I'll..."

"I want you to come outside onto the pavement in front of your office, madam." Lydia spoke calmly and clearly. "This is an emergency, and failure to comply with my request may result in unfortunate results for your firm."

Lydia turned and walked out of the front door. She was praying that the woman would follow her. She was already estimating how long it would take to unchain her motorbike and ride off if it all went belly up.

The door clicked behind her. The woman confronted her on the pavement, arms folded across her grey green jacket.

"This had better be good."

"What is your name?" Lydia asked.

The woman pointed to her name badge on her lapel, still seething.

Lydia tried to give her best impression of a police officer. "Nesrin Cevdet, we have reason to believe that a man dangerous to the security of this country has recently been in the flat above your office. I need you to open up the door next to your office, and to accompany me up to the flats."

"You haven't got a search warrant." Her mouth was a grim line.

"In a national emergency I don't need one. Being a solicitor, I'm sure you know that. My request is merely a courtesy. I didn't think you'd want your business tarnished by an open bust mid-afternoon in front of all the public."

"MI5 don't have the authority to make a bust. Since 2006 it's been the work of Counter Terrorism Command."

This woman was very well informed but Lydia ploughed on. "This man is dangerous, and you are obstructing the work of MI5. It's your call, but I'd advise you not to get on the wrong side of us. I can call in the Counter Terrorism boys if that's what you wish."

The woman licked her lips. "Who is this dangerous man? Bercu said he was a friend of yours from the army. What's he done?"

Lydia showed her the photo. "He's called Ian Forrester, though you may know him as Marcus Forest."

"I have never heard of this man. If he's so dangerous, why haven't you got an armed response team?"

"We don't think he's in the building now. But I need to search it."

"Well, I'm not going to give you access. It's not an emergency if he isn't in there." She smiled for the first time.

"MI5 decide if it's an emergency. Without your assent, I'll call in Counter Terrorism. We will force entry and search the entire premises, not just Ian Forrester's room, and I will report anything irregular to all the relevant authorities. If you give me access and accompany me, we will look only in Ian Forrester's living quarters, and I will not report any irregularities. That's the deal. It's your choice."

The woman shook her head. "We have powerful friends."

"So call them. Ask them if they want a scene made. Call the police if you want them to accompany us up to the flats. You've got two minutes before I call Counter Terrorism."

Nesrin Cevdet hesitated, before shaking her head. "I will phone them."

As the woman took her mobile from her breast pocket, Lydia noticed a bulge beneath the grey green jacket. Oh my God, she thought, this woman has a gun! Should I get on my bike and ride away now, while I can? At least there's no way she's phoning the police.

The woman walked away a few yards down the street, muttering furiously into her phone. Several passers-by gave her quizzical looks. Then the phone was jammed back in her top pocket and the woman turned back to Lydia.

"Let's go."

Lydia tried not to look relieved as the woman took out a set of keys from her hip pocket and strode over to the door with the buzzers. She unlocked both locks and threw the door open.

"After you," she said, holding the door open to Lydia. "Since this man is so dangerous and I don't want my head blown off, you can go first."

Lydia led up the narrow stairs. The walls were plain white, unadorned. At the top there was a small landing with three doors, all painted the same purple as the front of the building, numbered one to three. They were dimly lit by a single bare low-energy light bulb.

"Okay, which one shall we try first?" Lydia asked.

"How should I know?" the woman grumbled. She was far less assured now. "I've never seen this man. As far as I know, he's never been in any of these flats."

"Well, I'm going to leave you to have a random guess. If you get it right, we'll only search one flat. If you get it wrong, I will have to go through all of them."

The woman pointed to the number one.

Lydia rapped on the door. "Mr. Forrester! I have Mrs Cevdet, the lady from Ergun's, with me. There's no need to be alarmed. We just need to talk."

There was no response.

She tried again, with the same result. Lydia was aware this delay could enable Forrester to make his escape down a fire escape, but there was no real alternative.

"Mr. Forest, or Forrester, the lady from Ergun's has a key. We're going to open your door if you don't respond."

Still no response.

"Okay. Mrs. Cevdet, please unlock this door."

"You're making a mistake, a big mistake. Your superiors will hear about this."

"I'm sure they'll read my report. Now unlock the door, please, Mrs. Cevdet."

Muttering in Turkish, Nesrin Cevdet obeyed. She straightened, and turned back to Lydia. "It's already unlocked."

"Stand back," Lydia commanded. She was well aware that if Forrester was inside he might be armed, and she knew that Cevdet was armed. She could be shot from the front or in the back. What the hell had she got herself into?

Too late to go back now.

She opened the door slowly. The room ahead was dark – the curtains were drawn. Stale warm air flowed out into the hall.

"Mr. Forest?"

There was no sound or movement in the dark. Lydia looked back: Nesrin Cevdet had backed away and was standing a few steps down on the stairs. Her right hand was hidden from Lydia. She might already be holding her gun.

Pressed against the door of number two, Lydia snaked her hand round the doorpost, feeling for a light switch. She felt a double switch. She pressed down, and the lights inside the flat came on.

Still there was no sign of life inside the flat: there was the smell of dust on an electric bar fire, and possibly some old kebab takeaway, but no sound except the traffic out on the street.

"Mr. Forrester, I am coming into your flat. There is no need to be alarmed." She crouched down, as she had been taught, and put her head round the doorpost.

The bedsit was Spartan – a place to sleep rather than anyone's home. The walls were painted white and bare. There was a basin and kitchen surface in one corner, with a stool, a microwave and a kettle. There was a shower unit and toilet crammed into the far corner. A television was mounted on the wall. A double bar electric fire was glowing dully. Under the window, directly in front of Lydia, was a double bed with a blue duvet.

Under the duvet, head propped up on a couple of blue pillows, Ian Forrester appeared to be fast asleep.

"Mr. Forrester – wake up, please. There's nothing to be alarmed about."

No response.

Lydia inched forward, ready to throw herself to the side should he erupt from the bed with a gun or knife.

Still no movement.

Forrester's face looked waxy and pale under the bedside lamp. Lydia could see a syringe sitting next to the lamp and what looked like a tourniquet band next to it. It was a turn-up – she hadn't put him down as a junkie. Now he was zonked out, vulnerable and… no.

Ian Forrester was dead.

21

PERRY

"So..." Perry let his words hang. There was no easy way to tell Gerard, who was sitting, legs comfortably crossed, in his office. Although he feared the backlash, Perry wanted to savour the moment of Gerard's dismay. "So the upshot is that Lydia Twomey's suspension has been lifted and she is due back in H11 tomorrow morning."

Gerard's reaction was disappointingly calm. "I suppose you're going to tell me the DG ordered it, and that you, once again, were powerless."

Perry refused to be nettled by this snarky response. "We all have our place in the hierarchy, Gerard. I haven't seen Lydia yet, but I will, of course, offer her my full support – as will you tomorrow morning. The DG asked me to pass on this request to you."

"I can assure the DG that I will always carry out his orders." Gerard uncrossed his legs and stretched them out, toes pointing at Perry through his sandals. "I will have to inform my staff to put aside their consciences and do the same. I presume you will be informing Dennis Dunn's partner that the woman who hounded Dennis to his suicide has been exonerated."

"That's another thing, Gerard: the DG has decreed that Dunn's death is to be investigated as a murder until further notice. As is Froome's."

Gerard laughed, but it was a humourless bark. "Ha! Good luck with those, Perry. Some creative evidence will be required, no doubt."

The red light on Perry's desktop console began to flash. He glanced down at his screen. It was a message from Miss Parmenter:

Ms Twomey calling. She says it's urgent - more urgent than last time.

Last time it was to tell him Dennis Dunn was dead – what could be more urgent?

"Look, I'm sorry, Gerard, but an important emergency has cropped up. I need to give it my full attention immediately." For once Lydia had called at a good moment – to send Gerard packing was the icing on the cake.

Gerard got to his feet. "My, my! Such importance!" He walked stiffly to the door, waited for Perry to release the lock, and left without a backward glance.

Perry sat for a moment, relishing Gerard's undignified retreat. It wasn't often he got one over his old rival.

He pressed for Miss Parmenter. "Put Ms Twomey through."

Almost immediately Lydia's voice broke in. "Sir, I'm at the flat of Ian Forrester – he's dead."

"Remind me, who is Ian Forrester?" He was feeling so good that even Lydia in crisis mode couldn't immediately shake him out of it.

"The man in the baseball cap who followed Dennis Dunn on the tube and who followed me to Nuneaton."

"What on earth are you doing at his flat?"

"He is – was – a prime suspect in our murder case, if you remember, sir."

"What I do remember is that I suspended you this morning. Why were you pursuing this man whilst under suspension?"

"I didn't take any action until I received your message lifting the suspension."

Perry sighed. "So where is this flat?"

"188, Fore Street, Edmonton, North London."

"How did this Forrester man die?"

"Made to look like a drug overdose, sir, but I think it's another staged job."

"Jumping to conclusions again without any evidence, Lydia."

"I have evidence he wasn't a junkie. Anyway, sir, what do you want done? Do you want me to report it to the police?"

"Are there any witnesses?"

"Just one: a Mrs Nesrin Cevdet – she's the solicitor from the firm that owns these premises. She let me into the flat."

"Put her on, will you?"

There was a brief pause, and then Perry's ears were assaulted by a voice crackling with vehemence. "Are you MI5, like this girl says you are? I have never seen this dead man before. If he has been staying in my company's flat with your permission, then you are in big trouble. I mean really big trouble for you. You can't prove anything against me. I have powerful friends and I have already phoned them. You will be hearing from them."

Perry held the phone away from his ear. "Whoa, whoa! Hang on a minute, Mrs. Cevdet. You can't just go threatening MI5 like that. Can I ask you who you've contacted?"

"No, you may not."

"Was it the police?"

"No. It was someone more much powerful."

"Well, that's a blessing. Please put my colleague back on the phone." There was a brief pause then an exchange of angry words before Lydia was back on. "Lydia, why on earth did you allow that woman to contact someone? Do you know who she contacted?"

"I don't know, sir. I couldn't stop her because I was securing the crime scene, taking some photos. It's her property. And another thing: she's got a gun, and I haven't."

"Good heavens! Solicitors with guns? Has she brandished it?"

"No, sir. But I can see it under her jacket."

"Well, get her to hand it over – threaten her with MI5's unspecified might – then make sure she doesn't phone anyone else and that no one gets in or out of that flat. I'll have an armed response Counter Terrorism unit with you in a matter of minutes."

"You're promising a lot more than last time I phoned in a death."

"Just do as I say." He cut the communication, and immediately dialled into the emergency response protocol. If the DG wanted a song and dance made of this case, Perry would oblige. Counter Terrorism could put on quite a show – they could bring chaos to the traffic in a large area of North London.

It took just a few minutes to set the wheels in motion, but that wasn't the end of the procedure. Next he needed to inform the DG. Perry rummaged in his pocket, pulled out a card of pills, and popped one out into his hand; he needed to fortify himself.

The DG didn't sound exactly appreciative when he took Perry's call. "Please get down here, now."

It didn't get any better when Perry entered the DG's inner sanctum. Also present was the Head of Special Operations, Miles Mason, a thrusting up-and-coming chap, ex-SAS. Perry called him Perma-tan Man because he always looked bronzed throughout the English winter. The aggressive expression on Mason's chiselled face told Perry to expect some flak.

"Perry, take a seat." The DG indicated the chair to Mason's left. Perry sat down. "Now, Miles tells me there's a situation developing up in Edmonton."

"I reported it to you as well, sir." Perry had used the 'sir' word – an indication of the potential avalanche of shit that was about to fall. "As per protocol."

"Miles tells me one of your agents raided one of his department's establishments and has reported in the death of one of his freelancers. Is this true?"

Perry shook his head and tried to look innocent. "Not as far as I know. One of my agents – Ms Lydia Twomey, whose suspension you personally ordered me to lift this morning, was in pursuit of a major suspect in the murder cases you personally ordered me to pursue vigorously, a man called Ian Forrester. There is nothing on our records to suggest he was a freelancer working for Miles. Showing excellent initiative, Lydia tracked him down to an address in Edmonton. Again, there is nothing on our records to suggest that this place had any connection to Special Operations. The first inkling I had of this was when Lydia reported that the female solicitor who gave her access to the premises was carrying a gun – it sounds like something out of the Wild West. Lydia told me that this woman had phoned someone quote 'very powerful' unquote – I presume it was you." He looked across to Mason.

"It was." Mason's voice was dry like a robot, Perry thought.

The DG had his hand to his chin. "So this is a classic case of two departments in the same building not talking to each other."

"I can't forbid my agents to pursue prime murder suspects on the grounds that they might be one of Miles' freelancers, can I?" Perry felt he was on firm ground.

"I can't give everyone a list of all the people and addresses I use. Our internal security just isn't good enough." It was a snide attack from Mason, but it was a reasonable point.

"Hmm." The DG went into one of his long meditations. The grandfather clock solemnly ticked away, grinding its way into Perry's irritation. "Miles, what sort of work did you employ this man Forrester for? What were his specialisms?"

"Surveillance, clandestine searches, that sort of thing. He was ex-Army, not shy to get involved physically."

"Capable of assassinations?"

"Capable – but of course we've never used him for such things."

The DG smiled bleakly. "Of course not. Did you know he was a junkie?"

Perry was enjoying Mason's discomfiture, but he was trying to work out his answers when his turn came.

Mason shook his head. "I doubt very much that he was. Obviously we don't monitor freelancers with the same thoroughness as we do our regular agents, but we know he always kept himself fit. We wouldn't use people with a habit like that."

"Hmm. What was he working on when he died?"

"He wasn't. Forrester hadn't been employed by us for over four months. I don't have the precise date, but I can get it for you."

Another long pause, measured by the clock ticking. "So what do we think he was doing, using one of your addresses and getting mixed up in Perry's case?"

Mason spread his hands. "I have no idea. Perry hasn't told me anything about his case."

"Allow me to tell you now." Perry laid it on with a trowel. "Your freelancer was spotted following an archivist from H11 shortly before the archivist's death or possible murder, and then your freelancer followed Lydia Twomey when she was investigating the death or possible murder of another staff member of H11."

"He wasn't my freelancer when he followed these people." Mason kept a straight face.

The DG asked the obvious question. "So who was he working for?"

Again, Mason spread his hands. "It could be anyone. Forrester would be free to accept work from whosoever wanted to employ him."

Perry couldn't resist speaking. "But he's used your retained flat and your gun-toting solicitor. It suggests it's someone from within MI5 who knew about him and signed him up."

"That's your department – internal security – not mine," Mason sniped back.

The DG didn't need to raise his voice to regain order. "We can only guess it was someone from within MI5 who hired Forrester. Forrester may have used the Edmonton base on his own initiative. However, it's highly likely that he was engaged to carry out surveillance and maybe more on staff of H11. It suggests that whoever hired Forrester knew of his MI5 connections. That means either an insider or a leak in your department, Miles."

"I will investigate both possibilities." Perry tried to keep the gloating out of his voice.

The DG turned to him. "You have limited time, Perry. Forrester's employer probably decided his work was finished, and silenced him. They will have done a clean job. That avenue is almost certainly a dead end now. The answer lies in H11. Get Lydia Twomey away from disrupting Miles' assets in Edmonton, and down into H11, where I said I wanted her."

"Yes, sir." Perry hated using that word.

Lydia didn't arrive in Perry's office for her debrief until gone 7pm. He expected her to be full of herself, with her suspension lifted and the coup of having discovered Forrester's body, but she appeared tired and deflated. He, on the other hand, had perked up, courtesy of another pill.

Perry tried to cheer her up. “It was the Director-General himself who ordered your suspension be lifted. He has great faith in your abilities.”

“He’s never met me, but I’m glad someone has faith in me.”

“I, too, am delighted. I want to take this opportunity to offer you my full support for your future work.”

“Thank you. What is my future work?”

“The Director-General has asked that you be deployed back down in H11. He says, and I quote, ‘if there’s any shit down there, it needs to be stirred up’. So you have our full support if Gerard tries to make your life awkward.” Perry had expected Lydia to be downcast by the prospect of more H11, but there was no reaction. “Are you all right, Lydia?”

“I’m fine, sir.”

“I suppose a dead body plus Turks with guns are a bit unsettling.”

“Nothing I can’t handle, sir.”

“Well, once you’ve written up your report, you will have earned a good night’s rest. You look tired.”

“Thank you for the kind thought, sir.”

So she was playing the stoic martyr – that was her line. Perry tapped his desk lightly. “Well, if there’s nothing else, I won’t keep you from writing up your report.”

“Actually, there is something else, sir. I suppose you’ve thought about who would want to kill Forrester, and why they’d do it now?”

“We don’t know he was killed; all the evidence points to it being an overdose. The forensics team are doing their stuff now. We’ll get their report tomorrow. Plenty of time to start worrying tomorrow if something fishy is turned up.”

“With respect, sir, we both know it wasn’t an accident. Forrester had been used in surveillance against Dennis Dunn and me. If he was employed by Special Operations, would they admit it to you or the Director-General? If it was someone else, then it was probably someone within MI5 who knows of him. Why would such a person then kill one of their own assets? Forrester was employed by someone within MI5 to act against H11 and against me."

"It's been a long day. Write your report, go home, have a nice long bath, and have a good sleep, Lydia. We'll all see things much more clearly in the morning."

"There's more, sir: the reason they got rid of Forrester was because they knew we were after him, so they needed to silence him. Who knew we were after Forrester? You, me, Ashar and Jon plus anyone they briefed, and Gerard Bell. That's not many suspects, is it?"

"Plus anyone within MI5, including GCHQ, who can monitor our electronic activities and files. We're talking hundreds of people, and it's all based on your conjecture that this Forrester chap was killed." Perry put on his kindest smile. "Let's all sleep on it, eh? As I said, it will look clearer in the morning."

"It's good to know I have your full support, sir."

Why did Lydia always make life so awkward?

Pill time.

22

LYDIA

Lydia arrived home in Hanwell just after ten on a wet night. She checked out her garage carefully before locking her motorbike away then checked the street for surveillance before unlocking the door to the crumbling Victorian mansion in which she had her flat. She stopped in the vestibule, took off her helmet, and unzipped her leather jacket. She was cold, damp and unbelievably tired, but security routines needed to be adhered to. She reached out with her senses to detect any unfamiliar sounds or smells, even though there were six flats in the building, with maybe twenty inhabitants. There was a jumble of assorted smells – curries, damp, dogs and a multitude of muffled sounds – traffic outside, TVs, a child crying, a bath filling. Lydia took a deep breath and summoned the strength to climb the two flights to her attic flat.

She paused on the first landing. Hers was the only flat up the attic stairs. She paused, then resumed her way up. She looked down as she climbed.

Her heart somersaulted.

She stopped, her foot hovering above the stair.

The thin cheap stair carpet was damp; someone had climbed these stairs within the last couple of hours.

She remained frozen on the stairs as she thought about the possibilities. Someone had broken in and stolen Martin Froome's sheet of paper – had they returned?

She listened carefully: there was no sound emanating from her flat. There was no light shining under the ill-fitting door.

Whoever it was had probably left – or was waiting inside to jump her. It could have been a neighbour from one of the flats who popped up to see her – but she didn't know most of the neighbours well, and why would they have wet footwear? She could check with Bridget and Henry in flat 5 to see if they'd seen or heard anyone go up.

She turned and tiptoed back down the stairs to the first floor landing. There were the sounds of a TV programme coming from Flat 5, so she rang the doorbell.

It took a while for the door to be opened. It was Henry, in a dressing gown, without his glasses on, looking a bit grumpy.

"Look, I'm really sorry to bother you at this hour, Henry, but I wonder if you saw or heard anyone go up to my flat. I've had a few problems recently with, well… and there are wet footprints on my stairs."

"No – we haven't heard anyone go up, but we've been in for less than an hour ourselves."

She saw the struggle on his face: on the one hand he wanted to tell her to stop being a hysterical paranoid little girlie who had interrupted his Horlicks, and on the other hand he was trying to be a good concerned neighbour.

"Well, thank you anyway. I'm so sorry to have disturbed you." She started to turn away.

"Not at all. You look a bit freaked out. Look, it's probably inappropriate for me to come up to your flat dressed like this, but do you want me to ask Bridget to come up with you? Or we could phone the police."

"No, it's fine. Don't worry. Thanks for the offer." She turned back to the stairs, thinking that if there was an attacker waiting on the other side of her door, then he would have heard this conversation.

"No worries. Call us if you need help." Henry shut his door. She heard two bolts being drawn.

As she crept up the stairs, Lydia couldn't help thinking about Brian Powell. The way he had looked at her – it was the look of an obsessive, a stalker. What if it was him, breathing heavily and twiddling his long beard round his fingers, just the other side of her door?

She considered ringing Peregrine Webb. That was the correct protocol. No – the man was useless. He'd give her a patronising verbal pat on the head, tell her she was tired after a long day, and that she was imagining things. He'd say that after a nice hot bath and a good night's sleep she'd see things more clearly. And she couldn't tell him about the previous break-in. Gerard Bell had said paranoia was the natural consequence of working in H11. She had to be back in H11 tomorrow.

At the top of the stairs, she put her helmet on the landing floor and got her keys out. This was a moment when she would have liked to be holding a gun, but MI5 officers of her grade weren't routinely armed – she had a service pistol locked in her flat, but that was no use now.

There was nothing for it: either she had to sleep on the stairs or she had to put the key in the lock, turn it, open the door and fight off any intruder, with nothing more than the keys in her fist.

She inserted the key and turned it. The lock clicked. Wear her helmet or go bareheaded? Push the door open slowly, or throw it open?

She pushed the door open then threw herself through the opening, rolling over twice across the carpet towards the armchair and the TV, coming up in a combat crouch. She flinched, expecting a blow to the head or a bullet in her guts, but neither came.

The light from the stairs shone across the bed-sitting room. There was no intruder. Lydia breathed out, and hauled herself to her feet.

She saw a body on her bed.

It was Brian Powell. It had to be.

The body moved, sat up.

Lydia couldn't stifle her shriek.

The bedside lamp was clicked on.

Lydia looked into the sleep-befuddled face of her mother.

"Mum! What the hell are you doing here?"

"I'm sorry. I scared you." Sarah Twomey sat up on the bed.

"How did you get in?"

"You gave me James's keys when he moved out – remember? You said you didn't want to die and not be found for a year after."

"What on earth are you doing here?" Lydia was aware that she didn't sound welcoming, but she was shocked and furious. Her heartbeat was still battering her ribs.

"I was worried about you. You weren't answering your phone. I rang your office and they told me you weren't at work at present. I asked what that meant and they wouldn't tell me, so I knew you needed me. When I got here you weren't here either, and I was very tired from the journey so I thought I'd have a kip on your bed. I didn't mean to scare you. Where have you been?"

"I've been working late."

"But you're..."

Henry, hair dishevelled and still in no more than a dressing gown, burst wild-eyed into the room, brandishing a rolling pin as if he was auditioning for a West End farce. "Is everything all right, Lydia?"

"I'm sorry, Henry. This is my mother. She's come to stay without warning me." Lydia felt wretchedly silly. "I'm sorry to alarm you. Thank you for coming up."

"I'm sorry, too," Sarah said meekly from the bed. "It was my fault."

Henry clearly didn't know what to say. "Um, right. Um, well…"

"I don't suppose I can offer you a coffee or something stronger to say sorry, can I?" Lydia asked.

"Dressed like this? With your mother in bed? A bit inappropriate, but thank you. Sleep well, both of you." He turned and went back down the stairs, closing the door behind him.

Lydia shot the bolt on the door and turned back to her mother.

Sarah was smiling. "I imagine that young man isn't in a relationship with you. But he did come to your aid very promptly."

Lydia didn't know whether to laugh with her mother, or scream her anger. Most of all she wanted to rest her head on her mother's bosom and cry, but it would send out all the wrong messages.

She shook her head. "You're incorrigible, Mum." She giggled, but could feel her hysteria rising.

Sarah held out her arms. "Come and give your mother a hug, Lyds."

Lydia obeyed, kneeling on the bed. Her mother's arms enfolded her.

It was no good; she couldn't hold back the tears. She sobbed for a full two minutes, while her mother cooed and patted her head and back.

At last she regained control and disentangled herself from her mother's arms. "Sorry about that. And I'm sorry if my colleagues gave you bad information which has dragged you down here unnecessarily. I'm fine."

"Let me be the judge of whether I'm needed here. I haven't seen you cry like that since you were little. You're not fine, and I'm here until I've got to the bottom of what's wrong. I'm going to make sure you're all sorted."

"Mum, I've had a long day. I was just a bit fraught, and it was a shock to see you, that's all. I thought you were a burglar."

"Is that why you keep this in your bedside drawer?" Sarah pulled out the drawer to reveal Lydia's gun. "I hope you've got a license for it."

Lydia sighed. "It's for work – I have to have one."

"I don't know exactly what work it is you do, but if you need a gun then you need someone to talk to and to support you."

"It's not me who needs help – it's you. You've got MS. The last thing you need is to be traipsing up and down stairs, sharing my double bed, far away from your doctors. I'm not ungrateful – I'm very touched – but you're on the train back north tomorrow morning."

"We'll see. Maybe the best help for me is to feel I'm doing something worthwhile, supporting you." Lydia could see her mother's eyes filling with tears. "Get us a cuppa, will you? And you need to bring your helmet in from the landing. You always were careless with your possessions."

Lydia obeyed, like a good daughter. When at last they were sitting side by side on the bed, sipping their tea, she laid her hand gently on her mother's hand.

"Mum, you can't stay, I'm afraid." She paused. "Look, I'll be honest with you: there's some difficult, dangerous stuff going down with all security forces staff at present, and your presence here would simply add to my worries. I can cope on my own, but I'd be a lot weaker if I thought I was putting you in the metaphorical line of fire. If you return to Nuneaton tomorrow,

I promise I'll ring you regularly – every day – and I promise I'll tell you my worries."

Her mother turned to look her in the face. "I'll be honest with you, too, love: I haven't got a whole lot to live for up in Nuneaton right now. I need to have you to care for, to worry about. I can cope with metaphorical lines of fire, Lyds; I'm not so good with loneliness. If my life is put in danger, it might make me feel more alive – that's the truth. If I lost my life, I wouldn't be losing that much, but if I lost you I'd be losing everything." She turned away to hide her tears. "Now, tell me which side of the bed you want tonight. I'll leave you to set the alarm."

23

MADDY

Maddy King woke in a bad mood. For five minutes she lay still, listening to Toby snoring beside her. Yes, he was a hunk – a six-foot-two gorgeous rugby player – and yes, he was very well paid – a secure job with one of the most prestigious accountancy firms in the city. They lived in a lovely clean, safe, modern flat with the swankiest docklands postcode. Toby was well meaning – but he snored. At this moment, this one fact outweighed all his assets. Awake, he was really rather boring; that outweighed all his assets, too.

Not for the first time, she wished it was Vindi lying there beside her. Damian Curry could be capricious, mean and moody, but golly, he knew how to excite her, even when he didn't try. He moved with such grace, like a big cat, his hands were so sensitive, and his dark eyes smouldered like...

It was no good. She pushed back the duvet and got out of bed.

Toby stopped snoring and turned over to watch her slip to the bathroom in her short blue cotton nightie. "Nice arse," he muttered.

"Great chat-up line, Tobes," she said, and shut the bathroom door on him.

She inspected her face in the mirror, feeling the under-floor heating caressing the soles of her feet. Blonde hair, regular face, nice tits; even without her make-up, she had a classic beauty – 'deuced pretty' her father always told her – but it never quite delivered for her. Vindi played with her, Toby took her for granted, the Dong charmed her like a witty lecherous uncle, and the men on the train mentally undressed her each morning.

But today there was something more, something she couldn't quite put her finger on, that gave her a sense of unease.

She set her electric toothbrush to work on her immaculate teeth.

It was only when she was at Monument, making her way from the Dockland Light Railway to the Circle line, that she realised what had been bugging her: she didn't want to go to work. When she'd started in the service, fresh out of Exeter University, she'd always been bright-eyed and bushy-tailed and had regarded every day as a potential new adventure. Even after she'd been knocked back by the disciplinary panel and been sent down to H11, she'd stayed optimistic. She loved the men – Vindi and the Dong, of course, but also Double D – he was such a sweetie – and even Luther, though she didn't know him as well. The ladies, Farah and Maybe, were lovely, so supportive, always cheerful. It was such a close team. But now...

Now it had all turned sour. First Luther, then Double D – gone. The Dong had told them that Double D had committed suicide, and had hinted he'd been driven to it by an unnamed person. It had to be the new girl, Schizo.

Schizo seemed a nice girl, but she'd told Maddy the first time they met that she didn't believe some of what the Dong and other bosses told them; it was deeply unsettling. It undermined the foundations of professional trust like an earthquake destroyed your trust in the ground beneath your feet. Now she found herself questioning what the Dong told her, and she didn't like it. She didn't mind vigorous competition, but this was nasty. If Schizo had hounded Double D, then it was unforgivable.

She would be a naive idiot if she didn't think about the deaths of two colleagues: what if they weren't an accident and a suicide? Was there a serial killer in H11? No, that was obviously ludicrous, but all the same... she remembered Dennis had reported being followed on the underground on his way into work.

As she waited on the platform at Monument, she stood well back from the line, and carefully went through the security measures from her training.

Down in H11, Maddy was handed her duty schedule for the day by Maybe, who told her the Dong was busy upstairs. All the schedules were disrupted due to the deaths of Luther and Double D and Schizo's suspension. Maddy was surprised to see she was assigned to Schizo's induction.

"I thought she was suspended."

"We all thought so. Seems like it's been lifted. She'll be down very soon, I think," said Maybe, slightly raising her eyebrows. "She's getting briefed by her other masters upstairs. I believe she was caught up in another incident yesterday, involving another fatality."

Maddy's eyes widened in alarm. "Not one of our colleagues?"

Maybe smiled thinly. "I don't think so. The Dong didn't say. He just said to treat her sensitively when she gets down here. She's probably feeling a bit fragile. Mind you, I wouldn't stand too close to her if I were you."

"Why's that?"

"Death seems to be following her around right now." Maybe looked up at the monitor. "Speak of the Devil: here she comes now."

Maybe buzzed Schizo through from the corridor into the cloakroom.

When Schizo emerged into the office, Maddy noticed she looked tired and drawn. Perhaps these deaths had indeed made her feel fragile. Perhaps the Dong was correct and she was feeling guilty for driving Double D to suicide. Schizo had also made an effort to dress in summer shorts, although the message on her T-shirt – 'Modern Suffragette' – wasn't exactly within the beachwear theme.

"Hi, Schizo." She put on her bright-and-breezy voice to mask any antipathy she felt for the person who may have caused Double D's death. "I'm assigned to take you through the induction process today. I'll show you how we care for the archive, and how we keep it secure."

"Great. Thanks, George."

"Do you want a cuppa, either of you?" Maybe asked.

They both declined, and Maddy led Schizo through to the next room. "This is the archive work room, where Double D and I, and sometimes Luther and Vindi do – did – the practical stuff." She waved her hand airily round the workbenches, the basins and draining boards, the fume extractors and the pictures of tropical beaches on the yellow painted walls.

"What are those?" Schizo pointed to the cubicles screened off at the far end of the room.

"We call them the poison pens. It's where we paint the artefacts."

"Paint them?"

"That's right. Every artefact down here gets a tiny coating. We have to be very careful when we're applying it – it's mildly toxic, apparently. Once applied, no artefact can be taken from H11 without tripping the alarms which have sensors that can detect minute quantities of the substance on the artefact. And if you tried to smuggle out the artefact in an air-tight lead or heavy metal case, the sensors would be tripped by the lead."

"What is the coating substance?" Schizo's brow was furrowed.

"We've never been told. That's how tight security is down here. Even if you chopped up an artefact, burnt it and flushed the ashes down the loo, there are grills and sensors down the drain that would pick it up."

"Sounds radioactive to me." Schizo still looked worried.

"We take stringent safety precautions when we apply the stuff. No one has died of it yet." Maddy cut short a laugh. Today Schizo's critical mindset was stoking new doubts, eroding Maddy's trust. Why hadn't they been told what the substance was? What if they were contracting a cancer that would only show itself after they'd left H11?

"So no artefact in this archive ever leaves – ever?"

"Archives can be taken out if they're required in a court case or something, but the only person who can disarm the sensors and alarms is the Director-General himself."

"What happens to the old tapes when they've been rerecorded? Double D said he was 31% through replacing all analogue tapes."

Maddy was impressed that Schizo remembered the exact percentage. "There's an incinerator down the corridor. It can only be used by one senior manager – that's the Dong, Vindi or Luther (now you, of course) – in conjunction with one other member of H11 staff. Anything burnt has to be checked and signed off by both colleagues. Every few months the ashes are transported upstairs. When that happens, the sensors and alarms are turned off. The Director-General himself has to be present when it happens. The Director-General and the Home Secretary are the only people allowed to copy documents or artefacts and take the copies away, although department heads are allowed to view any document or artefact after the Dong has agreed their request. So you can see, it's pretty watertight."

"It certainly is." Schizo nodded, and sat down on one of the workbench stools. She looked very pale under the harsh lighting.

"Are you all right?" Maddy asked. "How do you feel – after yesterday?"

Schizo looked up sharply at her. "Yesterday? What have you been told about yesterday?"

"Nothing much. Maybe said the Dong had told her you'd been involved in another fatality yesterday. That's two in two days. And your suspension. Must be jolly upsetting. I mean, I can't sleep when my boyfriend Toby snores, but you…"

Schizo stood up. She was still shorter than Maddy, but she drew herself up, blue eyes shining fiercely. "I was not 'involved' in either fatality – I just happened to be the person who found the bodies. I want you to know that Double D had asked me to come to his flat – he asked me to help him. I wasn't suspended for any alleged harassment – it was due to a procedural oversight, caused by my trying to comfort Double D's partner. Anyone who tries to tell you that…"

Maddy took a step back. "No, no. No one has insinuated anything."

Was Schizo telling the truth?

"What did the Dong tell you about yesterday?" Schizo's eyes were still blazing.

"Nothing. I haven't spoken to him since it happened."

"Well, let me enlighten you: the body I found was that of the man who had been following Double D, the man who had so freaked him out, maybe the man who murdered him. I tracked him down, but someone got to him first."

It was Maddy's turn to sit down on a workbench stool. "You think Double D was murdered?"

Schizo nodded. "I do."

"But the Dong says it was suicide."

"We hold different opinions. I'm told the Director-General has ordered that all three deaths be treated as murders until proven otherwise, so I'm not alone in my opinion."

"If Luther and Double D were murdered…" She found it too awkward to continue.

Schizo finished Maddy's sentence for her. "Do I think you're in danger as well?"

Maddy nodded.

"I don't know. If they were murdered it was maybe because they knew something dangerous. If you don't know that same dangerous thing, then you're safe."

Maddy shook her head. "I'm just a bloody archivist; I'm not some secret agent. It's not fair. You know, I often sit in this room thinking about murder, but it's just for the novel I'm planning. And now this…"

"Until I or my colleagues up on the third floor find out more, I can't reassure you, but I shouldn't alarm you unduly. The Dong may be right and the Director-General wrong. At the moment we're all in the same boat; all we can do is to be vigilant, keep to all security protocols, and support one another."

"Hmm." Maddy looked round the workroom. Suddenly it looked a very dangerous place: biros to stab with, masking tape to choke with, and spray cans containing a toxic chemical.

Schizo picked up a metal filing case from the workbench. "All the documents and artefacts are housed in these, right?" Maddy nodded. "And these eight digit numbers denote the access number of the document or artefact – am I right?"

"You are."

Maddy watched Schizo nod to herself, as if she'd just confirmed some deep secret.

"And whenever any staff member handles any file, they have to write down in the logbook the numbers of the files they've handled – yes?"

"Yes."

"Can we have a look at that logbook next, please?" Schizo no longer looked tired and drawn; she had suddenly lit a spark of excitement in her eyes.

What it was all about, Maddy could only guess.

24

LYDIA

Maybe, or Maggie as Lydia still wanted to call her, explained that the file log needed to stay in the main office at all times, then left Lydia and Maddy to it. She said she needed to clean the Dong's office while he was upstairs.

Lydia was disappointed by her initial search through the logbook. There were columns for the date, for the name of the person handling the files, for the numbers identifying the files handled, another for the reason for handling them, and one for the signature of the duty officer. It was all very clear and simple, but there was just too much information, and she didn't know exactly what she was looking for. Try as she might, she couldn't summon up in her memory any of the numbers on Luther's secret list. She could flip back to the last entries made by Luther and by Double D, but without further investigation of what each file contained, she couldn't draw any conclusions. An added distraction was Maddy, who kept up an earnest commentary on everything Lydia ran her hand over.

"So the first two numbers represent the accession year – that is, the year we took possession of the file. So with eight digits it means we can accommodate up to one million files being added each year. We've never got close, of course. We only take the super-sensitive ones, the ones that can't be risked upstairs. All numbers are in order of accession."

"Would it be possible," Lydia asked, "for members of the H11 team to handle files and get away with not entering them in the log?"

Maddy looked at her blankly. "Well yes, I suppose so. There's nothing to physically stop it, but if you were caught you'd be up on a disciplinary charge. And why would anyone want to cheat on the system like that? It's not as if you can copy or take out the files. You can't do anything with them. Everywhere in H11 except the toilet is covered by CCTV cameras, so you wouldn't get away with it."

"And who controls the CCTV footage?"

"The Dong. I believe his line manager – the Director-General, I imagine – has to oversee his monitoring of it and has to sign it off whenever any coverage is wiped. Look, if you're implying that the Dong can subvert…"

Lydia could see Maddy was getting irritated or unsettled by this line of questions. "Not at all – I wasn't implying anything," she said quickly. "Anyway, presumably when the Dong goes on one of his famous foreign holidays, it's his deputy – me, at present, but Luther before he died – who gets to control the CCTV footage?"

Maddy's mouth formed a grim line. "We all have 'Triple A' security ratings down here in H11. Mutual trust is absolutely essential if you're to be a functioning team member."

"What about Bri – sorry, Nylon? Do you trust him?"

"Well, he's a bit intense. He's not exactly my type, of course, but I have total professional trust in all my colleagues."

Lydia smiled. "I'm sorry. Of course you do. I have total trust in you, too. It's just that I've been sent down here to ask those uncomfortable sorts of questions. I need to ask them so we can protect you." She wasn't sure whether she'd convinced Maddy.

A buzzer sounded above the main desk. They both looked up to the monitor to see Gerard Bell standing in the corridor outside.

Maddy buzzed Bell through into the cloakroom. "I'm allowed to do that if Maybe or Mo aren't present in the office. With such a small team, we have to be flexible in our duties. There are lots of new buttons for you to learn so you can take your turn on these duties." She looked up at the monitor, then pressed another button to open the door from the cloakroom into the office.

Bell stepped through. "Good morning, George. Good morning, Schizo. I hope George is doing a good job showing you everything and answering all your questions." He was geniality itself, beaming warmly.

"A brilliant job, thank you," Lydia replied.

"And I see you're dressing the part – excellent! I like your T-shirt: 'Modern Suffragette' – very good. Could you come along with me to my office for a chat, Schizo? Can I borrow her a few minutes, George?"

Maddy nodded. "Of course, Dong."

Bell swept out; Lydia followed him up the corridor. They met Maggie coming the other way.

"I've tidied your office, Dong."

"Thank you, Maybe."

As they turned into Bell's office, Lydia asked, "Does Maggie – Maybe – have full unaccompanied access to your office at all times?"

Bell turned, his craggy face still smiling expansively. "Trust – that's what it's all about."

"So do I have the same access?"

"Aha! Very clever! Nylon comes in to clean it once a week at a specified time, but I'm usually present. Maybe and Farah ask my permission to enter. I'd expect the same courtesy from you if I'm around, but as my deputy, you have access if I'm not down here. Of course, I wouldn't expect you to go through my drawers."

"Thank you." So this trust had limits.

Bell sat down behind his desk, and waved Lydia to one of the rattan chairs. "Now, I just wanted to have a little chat with you so I could reassure you that you have my full and unconditional support."

It sounded like a prepared speech that he'd been ordered to give, but she kept her counsel. "Thank you."

"I know we got off to a rocky start, but I want to tell you I am delighted to have you down here in our hour of need. It's fantastic to have such a committed, bright woman as you join our team. I'm sure you'll have some great suggestions on how we might tighten up our security, so please go ahead and speak out whenever you want – just as long as you think about maintaining team morale. Everyone is very tense after the deaths of two of our much loved colleagues, as I'm sure you're aware. I'm guessing that you, too, are feeling the effects of the last few days – you'd be superhuman not to."

"I'm fine, thank you – without being superhuman."

They both had a little chuckle. Lydia felt vaguely uneasy that they seemed to be getting on so well.

"Anyway, you'll have your first experience of deputising for me tomorrow, or at least being joint deputy. It's Luther's memorial service at 10am, and I'm leaving you and Vindi to hold the fort here while I take George, Farah, Maybe and Nylon to pay our last respects to dear old Luther. It's down in Canterbury and there are drinks and eats after, so you'll have most of the day to get to know each other, and Vindi can take you through the processes of being in charge down here. Is that okay?"

"Of course it is." She was going to be alone with Vindi for the day. Could he hear that her heart was beating just a little quicker? Control this schoolgirl reaction, she told herself.

The chat went on for another ten minutes, and it was very pleasant. They discussed their common interests in art and literature. She was surprised and pleased he was a fan of Frieda Kahlo. He was delighted she was a fan of Reza Hamid, told her that his wife Louisa was Reza's agent and offered to invite Lydia to meet Reza sometime in the near future.

The chat was so pleasant that Lydia almost forgot to ask Bell the question she had been rehearsing all morning.

"Tell, me, Dong," she really didn't like using his nickname but she made a good attempt at hiding it, "have you heard the name Ian Forrester?" She scanned his ravaged face for the slightest hint of guilt.

There was none. "Yes, of course I have."

"When? In what context?"

"Half an hour ago, upstairs. Perry briefed me on your adventures of yesterday. You showed great bravery and initiative to go after him, especially as you were suspended at the time."

"What light do you think it sheds on Double D's death?"

"I honestly don't know." Bell creased his brow. "It's too early to say. He could have been employed by anyone, and he may not have been following Double D. I agree that it does show Double D had cause to be worried and this Forrester chap may have pushed him closer to suicide. It does suggest I was certainly hasty and may have been wrong to imply it was your pursuit of Double D that contributed to his suicide, and for that I would like to apologise sincerely and unreservedly. I hope you can accept my apology."

"Of course."

"Splendid. Let's go to work together and get through this crisis. I'm sure we'll make a great team."

It was only when Lydia was walking back down the corridor to Maddy in the main office that she started to evaluate how much of Gerard Bell's new charm offensive was genuine.

At the end of her shift in H11, she had a session scheduled with Perry Webb, but he was busy and had left a message that no significant progress had been made by the team 'above ground'; he obviously didn't think Lydia was going to offer up any new developments either. Miss Parmenter sent Lydia home early, which was good – Lydia had been fretting about her mother for most of the day. She phoned to say she was on her way; her mother said she was fine and that there was no hurry.

When she climbed the stairs to her flat, she found her mother sitting in her armchair watching *Coronation Street*. The tiny flat was immaculately tidy and had obviously been cleaned from ceiling to floorboard. There was the enticing smell of a stew, with vegetables being boiled on the other gas ring.

Lydia kissed her mother on the forehead. "Oh Mum, you shouldn't have! You're very naughty."

"What was I expected to do? Sit around all day in your pokey little place? I've had a lovely time! I haven't felt as alive for ages, though I must admit I feel a bit pooped right now. I'm going to watch the end of this. You can drain the veggies."

Lydia dished up stew, potatoes and broccoli as the *Coronation Street* theme played and the titles rolled. They sat at the little table, eating.

"Good wholesome food – just what the doctor ordered. Thank you, Mum."

"Aren't you going to ask me what I did today?" Sarah Twomey beamed.

"I can see it, without asking you. I'm a spook, remember? I can use my training to make amazingly complex deductions. You've been shopping, you've cleaned my flat, and you've cooked our dinner. That's far too much for someone in your condition."

"I'm very proud of myself. I usually have trouble with... well, you don't want to know. And what you've seen and deduced is only part of it. I've been on my laptop, doing research."

"Into what?"

"Into your world. You seem to be all bothered with surveillance men following you, spying on you, so I've been researching surveillance. I'm an expert on bugging now – all the different types of bugs they can put in a home or workplace. And..." she paused for effect. She put down her knife and fork. "I found this." She reached down, fumbled in the handbag at her feet and pulled out her glasses case.

"It's your glasses, Mum."

"No it isn't, dear. It's something much nastier. I wrapped it up in cotton wool and then tin foil, and put it in my glasses case, because I thought it might still be live."

"Alive?"

"My, for a spook you are slow today!" Her mother was enjoying this. "Live, not alive. If you look up to the bracket holding up your bookshelf over there, you'll see it's missing one of its Phillips screws."

"Go on."

"I'd researched all the types of bugs that buggers use, and one of them is to plant tiny bugs in fake Phillips screws. They contain a camera and microphone – it's amazing how small they are. Then I looked for the best vantage point for a bug in your flat." She pointed to the shelf bracket. "It was there."

"Oh my God, Mum. You found a bug in my flat?"

Sarah nodded. "And now it's safely wrapped up in my glasses case." She put the case down on the table between them. "What do we do with it?"

For a moment Lydia was lost for words. She just stared at her mother's glasses case as if it was a bomb. It must have been planted when the list of numbers was stolen. Her enemies had penetrated her place of refuge – but who were her enemies?

"You, Mum, don't do anything with it – I'll sort it and then I put you on a train tomorrow morning. Look, you're incredibly clever to have found this, and you're wonderfully brave – but this bug just proves this place is way too dangerous for you to be here. Some bad person has had access to this flat. They could return. I love you too much to expose you to this danger. This is non-negotiable."

Sarah picked up her knife and fork and continued to eat her stew and potatoes. "We'll see."

25

LYDIA

Next morning the alarm woke them in plenty of time for Lydia to get her mother up and to Euston Station, but her plans ran into trouble immediately.

Sarah sat up in bed, a weary dazed look on her face. "I'm sorry, dear, I must have done too much yesterday. I feel really rocky. I know my condition well enough to…"

"You mean you're not well enough to travel home today on your own."

Her mother nodded.

Lydia looked at her mother carefully. It was difficult to tell if her mother was shamming, but it would be impossibly heartless to call any bluff; she couldn't thrust a suitcase in her mother's hand and tell her to piss off back to the Midlands, and she couldn't take her back herself – today she was holding the fort with Vindi down in H11.

"So what do we do?"

"You leave me here in bed for the day. That should give me time to recover."

Lydia shook her head. "I explained it already: someone has broken into my flat before. They could do it again, especially now their bug has been removed."

Sarah smiled. "I've got your gun. I looked up on the internet how to use this model. It's amazing what you can find. I've already practised flicking the safety catch."

Lydia's mouth fell open. "Absolutely no way are you getting involved in a shoot-out in my flat, Mum! Jesus Christ, has your condition sent you mad?"

"Quite the opposite, Lyds: I'm crystal clear – but very tired. I'm not frightened of some bugger. I shall rest up in bed all day with my laptop, doing some research for you. I'll have a great time. Then this evening we can discuss me going back to Nuneaton. Now, what do you want me to research on my laptop? They've probably got yours bugged but the spooks won't know about mine."

Lydia sighed. Her mother had her over a barrel. "Okay, if you want to spend your day playing at being a spook, see what you can find about these names and places."

She sat at the table and wrote a list on a torn-off cereal packet lid:

> Ergun Solicitors, 188, Fore Street, London. Nesrin Cevdet, Solicitor. Ian Forrester, aka Marcus Forest, ex-army. A & C Foodstore, Fore Street, London. Louisa Bell, Literary Agent.

She handed the list to her mother.

"Well that's a varied bunch if ever I saw one. I hope you haven't made these up just to divert me." Sarah was beaming with pleasure.

"Mum, this isn't a game, I promise you. This is deadly serious, and if you get into any trouble I will never forgive myself."

"I won't let you down, Lyds."

As she descended the stairs from her flat on her way to work, the pangs of guilt were already gnawing at Lydia's insides. Why had she given in to her mother so easily? What if the enemies did return to her flat? What if her mother's enquiries brought her into danger?

But it was wonderful to have someone to trust; she had been missing it for so long, ever since James had moved out. To have someone beside her in bed, someone to talk to, someone to cook stew – God, it was lovely!

When she got into work she went to see Perry, but he wasn't yet in. She left the bug with Miss Parmenter, wrapped in cotton wool and tinfoil, with a note: 'Urgent: Dear Mr Webb, please find out who screwed this into the wall of my flat. Yours in expectation, Lydia Twomey'.

Lydia hurried down to H11. For the first time she didn't feel a pall of dread as she walked out of the lift and along the corridor, past the biometric tests, to where Damian Curry was waiting for her outside the door to H11. He was wearing shorts and a blue athletic vest; he was doing press-ups, quickly and with ease. She watched him for a few seconds, until she realised he'd noticed her enjoying the show.

"Sorry," she said, moving forward. "Have I kept you long? I didn't realise we had to go in together."

He stopped the press-ups, and sprang lightly to his feet. "Only the Dong is allowed in H11 on his own. It's no hassle to wait here – I can do my exercises just as well here as in the archive stacks. We haven't exactly been set an arduous set of tasks for today."

They went through the codes and the biometrics; the doors to the cloakroom slid open. As she took off her bike jacket and boots, she was acutely aware of Damian's presence – she couldn't help but watch him towel some sweat off his face and arms, then change his trainers. She saw him appraising her as she peeled off her leather bike trousers: underneath she was wearing a pair of pastel blue culottes below a classy white cotton shirt that she'd bought in Morocco. She noted that Damian didn't disguise a brief smile, but he said nothing.

They went through into the main office. Damian picked up the duty sheet left on Farah's chaotic flower-bedecked desk. "Here's yours." He handed it to her. He looked full into her face for just a little too long, she thought, but there was no hint of an expression to tell her what he was thinking.

She looked at the tasks. It was mainly getting familiar with the nature of the files and how to find specific ones. "Thank you. I may need to ask you for a bit of help when I get stuck, Damian."

"It's Vindi down here." He said it coolly, without reproach. "I'll be in stack four if you need me. Feel free to interrupt me – the work isn't stretching." He put his hands behind his head and stretched in such a way that his vest rode up, exposing his midriff, a mass of black curls around a neat navel. "See you."

He was off, leaving Lydia chewing her lip in the office.

What game was he playing? He was obviously displaying his charms – he'd probably been waiting for her in the corridor before starting his press-ups, then the towelling was just too theatrical and the stretch was the same. He wouldn't try to seduce her down here, surely? He'd know that she wouldn't keep quiet about any possible sexual harassment. Perhaps it was all part of his way to assert his power. The annoying thing was that it worked: Lydia was definitely attracted, even though she knew it was unprofessional and very unwise.

Jesus, this was all too much like some Year Nine adolescent fantasy – just get on with your job, and stop obsessing about something that isn't going to happen.

She got down to the work outlined on her task sheet: to familiarise herself with the files, she chose file 97000161 at random, found it in Stack 2, brought it back to the office, entered it in the log, and opened up the metal box. Inside there was a cassette audiotape and a paper transcript. She set up the office cassette player, inserted the tape, and sat back to listen. It was obviously a covert recording because the sound quality was poor. The dialogue was tedious – a lot of clichéd flirting between an older and a younger man – but the significance was that the older man was a top British industrialist and the younger man was a rent boy who had moved to London from Budapest only the year before, and who met with an 'unexplained' death just months after the tape was recorded.

Lydia stopped the tape and ejected the cassette. It was easier to read the transcript. She noted the transcript had been done by Maggie Willis and had been signed off by Gerard Bell as being accurate.

So what?

It told her that Bell had enormous potential blackmailing power over prominent people, but nothing more. The trouble was, she didn't know what she was looking for. There were hundreds of thousands, even millions, of deadly secrets down here, and she had no idea which ones held the key to her investigations. She would start on going through Dennis Dunn's recent work first but it could be a long and hopeless task, because there would be nothing to say that one secret was any more vital or toxic than another.

"How's it going? Discovered the vital clue yet?" Vindi was lounging against the doorpost.

Lydia tried not to show she'd jumped when he spoke – she hadn't heard him arrive at the door. "Give me another half an hour and I'm sure I'll have it all sorted and the bad guys banged to rights."

"What are you looking at?"

"I'm going to start with Double D's schedule – try to see what spooked him."

"Good luck with that."

"Did he say anything to you about the work he was doing?"

Vindi shook his head. “We didn’t talk much. He was on the morning shift, I’m on the evening shift and we didn’t share the same interests and tastes.”

“So you’re not into musicals, then? What do you like? What’s on your headphones when you’re doing all those exercises in the stacks?”

“Loud aggressive testosterone-fuelled stuff when I’m burning the calories, blissed-out new age stuff when I’m relaxing or meditating.”

“Meditating? How on earth do you get away with meditating on duty? Surely Bell checks the CCTV footage of you zonked out in the stacks – does he allow it?”

“Oh, I know all the CCTV blind spots down here – believe me. I’m an expert on evading CCTV. I even did a course on it once, way back. And what’s Bell going to do if he does catch me – transfer me back upstairs?”

Lydia felt they were making progress but she knew the next question was pushing her luck. “So tell me, what was the real reason you got transferred down here, if it wasn’t Webb’s daughter?”

Vindi laughed. It was supposed to sound casual, but Lydia could detect the bitterness. “Vanessa was a nice girl – probably still is – but she was out of her depth. Webb had wangled her a gap year internship in our department – I ask you, interns in MI5! She developed a crush on me. Daddy didn’t like his darling daughter, destined for Cambridge and a career in something glittering and vacuous, consorting with a grubby pleb like yours truly. So I had to go. The vacancy in H11 was the first that presented itself. And here I am, four years later.”

“Ah. It’s truly a sad story.” If it’s true, she thought.

“I’m not looking for any sympathy. But you asked, for some reason.” He moved forward towards her desk. “Why were you interested?”

She took a deep breath.

The buzzer sounded above their heads.

Vindi stepped back. "Someone in the corridor outside."

They both looked up at the monitor on the wall, which automatically showed any motion in the corridor. There was a man waiting to be admitted to H11. He was middle-aged, greying, with a smart suit and rimless glasses.

"Oh my God," said Lydia. "You know who that is?"

"I've never met him, but we all know who he is. It's our Director-General. What the fuck is he doing down here?"

26

LYDIA

The Director-General of MI5 was sitting at the desk surrounded by metal box files neatly stacked around him when Lydia entered Gerard's office.

"You called, sir?"

"Yes. I'd like you to sign off my use of these files, please." He pushed the logbook across the desk, between the files.

Lydia moved forward, pen in hand, to inspect the list of numbers. She ran her eyes down the numbers listed in the log, and then inspected the metal files. She went back to the log. She looked at the Director-General.

"Sit down, Ms Twomey."

She obeyed. She looked at his impassive calm face framed by the files. "Sir, you're asking me to sign off for a different set of files."

"That's right, I am."

"You're asking me to falsify the records."

"Correct. I know I owe you an explanation, but it's a matter of national security. I can't let anyone, apart from you of course, know I have seen these files."

"With respect, sir, I have been told it's a matter of national security that I only sign off for the correct files that have been opened. I would be endangering national security if I falsified the records. I cannot do as you order."

The Director-General sat in silence for what seemed an age. "I understand your position, Miss Twomey, and I commend your integrity. You might already be aware that I personally requested that you be embedded down here in H11 precisely because of your integrity and your strength of will. I was going to brief you on the case you're investigating; the discovery I have made today has merely pushed things forward." He paused.

Lydia waited – she had nothing to say.

"The files you see on this desk have been corrupted." He patted the files on his left. "They do not contain what is listed on your H11 catalogue. Instead, these file boxes contain old material from other files, which has been dumped in these files to replace the missing material."

"Have you checked that these other files, where the old material came from, are empty?"

The Director-General patted the files to his right. "They're not empty. They contain material that has recently been rerecorded plus renewed material – material that, once copied, should have been incinerated. Somebody has stolen the crucial material and replaced it with this old copied stuff."

"It's what Dennis Dunn had been doing before he died – renewing and replacing. You're saying that he never destroyed the old material once he'd copied it."

The Director-General nodded. "Of course it's possible he killed himself in remorse for what he'd done or not done, but it's much more likely he's been killed to cover it up, albeit possibly without being aware of what he'd done."

"But I don't understand why you want me to falsify this log." Lydia's brow creased. "Now you've discovered this scam, surely you can look up in the log which members of the H11 team entered the false incineration of the material that's in these files, and then arrest them. Why hide the fact you've inspected these corrupted files?"

"It's the missing information that is vital to this case. If the material is destroyed or has been smuggled out of H11, then the country's national security is at risk."

She was aware he hadn't answered her question. She asked another. "Why?"

"It's best you don't know that for the time being."

She shook her head. "I think it's unlikely the material has been smuggled out of here, sir. From what I've learned so far, the system is pretty foolproof."

"But it could have been destroyed. All that had to be done was to switch the sensitive missing material with the old material that was being replaced, and put it in the incinerator."

"So why aren't you open about it? Why not arrest the people who were logged as carrying out the incineration, sir?"

"Because, Ms Twomey, the people logged as carrying out the incineration were..."

She saw the pattern. "Martin Froome and Dennis Dunn."

The Director-General nodded. "We can't discount the possibility the log has been falsified. This is an elaborate and complex plot, involving many more people than just two H11 staff."

As she listened, Lydia found her eyes drawn to the numbering on the file to her right. The eight digit number was somehow familiar. Why? She forced her mind back to what the Director-General was saying.

The DG continued. "Until we can ascertain if the log has been falsified and if so, who has falsified it, we have no one to arrest."

Lydia frowned. "But if Martin Froome and Dennis Dunn were the only conspirators within H11, the other plotters won't know for certain that the files are indeed destroyed. They will only have Froome and Dunn's word for it."

"Exactly. You have a sharp mind, Ms Twomey. That's why we must pretend that nothing untoward has happened. We can pretend to the outside world that the files are still intact, and that we still control the critical evidence. It's why I am asking you to falsify the log and sign off for a different set of files."

"If I do it, sir..." she paused, feeling her heartbeat hammering at her ribs. "If I falsify the log, I'd like some help from you."

"Yes?" He sounded wary, as if he was expecting some tawdry deal.

"On my first day down here, I... I removed a piece of paper that had been stuck to the bottom of Martin Froome's desk. I don't know why I did it. I suppose I felt pressured and I didn't trust Gerard Bell enough to hand it over. I smuggled it out of H11 and hid it in my flat."

"What was on it?" The Director-General leaned forward, hope suddenly in his eyes.

"A list of H11 file numbers. I can't be certain, but one of those numbers may have been the same as the number on that top file you've got on the desk."

"Where is this piece of paper now?"

"That's where I need your help, sir: it's gone."

"How do you mean, gone?"

"It was stolen from my flat. I'm truly sorry. I didn't have time to memorise it, and I didn't back it up. At the time I didn't even recognise that the numbers were file numbers. Now it's gone and the conspirators have it and they know I've seen it. I know I've been incredibly stupid."

"If Gerard Bell is a conspirator, you've been very wise not to hand it over."

"There's a bit more: the numbers were in two columns. The file you've got there was listed in the left-hand column."

"So?"

"I'm just wondering whether the left-hand column listed the emptied files and other side was the destination of where the material had been hidden – in other files."

"Go on."

"What if Froome and the other conspirators didn't incinerate the material because that was too difficult or risky, and they couldn't smuggle it out, but instead hid it within other file boxes that had space in them? It's an effective hiding place – there are hundreds of thousands of files – it would take months or years to search through all of them."

"Hmm." He put his hand to his chin, and closed his eyes.

Lydia waited. She didn't know this man; was he going to fire her for losing the list? She looked around: the plasma screen and computer were turned off so there was no tourist image dominating the claustrophobic room. The statuette of Baal gazed impassively from the bookshelf.

At last he spoke. "We need each other, Ms Twomey. I need you to sign off this log, and then I need you to find these missing items, if indeed they are hidden somewhere down here. I need you to flush out any other conspirators in H11. You need me to overlook your purloining Froome's list and then losing it without a back-up. And you need me to protect you. Believe me: your life is in danger. These people have killed already, and they will be prepared to do so again. Your list may have been crucial. I will pull strings to have you protected, but I need you too much down in H11 to have you withdrawn to some MI5 safe house."

"I wouldn't feel safe in a safe house, anyway." She took a deep breath. "I believe there's someone in Internal Security or maybe in GCHQ who is part of this conspiracy." She almost flinched; if the Director-General was like Webb, he would laugh and patronise her.

"Why do you think that?"

"Before I went to interview Dennis Dunn, someone must have been tipped off, because they got to Dennis first and killed him. Then before I got to Ian Forrester, someone got to him first. The only people who knew I was after Dunn and Forrester were in the Internal Security team investigating this case. It's being led by Jon Small and Ashar Chowdry, but they're not the only ones in the loop."

"I hear what you're saying, and I will try to tackle that side of things. In return, you need to report directly to me, as well as reporting directly to Gerard Bell and directly to Perry Webb. You need to discriminate very carefully what you report in each case." He smiled. "I'm the only one to whom you give the full unvarnished truth. I have faith in you. I'm sure you can work it out."

"I can."

"And not a word of our conversation to Damian Curry, either. He'll be waiting down the corridor, wondering what's being said."

"Of course. One other favour, sir: my mother."

He raised his eyebrows. "What about your mother?"

"She's at present guarding my flat, as she sees it. She heard about my suspension and came down from Nuneaton to be with me. She found the bug in my flat – did Perry Webb tell you about it?" The Director-General shook his head. "Anyway, she's vulnerable – she's got advanced MS, and I need to be sure she's being looked after somewhere safe. I can't do what you need if I'm trying to look after my mother as well."

"I quite understand, Ms Twomey. My own mother isn't well and needs help. Phone your mother to say we'll be sending someone round to discuss what help she needs…"

"And discuss what help she'll accept. She's stubborn and proud. Thank you very much, sir."

"Take this card. It has the details on how to contact me directly. Feel free to use it whenever you need to. There – I think we've made all the deals we need to forge our alliance. Let's hope we turn this around."

He didn't smile.

27

PERRY

Another visit to the DG's Inner Sanctum: Perry wasn't sure whether he should feel honoured or alarmed, but his guts told him to be apprehensive. The pill told him to stand firm.

"Sit down, Perry." The DG looked in pensive mode, hand already on his chin.

Perry took the seat underneath the damned grandfather clock.

"You may recall, Perry, I told you in strictest confidence a couple of days ago that some very nasty political issues were bearing down on us."

"My lips have been sealed."

"Of course they have. Well, these political issues have well and truly arrived, and although they are yet to break over our heads, it's probably only a matter of hours." The DG paused. Perry wondered whether the DG took his rhythm from the ticking clock. "I'm confiding in you, Perry, and in no one else at present. That's because I know I can trust you."

"I'm glad." Perry sat straighter in his chair and adjusted his tie. Perhaps this was going to be a good meeting after all. He'd always liked the Matisses on the wall of this office; maybe he too would get his office decorated with government-lease fine art before too long. "How can I help?"

"You'll recall the case of the prominent government minister who astonished the press by resigning so meekly over the defence crisis a few years ago. Let's give him a codename: Vilnius – I don't want any added risks of a slander case."

"I recall it very well."

"You will recall that the real reason why the PM was able to get rid of Vilnius so easily was because of the material we had on him down in H11. That material had been stolen from his flat by a burglar who'd then attempted to sell it to the press."

Perry nodded.

The DG resumes. "What you may not know is that this material implicated as members of a ring of paedophiles not only Vilnius but also a number of politically active men on one wing of the political spectrum."

"I'd heard the rumours it extended out from Vilnius, obviously."

"Those rumours, and the threat of the damning material held in H11, has held back the careers of those men for the last decade. They and their families have been very bitter about the whole thing."

"Damned cheek. They were guilty."

"I know, but they were never convicted of anything, and that group of families have an unshakable belief that they have a right to rule come what may. Their ancestors did far worse and never lost their positions of power. They've always wanted their entitlement, as they see it, restored to them."

Perry shook his head. "So we need something to knock them down. Can't we pin something on them?"

"We carried out a few discreet enquiries of our own, but the only concrete evidence of their guilt sits in H11. Or rather, it did sit there."

"What do you mean?" Perry was on the edge of his seat. This was genuinely exciting.

"I chose today to visit H11 because Gerard and most of his staff were at the memorial service for Martin Froome. I dug out the Vilnius files and found they've all been corrupted. All the damning information has been removed and replaced with copied information from other files."

"Good Lord!"

"We no longer have anything incriminating on Vilnius and his cabal. We can expect an attack from them in the very near future."

"What sort of attack are you expecting?" Perry could feel his palms sweating. He wiped them on his trousers.

"Elements of the press – you can probably guess which journalists they'll use – will trumpet the innocence of these 'true British patriots' and will demand a full inquiry to rehabilitate their reputations. The Home Secretary will demand I rebut this attack with the H11 documents. The documents will be found to have gone missing, and I will pay for this security lapse with my job. The other person who will lose their job will be the Head of MI5 Internal Security, who allowed this security lapse to occur."

"Me." Suddenly this meeting was far less congenial and the Matisses on the wall looked like impossible dreams.

"Now you see why I have confided in you. The plotters will have our replacements already lined up. They will have already sounded out supporters within the service. Our removal will be the first step of their coup d'etat. Control of MI5 will enable them to move to the second stage of their plot. They'll go after the Home Secretary, and eventually the Prime Minister. The government will fall and they will introduce some radical new legislation which, amongst other things, will convert MI5 into a service curbing freedoms rather than defending them. That's the Doomsday scenario, but don't think it won't happen." The DG fell silent.

"Oh dear." Perry searched for something useful to say. "How do you read Gerard's role in all this? Do you think he's one of the plotters? He doesn't strike me as a fascist, but surely these documents couldn't get destroyed or stolen without his connivance. Surely he's got to be in on this? I know Lydia Twomey doesn't trust him."

"As you're so fond of saying, Perry, mere suspicion and distrust doesn't hold up in court. The missing materials' file boxes have been filled with artefacts supposedly incinerated – the logbook suggests the incinerations were carried out by Martin Froome and Dennis Dunn. I don't have to remind you that you advised me that there was nothing suspicious in either of their deaths, but they put Gerard in the clear – for the moment."

Perry tried to ignore the DG's dig. He shook his head. "But if we're going to lose our jobs through accusations of negligence, surely Gerard is guilty of much greater negligence? He's bound to lose his job if this ever gets out. In fact, you have grounds to sack him immediately, even if he's got nothing to do with the plot."

The DG almost smiled. "Ah, Gerard! You may not like him, Perry, but you've got to respect him. He's a very subtle player."

"What do you mean?" Perry hated any implied praise of the bastard.

"Even if he's not involved in their plot, he'll have intelligence about Vilnius; he will have made arrangements to deflect any flak from himself – you can count on it."

"How?"

"I don't know yet, but Vilnius will be very wary of Gerard Bell's knowledge."

"Surely what we need to do is to suspend or arrest Gerard immediately, suspend all other H11 staff pending an inquiry, seal the department then send in the search teams. Only decisive action will save our bacon."

It was the DG's turn to shake his head. "It's not like you to be so impetuous, Perry, but it's not wise this time. Your Lydia

Twomey believes the material is hidden, not destroyed; if we could guarantee to find the material within hours, I'd agree with your plan, but there are hundreds of thousands of file boxes to examine, and potentially explosive secrets in most of them. We don't have enough staff with the requisite security clearance to tackle such a huge task in the available time."

"Why does it have to be done so quickly?"

"As soon as I move against Gerard or close down H11, the Home Secretary will need to be informed. She will demand an explanation, and when she hears it, she will suspend or sack both me and you. She will do whatever she can to insulate herself and the government from the crisis. Gerard, of course, knows I can't move against him, even if I had evidence."

"So what do we do? We can't just pretend nothing is wrong and wait for this storm to break over our heads."

"Firstly, your department goes all out to investigate Martin Froome, Dennis Dunn and Ian Forrester. One way or another, they were involved in this plot. Put maximum resources into this. I want to know everything there is to know about their lives, who they had contact with, their political views – everything. We need to identify their connection to this conspiracy. I want this information from you by this time tomorrow."

Perry gulped. "Of course."

"And there's another thing, Perry: Ms Twomey has convinced me that you have a security leak somewhere in the team you set up to investigate Martin Froome's death. They got to Dunn and to Ian Forrester before she could. She mentioned Ashar Chowdry and Jon Small by name, but it could be anyone whom you or they have briefed, or anyone in GCHQ with access to your communications. Get that leak cauterised immediately."

"Right-oh." Perry tried to sound as if he was in effortless control, but it sounded too casual.

"I can rely on your complete discretion about our conversation today, and I know I can rely on your efficiency and dynamism to deal with the matters I've put into your hands."

"Naturally."

Great, thought Perry. I may be efficient and dynamic but I'm not a miracle worker. I've got a team of less than thirty operatives, a probable deadline of twenty-four hours and no obvious clues.

Not good, not good at all.

28

SARAH

Sarah Twomey was excited. Any tiredness she'd complained about to her daughter was long gone. She'd got up, washed, had some breakfast and got dressed. Now she was sitting at the table, tapping away feverishly on her laptop in her new role as investigative researcher.

Sarah prided herself on having a methodical, tidy approach to problem solving so she started with A & C Foodstore, as they came first alphabetically. A & C Foodstore's Turkish Cypriot owners were clients of Ergun's the solicitors, but she was disappointed not to dig up any dirt on them. All she could find was that they were involved in importing foodstuffs from countries around the Eastern Mediterranean. Of course it might mean that they were involved in people trafficking, or even drug smuggling, but she found no evidence of it.

The Bell Literacy Agency, headed by Louisa Bell, didn't yield many secrets at first. Its bland but glossy website was full of advice for first-time authors on how to present their submissions, and then informed them that they weren't actually taking any submissions at present. There was a fairly short list of authors they represented, with biographies and pictures, together with plenty of glamorous pictures of Louisa Bell standing next to various celebrities and politicians.

But Sarah was resourceful, and she knew how to dig deeper. The picture that emerged didn't quite stack up. This was just a small agency with no big-selling authors, but it seemed to be doing extraordinarily well. Some of the clients seemed to put huge sums of money into publishing their work. Digging further into the background of the clients, although most were not names Sarah had ever heard before, they seemed to be an extremely rich and powerful group, quite unlike normal authors. There were also some very quirky anomalies on the website. This was no ordinary literary agency.

With Ergun Solicitors she was delving into the nitty-gritty of North London streets. Ergun's office in Fore Street was just a branch office; their head office was in Green Lanes, but they had a network stretching across the area. They specialised in compensation claims, issues with the police, robberies – anything involving the nasty side of life. Nesrin Cevdet was one of their lawyers, specialising in security services. Sarah came across all sorts of vague terms describing what Erguns offered: personal protection, phone records investigation, recovery of property, enabling privacy, internet security, interface with government agencies (what sort of interface, and which agencies?). Some of these activities certainly sounded dodgy to Sarah – they seemed to be the champions of the criminal fraternity.

When she dug deeper into Nesrin Cevdet's past, she decided to try some 'shots in the dark', as she called them. One of these came up with a remarkable 'coincidence', one she knew Lydia would be interested in…

Sarah sat back and sighed contentedly. The day had flown by, and she felt proud of her work, though now she was ready for a cup of tea and a chocolate biscuit, maybe two. She had plenty to tell Lydia when she returned. She patted Lydia's gun that she kept by her laptop, as if she was a true secret agent.

Her mobile phone rang. It was Lydia.

"Hello, Lyds."

"Are you all right, Mum?"

"I've had a great day, although I'm still feeling tired. I've found out some very interesting information on those Turkish solicitors, and also on Louisa Bell and her agency."

"Look Mum, you probably won't like this, but I'm worried about you, so I mentioned it to my boss and he's agreed to do something to help me to look after you; he's going to send someone round to talk to you, to assess what can be done to help you, at least in the short term while we have this crisis at work. You need to co-operate with them for your own good and for my peace of mind."

"You're right: I don't like it. I don't need any help. I'm not a geriatric. I'm not even an old age pensioner."

"I need the help, even if you don't. You can't stay in my flat, and I don't have the time to escort you back to Nuneaton."

"I've had a lovely time today in your flat, dear. I don't need to go back to dull old Nuneaton just yet."

Sarah could sense her daughter weighing things up in a brief pause. "Mum, I have to tell you that it's not safe for you to stay in my flat. I don't want to alarm you unduly, and you're probably not in immediate danger, but..."

"So it's settled then: I send your boss's fixer away after a nice cup of tea and a biscuit with the message that I don't need any help."

A groan from Lydia. "I'll talk to you when I get back. I won't be late – maybe six."

"Bye then. Love you."

"Love you, Mum."

Sarah made herself a cup of tea, and put a couple of biscuits down beside her mug. All that concentration on her laptop had made her feel just a little faint.

The doorbell rang.

Sarah got slowly to her feet. She picked up the gun and put it in her pocket – she didn't want Lydia's boss to think that Lydia carelessly left her gun lying around on the table. As she walked across the room to the door she rehearsed what she was going to say to the well-intentioned bureaucrat who would try to persuade her to go back to Nuneaton or to go into assisted living. 'Bugger off' was the phrase that came to mind.

She looked through the spy-hole. She saw a woman in what looked like a police uniform.

Hmm. She hadn't realised that Lydia was in the police.

She pulled the bolt, undid the chain, opened the door a few centimetres, and peered round it at the two figures on the tiny landing. The policewoman stood in front; she was maybe thirty, dark Mediterranean-looking. Behind her was a man of maybe the same age, also dark skinned, in plain clothes – a sharp dark suit and a black tie. He was standing one stair down, in profile, his right side hidden from Sarah, as if he was holding a gun.

"Ms Twomey?" asked the policewoman, sliding her foot into the door.

"Mrs. Twomey." Sarah didn't like the policewoman's lack of trust. She wouldn't slam the door on a policewoman – maybe things were different in London.

"Are you the occupant of this flat, Mrs. Twomey?"

"I am occupying it right now, as you can see. Have you been sent by my daughter's boss?" Something in their stance, in their aggressive manner, suddenly put doubt in her mind.

"Are you Lydia Twomey?" the man asked. He had a foreign accent, very like her Kurdish neighbours in Nuneaton, the Kamkars.

"No – I'm her mother. You're not from Lydia's boss, are you?" Sarah had a growing bad feeling about this.

She saw the man mutter something. She thought she caught the words 'fuck-up', and it confirmed that something was very wrong. She could feel her stress levels rising by the second.

"Are you alone in this flat, Mrs. Twomey?"

She nodded, feeling sick. "Why do you want to know?" She tried with her foot to dislodge the WPC's foot from the door, but the woman just stared in her face and didn't remove it.

The man nodded to the policewoman, then addressed Sarah, his right hand still hidden. "Mrs. Twomey, we have reason to believe that someone in this flat has used a computer to breach government security. We have the authority to seize your computer and to take you in for questioning."

Sarah dredged up a flare of anger. "That's absolute rubbish! I haven't been near a government website. Where's your warrant card?"

"We don't need it, madam. We're from Counter Terrorism."

"What? And you think I'm a terrorist – me?" She laughed.

"We need to discount that possibility, madam. Now, please step back from the door, or I'll have to ask my colleague to force an entry." The man spoke quietly and calmly, but there was an unmistakable menace in his voice.

The WPC didn't wait, but pushed open the door and moved past Sarah into the room. She marched over to the table, closed down Sarah's laptop, unplugged it and picked it up.

"Stop!" Sarah held up a shaking hand. "Stop right now. Until you show me your warrant card, and until you show me your search warrant to give you permission for breaking into my daughter's flat, you are breaking the law, and I will report you to the police complaints board, and I will tell every news reporter in the land what you're up to."

The man, who had stepped into the flat and shut the door behind him, at last showed his right hand. As Sarah feared, it held a gun. He didn't need to point it at her – she got the message.

"Madam, you will get your opportunity to complain, but first we are taking you in for questioning and your computer for analysis. This is a matter of national security – your daughter will understand. Now, we need to leave with as little fuss as possible. I promise you I will not fail to shoot you if you cause any trouble. Is that clear?"

"It's clearly ridiculous."

"Do you understand me?"

"Can I phone my daughter first?"

The man shook his head. "No. Sorry, madam."

"My daughter works with you, in Counter Terrorism. You told me that yourself." Sarah knew she was clutching at straws. "I have MS, and she worries about me. I need to phone her to tell her where I'm going."

The WPC was already at the door with Sarah's computer. "Come along, madam." She smiled nicely at Sarah. "I'm sure this can all be cleared up quickly and you can be back here before your daughter gets back from work."

The man put his gun hand back in his pocket. "Please follow my colleague, Mrs Twomey. I will be right behind you."

She had no option. She doubted a man in the security forces actually would shoot her if she tried to resist, but it wasn't worth taking the risk. She clung to the hope the WPC had held out: that they really were Counter Terrorist officers and that this could all get cleared up swiftly. If things got really bad, she could always make a scene in the street and attract the attention of passers-by.

Descending the stairs, Sarah found it hard to focus on each stair. She was terrified she would fall. She stumbled. The man behind her grabbed her by the armpits and yanked her upright. "No, you don't," he hissed.

"I didn't mean it," Sarah said. "It's my MS – I miss things sometimes." For a moment she wondered if this whole nightmare was the product of her MS cognitive decline – that something very normal was happening and that she was misinterpreting it all.

Outside in the street, it was raining and there were no passers-by to call for help. Her abductors (that was how she saw them now) had parked their car in the forecourt of the house, so she was hustled straight into the back of the large Mercedes with blacked-out windows. She tried to memorise the number plate, but they were too quick for her. The WPC sat in the driver's seat with the computer next to her and the man got in the back with Sarah. The WPC drove off in a hurry.

Sarah looked down at the man's shiny black shoes. They looked like gangster's shoes, not a policeman's. And he smelt of nice cologne – no policeman in Nuneaton smelt so expensive. Gangsters – is that who'd abducted her?

"How come you knew I was using my computer in the flat?"

"We have sophisticated surveillance equipment in the service. GCHQ can monitor any computer in the land that's connected to the internet," the man said.

It reassured Sarah: surely gangsters wouldn't have the means to remotely monitor her computer? She looked out of the darkened windows. They were travelling quite slowly through residential streets.

The man was on his phone now, gabbling in some foreign language. He seemed to be angry and frustrated. In the torrent of Middle Eastern words, she made out a few English words, including 'fuck-up' for the second time.

Sarah cursed herself for being a self-deluded fool. No policeman or security man would be talking on a phone in a foreign language. She had been desperate to believe these two, but now it was becoming clear to her: they had gone to the flat expecting to capture or even kill Lydia; instead they were lumbered with some middle-aged woman, and they didn't know what to do with her.

The man finished on the phone and said something unintelligible to the woman in the front. The woman took a swift left turn under a railway bridge, and then another left turn.

"You don't have to kill me, you know." Sarah said it as calmly as she could. "If you just set me down here I'll find my way back home. No one will believe anything I say: my MS means I have cognitive malfunctions so I can't remember things. You can keep my computer."

The man turned full face to her and smiled. It was supposed to reassure her, but his gold fillings gleamed and he looked predatory to Sarah. "Don't you worry, madam. We're just taking you to our base for a few questions. Then we'll take you back to your daughter's flat. No worries."

There was now a park to their left and a row of smart houses on the right. They slowed down into a small cul de sac, and then parked. There were a couple of other cars parked there, but Sarah couldn't see any people about. Ominously, the man and woman appeared to be checking that the coast was clear, too.

The woman got out of the car, into the rain, went round to Sarah's door and opened it.

"Please get out of the car, madam."

Sarah looked out. She could see the blue board of the parish church of St Mary, Hanwell, behind a low stone wall.

She didn't move. "This isn't a security forces HQ," she said. "I'm not getting out."

With no warning, the man next to her violently pushed her out of her seat and into the arms of the woman, who hauled her up to her feet. The woman hissed in her ear. "We haven't got time for fucking about, lady. If you don't fully co-operate, you get a bullet in the head. Now walk."

Sarah's head had snapped back when she was pushed out of the car; now she had a pain down her neck and her eyes were struggling to focus.

Stop feeling sorry for yourself, and do something, she told herself. They're going to kill you.

The man was out of the car now and they were hustling her along a path at the end of the cul de sac. The sign said it was the Brent River Park Walk. There were trees on either side. Sarah prayed some jogger or dog walker would appear, but the rain was unrelenting and no one was around.

She saw that the man, walking to her left, had his hand in his pocket, obviously holding his gun.

"Please walk on ahead for a minute, madam." Even in her dazed state, Sarah could tell from the man's tone that this was no ordinary request.

This was it: this was where she was going to die. They were going to shoot her. It was now or never.

She shrugged off the woman's hold of her right arm, and snarled at her. "I don't need help to walk, thank you very much." She knew what she was going to do, but she had a stab of doubt: would she be able to co-ordinate her actions well enough to…? She couldn't think of the words.

Just do it.

The next seconds went by in what seemed like a series of freeze-frame photos.

She reached into her trouser pocket.

She felt her hand on Lydia's gun.

She flicked the safety catch.

She brought the gun out of her pocket and swung round towards the man, nearly overbalancing.

She saw the man's eyes widen with disbelief and alarm.

The man struggled to get his gun out of his pocket.

The man cleared his gun and brought it up towards her.

A gun fired: a sharp 'pop'.

Another gun fired. It was like a small firework.

There was a ringing in her head.

The man seemed to have some problem standing on his feet. He had red liquid running down his face.

The man crumpled to his knees.

He fell forwards, his head smacking the tarmac of the walk face first. His head bounced on the tarmac.

She turned to face the woman, who was saying something Sarah couldn't understand.

The woman was pulling a gun out of an underarm holster.

Another gun fired.

It fired again.

Firecrackers; who was letting these things off?

The woman was on the path, writhing around in her police uniform. Her stockinged legs were thrashing as if she was in extreme pain.

Another firecracker.

The legs still now.

A wave of pain swept through Sarah. Someone had punched her harder than she had ever been punched before. How had that happened?

She felt like she was losing consciousness but she knew you should never give in to that blessed relief.

Got to keep awake. Got to keep moving.

She lost her balance. She waved her arms, trying to stay upright.

She was sitting on the wet grass, her clothes soaked through.

Get up, you lazy cow. Get moving.

None of this is really happening.

The rain cascaded down.

None of this is really happening.

29

LYDIA

It was gone six by the time Lydia finally made it back to her flat in Hanwell. She was worrying about her mother – again. She'd phoned to say she was on her way home, but had got no response. Maybe she had gone out shopping, or perhaps she was asleep.

Lydia wanted to rush straight up the stairs, but she went through all the routines while locking up her motorbike, entering the house and making her way up past the first floor to the attic flat.

She rang the doorbell before putting her key in the lock. No response. She turned the key, opened the door and poked her head round.

"Mum?"

The flat was empty. Maybe her mother was in the bathroom.

"Mum?" A bit louder this time.

No response.

Fighting a rising tide of panic, she sped across to the bathroom. It was empty.

Back to the table: no note explaining her mum's absence.

No computer on the table, just the electric cable from the plug in the wall. Perhaps she had packed up and gone back to

Nuneaton. No – her mother's suitcase was on the floor by the bed and her pyjamas were folded on the pillow.

She felt the kettle. It was still faintly warm, but the full cup of tea on the table was cold. Sarah Twomey would never leave a cup of tea un-drunk, unless...

She took out her phone and rang the Director-General.

"Yes?"

"Lydia Twomey here, sir. Sorry to bother you so soon, but this may be an emergency. Did you send someone round to my flat to help with my mother?"

"No, I'm sorry. I hadn't got round to that yet. I'm actually in a meeting now."

"I'll be quick. My mother has disappeared from my flat, along with her computer. Everything else is still here."

"Could she have wandered off?"

"It's possible, but unlikely."

"What do you think has happened?"

"She may have been abducted or even..." She couldn't bring herself to say it. "She was doing some research for this case on her computer and..." A wave of guilt swept through Lydia, nearly choking her. "I think I may have dumped her into some serious trouble."

"Sit tight, Ms Twomey. I'll have an emergency team round to your flat within forty minutes. Please contact Perry Webb, tell him what's happened, and get him to alert all the emergency services to get a search going. Keep me informed of developments."

"Thank you sir."

"Goodbye." He rang off.

Lydia searched the rest of the flat for any clues as to what had happened, but there was nothing – no signs of a struggle, nothing broken, nothing missing except her mother's computer... and the gun.

By 9pm the team sent by the Director-General had searched the flat, found nothing and had fanned out to interview the others in the building and neighbourhood. Lydia had been driven back to Thames House, had reported the loss of her firearm, had been interviewed, had drunk numerous cups of coffee and had chewed her nails to the quick. GCHQ in Cheltenham were monitoring all the cameras in the area of the flat and the train and bus stations.

Nothing.

Lydia paced the corridor of the Internal Security offices. She should never have left her mother alone in the flat, but worse, she shouldn't have given her mother those names to research. What had she been thinking? She might as well have hung a sniper target on the back of her mum when she kissed her and blithely went off to meet Vindi in H11. On the other hand, it may have been nothing to do with the computer research – it may have been a hit squad come to kill Lydia. Jesus, either way she was guilty.

Maybe her mother would turn up, smiling, and say she'd taken her computer for a walk by the canal, and what was all the fuss about? That would be just like her, but Lydia didn't think it was likely this time. Too much time had passed. With every hour, it became less and less likely this was going to have anything but a nightmare ending.

The first piece of possibly relevant information came at 10pm from Ealing Broadway Metropolitan Police station. They had been called to a double shooting in the parkland behind Hanwell parish church. A dog walker had come across two bodies, one in the uniform of a policewoman. The Met Police thought they were investigating the loss of one of their own, but when they arrived at the scene they couldn't identify either of the bodies. The male had died from a single shot to the head, the female had been repeatedly shot in the body. There were three guns found at the scene, so it was assumed a third person had killed them and made their escape.

Even though it was clear the female corpse was too young to be Sarah Twomey, Lydia insisted that the pictures be sent across to Thames House. Any abnormality in the vicinity had to be chased up.

When the pictures came through, Lydia sent them upstairs to be identified in the MI5 files. There was only one person left on duty at this late hour, and he grumbled about 'a wild goose chase at silly o'clock', until Lydia said if he failed to get an identification within fifteen minutes she'd come up and personally slice his balls off.

Two minutes later she phoned up to apologise, explaining that her anxiety had got the better of her, that her mother was in danger and that this lead could be vital.

Seven minutes later, they had a matched identification: the dead man was Aydin Cevdet, and the girl was his sister, Merak Cevdet. The files showed that Aydin had prosecutions for a string of offences but he had never been convicted; a gangster with a good lawyer, Lydia guessed, and she could also confidently predict that the solicitors who defended him each time were from a firm called Erguns.

By this time Perry Webb had emerged from his office and joined Lydia and Jon Small in the incident room. He apologised for not coming earlier – he said he'd been working on an urgent project for the DG. He looked awful, Lydia thought, but she knew she looked even worse.

"These Cevdets – you're sure they're connected to your mother's disappearance?" Webb asked.

"Of course. Cevdet – I'm sure you remember that Nesrin Cevdet was Ian Forrester's landlady. It may be a common surname but this is too much of a coincidence. We need to confirm a connection and pull her in."

Webb frowned. "We need to be careful on this, Lydia. If you remember, Nesrin Cevdet was also the landlady for our own MI5 Special Operations freelancers. I got my knuckles rapped last time we took action against them."

"So run it past the Director-General – tell him what we're doing. But don't let's sit on our hands for fear of offending someone. They may have killed my mother."

"So who killed the two Turks?"

Lydia wanted to throttle him. "Does it matter right now? Please get permission to bring in Nesrin Cevdet. Quickly."

Perry got to his feet. "I think the DG's working late. I'll be back."

While he was gone, Lydia got back on the phone to Ealing Broadway Police Station. She told them that the dead pair of Turks were vital evidence in a terrorist context, and that they should not allow access to the bodies to anyone until Internal Security at MI5 authorised it.

She also asked about the three guns found at the crime scene. One was a Beretta Bobcat .22, another was a Beretta Tomcat .32, and the third was a 9mm Glock.

Lydia's own missing gun was a 9mm Glock.

She asked whether ballistics had reported on which gun or guns had fired the fatal shots, but there was no news on that front yet. Lydia asked them as nicely as possible to hurry along the inquiry, but was told that if MI5 or Counter Terrorism wanted to take over the case, they could do it whatever way they wanted.

There was no word from Webb and he wasn't answering his phone; nor was the Director-General. So much for his promise to always be available. Meanwhile the Cevdets and Erguns would be covering their tracks.

There was nothing more she could do. She examined her fingernails, looking for a fragment left unchewed.

30

MAGGIE

"What time do you call this?" Dean hardly looked up from football on the TV when she came in.

"It's ten o'clock and I've had a horrible day, so don't you start." Maggie Willis dropped her raincoat on the back of the settee. "Did you get the kids their tea?"

"I had a fare to Heathrow, and the traffic was murder getting back, so I was late. They got pizzas."

"Not again! I left out defrosted cod fillets for you."

"I can't just turn down fares, can I?" He was whining, defensive, now. "So what was horrible about your day? Why are you so late?"

"Turn off the football and I'll tell you."

Dean sighed, pressed the remote, and took his feet off the black leather settee. He made a token effort to kiss his wife as she sat down next to him, but she brushed him off. He wasn't going to get away with it that easily.

He sighed again. "Ooh, you really have got the hump, ain't you, girl?"

"Has Michael done his homework?"

"I dunno. Probably. He says he has."

"Have you checked it and signed his homework diary?" She was relentless – as always.

"No. I was going to do it at full-time. We're up to eighty-nine minutes."

She gave him the hard stare. He looked away.

"And where's Lara?"

"She's out with Ellie and Vee."

"Where?"

"Round at Vee's – that's what she said."

"What time is she getting back?"

"I dunno. Bedtime. I didn't give her a curfew hour."

"It's after 9.30 and she's a thirteen-year-old girl."

"Blimey. This is like the Spanish Inquisition. You really have had a horrible day, haven't you, girl?"

"Memorial services aren't a bundle of laughs."

"They can be. Remember old Uncle…"

"This one wasn't." Maggie closed her eyes. It had rained all the way down to the village just outside Canterbury and the wind had rattled the windows of the church when they were inside. There were about thirty friends and relations, all downbeat. Afterwards, in the drab function room of the local pub, they'd chewed on cold lardy sausage rolls, chicken legs coated with some disgusting curry gel, stale egg sandwiches with a free drink from the bar (not to exceed £4, the barmaid had said). The relatives had wanted to ask about Luther's work but of course they couldn't say anything, and the lurid post-mortem report hung over the whole thing like a Chernobyl cloud. It had rained all the way back as well, so there were extra cars out for the afternoon school runs; there were roadworks and tailbacks on the M2.

Her colleagues hadn't made it any better. George had said very little the whole day – she looked worryingly shifty or paranoid. Maggie had made a mental note to keep an eye out for her in future. Mo spent most of the day either in floods of tears or sniffing into her handkerchief; after a while Maggie had found it intensely irritating. Nylon kept making that disgusting noise, even in the church service – Maggie assumed that he couldn't help it but it seemed disrespectful. She wasn't sure that Nylon should have been dragged to Kent anyway – he wasn't a real member of the team.

The Dong had been the worst. Usually he was so relaxed and charming, but today he'd been snappy and irritable, constantly nipping off to take phone calls. He seemed to blame Maggie personally for the whole tragedy – he'd looked at her pointedly on several occasions.

"If Double D's funeral is half as bad as this one was, I think I'll skip it," she said.

"That bad, was it?" Dean put his arm around her and gave her shoulder a squeeze, but she felt no empathy, only duty. She knew he was itching to turn the football back on. They'd be into injury time now.

She opted to keep him waiting. "It's the end of an era, Dean, the end of an era."

"What is?" She could hear the resignation in his voice: the football wasn't coming back on.

"We used to have good things going, down in our cosy little basement. But it's all gone now. Two are gone forever, and the new girl is driving a wedge between those of us who are left."

"Put in for a transfer."

"You don't do that in our department. But…" she paused.

Dean patted her knee. "Well, who knows? Our ship might come in. I might win the lottery. Stranger things have happened in this world." He wore the resigned face of a habitual loser. Then a smile broke out. "But you know, Maggie, I've already won the lottery. You're my winning ticket."

"Who knows? Stranger things have happened." She was moved to kiss him on his stubbly cheek. "Now, go and check Michael's homework."

31

PERRY

"I've just been speaking to Miles Mason." The DG was in his familiar pose, chin resting in his hand. "He's confirmed that these two dead Turks, Aydin and Merak Cevdet, worked for Ergun solicitors, and occasionally worked freelance for our Special Operations Department. He's furious they've been killed. He's suggesting your Internal Security chaps may have done it. If it wasn't MI5, who else would dare kill them?"

"With the greatest respect, Miles is talking absolute tosh – they were gangsters, for heavens' sake. Gangsters shoot each other all the time. Anyway, what on earth was Miles using Turkish gangsters for?"

"Come on Perry, you know we all have had to use some unsavoury sources to keep abreast of security threats. You've done it yourself in your time. Miles says they were used for gathering information relating to illegal entry of terror suspects into this country. He alleges that this crusade by Lydia Twomey and your department is severely disrupting assets his team has taken years to build up."

"These gangsters have been used in the illegal abduction of Lydia Twomey's mother. Did Miles Mason order that?"

"We can't be certain yet that they've been used to abduct Mrs. Twomey. As for Miles himself, I'd like to censure you for making such an outrageous suggestion against a colleague, but..." It was one of the DG's trademark pauses. "But I cannot be totally certain that you're wide of the mark."

Perry sat forward. It was approaching midnight and he was dog tired, fuelled only by his white helpers, but any shit on Perma-tan Miles Mason was going to be music to his ears. "What do you mean?"

"If this plot is designed to get rid of the 'old guard' of MI5, people like you and me, then the plotters must have sounded out and probably recruited our replacements."

"You think Miles could be one of them?"

"He fits the profile: he's younger than us, fiercely ambitious. Of course we have no hard evidence to tie him to the plot or to this abduction, but we shouldn't discount the possibility that there are senior colleagues batting for the opposition. If it isn't Miles, then it's someone else."

"So you would like my chaps to investigate the connections between the Cevdets and our own Special Operations Department?"

"You're the Head of Internal Security; it's your show, your call. Do what you need to do to maintain our security. Just do it quickly."

"I'll try. My resources are stretched. I've already got quite a few of my chaps in here doing overtime tonight, working on connections with Martin Froome and Dennis Dunn. They'll need some sleep at some stage."

"We're all stretched, Perry. It's your job to know who is being lined up to replace us – think of this as an overdue catching-up exercise. My sources tell me Vilnius and his cabal are likely to call a press conference tomorrow, with the less-than-charming Lord Brooke slated to be their front man. They're ready to show their hand. We've got to hold more in our own hand than just an empty bluff. I'm counting on you to come up with something substantial, Perry."

"Thank you for your faith, sir."

It was a faith he didn't share. He got the distinct feeling the DG was distancing himself, hanging him out to dry.

32

LYDIA

"Lydia, wake up." A hand was shaking her shoulder.

She raised her head from the desk. The clock on the wall said 2.36am. She must have fallen asleep – another wave of guilt. How could she sleep when her mother was missing, maybe dead?

It was Jon Small standing over her. "We think we've got news of your mother. Come and have a look."

Lydia scrambled up and crossed to Jon's work station. There on his screen was a picture of her mother's face. Her eyes were shut.

"Oh my God! Yes! That's her. Is she dead?" Her hand went to her mouth. She could feel bile rising in her throat.

"She's alive. She's sedated."

The tears came. Lydia fought them but it was like a tsunami, shaking her, wracking her. "Thank God, thank God, thank God." She doubled over.

Jon stood back awkwardly, his hands at his sides. He obviously thought he should be doing something to comfort her, but he had no experience of crying women in the office.

"Um, yes. They say she's not seriously injured – just a flesh wound."

Lydia straightened, and turned to examine her mother's face on the screen. "What wound? Where is she?"

"She's got what appears to be a gunshot wound in her left arm. She's in the Central Middlesex Hospital. She was brought in several hours ago, but they had no way of identifying her, so they didn't connect her straight away with our calls for your missing mother."

"Why couldn't she identify herself? Was she unconscious?"

Jon shook his head. "They didn't say. They still don't know she's your mother. They're waiting for your confirmation of identity."

It took ten frustrating minutes for Lydia to get through to the relevant ward and confirm the identity of her mother. "Why couldn't my mother identify herself?" she asked the ward sister. "Was she unconscious when she was admitted?"

"Not exactly, but she wasn't fully conscious, either."

"What does that mean?"

"Look, Miss Twomey, your mother's situation seems to be very complicated. I suggest you come over to the Central Middlesex now and we can give you a full briefing."

"She's not in danger, is she?"

"Her life is not in danger, no."

"You know she's got MS, don't you? She has cognitive issues. And her life may be in danger from people who…" Lydia struggled to find the words that wouldn't compromise MI5's position. "Don't let any strangers get to her."

"Don't worry, Miss Twomey. She already has a police guard. That's part of the complicated situation."

"I'll be with you as soon as I can."

Lydia left messages to inform the DG and Perry Webb that her mother had been found and was now in need of an armed guard. Then she was driven by a MI5 duty driver to the Central Middlesex.

She was directed up a floor and along a series of corridors where her squeaking shoes echoed, to a ward tucked away in the corner of the building; Lydia hated the smell of hospitals – the disinfectant reminded her too sharply of her father's death.

She was met by the ward sister. "Hello, Miss Twomey. I'm Sister Ngidi."

"Thank you for helping my mother. Can I see her, please?"

Sister Ngidi led Lydia through the swing doors before turning to her. "You'll need to get permission from that man there." She pointed to a large man in an anorak who seemed to be asleep, slumped awkwardly across two plastic chairs. He had a bulbous nose and the sort of large moustache that had last been fashionable in the 1970s. "He's Detective Sergeant Beamish."

"He's my mother's guard?"

Sister Ngidi pulled a face. "Sort of."

Lydia stood in front of the snoring man. "Excuse me, sir." She said it loudly.

Sergeant Beamish woke with a start and a grunt, shaking his head. He squinted up at Lydia. He smelt of cigarettes and kebabs.

"What?"

"I'm here to visit Mrs Twomey. I'm her daughter."

"You're not her lawyer? We've sent for a lawyer." He remained seated, legs splayed out.

"Why does she need a lawyer?"

"She needs to be questioned urgently."

Sister Ngidi shook her head. "She's in no fit state to be questioned."

Lydia took out her MI5 identification and held it up. "Have you spoken to MI5, Sergeant Beamish?"

He didn't seem impressed. "Yes, but you don't understand: your mother is in the custody of the Metropolitan Police for the suspected murder of two members of the public. Just because her daughter works for MI5 doesn't change the rules."

"My mother – you think she's murdered those two gangsters?" Lydia let out a hollow laugh. "My mother is sixty-one years old, suffers advanced Multiple Sclerosis symptoms, and has never been near a gun in her life."

Sergeant Beamish stood up, towering above Lydia. "Well she has now, Miss Twomey; she's got a gunshot wound in her left arm and what looks like powder residue from a gun on her right hand. These two members of the public were shot dead, so we're interested to know how the suspect came to have such a weapon in her possession. Can you show us your service weapon, Miss Twomey?"

"You have no proof my mother fired any gun. The guns were found by the bodies, not with my mother."

"Sounds like you want to act as her lawyer after all. Perhaps you'd like to avail yourself of a lawyer, too, and join your mother in a session with us at Ealing Broadway."

Lydia wasn't going to be intimidated by this bloody-minded cop. "I'm sorry you've been called out here in the middle of the night, Sergeant Beamish, but I'm here on MI5 business. We've already explained to your bosses at Ealing that this case concerns national security."

"Yeah, well, we've already explained to your bosses that this is a case of local sensitivity, too. The victims of this shooting are very, very well connected. There are shock waves running across London as we speak. There'll be all sorts of shit hitting all sorts of fans, and the Metropolitan Police must be seen to be pursuing leads."

Sister Ngidi broke in. Arms folded, she stood in the doorway to the single bed room. "Neither of you can interview Mrs Twomey. She arrived here to be healed, not questioned. She's exhibiting symptoms of extreme trauma. She wasn't able to say a word before we sedated her. She's lost a serious amount of blood and she was suffering from hypothermia when admitted.

If you need to guard her, then I suggest you both make yourself comfortable here for the rest of the night."

Lydia and Sergeant Beamish got little sleep. At 3.30am two Met Police detectives from Ealing arrived to reinforce Beamish. They stood around chatting. Lydia positioned her plastic chair between them and the door to her mother's room – she wasn't confident that these coppers wouldn't try to take her mother away for questioning. The detectives' phones kept up a barrage of ringtones.

Lydia, too, had been on her phone back to MI5, requesting back-up, but Perry was unresponsive. He sounded very tired and stressed. He said he had no one to spare from Internal Security, and Special Operations were unlikely to lend any of their staff, considering who had been shot dead. When Lydia asked him to explain what he meant, he refused to answer.

It wasn't until 4.45am that three officers from the Counter Terror Command arrived. Two were in full combat gear and carried machine guns. Their leader wore an expensive overcoat. They presented their ID cards and then had a short but noisy argument with the three Met Police detectives before persuading them to stand down. Sergeant Beamish said this wasn't a terrorist matter, but the man in smart coat said it wasn't for the plod to judge matters of terror.

Sister Ngidi hissed at them all to keep their voices down. The Met officers went, grumbling that 'all sorts of shit would be hitting the fan', while the Counter Terror boys told them to think of their overtime payments. The doors shut behind the detectives, and Lydia closed her eyes.

"Miss Twomey, I need to have a word with you."

Lydia opened her eyes. She really didn't need to have a word with the man with the gelled black hair and the camel coat. She restrained herself from telling him she was Ms, not Miss. "How can I help you?" She struggled to an upright position.

"We've received information from Ealing Met Police ballistics that a 9mm Glock was the murder weapon in this case."

"Very quick work." She knew what was coming.

"It's a very sensitive case, as I'm sure you're aware. The owner of the gun in question has been identified: it's you, Miss."

"So? It's my MI5 service gun. It's my mother in there. She's been shot too, most likely by the so-called victims, the Turkish gangsters."

"In light of this new revelation, I have orders to escort you down to your driver, who is waiting outside the hospital. He will drive you back to Thames House."

"Ridiculous. I've come here as a daughter to see my mother, and I've come here as an MI5 officer to interview a witness in a serious case. I am not a suspect – I was at Thames House all day yesterday."

"I have my orders, Miss; I am merely carrying them out."

"Who gave you this order?"

"I am not at liberty to say, Miss."

"Can you let me see my mother first, please?"

He shook his head. "I've been told specifically not to let you discuss the case with your mother – contamination of evidence."

"She's heavily sedated, for Christ's sakes! She hasn't said anything since she was admitted. I'm worried sick about her. I don't want to talk about the case – I want to know she's okay."

A compromise was found: Lydia, flanked by Sister Ngidi and the Counter Terror officer, was allowed to view her mother through the glass screen.

Sarah lay as still and pale as a waxwork, hooked up to monitors, with drips into her arms.

Lydia clenched her fists as she was led away.

33

PERRY

Perry knew from the start it was going to be one of the worst days of his life. It began with a 7am call from the admin desk to wake him after less than four hours of fitful sleep in the cheerless little room at the top of Thames House laughingly called 'The Executive Bedroom Suite 2'. The DG had Suite 1, he presumed. He didn't have his shaving kit with him – he always felt seedy without a shave. He skipped breakfast and was at his desk by 7.30am, sipping a cup of coffee, taking a white helper instead of his blood pressure pills which were at home, and scanning down the avalanche of emails Miss Parmenter had chosen not to whittle down for him.

Jon Small and the night shift had gone home to sleep while Ashar and the day shift were not yet in, so it was the perfect time for Perry to start identifying the leak in his team that the DG had ordered him to 'cauterise'. The trouble was, he had no idea where to start, or what he was looking for. Perry judged himself a pretty shrewd judge of character and mood but was the first to admit he didn't know his team as well as he should; he was rather too old to socialise with them, and because things had been relatively calm over the last few years, he hadn't needed to work too closely with any individuals.

At 8am he took a call from Glenys. She gently asked him if he would be home this evening, given that it was their wedding anniversary and they were due to dine at La Gavroche at 8pm. He groaned and apologised. He said he'd bought her a card – it was in his bedside table but it wasn't yet signed. Glenys said she understood perfectly, but she rang off with a rather frosty 'Have a good day'.

Perry logged onto Ashar's work account, and trawled through it. He could see nothing amiss, and he logged off hastily when Ashar herself logged on at 8.20am. He called her up on the phone and sent her off to the Central Middlesex to interview Lydia's mother.

"May I ask, sir, why it's such a priority to speak to her? We're incredibly busy here. I mean, she's just a member of the public. Just because she's Lydia's mother..."

"The Turks she allegedly killed are part of the conspiracy that threatens national security. Her laptop may contain vital information about the case you're investigating – yes, the Martin Froome H11 case."

"How could that be, sir?"

Perry was too tired, too unshaven, to waste time with this. "Just go and interview her, and bring me back her laptop. I want your report on my screen by 10."

After that he trawled through Jon Small's work account, but again, it was a huge haystack with no obvious needles protruding.

When Miss Parmenter arrived on the dot of 8.45, he called her in and asked her to sit down for a chat. Desperate times called for desperate measures.

"Miss Parmenter, Audrey, you see and hear a lot that I probably miss. I have been told we may have a security leak in our department. If you had to pick one person in the whole of Internal Security who was leaking information to a hostile power, who would be your most likely candidate?"

She sat perfectly still for a moment. The light caught in her glasses, so he couldn't see her eyes. She was a plain woman in her forties. He'd never really looked at her carefully or thought about her much – she was almost like part of the furniture, always there; what he liked about her was that she was uncomplicated, in that he could rely on her to carry out orders without questioning them, and she could often anticipate his needs.

"Lydia Twomey."

Perry groaned inwardly, but outwardly he smiled encouragingly. "What prompted that choice?"

"She's very independent. She's clever – she wouldn't get caught. I have detected some left-wing sympathies."

"Okay. Thank you. If I asked you who might be leaking information to a right-wing source, who would be your best guess?"

Again, there was no immediate response. "Maybe yourself, sir. You have a strong belief in law and order. But I know you're loyal to the service."

Perry thanked her and sent her back to the outer office with a list of jobs. Thinking outside the box rarely worked in his experience, and it hadn't worked so far today.

He dragged himself out of his chair and went down the corridor to brief the rest of the team on the task of digging the dirt on Froome and Dunn. He emphasised how vital it was (without giving the reasons) to have something to give the Director-General before the end of the day. They all nodded and assured him they'd do their best to crack the case, but he saw only blind ignorant optimism in their eyes. They weren't going to come up with anything – the conspirators had covered their tracks too well. He shuffled back to his office.

The next piece of bad news came in a phone call from Ashar. "I can't get Sarah Twomey to speak to me, sir."

"She's refusing to speak?"

"No, sir. She seems unable to speak. The nurses say she may be severely traumatised by her experiences. She's come round from her sedation, but she's not speaking to anyone. She seems catatonic."

Perry slapped the top of the desk in frustration. "Is there any sign of the woman's laptop?"

"None at all, sir."

He ordered Ashar back to Thames House, and then rang Ealing Broadway Police Station. Predictably, they weren't very helpful.

No, there was no sign of the woman's laptop.

Yes, they had found the vehicle used by the murder victims and 'alleged' murderer – it was a black Mercedes – but no, there was no laptop found inside it.

The Mercedes had been discovered near the crime scene two hours after the bodies, so yes, it was possible the laptop had been removed by the associates of the victims (or the associates of Sarah Twomey) before the car had been secured.

No, it wasn't possible the laptop could have disappeared after the car had been found; they very much resented such an insinuation.

Perry thanked them for their help and terminated the call.

Next he had to deal with Lydia. She had been interrogated by Counter Terrorism until five in the morning, she'd had no proper sleep all night, yet here she was in his office demanding access to her mother.

Perry sighed. "Lydia, you are barred from talking to your mother due to your own part in the killing – namely, supplying the gun. Anyway, the DG wants you down in H11 right away. It's only a matter of hours before this whole thing blows open, and when it does, we need to have our hands on those missing files, or to have caught those responsible for destroying them." He kept his voice admirably calm and patient.

Lydia also stayed calm. "Has anyone on your team interviewed my mother?"

"No. She wouldn't or couldn't talk to Ashar. The nurses say she's traumatised."

"I am the only person she will talk to. Please give me a few minutes with her. It's clear she's found something important that alerted them. They took a big risk in trying to silence her, so they must have had a reason for it. We must find out what my mother knows. I am your only hope of getting that information."

Perry was too tired to argue, so he wearily gave her the authorisation. Lydia went off with a driver to the Central Middlesex.

Perry steeled himself against the inevitable outrage from the Met Police and from the DG.

Miss Parmenter buzzed through. "The Director-General has asked to see you in his office."

That was quick, Perry thought. Hasn't he got anything better to do than to bollock his loyal lieutenants? He hauled himself out of his seat and made his way down to the DG. He'd never expected this day to be anything but a disaster.

Disconcertedly, the DG was smiling. "Take a seat, Perry. Well, it seems as if we've got a stay of execution. Lord Brooke and the Vilnius cronies have postponed their scheduled press conference."

"Do we know why?"

"The only thing we know that could have prompted them to change their plans is the attempted hit on Lydia Twomey's mother and the death of the two Turks. Something went very wrong for them when they bungled that, and Mrs Twomey must have discovered something to rattle the conspirators. What's your news on the case?"

"The good news is that she's out of danger, guarded tightly in the Central Middlesex by Counter Terrorism, but the rest isn't good. She won't – or can't – speak to anyone, and her laptop has gone missing. Either the police who found it have handed it over to someone other than us, or the Turks' associates got to it first."

"So what are you doing to retrieve this potentially vital information?" The DG fixed him with a stare.

"I know you wanted her down in H11 immediately, but I've sent Lydia over. If anyone can get her mother to speak, it's her."

"Good move. How's Lydia bearing up?"

Perry had no idea – he hadn't asked her. "Pretty well, I think. She was questioned by Counter Terrorism last night concerning the fact that it was her gun that killed these Turks. Now of course the Met want to interview her as well."

The DG waved his hand in annoyance. "Tell them to get lost. Smack their wrists for losing the laptop and get the mother moved to somewhere secure. This is not the time for pussy-footing, Perry – we've got an extra few hours, but we can't spend it tiptoeing around the Met. How is the identification of the mole in your department coming along?"

"Slowly, so far. But I've sown a few seeds that will hopefully come to fruition."

"What seeds are those?"

Perry had hoped the DG wouldn't ask him that. "Um, I'm asking a cross section of my staff who they think might be the traitor."

"Interesting." The DG's face remained a cipher. "What's your thinking behind that?"

"If the traitor knows we're onto him or her, it might pressure them into making a mistake. And it's possible that someone on my team has spotted something but hasn't reported it – hasn't connected it up with leaking to the opposition." Perry was aware that he hadn't put it too clearly, but the DG nodded solemnly.

"I see. Stalinist denunciations – they've worked in the past, or at least they did for Stalin and for Matthew Hopkins."

Perry looked at him blankly.

The DG continued. "Matthew Hopkins – Cromwell's Witchfinder-General. Denunciations tend to leave a messy residue, but these are desperate times. Good luck, old chap. I'm sure you have a few other avenues of inquiry that you're pursuing, but I won't keep you from your tasks."

Although the DG had stayed politely neutral throughout, Perry couldn't help feeling rebuked as he slunk from the DG's office. The tasks he had been set were impossible, and good luck was the least he needed.

Back behind his own desk, he pressed on with his only strategy. His next interviewee was his number two, Andrew Elms. Perry had always considered Andrew a rather wet fish.

Andrew was horrified there might be a leak, but was useless in providing any leads. All his suggestions involved processes that would take weeks. Andrew was formidably intelligent, a superb bureaucrat and a decent chap, but not an inspired spook.

Next Perry called in his number three, Sophie Hutchings. Sophie was a sharp, ambitious lady who dressed like a Tory politician and who had always made Perry a bit nervous. As soon as she started to answer his question, his nervousness tipped over to outright fear. She knew everything about everyone – God knows what she had on him.

Sophie rattled through the indiscretions and dodgy affiliations of nearly everyone under his command. He learned more about his team in fifteen minutes than he'd learned in the previous five years.

"How do you know all this… this fantastic information, Sophie?"

She looked at him squarely. "It's no fantasy, Perry. I ask people about themselves. I show personal concern. And then I check up on what they've said."

Perry could only take it as another rebuke – she'd implied he'd failed to do these things. "Okay, so where does this knowledge take us? Who is your number one suspect?"

"Lydia Twomey."

"Why choose her?"

"I suppose you know her ex-boyfriend James Haddon has taken a job overseas."

"Go on." Perry didn't even know she had a boyfriend in the first place. He'd vaguely assumed from her short hair and motorbike gear that she was a lesbian.

"Their break-up was sudden, and he went off to work for a lobbying firm in America. He works at the United Nations these days."

"Why do you judge that this makes Lydia a security risk?"

"James Haddon now mixes with a wide variety of political movers and shakers. Lydia was very cut up when he left, as you probably know. She still follows him on social media, and I suspect she's in closer touch on a daily basis. If James Haddon is working for a foreign power, then she might be too."

"Hmm. Thank you. Lydia herself has suggested that Ashar may be behind the leaks. What have you got on her?"

"Lydia and Ashar don't get on, as must be obvious to you."

Perry nodded sagely.

She continued. "Ashar's family are hiding a debt mountain on their retail business. They've been transferring balances from their importing arm to cover it up. It's possible Ashar could be looking to earn big money to bail them out, but I think she's too smart to put her own career in jeopardy."

"What about Jon Small?"

"He works out in the Virgin Gym in Clapham. It's frequented by all sorts of security nightmares. But I think he's too drippy to do anything off-piste."

"Ouch! Thank you, Sophie, for sharing your insights with me. I'm very impressed by your phenomenal knowledge."

"Well, you know what they say: knowledge is power. I do my best."

He took it as a threat.

After Sophie had gone, he scribbled down some notes. He had the interview recorded on audio, but she had given him much food for thought – an oversized feast, in fact. He wondered whether all her knowledge about the human frailties around her actually blinded her to the positive side of her colleagues and made her paranoid. It also served to remind him to dig up some shit about her – she was bound to have some dirt on him, and she could be angling for his job.

Time for a little white helper.

The longer he scribbled away and the more convoluted and tangled his causation arrows became, the more he came to the conclusion that Sophie Hutchings herself was the mole: with all her powerful knowledge, she would be the person any Vilnius conspirator would want to recruit; she was ambitious and not above poison pen portraits of her colleagues. Yes, she was a prime candidate. But how could he prove it?

He ploughed on with the denunciations, as the DG had called them. Jon Small was next up.

"We think it's Lydia Twomey," Jon said, looking guilty himself.

Perry could see what Sophie Hutchings had been getting at: this man was indeed wet. "Why do you think that?"

"Oh, it's not me personally, of course – it's the team. We've put our heads together and we've worked out that Dennis Dunn, if he didn't commit suicide, must have been killed by someone he knew and trusted, or someone he was expecting. He had double deadlocks on his front door, and a chain. He wouldn't have unlocked those if he was going to commit suicide, and he wouldn't have opened his door to a potential assassin. We know he was expecting Lydia. All she had to do was to turn up a bit early, be let in, kill him, wait outside the flat for the boyfriend to arrive and then call you for help."

"If you've identified the murderer, what are you doing about assembling the proof? It's all conjecture so far, isn't it?"

Jon looked bereft of ideas, and just a little hurt his boss should have asked such a question.

Perry took pity on him. He knew how it felt to have a demanding boss. "I'm sure you'll find a way forward. Lydia's flat is a crime scene at present – you could send someone round to ferret around for incriminating evidence."

"Thank you, sir."

Perry was tucking into lunch – a ciabatta tuna sandwich that Miss Parmenter had got him from the canteen – when Lydia fetched up in his office. His mouth full, he gestured for her to sit in the high-back chair in front of him.

Eventually his mouth was clear. "Well? How is your mother?"

"Not well."

Perry wiped a piece of cucumber from the corner of his mouth. "Did she talk to you?"

"Yes and no: she managed a few words, but…" Lydia shook her head.

"Yes?" She really did look awful. There was no point in asking her how she was – it was only too obvious.

"She doesn't remember anything. She knew who I was, but she didn't know where she was, and she couldn't tell me anything about the Cevdits or how they abducted her. She has no idea what happened to her laptop or what she'd researched before the trauma occurred. She doesn't recall shooting anyone."

"Do you think she's just putting it on because she knows she's going to get interviewed by the police?" He saw Lydia frown. "Or because it's just too awful for her to face?"

Lydia's voice trembled with rage, but she held it together. "My mother is a strong person, sir. She would never 'put anything on'. She was very ill with what her doctors call cognitive malfunctions before this trauma. She will do everything she can to help us. Have you any other questions, sir?"

"Of course, of course. No, no, I didn't mean to imply…" He gave up trying to dig his way out. "As soon as she's well enough, we will move her to a better guarded location. I will see to it that the Met Police don't bother her, and that all charges will be dropped. Don't you worry about any of it."

"Thank you. I blame myself for what happened. If I hadn't asked her to do research for me, none of this would have happened to her."

At last Perry began to see some light at the end of the tunnel. "Ah! She was researching for you. Can you tell me exactly what research you asked her to do?"

"I asked her to dig up anything she could find on Ian Forrester, Erguns Solicitors, Nesrin Cevdet, A & C Foods – a shop opposite Ergun's on Fore Street, and lastly on Louisa Bell."

"Why did you ask for material on Louisa?" He hoped he'd kept the antipathy out of his voice. Anything on that bitch would be a bonus.

"Because there won't be anything on the internet about Gerard Bell, but I'm sure he's behind the disappearance of the files in H11 and the deaths of his staff. I thought details about his wife might shine a light on him."

"Be careful: that's a radical idea." This girl was sharp. "And you think someone monitored your mother's research and came to your flat to put a stop to it?"

"It's obvious, isn't it? What I want to know is whether the Turks could monitor it themselves, whether it was picked up by a second bug in my flat, or whether they were alerted by some mole in GCHQ."

Perry smiled for the first time that day. "We can find out. You've given us some very valuable lines of inquiry. I'll get a team to look for a bug in your flat, another team to investigate from the GCHQ end, and a third team to do exactly the research that your mother would have done yesterday. We're pretty certain she turned up something that alarmed our enemies. If my team can find the same information (always supposing the opposition haven't covered their tracks in the meantime), we'll be in business. Well done!" He paused, and put on his 'concerned' face. "Of course, I deeply regret what's happened to your mother."

"So do I."

"One more question, Lydia: you've suggested there's a leak from this department. If you were pushed to guess who it was, who is your prime suspect?"

Lydia got up from her chair, walked round the side of Perry's desk, and bent down, putting her lips to his ear. He smelt her perfume – honeysuckle, was it? It was remarkable that she could smell so fragrant given the thirty-six hours she'd just had. A frisson of erotic fear ran through his body – what was she about to do? Kill him or kiss him?

"Meet me by the lifts in three minutes' time. I'll give you the name." Her warm breath on his neck and the whisper of her voice in his ear gave him goosebumps.

She turned and marched over to the door of his office. He buzzed her out then sat sweating under the picture of the Queen. Good Lord – he was shaking!

Get a grip on yourself, man.

Should he meet her? What if this was some stratagem to entrap him into some indiscretion? She was a very attractive woman, and currently unattached, apparently, but she was dangerous – just the sort who might be playing some complicated game. The rest of the department were almost unanimous that she was the traitor. What if the DG was wrong and they were all correct? Why hadn't she just answered his question right there in the office? She wasn't usually a shrinking violet.

On the other hand, what harm could there be in him meeting her out by the lifts? It was public enough – she wasn't luring him into a dark alleyway or a sleazy nightclub. Not yet, anyway. The third floor of Thames House was his kingdom – no harm could come to him here.

He got up, necked a pill, and on slightly unsteady legs made his way to the door of his office, then out past Miss Parmenter.

"Just popping out for a few minutes," he told her.

She nodded, and went back to her word-processing. She had earphones on so she probably hadn't heard him anyway.

He made his way down the corridor, his heart beating in time with his footfalls. He felt like a fifteen-year-old on an assignation.

She was standing by the lifts. There was no one else about. He hoped she couldn't spot his nerves.

"What's all this about, Lydia? Why the cloak and dagger?"

"Miss Parmenter." She said the name very quietly, looking past him up the empty corridor.

"What about her? I didn't tell her I was coming out here to speak to you."

"Miss Parmenter – she's your leak."

"Don't be ridiculous." He couldn't keep the disappointment from his voice. She'd lured him out here, got his hopes up, all for some silly wild allegation.

"The reason we're out here is because she listens in to everything said in your office."

"This is absurd! Miss Parmenter has been with the service since almost before you were born. She's..."

"She's the only person who monitors absolutely everything you receive. She has listened in to all our phone conversations – on your supposedly secure line. I've worked it out: there's no one else who could have tipped off our enemies about my meeting with Dennis Dunn."

"Audrey Parmenter is as loyal as the day is long. I'd know if she wasn't."

"Loyal to whom? Have you ever discussed real issues with her? If you scratch the surface you'll find that politically she's somewhere several miles to the right of Genghis Khan. She wants to save the world from sloppy dressers and hippy idealism. She supports the death penalty, and not just for murder and treason."

Perry took a deep breath. "Thank you, Lydia, for your ideas. You always come up with something original and thought-provoking. I will consider it carefully. Now I must get back to my office. I'd be grateful if you made your way down to H11 now. The DG is most insistent that you stick to your tasks down there."

"Yes sir." She said it without emotion. She turned and pressed the lift button. The lift door opened immediately – it must have been waiting. She stepped into the lift and was gone.

Perry leant against the wall. He felt emotionally wrung out. She had stirred emotions of hope and even lust up so powerfully. He was so disappointed, and also ashamed of himself.

"Are you all right, sir?" One of the office juniors pressed the lift button beside him.

"Perfectly fine, thank you." He searched his brain for the name of the young man, then gave up and walked off, back to his office.

He walked past Miss Parmenter, trying not to catch her eyes. He wondered if he'd ever be able to look at her squarely again, after what Lydia had just said…

What a stirrer Lydia was, he thought, pushing the door into his office. No wonder the DG wanted her to be the one stirring down in H11. God help Gerard if she really got going. She was a human wrecking ball, that girl.

But…

He slumped into the swivel seat behind his desk, and turned to the Thames. His mind was whirring. Past events, past remarks, they all needed calibrating to get the clear picture. Perry knew he had a good memory and an analytical brain, so when it all clicked into perfect alignment he could work out…

Bloody hell.

So the day didn't turn out as badly as Perry had feared: he was able to go down to the DG with new lines of inquiry on the websites of the Erguns and Louisa-bloody-Bell, and even more satisfyingly, with the mole identified.

"Well done, Perry. Your denunciations worked after all. Have you any idea how long Miss Parmenter has been supplying the enemy with your secrets?"

"No idea, yet."

"Well, better late than never."

"Actually, in the nick of time, I'd say." Perry was rather miffed not to garner higher praise for his discovery. "I'd rather not be around when Miss Parmenter is carted away for questioning, if that's all right. She's looked after me very well over the eight years."

The DG wasn't impressed. "There's no room for sentimentality in this game, Perry. It's actually your role, not just to arrest her, but to question her. It's an internal security issue." The DG paused. "However, I think it would be better not to take any immediate action against her."

"Why?" Perry felt relieved he wouldn't have to confront her, but he felt uneasy about sharing his office space with a traitor.

"We'll use her to feed the enemy with false information. It needs to be handled carefully – you may find that vital information doesn't flow straight to you in your office anymore – but, handled carefully, she could yet be very useful."

"I see."

“Now, tell me what your teams have found on the websites of Ergun’s and Louisa Bell.”

Perry confessed that the results were rather disappointing so far. Ergun’s were involved in murky activities and boasted of their access to government; perhaps the DG would like to speak to Miles Mason about allowing that. As for Louisa, Perry was gratified to learn that her clients and profits seemed to be more about vanity publishing than about genuine literature, but it was hardly treason.

“Keep digging, Perry. Lydia Twomey’s mother managed to find something that rattled their cage so severely that they felt obliged to try to kill her, and caused them to postpone their press conference. It shouldn’t be beyond your team to find it as well.”

Why did the DG always dish out such tepid praise? Perry grumbled to himself as he made his way back up to his office. He’d felt really good when he’d entered the DG’s sanctum, and now he felt wretched again.

His mood wasn’t improved when he found Miss Parmenter still at her desk – she said she was putting in overtime today.

Half an hour later Lydia reported in to him on her way to visit her mother. She had little progress to report, except that Gerard had invited her to a soiree at his flat on Wednesday night. She was more interested in what was being done for her mother. Suddenly Perry was conscious that Miss Parmenter would be listening in, so he hummed and hawed and sent her away with no satisfactory answers.

He felt some sympathy for Lydia: she wasn’t allowed to return to her flat except for a brief escorted foray to pick up some clean clothes, her mother was going gaga, she was stuck down in the H11 hellhole with that shit Gerard Bell obviously trying to seduce her and that other shit Damian Curry probably after her as well. What she needed was a proper night’s sleep. Or a knight in shining armour. But… much as he might like to be that knight, Perry knew it wasn't an appropriate role for him.

A call from Glenys cut into his thoughts: she presumed he wouldn't be back for their wedding anniversary meal at La Gavroche, but would he be back at all tonight?

He always knew it was going to be a long day. It called for a double ration of white helper.

34

MO

Mo Dennis woke with a start.

She had been drifting through a vaguely disturbing dream about swimming in the South Norwood Leisure Centre pool – she knew she shouldn't swim in the deep end, out of her depth, but she was being sucked there – but it wasn't the dream that woke her; it was a cat's tail in her face, and purring in her ear.

She pushed him off. He jumped lightly onto the floor, then back onto the bed. It was Rajah, her gorgeous three-year-old Burmese, the light of her life.

"What is it, Rajah?" Her digital clock told her it was 3.34am. He didn't usually come up and bother her in the middle of the night; at this time he would normally be curled up on the boiler in the kitchen or out through the cat-flap giving the neighbourhood cats and rats a hard time.

She tried to push him back off the bed, but he dug his claws into her duvet, so she cuddled him instead.

"Something's up with you, my darling. What is it, eh?" She stroked under his chin – he always liked that.

Rajah jumped off the bed, and stood by the open door, tail twitching.

Mo always marvelled at how human Rajah seemed to be; he seemed to be able to tell her exactly what he wanted: he wanted her to go downstairs with him. But she was warm and comfortable in her bed. "What's wrong, Rajah?"

He made a soft answer, half mewl, half growl. Mo knew she was going to have to get up – she was, after all, his servant, as she often told him.

"All right, I'm coming, my darling. Might as well have a cuppa while I'm about it." She sat up and swung her legs over the side of the bed. Her feet found her fleece slippers and she stood up. The floorboard creaked beneath her like it always did, as if telling her off for being a few stone overweight. That's why she went swimming in South Norwood pool. What was it she'd been dreaming?

Click.

She knew that sound well. It was the lock on the French windows that led out from her lounge to her little back garden.

Someone had just unlocked her door. Someone had just heard her getting up and was preparing to flee into her garden.

Rajah mewled again, but Mo stood stock still by her bed.

There was silence from downstairs. The burglar was standing by her French windows, still and silent like her, almost directly below her, waiting for her next move.

Five seconds passed. Rajah rubbed himself against Mo's pyjama legs, purring. Mo didn't move.

Ten seconds. Mo picked Rajah up. She didn't want him wandering downstairs and getting killed by the burglar.

She thought about calling out – telling the burglar to make his escape while he could. She thought about phoning the police, but her phone was downstairs.

Twenty seconds. Mo wondered if it was a burglar or… no, she couldn't say the word – it was too dreadful to even think. Killer – there, she'd said the word. Of course she believed the Dong when he said that Luther had died in an accident and that

Double D had taken his own life, but both George and the new girl, Schizo, had been burbling on about how maybe they had been murdered. Maybe it was her turn to be killed.

She stood there, fear flooding into her veins. Rajah struggled in her arms – she was squeezing him too tightly.

Why would anyone want to kill her? Why would they want to kill Double D and Luther? No, no – she was getting paranoid. The Dong always warned them about paranoia. It was a burglar, plain and simple.

She'd had the security training, of course, but she couldn't think what she was supposed to do now, except deep breathing. She wasn't a high enough grade to be issued with a gun, and anyway, she knew she was too nervous to hold one straight. She was shaking so hard that Rajah had stuck his claws in her arm. She could see his tail had turned bottle-brush.

She started to pray.

Another minute, but it felt much, much longer. She'd got through the Lord's Prayer and the Creed.

Click.

That was a different click, she knew: it was the sound of the door opening. The intruder was leaving! Please let him leave!

She turned, gently put Rajah on the bed, and moved to the window. She tweaked the curtain to give herself a view of the garden. It was bathed in the dim glow from the millions of streetlights that permanently blurred London's nights.

The intruder was dressed all in black and wore a balaclava over his head. He seemed to float over the patio paving stones, then across the grass, past the dwarf willow, before disappearing through her garden gate, which he must have unlocked on his way in.

Mo knew the danger was over for now, so she ought to have been shuddering with relief – but it was fear that was still wracking her.

The intruder had looked back briefly as he crossed the patio and she had caught a clear glimpse of his eyes through his balaclava. Then the way he had glided across the garden with such easy athleticism – she recognised it. She had seen that motion before. It came to her in an instant, instinctively: she knew the identity of the intruder.

It was Vindi.

Her legs failed her – it was as if someone had kicked her in the back of the knees. She slumped to her bed.

What was Vindi doing in her little terraced house? What could he possibly want with her? Why had he got a balaclava on? He always seemed a nice young man, even if he was a little serious, a little intense. She could make no sense of it. She shook her head, but it didn't clear. She pinched herself, just to check she wasn't still dreaming.

Eventually she felt strong enough to get up off the bed and make her way slowly down the stairs. She shuddered to think what chaos might greet her downstairs, but she knew she had to relock the door so he couldn't get in if he returned.

She rushed over to the door and locked it. She went into the kitchen. The door was open and the cat-flap was wedged open; so that's how he'd got in – some sort of lever up from the cat-flap to the door lock.

She made sure the blinds in the kitchen and the lounge curtains were drawn before she turned on the lights. She flinched as the light made her screw up her eyes. She half expected to see a dead body, or maybe Vindi still hiding behind the sofa, ready to leap out on her.

There was nothing to hint that there had been a break-in. Mo was never the tidiest of people, but she'd know if the place had been searched. Perhaps Rajah had disturbed her before Vindi could find what he was looking for.

She picked Rajah up and gave him a big cuddle. She kissed

his warm furry stomach. "You're a good boy," she said. "You might have saved me from the bad man. This calls for a treat for you and a cuppa for me."

But Mo was a good MI5 employee, so the first thing she did was to ring the duty desk at Thames House to report the break-in. The duty officer didn't sound interested, but Mo knew he would ring the Dong to inform him.

It wasn't until she was sitting on her sofa with a cup of hot tea that the tears came. At first she was shocked, but as she looked round her dearly beloved room, all sorts of emotions cascaded out, most of them too complicated for her to identify.

The two security officers from MI5 arrived at 4.20am. It took them several minutes to convince Mo to open the door, and it prompted another flood of tears before Mo calmed down and got the officers a cup of tea each. The female officer, whose name was Penny, sat in the lounge with Mo, while the male officer checked the locks on the kitchen and lounge doors, before going outside to investigate.

Penny remarked on how beautiful Rajah was, and said Mr Bell would be arriving shortly and would take her through the official questions. She said she lived not far away, in Thornton Heath, but she'd been on duty at Thames house when the call came in. She said she liked Mo's crochet work on the back of the sofa, and she thought Mo's nieces looked very pretty in the photo on the mantelpiece.

Mo began to relax. She liked Penny.

The Dong arrived just before 5am. His grey face looked like a scrumpled-up duvet cover; he obviously hadn't had time to shave, and Mo thought he hadn't had much sleep from the look of him. He declined a cup of tea, but sat in the armchair Penny vacated for him. Penny left to help the male officer.

"Have you contacted anyone else, Farah?"

"No."

"Good for you. Please keep this incident under wraps for now. How do you feel?"

"I'm scared and I'm angry. I've lived in this house all my life. I inherited it from my mum when she died. My parents bought this house back in 1975 and we took thirty years to pay it off and…" She could feel the tears returning. "I feel violated."

"I understand. I'm so sorry. Would you like to tell me what happened?"

She told him everything. "And what's so terrifying is that I know who it was."

"Who?"

"Vindi."

She saw him start at that. "How could you tell? You said he was wearing a balaclava."

"The way he moved. I saw his eyes."

"It was dark."

"It never gets dark here; the street lights see to that."

"But you can't be certain, not in that light." He was trying to sound gentle, but he wasn't really listening to her anymore. She could see his mind was racing ahead, on other matters.

"Mr Bell," she said, marvelling she'd called him by his real name, "I am totally certain, as God is my witness: it was Vindi in my garden."

He shook his head. "The problem is, it would never stand up as proof in a court of law. Of course we'll check for fingerprints and DNA traces, but you say that nothing has been disturbed. If it was indeed Vindi, he's professional enough to have been wearing gloves. We'll check all CCTV in the area, but I wouldn't hold out any hopes of identifying your intruder. We may not even find any concrete evidence that there has been a break-in at all."

Mo felt betrayed. This man was supposed to be on her side. "Please don't tell me I'm being paranoid, Mr Bell. I know what I saw, and I know who I saw."

"Of course you did, Farah."

"Miss Dennis here."

"I apologise: Miss Dennis it is."

"And I don't think I can face coming back to work if he's around. I mean, I love work but I don't think…"

"I totally understand. You will need to give a full formal statement to the officers here, but after that you're free to take some holiday. I would advise you to get away from London for a few days. You've had a nasty shock, and being alone in the place where it happened isn't always healthy. Do you have any relatives or friends you could stay with?"

"Yes, but…"

"You need to keep me informed of your location and contact details at all times. I will see that your allegations are investigated fully, and I will keep you informed. I'll inform personnel and ask for a temporary replacement." He paused, and dredged up a smile on his tired face. "But you are irreplaceable, Miss Dennis, so I hope you recover quickly."

She'd always been charmed by the Dong, and she'd always felt that he'd do anything for her and that she'd do anything for him. But suddenly she wasn't so sure.

35

ADAM

The Director-General stared at himself in the mirror by his office door. He was looking for changes. The suit was still the same: immaculate Gieves and Hawkes lightweight blue. The figure beneath was still as trim as when he'd been fitted for the suit. His salt and pepper hair was receding, and he knew that the hair on the top of his head was thinning like the ice of the Arctic, but it was a slow loss – the shock of present events wasn't going to send him instantly bald. He was in good shape considering his fifty-six years. No one would detect any change to his grey eyes, either: they were hidden behind his rimless glasses.

He'd loved the fact that at work he'd always been nameless, almost anonymous. Ever since he'd got the top job he'd been an institution rather than a person. No one, not even the Home Secretary, called him by his name – he was either 'Director-General' or just 'sir'. No one dared ask him about his wife or children or home life, no one remarked on his appearance or health, no one questioned his decisions – not to his face, anyway. He was simply the boss, the rock on which the service was founded. He had always been able to be impersonal, unbiased, passionless and cerebral.

But everything had changed forever today. He had fallen from grace, rather like his namesake in the Bible. Now he was looking in the mirror at Adam Thornton, a mortal rather than an institution, a mortal with all the human frailties and vulnerabilities. Look carefully: the grey eyes look hurt, the thin mouth turns down at the corners and the hand is fiddling with the club tie.

Lord Brooke had gone ahead with the promised press conference this morning. They'd chosen the Hyde Park Hotel as the venue. An extravagant array of pastries and coffees had been laid on for the assembled hacks. Lord Brooke had swanned about in the limelight, pressing the flesh and then basking in the television lights. He'd outlined the 'baseless and outrageous smears' against his clients and then had demanded from the government a full, unreserved apology. He'd called on the press to support him in a 'crusade' to get these patriots, all spotless servants of the British state, back doing what they did best: serving the people, making Britain great again. He called on the Home Secretary personally to right the grievous wrongs.

The Home Secretary was on the phone to Adam even before the charade was over. She got straight to the point: we still hold the dirt on Vilnius and the other bastards down in H11, don't we?

This was the moment when Adam Thornton threw the dice, fell from grace, crossed the Rubicon, embarked on the slippery slope and a thousand other clichés: yes, Minister, of course the documents and artefacts are still safe down in H11.

Adam lied to the Minister.

The Home Secretary wasn't done: why on earth would they come up with this attack now, if they knew the dirt on them was still available to the government? Lord Brooke was the very antithesis of a Kamikaze pilot – he always bet on winners.

Adam had tried to sound confident, assuring the Home Secretary that she had nothing to worry about: even the most confident odds-on bet could go wrong, and Lord Brooke was only mortal – he had got it wrong this time.

Now Adam was committed to more lies and more justifications for the lies. He'd entrusted his only chance to a young agent called Lydia Twomey, whom he'd only ever met once, briefly. If she didn't find the missing artefacts and documents, he personally was finished, and democracy in Britain itself would be on the brink.

Now he was about to dig himself deeper into the pit.

"A Ms Lydia Twomey to see you, sir."

"Buzz her through please, Sandy." He walked over to his desk and sat down.

The young woman who carried all his hopes entered and stood beside the grandfather clock. She was dressed in a T-shirt from the Tate Modern and calf-length blue trousers. She didn't look like someone with the vital burden he was heaping onto her.

"Please take a seat, Ms Twomey."

She sat in front of him, waiting for him to begin. He reflected that it wasn't every day that a girl in casual clothes sat in front of his desk.

"I hear you've been over to visit your mother. How is she?"

"She's talking more clearly now, thank you. But she's not able to walk and she still remembers nothing. It may be the morphine. Her gunshot wound is painful but not causing concern. Thank you for removing her from the Met Police and for taking her security seriously."

"It's the least I could do." He paused. "Especially in the light of what I'm about to ask you to do."

"I warn you sir, I don't sing for weddings and I don't walk dogs."

He smiled. When had he last smiled? “I wish it was that simple. You remember the artefacts and documents that have gone missing from H11?”

“I’m unlikely to forget them. I haven’t picked up any trace of them yet.”

“Well, today I had to lie to the Home Secretary: I told her that they were still there in H11. You’ll understand the reasons when you catch the next national news.”

“Technically, you didn’t lie. At least, that’s my theory. I believe those file contents are still down in H11.”

“Thank you, Ms Twomey. I hope to goodness you’re right. If we – you – don’t find them very soon, there will be dire consequences. Meanwhile, I am anticipating that the Home Secretary will want to personally reassure herself that the documents are safe in H11.”

“I can see how this could present a problem.”

“That’s why I want you to smuggle into H11 this stuff I’ve got here and put it into the correct file boxes.” He patted a small pile of transcripts and cassettes sitting on his desk.

She looked at him, eyebrows raised. “What is ‘this stuff’?”

“They’re replacement documents and audio recordings of the Vilnius case.”

“Replacement – as in ‘fake’?”

Adam nodded. “They’re not perfect, but they’re good enough to fool a quick perusal by the Minister. It will give you more time to retrieve the real material.”

“They won’t fool Gerard Bell, though.”

“I’m counting on him not wanting to admit the loss – his job is on the line if any loss becomes public. The Home Secretary won’t want to admit to any loss either.”

“So it’s like the Emperor’s new clothes, then?”

“Let’s hope so.”

“How am I to smuggle this stuff into H11 and then get it into the right files? I’m not allowed to be down in H11 on my own, and CCTV coverage is total. Gerard Bell will be down there for the rest of the day, and Mo Dennis, too."

"Once upon a time I used to be a spook myself, believe it or not; I will arrange it all. I am going to take this stuff down to H11 in my case. You will collect it from my unlocked case which I will leave in the cloakroom. You will place this material in the correct file boxes. The file numbers are attached to each item. Remove the corrupted material that is presently in the files and shove it any file box that has room for it – try not to make it too obvious, but do it as quickly as you can. I will ensure you have at least twenty minutes to complete the transfers. Any questions?"

"What you're asking me to do is a criminal offence. I could lose my job and be imprisoned for an unlimited time."

Adam took off his glasses. Let her see his desperate eyes. "Yes, I know. If there was another way of doing this, I would take it. We must have this material in place before the Minister gets too twitchy. Of course, I'll vouch for you if your role gets discovered."

"But if I get discovered, you will have lost your job as well. I imagine you can't give me a 'get out of jail' card in advance."

"I'm afraid not."

Lydia sighed. "Well, at least it isn't going to get me shot. It's my mother who has taken the bullet."

"Yes – I regret it very much. I'd be grateful if you didn't report this substitution to your other bosses, Perry Webb and Gerard Bell."

"You can rest easy on that one."

"I'm afraid Perry has discovered a leak close to his office, but we're not going to plug it yet."

Lydia nodded. "Miss Parmenter," she said, showing no surprise.

Adam looked at her carefully. How had she known? What had Perry not told him? Was Lydia the one who had made the discovery?

He continued. "Next: there is good cause to believe your life could be in danger. I'm going to insist you carry your gun whenever you're out of this building."

"My gun is impounded by the Metropolitan Police."

"Go to Armoury and draw another one. Are you up to date with all your firearms training? Are you confident in being able to use a gun?"

She nodded. Adam didn't think she looked totally convincing.

"One other thing, Miss Twomey." He paused.

"Yes?"

"I'd like to call you Lydia when it's just the two of us." She nodded, and he hesitated, summoning up the courage. "And I'd like you… to call me Adam. I feel our fates are bound together in this enterprise and…" He wanted to tell her about his fall from Eden, but it was definitely a step too far.

The young woman sitting opposite him took his turmoil in her stride. "Okay. No worries, Adam."

Adam put his glasses back on.

36

LYDIA

Lydia waited in the corridor outside H11, waiting to be buzzed through.

"Come through." It was Gerard Bell, not Farah.

The door slid open and she walked into the cloakroom. She didn't glance up at the CCTV camera, but she could sense his eyes on her. She calmly put her bag down on the bench beside her, composed her face, and waited to be buzzed through into the main office. If ever there was a time to use her yoga training, this was it.

Bell was sitting at Farah's desk, surrounded by the gladioli, with the latest logbook open in front of him.

Lydia put on her best smile. "Morning, Dong."

"Good morning, Schizo. I see you've no helmet and motorcycle gear today."

"It's the only benefit of having to sleep upstairs in this building."

"But you've been out to see your mother. How is she doing?"

"Making progress. Once she's off the morphine I think she might be back to normal."

"Has she remembered what happened to her yet?" Bell sounded casual and chatty, but Lydia could detect tension beneath the surface.

"It's coming back slowly." There, let him stew.

"Splendid! Well, as you can see, it's like the Marie Celeste down here this morning. I've been all on my own, doing the admin. I've been relearning how to make a cup of tea for myself."

"Where's Farah?"

"She's taking some leave. This may have some relevance to your investigation, so I'll give you the details. I got a call at 4am last night from the duty desk; they told me that Farah had phoned in to say her house had been broken into by an unidentified male wearing a balaclava."

"Was she attacked? Is she all right?"

"When I arrived at her place in Penge, the duty team were already there. There were no signs of a break-in, no damage done, no items missing. Farah herself was very shaken up, though."

"I bet she was, especially after what happened to Luther and Double D."

"Quite. I wonder whether she let their deaths colour her fears and imagination."

"You think she made it up?"

"I don't know what to think. The duty team found no evidence to back up her story. The important thing is that she believes it and is in no fit state to come to work. So despite our staffing crisis, I have given her the time off to recover. The welfare of staff must come first."

"Of course. So if I wanted to interview her, where would I find her?"

"She's going up to stay with her cousin in Yorkshire, near Doncaster, for a few days."

"Can I talk to her over the phone, then?"

"I'm sure we can arrange it, as long as she's up to it. I'll talk to her later today, once she's arrived up there."

"Thank you. Well, I must make up for lost time, and get on with my work." She clapped her hands together, and made for the door to the corridor.

"What work is that?" Bell said it so casually. "I've got a list for you to do when you're free. There's Farah's work to share as well."

"I'm going through Luther's work record as shown by the logbooks. I believe he came across something that got him killed." She looked at Bell unflinchingly. I think it's you who had him killed. I'm down in a hermetically sealed basement alone with a killer, and somehow I've got to show no fear.

Bell's face had turned to the monitor above him. "Oh, look who we've got here." He said it softly, but a smile spread across his face.

Lydia followed his eyes. The Director-General was standing in the corridor, waiting to be buzzed in. "Don't let me detain you, Lydia; the DG and I may have some important talking to do."

She picked up her gloves for archive handling, left the main office, heart hammering, went to her own office and stood against the door, waiting. She told herself that what she was about to do was no worse than smuggling Martin Froome's list out of H11 – she was waist deep in the shit already.

A couple of minutes later she heard their voices in the corridor, moving away, down to Bell's office. She heard the office door close and the voices were extinguished. It was time for her to act.

She slipped on her archivist gloves. She walked slowly back to the main office, pressed the button to gain access to the cloakroom, walked through into the cloakroom and opened the DG's case which was on the bench. The cassettes and transcripts were all there, neatly labelled with the file box numbers. She picked up the packets and walked back into the main office.

Everything she'd done had been captured by the CCTV. What if the Director-General – Adam, he wanted to be called – hadn't sorted that aspect out? What if he was setting her up?

It was too late to go back.

She walked into Stack 3. The strip lights flickered on automatically, triggered by her presence. The motion-sensors on the CCTV cameras clicked into gear and the little red lights on the cameras signified that they were now recording. She forced herself to walk slowly. She found the corrupted files; all four were neatly in a line on the second-from-top shelf, looking like all the other hundreds of thousands of others.

Four minutes gone: plenty of time.

She took down the first file, placed it carefully on the wheeled table beside her, opened it up, took out the corrupted material, picked up the material given to her by Adam, placed it in the box file, and replaced it in its place on the shelf.

There – that was easy.

She did exactly the same with the second box file.

She looked at her watch. Six and a half minutes gone.

She replaced the contents of the third box – no problems. She could feel her heart rate falling. It was going to be all right.

The last box. She lifted it down from the shelf, placed it on the table, opened it up and lifted out the materials. She picked up the last set of fake materials – a sheaf of papers.

An audio cassette she hadn't seen fell from between the papers, tumbled to the floor, bounced and skittered underneath the bottom shelf.

Lydia knelt down. She could see the cassette clearly. She reached under the shelf, but her hand didn't fit into the small gap. She felt the cassette on the tips of her gloved fingers – she'd pushed it further under!

She got back up, took a sheaf of documents and slid them under the shelf to push the cassette out of the other side of the shelf. It budged the cassette, but not far enough to be out the other side. She peered under the shelving.

Nnnrrnnggg.

That sound! Her heart lurched; she nearly hit her head on the shelf as she straightened.

"Need any help?" Brian was standing by the door behind her in his green overalls. His pale face was impassive but his dark eyes glittered.

"Jesus, you gave me a shock!"

"That'll be one all, then." He said it without a glimmer of a smile.

"Oh yes – your cup of tea; sorry about that." She struggled to her feet. "I didn't realise you were down here."

"It's my day. I was in Stack 4. Cleaning. You wouldn't think you'd get much dust down here, but you do – very bad for the artefacts, I'm told."

"Yes, of course." Lydia had regained control of her galloping heart. She resisted the urge to look at her watch.

"No spiders ever make it down here, though. So you don't get cobwebs."

"Well, that's a relief, then." Why was he so chatty all of a sudden? How much had he seen?

"So, do you need some help?"

"No, no, it's fine. I can manage. Don't let me stop you getting on. Have you come in here to clean?"

He nodded. His black beard was dark against his fluorescent overalls.

"Do you think you could do another stack first? I must get this done now. I won't be long, I promise." She hadn't got long – Adam had given her twenty minutes maximum. If she couldn't get Brian out of the way quickly, she was going to be in serious trouble.

Brian thought about it for several seconds.

Nnnrrnnggg. It sounded as if his guts were being ruptured.

She wondered if he was enjoying the power – he must have noticed how agitated she was.

"Yeah, okay." He turned and was gone through the door before she could thank him.

Lydia slumped against the shelves. That was horrible, and she had no idea if he'd seen what she was doing. She looked at her watch: she had just eight minutes left to find hiding places for all the corrupted materials that Adam had told her to hide.

She shut the file box, minus its cassette, and replaced it on the shelf. She then scooped up the corrupted materials and made her way out of Stack 3, along the corridor, and into Stack 4. Brian said he had cleaned here already, so he shouldn't be back.

Again the lights came on and the CCCTV silently began to record her actions.

The first file she chose was on the bottom shelf furthest from the door. It was full to choking: no room for any fugitive material. The second file she chose was the same.

Six minutes left.

At last she found a relatively empty file on a top shelf. She stuffed as much as she could into it, snapped it shut, mentally noted its number and moved across the room to find another file for the rest of the material. Again, the first file was full. With shaking hands, she snapped it shut and shoved it back on the shelf.

She stopped, and fought the instinct to look at her watch. She needed to do this properly. She looked up at the file she had replaced: it was slightly out of alignment with the others. Carefully, she readjusted it.

The next file had space for the remaining corrupted material. She jammed the papers into the file, shut the file, shoved it back on the shelf and turned away.

She exhaled. The task was complete with four minutes to spare… except of course it wasn't complete. Now she had to go back, get the cassette out from under the shelf, and put it in the allocated file box.

She left Stack 4 and hurried back along the corridor towards Stack 3. She was just about to open the door, but stopped.

The light automatically stayed on for a full three minutes after anyone left the room. If she re-entered now, the light would still be on beyond the Director-General's twenty minute limit. If Bell came back down this corridor with the DG, he would see where she had been.

She put her hand to the door: risk it!

She withdrew her hand. She could always pick up the cassette later. She looked at her watch – not enough time. She turned and pushed open the door to the office she shared with Vindi and the archivists.

It was less than two minutes before she heard voices in the corridor. He hadn't given her any margin for error.

But she had made an error. That cassette was still lying under the shelves.

The voices faded as they went into the main office.

A minute later there was a knock on her door, and Bell popped his head round. "Got a minute, Schizo?"

She nodded. "Sure."

He came in and sat in Double D's old chair, opposite her. "Well, that was interesting. The Director-General was asking for our special help and vigilance." He was observing her intensely, as if he suspected something.

"What about?"

"This big press conference this morning. Did you hear it?"

She shook her head as if it was no concern of hers.

"Some right-wing loony has-beens are trying to make a political comeback. They've claimed today they were smeared without evidence; in fact we hold the evidence of their guilt down here in H11." He picked up one of Double D's novelty pencils with tassels, and twiddled it round his long bony fingers.

Lydia attempted a casual smile. "So their attempt is doomed."

"Should be. But the DG and the Home Secretary have got their knickers in a twist about the whole thing. They fear that the evidence may get tampered with, so we're to be on our guard. The DG is so paranoid he's just walked off with all the CCTV recordings for the last week, right up to the moment he left. So I hope you weren't up to something naughty while we were chatting; if you were, the DG will enjoy watching it."

It was hard not to smile, but she knew Bell was watching and analysing every twitch on her face. "No," she said, "I've been a good girl, slogging through these logbooks."

"And be careful in future. The DG has ordered that all CCTV footage from H11 be streamed directly to his office. Either he doesn't trust you, or he doesn't trust me."

"You've just told me he's paranoid."

Bell's eyes narrowed. "Did you talk to the DG this morning?"

"I report to you and to Perry Webb."

"So what have you been up to?" He definitely suspected something.

"I told you: slogging through these files."

"Well, prepare yourself for a very special occasion. We are receiving a huge honour: the Home Secretary herself will be visiting us before the close of play today. The DG says she wants to check this vital evidence herself. The DG has asked us to sit on Stack 3, where this evidence lies, as if it was a nest with golden eggs."

Oh great. There'll be no chance to pick up the cassette before the Minister arrives.

37

LORD BROOKE

TELEGRAM ENCRYPTED TEXT MESSAGING SERVICE

A I'VE GOT YOUR SERVICE CHAPS BUZZING ROUND ME LIKE A PLAGUE OF BLUEBOTTLES. NO CHANCE TO MEET.

B THEY'RE ON ME TOO. AND WE HAD A VISIT FROM THE HOME SEC HERSELF TODAY.

A SO WHAT HAPPENED? THE HOME SEC HAS REFUSED TO GIVE A PUBLIC APOLOGY. SHE SAYS SHE'S HAPPY THE EVIDENCE IS DOWN THERE IN H11. WHAT THE DICKENS DID SHE SEE?

B FAKES. DG HAS BEEN CLEVER. HE'S SMUGGLED FAKES INTO THE FILE BOXES.

A HOW?

B IF I KNEW I WOULD HAVE STOPPED IT. I SUSPECT TWOMEY.

A WHY DIDN'T YOU DENOUNCE THEM AS FAKES?

B I WASN'T PRESENT WHEN HOME SEC INSPECTED THEM. I ONLY SAW THEM AFTER.

A CAN WE GET THE FAKES OUT?

B AN UNNECESSARY RISK.

A YOU'VE BEEN FUCKED OVER.

B ONLY TEMPORARILY. THE FAKES ARE CRUDE. ENOUGH TO FOOL A MERE POLITICIAN, BUT WHEN THEY COME TO COURT IT WILL BE SO OBVIOUS THAT THEY WON'T DARE SUBMIT THEM. THEN THEY'LL LOSE EVEN MORE FACE, FALL EVEN MORE HEAVILY.

A WHAT'S THAT BLOODY TWOMEY DOING NOW? I HEARD THAT SHE'S STILL LOOKING FOR THE MATERIAL YOU SAID HAS BEEN DESTROYED.

B CORRECT.

A WE NEED TO GET RID OF HER.

B I'VE ALREADY SAID: NO MORE DEATHS.

A THERE'S AN UGLY RUMOUR THAT THE MATERIALS HAVEN'T BEEN DESTROYED, AND THAT TWOMEY HAS A CHANCE OF FINDING THEM.

B JUST THAT: A RUMOUR.

A IT BETTER BE. OTHERWISE YOU'RE NEXT AFTER TWOMEY.

B IF I DIE, YOU CAN BE SURE THE WORLD WILL FIND OUT WHETHER THE MATERIAL STILL EXISTS.

A I'M NOT A GOOD PERSON TO THREATEN.

B NOR AM I. LET'S HOLD OUR NERVE. TWOMEY WON'T FIND ANYTHING, AND WHEN THE COURT ORDERS THAT THE EVIDENCE BE HANDED OVER, THE DG'S BLUFF WILL BE EXPOSED. THEIR HOUSE OF CARDS WILL FALL. I'VE GOT MY END UNDER CONTROL, NOW YOU GET YOUR END SORTED. ARE THE TURKS SORTED?

A TERMINATES DIALOGUE

38

LYDIA

"You must be Lydia. Gerard has told me everything about you. I'm so glad you could make it here this evening to our little gathering." Louisa Bell took Lydia by the hand and drew her over to a waiter with a silver drinks tray. She took a champagne flute from the tray, and without asking Lydia, held it out.

Lydia took the glass. "You must be Louisa. Gerard has told me nothing about you at all."

"Oh, is he always boringly business-like at work?" Louisa laughed in the musical way cultivated by the privileged. Her dark brown eyes were scanning Lydia like a security sensor. She looked the identikit of Bohemian sophistication: lustrous black hair cut artfully asymmetrical, a lean body under a multi-fabric gown of deep reds, long slender hands with immaculate nails, and the face of one of the middle-aged models from the *Guardian* colour supplement.

"He's never boring. But he's very discreet." Lydia wasn't going to be cowed by this woman. She was acutely aware that her Zara red top and black trousers were painfully clunky next to Louisa's sophisticated gown, but she didn't care. She'd done her homework about Louisa's literary agency, and she wasn't impressed. What she still hadn't worked out was why on earth Bell had invited a scruffy girl from Nuneaton to mix with the great and the clever at this soiree in his palatial Kensington house.

"Are you talking about me? All good, I hope." Gerard appeared behind Louisa. He slid his arm around her waist and kissed her neck. "Louisa, my darling, you are talking to the one genuine intellectual, the one ray of light in my dismal place of work. Lydia is an expert on matters as diverse as WH Auden's scrotum and the funk career of Luther Vandross. She is a veritable polymath."

"Should I be jealous?" Louisa laughed musically again.

Lydia didn't blush or simper; she stood waiting. This was all play-acting. She hadn't been invited to be praised or to be humiliated. The real purpose of her invitation would become apparent soon enough.

"Anyway, let me introduce you to some people you might like." Gerard took her by the elbow and led her away from Louisa. "There's someone special I want you to meet, but she hasn't arrived yet." He surveyed the room.

There were maybe thirty people engaged in loud conversation. Ages ranged from bright young things in their twenties to grey-haired politicians and their wives. Lydia recognised several people from late night BBC arts shows. The walls of the room had tasteful 18th-century etchings and lovely Victorian watercolour landscapes. The curtains were opulent Persian fabrics.

"Lydia, meet young Fabian here." Gerard put his arm round the shoulder of an intense-looking man with an angry haircut and round John Lennon glasses who was inspecting one of the pictures. "He scribbles excruciating pieces for the progressive press – and for *Private Eye*." Gerard winked. "We need to keep in with the enemy."

He glided away, leaving Lydia with the journalist.

"I was just looking at this daub." Fabian turned back to examine the scene of a young woman on a swing, her skirts rising as a young man admired her from below. "It's by Boucher, done shortly before the French Revolution. It's amazing how the patrons of Boucher didn't see their doom coming." He turned back. "Are you a writer, Lydia?"

"No." She took a sip of her champagne. "I'm surprised a left-wing writer like you is at a gathering with so many people with right-wing views. Are you gathering material on them?"

He didn't laugh. "That would be a bonus. Anyway, Gerard labelled me 'progressive', not left-wing. Gerard and Louisa like to invite people of all political hues – some for business, some for..."

Lydia supplied her own word. "Credibility?"

"I was going to say 'pleasure'. They're very... eclectic. What are your political views? Why are you here?"

"Good question. That's what I'm asking myself."

"You're not here to sing, are you? They'll have some ghastly performer on later."

Fabian was barged out of the way by a large florid man wearing a blazer and cravat. "Hello, hello, we can't have you lefties monopolising the totty, can we, Fabian?" He turned to Lydia with a wink. "You watch out for Fabian: he's a little shit, y'know. He's not interested in you – only in your revolutionary potential. You're better off with a reliable old codger like me, m'dear. What's your name?" As if to validate this assessment, Fabian moved off, leaving Lydia backed up by the boor against the Boucher.

"Lydia."

"Nice name. You've got to hand it to the Bells, they do get some cracking 'guests' along. What do you do, Lydia? Let me guess: you're a dancer. No?"

She couldn't be arsed with this. "Espionage."

"Oh." He took a step back, disappointment flooding his face. "Gerard bringing work home now, is he?"

"Not at all, Charlie." Gerard had materialised at the boor's shoulder. It was the first time Lydia had been glad to see him. "I know that Molly Henderson over there is dying to meet the author of 'In My Time'. She said she couldn't put it down, and she wasn't talking about her dog. She's the appreciative type, I think you'll find."

Gerard gently propelled Charlie in the direction of a blonde lady in a very tight aquamarine dress.

"Thank you," said Lydia.

"Don't mind Charlie Houghton – he's relatively harmless. He was once a junior minister a very long time ago. If you multiplied the number of his wives by the number of his insolvencies you'd get the number of women he propositions daily. He's a serial failure."

"So why do you invite him?"

"Louisa is his literary agent. He's very well connected, and possibly due a comeback in the near future. Come on, there's someone I want you to meet."

He whisked Lydia through the melee to the far side of the room. A woman with her back to them, wearing a calf-length white linen dress, was arguing vehemently with a large angular man in a dinner jacket.

"Simon, may I butt in for a minute? I'd like you both to meet a colleague of mine, Lydia. Lydia, meet Simon Gordon, soon to be Minister for Culture and the Arts if rumours are to be believed, and Reza Hamid, revered writer."

Reza turned to greet Lydia, a dazzling smile on her face.

Lydia gulped. She was truly star-struck. Her favourite writer was smiling, holding out a hand to her.

"Pleased to meet you, Lydia."

She shook Reza's hand. "I'm your most ardent fan – believe me." Oh shit – she'd gushed. She wanted to start again.

Simon Gordon backed away, muttering that he was outnumbered now. Gerard led him away, hand on his shoulder, to meet some 'incredibly interesting new talents'. Lydia was left with Reza.

Now she understood why she had been invited. How wonderfully kind (or clever) of Gerard to arrange this! If he wanted to charm her then he was going about it the right way. He obviously knew the way to a woman's heart was through her reading.

Reza laughed. "If that man ever gets to be Minister for Arts and Culture, we might as well all become farmers."

Lydia knew she was going to get on with Reza. She liked her friendly but strong face, her dark eyes and black hair, her plain gold earrings.

They spent the whole soiree together, warding off the attention of increasingly inebriated men, suppressing giggles at the vocal performer, discussing a never-ending kaleidoscope of issues: the harassment of women, whether you turn into your mother with age, Sylvia Plath, Miles Davis and Charlie Mingus, the relative merits of Hemingway and Steinbeck, sexuality in the feminist novel, first memories and favourite places. Lydia wanted to ask Reza about her books, but Reza never once directly mentioned them.

The night slipped by. Lydia didn't count her drinks.

The room began to empty – in fact almost everyone had left before Lydia realised.

"Where do you live?" Reza asked. "Perhaps we could share a taxi."

Lydia pulled a face. "I'm not allowed back to my flat. It's a long story – too long to tell. I'm hoping to be allowed back on Monday. I'm staying in a sort of dormitory at work."

"That's miserable. Look, come back to mine. I live quite centrally – in Fulham. I've got a sofa, or if you're cold, you could share my double bed." She said it with no embarrassment – Lydia liked that.

"Yeah – okay. Thank you – it would be great. I'll have to phone work to say I won't be back, and I'll have to be up early in the morning to visit my mum in hospital – another long story. Just give me a minute."

They were handed Reza's long coat and Lydia's short jacket by the waiter in the entrance hall. Lydia made her call to Thames House. Gerard and Louisa hugged both of them goodbye and said it had been lovely to have them both there. It gave Lydia a warm feeling.

As they descended the steps to the street, Lydia said, "It was really nice of Gerard to invite me."

"They're lovely people."

Lydia nodded. She could almost agree. She realised she wasn't entirely sober but what the hell, she was off duty at last. God knows when she would next have the opportunity to let her hair down.

They linked arms against the chill of the April night and made their way down to Kensington High Street to hail a taxi. As they turned out of Phillimore Place into Argyll Road Lydia heard a scooter start up behind her. She turned back.

A man in a bulky jacket, his faced wrapped in a scarf, was walking briskly along the pavement fifteen yards behind them. His eyes were fixed on Lydia. He seemed to lean towards her like a hunting dog. The scooter, ridden by a figure in a full helmet, was taxiing a few yards behind the walker.

Even in her euphoric befuddled state, Lydia's training came through: DANGER! This man was going to shoot her.

"Shit! Get down, Reza!"

"What?"

Lydia pushed Reza behind the car they were passing, and turned to the walker. Sure enough, her nightmare was unfolding: he had pulled a pistol from his clothing and was levelling it at her.

Oh my God, oh God, oh my God! Her mind froze. What should she do? What the fuck…

As she lurched sideways, a report sounded and something zinged past her ear.

She threw herself down behind the next car. She heard the scooter speed up. In a second or two it would be level with her. She scrabbled desperately in her jacket for the 9mm Glock she'd drawn from Armoury just yesterday. Shit – she couldn't get it clear – she hadn't had time to practise. She could hear the man's boots thudding on the pavement as he ran forward.

She heard him shout. "Out of the way, or you get a bullet, too."

Still Lydia struggled to clear her gun.

She heard Reza yell something, then the man screamed. "You bitch! You fucking bitch!"

Lydia had her gun in her hand now. She stood up.

The scooterist had stopped and the man with the gun was doubled over, hands on his eyes. Reza was backing away, aerosol in her hand.

"The bitch maced me!"

The scooterist was looking at Lydia. "She's got a fucking gun! Get out of here!"

Lydia levelled her gun at the scooterist. Her rules of engagement were clear: don't fire unless you are in extreme danger from your target.

She squeezed the trigger. Nothing. The safety catch was still on.

The man on the pavement had jumped on the back of the scooter by the time she clicked the safety, and the scooter had blasted past them and off northwards up Argyll Road. No way could she fire in self-defence now.

Reza was now on her knees, heaving in the gutter. Little sobs came from her between the retching. She had dropped her can of pepper spray.

Lydia hauled Reza to her feet. "Come on. We must get away!"

"Get back to Gerard's house," Reza slurred, wiping her mouth.

"No!" Lydia squeezed Reza hard. "That bastard set this up. Come on!"

They half ran, half staggered down Argyll Road to Kensington High Street. Lydia's thoughts churned, panic fighting her training. Get to somewhere with light and CCTV cameras, get a taxi, get away.

They careered onto the High Street and turned right, stopping to get their breath in the doorway of the Metro Bank.

"Have they gone?" Reza whispered. Her lips looked pale in the street light.

"Yes, they've gone." Lydia hugged her. "Are you all right?"

Reza nodded. Her face looked oddly bloodless – Lydia worried she'd taken a bullet. "Will they come back?"

"No, they won't. They're cowards. They've seen my gun." She squeezed Reza's hand.

Reza looked over Lydia's shoulder. "A taxi!"

They staggered out into the road, waving furiously at a black cab. The taxi swerved round them and kept going.

Reza shook her fist. "Bastard!"

"He thought we were drunk. We've got to calm down." Lydia could see another taxi approaching.

"He just drove past. We might have been attack victims." Reza shook her head in fury.

"We are attack victims, in case you missed it."

Lydia stood rock-still in the road, arm outstretched. The taxi slowed, then stopped.

"Where to, love?" Sometimes the simplest words sound better than the greatest poetry.

Lydia hauled Reza into the back of the taxi and slammed the door behind them. "Fulham, please."

"Where in Fulham?" The cabbie sounded bored; he was obviously used to having hysterical women in his cab.

"Reza, you need to tell the man."

"Radipole Road."

"Right you are, ladies."

"Do you think we're safe now?" Reza asked. She clung to Lydia's arm as the taxi seemed to crawl through the streets.

"You've always been safe; those men were after me. You saw that they had no interest in you. They won't know who you are or where you live. Now, I just need to report this to my boss, so if you could just…"

She disentangled herself and rang Adam Thornton.

He picked up after less than ten seconds. "Hello, who's speaking, please?"

"It's Lydia. There's been a shooting incident – an attempt on my life."

"Where?"

Lydia outlined what had happened.

"You need to get back to Thames House."

"No. I'm taking home the woman who saved my life. She may be in shock."

"I'm all right," Reza called out.

Lydia ignored her. "The assassins won't know where she lives, and I need to keep her safe. I owe her that at the very least."

A pause. "Okay. Keep in touch. Inform me of any developments. I have your phone location on my screen. Keep it turned on." He rang off.

"Do you think I saved your life?" Reza sat up.

"I'm sure of it. I couldn't get my gun out. That guy would have plugged me where I was cowering if you hadn't filled his face with pepper spray. You were very brave; you didn't have to do it – you could have run for it and they wouldn't have touched you."

Lydia marvelled how perceptions can change; when she had read Reza's books, she'd always thought of the writer as the quintessential strong woman, passionate but confident, always in control. The flesh and blood Reza was so different: a mixture of instinctive bravery and panicked reaction, subject to the violence of others.

They hardly spoke when they arrived at Reza's flat. Reza took Lydia's hand and led her through a small living room to the large bed in an alcove.

Lydia freed her hand.

Reza smiled. "Don't worry – I'm not going to jump you."

Reza took off her white dress and laid it on the chair beside the bed. Lydia slipped off her jacket, shoes, trousers and top and laid them on an armchair. She felt too tired to analyse anything. Reza climbed under the blue duvet in her underwear; Lydia followed from the other side of the bed. Reza kissed Lydia on the cheek then turned over, clutching a pillow. Less than two minutes later Lydia could hear her gentle snoring.

She lay on her back, staring up at the dark blank ceiling. The events of the evening were just too weird to get her head round. She had just met one of her heroines – my God! She was actually lying in bed with someone she'd idolised from afar, who had undoubtedly just saved her life. How the hell had it all happened?

It had to be Gerard. All that charm over the past few days, getting her to lower her guard. Next: invite her to his house, ply her with drink and flattery, and dazzle her with celebrities.

Then the master-stroke: introducing her to her heroine – it had flattened any guard she might have retained. Finally, once she was pissed and comfortable, her gun zipped into her jacket, Gerard had sent in the assassins.

He'd played her like a concertina.

Well, she was still alive, and he wouldn't get away with it.

"Good morning."

Lydia opened her eyes.

Reza was sitting on the side of the bed, dressed in a kimono that was tied at the waist, revealing the soft curves of her cleavage. She was smiling broadly at Lydia. The sun had crept through a crack in the curtains and a shaft of golden light played on Reza's long unbound black hair.

"Coffee or tea?"

"Coffee please. Black no sugar. What time is it?"

Reza stroked her cheek. "Don't worry – it's just gone seven. Plenty of time to visit your mum."

"How are you this morning? You seemed pretty shaken up last night."

Reza shrugged. "It's not every day you witness an attempted hit in the street."

Lydia shook her head. "I'm so sorry. I should have seen it coming, but I was distracted, too happy. I should have left the party alone."

"You might be dead if you'd been on your own."

"No – I led you into danger..."

"Shh." Reza reached out and put her finger on Lydia's lips. It was powerfully erotic. "Don't beat yourself up about it. It's me who should be apologising to you."

"What are you talking about?"

Reza shook her head. "We... I got you into that danger. I should have anticipated it."

"You're making no sense." Lydia sat up. She pulled the duvet over her bare shoulders. Suddenly she felt half naked and vulnerable.

"Look, I have a confession to make, Lydia." Reza paused.

"Go on." Lydia said it with anger and dread rising in her.

"I was given the task of recruiting you to our group."

"What group?" She didn't want to hear this.

"We're a small underground group, led by Gerard and Louisa, dedicated to fighting the rise of fascism and sexism in this country."

"Oh yes?" Anger was winning out; Lydia could feel herself shaking.

"Yes. We'd like you to join us."

Lydia felt the blood pounding in her neck. "Do you realise what your precious Gerard is mixed up in right now?" She paused, reminding herself of her professional code. "Well, I'm not allowed to tell you about it, but I can assure you that you wouldn't like it one little bit. Has he told you about it? Are you part of the conspiracy?" She looked across the room to her jacket, with the gun zipped in the pocket. It lay on an armchair, out of reach.

Reza shook her head and smiled sadly. "You've got him completely wrong. Of course he has to appear like he's going along with those fascists, but he's the only thing between them and the coup d'état – believe me." Her voice rose with passion.

Lydia wanted desperately to believe her. But she didn't.

"Bullshit! He's used you to seduce me, and once my guard was down he sent in the assassins to kill me. He's played me. You've played me too, and now you expect little-girlie-me, the simpleton from Nuneaton, to melt to his will."

"No! It was the fascists who sent the assassins. I was as shocked and unprepared as you were."

"Don't give me that! Some of those fascists were at his party last night. Louisa is their literary agent – she promotes their shit. Your leaders are in bed with the worst in the land, Reza."

Reza took Lydia's hand. Lydia tried to pull it away, but Reza gripped her tightly. "Gerard has to go along with the fascists for now. He needs to recruit you, not kill you. He's against all killing. You may not know it yet, but you are in a position to destroy everything he's working for. The fascists, they fear you too – it's why they're trying to kill you. If you join with us, Gerard can get them to call off their assassins." She paused. "The main reason for Gerard taking the huge risk of asking you to join us is because he knows you're on their hit list, and the only way of stopping them is to have you join us. He wants you to live. Lydia darling, I too want you to live."

"I want to believe you, Reza." But I don't. "What does Gerard want me to do?" She worked her hand free of Reza's grip.

"He wants you to stop your present lines of inquiry, or to just go through the motions. If you succeed in what you're doing, it could prove a disaster for everyone."

"What else?" She felt the dull ache of disappointment.

"He thinks you've been involved with Adam Thornton, your Director-General, in carrying out some illegal activities. You need to convince the fascists that you've come to our side. If Gerard held the proof…"

"Hand me my clothes, will you?" Lydia said it without bothering to disguise the disgust in her voice. She looked Reza square in the face. "You know, I worshipped you and your books."

Reza looked down at the rug on the floor. "I'm so sorry. I really like you, Lydia. I was sure you'd join us in our battle against fascism. I am sad." She looked up again at Lydia. "I'm not ashamed of what I've asked you to do. I am only an exile in your country, so if you want to report me to your superiors, they can have me extradited to face torture and death. In my own country we have real fascism: as you know from my writing, they killed my father."

Lydia didn't stay for coffee.

39

PERRY

Perry Webb was waiting in the anteroom when the DG arrived at his office at 7am. The DG raised his eyebrows, then invited him in and offered him a seat.

"This is an unexpected treat to see you so early, Perry. I trust it's good news you've come to share."

"My team have been working round the clock, and yes, we've come up with some pretty interesting material." He fished about in his case and pulled out a couple of data discs, which he deposited on the DG's desk. "That top disc contains evidence which links the Turkish solicitors, the Erguns, with our Special Operations team, led by Miles Mason."

"Have you found evidence to link Miles and his department with the Vilnius case?"

"No, but we know that the Erguns, through the Cevdets, tried to kill Lydia's mother, and we know that Ian Forrester, who was shadowing Dennis Dunn, was found dead on their premises. I think we've got enough to move against Miles."

The DG's voice was the model of forced calm. "With respect, I disagree. We've known for some time our Special Ops use the

Erguns for accommodation, information and other outsourced services, but that doesn't preclude the possibility that someone else, maybe Gerard Bell, has also used them in the Vilnius dealings. Until you can link Miles Mason or the Erguns to this case, we have nothing."

Perry could feel his cheeks redden. He ploughed on. "The second disc is a collection of material on Vilnius, Lord Brooke and the others. My team have come up with some very grubby details about them."

"Does it link them to the missing H11 evidence?"

"No, but we could use it against them – leak it to the press. We could fight back against these bastards – show them we're not totally supine."

Again, the DG shook his head rather sorrowfully. "Perry, digging this dirt falls outside your internal security remit. It's probably stuff we've already got. If we leaked it to the press it would look like we've something to fear from Vilnius and Brooke. That would bring the Home Secretary down upon us – precisely what we're trying to avoid. Thank you for this file, though – I'll keep it for use if things look desperate."

"Oh, terrific!" Perry knew his reaction was unhelpful, but sometimes a man just had to let off steam. "Look, my team are working round the clock, and, well, a bit more appreciation wouldn't go amiss."

"I'm sorry, Perry. I know it's difficult. We're all under a lot of pressure and…"

"You've totally sidelined me since we – I – identified the leak as being Miss Parmenter. These bloody gangster Turks and their friends in Special Ops and GCHQ have killed two members of H11, and we're taking no action against them. I don't mind admitting that I'm pretty damned frustrated."

The DG didn't reply for a moment. Instead he closed his eyes for a full five seconds before opening them. "The Turks didn't murder Froome and Dunn. Those were skilled jobs. The Turks use motorbikes and guns. Did you know that Lydia Twomey was attacked by them last night?"

"No, I didn't. That's exactly my point: I'm no longer in the loop. She's one of my staff – I should be the first to know."

"You needed the sleep last night – you've been working too hard. How's Glenys coping with it all?"

"Please don't try to soft-soap me." He wasn't an idiot.

"Anyway, Perry, I want you to go down to your office, and get ready for an important phone call from me. Please make sure that Miss Parmenter is listening in."

As he stormed off to his own office, Perry fumed to himself; his role in this whole affair had declined to being a mere recipient of disinformation, or a purveyor of dirt which would only be used if things got desperate.

It was time for a chill pill or two. And maybe, just maybe, he could do something off his own bat that would blow this thing wide open.

Half an hour later the promised disinformation call came through from the DG. He presumed Miss Parmenter was listening in, but Perry could hardly be arsed to give replies to the DG's hints that the net was closing round Gerard Bell. He was too old to act the stooge, he was tired and the pills had kicked in nicely.

40

LYDIA

Lydia was picked up by a service driver from Reza's flat to visit her mother in the Central Middlesex. She was pleased to see the armed guard in the ward had been increased to three, and she was even more pleased to see her mother sitting up in bed, eyes alert.

"Hi, Mum. You look a lot better. Give me a hug." They hugged and kissed, and Lydia sat down by the bed. "Have they reduced your drugs? You don't look zonked out any longer."

"I've told them I don't want any more drugs. I don't want to become a cabbage. My fingers feel all puffed up."

"It's probably the MS. What about the pain in your arm?"

"It hurts, but it's no worse than some other things that have been done to me in hospitals."

"You do know what caused it, don't you?"

"Sister Ngidi said it was a gunshot wound, but I think she was joking."

"Mum, she wasn't joking. Don't you remember what happened?"

Sarah shook her head. "This is ridiculous. I said I wanted to discharge myself and get back to Nuneaton, but they said I can't go anywhere. They said that as soon as I'm well enough they're going to send me to somewhere called Frimley. Where on earth is Frimley? It sounds like it's where the Teletubbies live."

"It's in Surrey."

"Same difference."

"They've got a military unit in the hospital at Frimley. They obviously think you'll be safer there."

"Safe from what? Do you know, there are men with guns out there in the corridor? I feel like I'm in prison. I haven't done anything wrong, so why am I not free to go home? The liberties of an Englishwoman say that if I'm not charged…"

"Mum, you don't remember it yet but…" Lydia took a breath, "you shot and killed two Turkish people who were trying to kill you. At least, it's what we're guessing. There were no witnesses. It's why it's so important that you remember what happened."

Sarah's face went blank. "How could I shoot anyone? I don't have a gun."

"You fired my gun. In self-defence, we assume. Remember? The gun was in my drawer in my flat. They're not arresting you – they're protecting you."

"Well, that's something, then."

"Mum, can you remember anything about what you were doing in my flat before this – anything about some work you were doing on your laptop?"

Sarah looked carefully at Lydia. "You look sad, my love. You look like you did when 'he' left. Are you all right?"

Lydia sighed. She obviously wasn't going to restore her mother's memory this session. "Yes, I'm all right. I'm just a bit… well, I've got a difficult decision to take, and I don't know what to do. The stakes are high."

"Is it about a person?"

Lydia nodded.

"Can you tell me who?"

Lydia shook her head. "This is not about James. That's all in the past."

"Do what your heart tells you, not what the laws or conventions or bosses or whoever might say. Even if you get it wrong, you'll have a clear conscience, and you're tough – you can live with the consequences."

"It's my heart that's giving me the conflicting messages."

Throughout the journey in the car to Thames House Lydia wrestled with her dilemma. Her mother had advised her to go with her heart: Reza Hamid was a victim of Gerard's charm and her own idealism, and she didn't deserve to be sent back to be tortured in her own country. They had enjoyed a genuinely good time at the party, and there were real emotional bonds between them.

But her heart was also very angry.

She was still undecided as she walked into the Director-General's office. She looked up at the gorgeous Matisse prints, but they gave her no guidance on what to do.

"Good morning, Lydia. How's your mother?"

"Hello, Adam. She's recovering, but still not remembering anything. She doesn't want to go to Frimley and I don't want it, either – she needs to be near to me."

Lydia knew the decision about Reza had to be made, but she still wanted to put it off – she was happy to talk about her mother.

"So tell me about last night," Adam asked calmly.

It was easy to recount most of it. It was the details of this morning that were so hard. She raced through the party and the attempted hit. She trusted Adam, correctly, not to be judgemental about her sharing a bed with Reza: he made no comment.

Then she disregarded her mother's advice. "This morning Reza attempted to recruit me to a group headed by Gerard and Louisa Bell, dedicated to holding back fascism."

The Director-General betrayed no emotion. "Tell me more."

She told him everything. "I turned them down. I feel like I've been taken for a fool, but I don't want Reza punished, sent back to her country; I think maybe she's been taken for a fool, too."

He put his hands to his chin and closed his eyes. Lydia was getting used to these long pauses. Eventually he opened his eyes.

"You needn't worry about Reza Hamid. We haven't got anything on her – at least not yet. She was careful not to put the offer to you until she'd seen you undress, so she knew you carried no wire. It's your word against hers, and there's no way we could deport a well-known liberal writer to a savage regime – the press would crucify us. She knows that, too."

Lydia nodded. She realised that she had been holding her breath. "I suppose that goes for the Bells, too. We can't prove they work for an underground group, or that they tried to recruit me to pass secrets about the Director-General of the service."

"Exactly. But we can use this clumsy attempt." He took off his glasses.

"How?"

"Firstly, it confirms that Gerard Bell has indeed removed the Vilnius files. It suggests he has hidden them rather than destroying them in the way he would have been ordered by the Vilnius cabal. We can assume there's tension between the Bells and the Vilnius cabal."

"You don't think he really is fighting against the fascists, as Reza said – that he has a plan to destroy Vilnius?"

"We can't afford to sit back and rely on Gerard; he's always had his own agenda. We need to defeat them ourselves. Do you think that you could turn Reza – get her working for us?"

"She seemed very passionate and sincere about the cause. And Louisa finds publishers for her books. She has no incentive to betray the Bells."

The Director-General tapped his glasses on the walnut top of his desk. "In which case the best plan is for you to agree to join Gerard's group, or at least give him some encouragement. That way you can learn more about exactly what he's up to. Of course, you'll have to stall on supplying him proof that you and I have falsified the records held in H11, and you'll have to pull the wool over his eyes in order to continue searching for the Vilnius evidence. But he might give you some protection against Lord Brooke's assassins if you pretend to join his group."

"Do you think Gerard ordered the hit on us outside his house, or do you think it was the Vilnius fascists?"

"Let's not assume yet that they're two separate groups. I've put a team onto investigating the hit. Of course, there's no CCTV covering the place where they attacked you. We traced the scooter via various cameras, but the two men knew where to abandon it and disappear without trace. The scooter had been stolen from Acton earlier in the day. It was a smooth job, but not difficult."

"Who do you think it was?"

"Because of the MO and because they weren't very competent we're assuming it's our Turkish friends, but we're not discounting the possibility that it's rogue elements within our own service, or even other contractors brought in."

"The fact that they failed – do you think it shows they were only trying to frighten me?"

"We simply don't know yet. But one thing is for sure: your life is in danger. That's why I'm not authorising you to go back to your flat. You will need to sleep here in Thames House until this crisis is resolved. If you leave the building, it will be with an armed escort chosen by myself. Now, I want you to go down to H11, charm Gerard Bell, tell him you'll do what he wants. Then I want you to find the missing material."

"Just like that?" Lydia rolled her eyes.

"Just like that. By tomorrow, please." He smiled.

"No problem. Adam." She smiled back.

Lydia was buzzed through into H11 by George. Since the death of Double D and Farah's sudden holiday to Doncaster, they had all been swapping roles to keep the place going.

"The Dong says he'd like to see you in his office, Schizo," George told her as Lydia passed through the main office.

"Thanks, George."

She knocked before walking into Gerard's office. He was sitting in one of the rattan chairs, dressed in baggy white linen trousers and a cotton shirt with pastel deckchair stripes. As usual, his feet were bare in his open-toed sandals.

"Ah, Schizo – the sensation of last night's party! Take a pew. The tongues were wagging, I can tell you – or just hanging out. All the tired old roués were dying to know who you were."

"Sounds like a scene from *My Fair Lady*." Lydia sat down. "Thank you very much for inviting me. I enjoyed it greatly – but not the journey home."

"Why? What happened?" Gerard's wrinkles creased into a concerned frown.

"You know perfectly well what happened. There was an attempted hit on me in the street outside your house."

He sat up straight. "My dear girl, I'm so sorry." He was a good actor, Lydia had to give him that. He looked genuinely horrified. "Are you all right?"

Lydia ignored his concern. "Reza will have given you my answer by now."

"I don't know what you're talking about." His voice and face were deadpan. The look of concern was gone.

"I know you do. Look, I've reconsidered the offer put to me by Reza, and I'd like to accept your offer."

"My offer? My offer of what?"

"To join your anti-fascist group – in return for your protection."

"My dear girl, what on earth are you talking about?" His grey eyes widened, the picture of innocence. "Whatever Reza said to you last night didn't come from me, I can assure you."

"You're cutting her adrift, then? You know she's in a very vulnerable position. She could be deported."

He gave a short laugh. "Don't you worry about Reza. She's lovely, but she's as tough as old boots. I don't know what you've been saying to the Director-General, or what he's been saying to you, or indeed what Reza's been saying to you, but she will always be fine."

Lydia nodded. "I understand you can't say anything to me if you think I'm recording our conversation, but rest assured I will call off my search in return for no more attempts on my life."

He leant forward, fixing her with his green eyes like a mesmerist. He spoke slowly and deliberately. "My dear, if Adam Thornton genuinely wanted to protect your life he would have you withdrawn from this department today. The fact that he's sent you down here again tells us he doesn't give a fig for your well-being. Whatever he's told you to say, you can tell him I'm not playing." He sat back, then looked up at the camera. "Mind you, I don't need you to tell him. He's probably sitting in his office listening to every word we say via the CCTV that is now streamed through direct to him." He bowed his head to the camera.

41

MAGGIE

She knew at once that something was wrong. It was years since Maggie had been trained to deal with computers, and down in H11 there was no internet, but she could tell when her personal laptop from home wasn't quite right. It had booted up just a bit too slowly. It had bleeped when it never bleeped before. Someone had…

"Dean!"

Her husband put his head round the door from the living room. "Yes, girl?"

"Have you been on my laptop?"

"What's the big deal? You sound like someone's stung you on the bum."

"Yes or no: have you been on my laptop?"

"No, I ain't. I don't even know your password. What's the panic?" He came over and put his hand on her shoulder, looking down at the screen.

She brushed it off. "Has Lara been on it?" She was sure that Michael wouldn't bother – he was only interested in his games.

"How would I know? Ask her yourself."

"I hope she's at school." Maggie chewed her lip. "We pay enough for that school – she better not be skiving."

"Can't it wait? What's up, anyway?"

"I think it's been hacked. It's behaving oddly."

"I wouldn't worry, girl." Dean turned away. "Call me if Viagra ads start popping up." He disappeared back into the living room.

She checked her emails, Word files and her list of installed programs, but there was nothing amiss. She hesitated about checking her online bank accounts – what if someone had remotely accessed her laptop, installed malware and was even now monitoring her every keystroke?

She logged off and shut down the computer, slamming the lid shut. She felt that it had gone from being her friend to something toxic, an enemy, overnight. She felt stifled to be in the same room as it.

She shut the door behind her as she went into the living room. Dean was lying on the sofa, flicking through the daytime TV channels.

"I'm off out for a run. When are you out on your shift?" She picked up her phone and slid it into her tracksuit bottoms.

"I'll be gone before you're back. But I'll be back for the kids. Listen..." He reached out and grabbed her knees, drawing her down onto the settee. "Don't worry about your stupid laptop. It's probably just some new automatic upgrade or something. Worst case scenario: I have to take it down Curry's to get it cleaned up – cost a few quid."

She disentangled herself and got to her feet. "Don't you dare take my laptop anywhere – you hear? You have no idea what they would do down at Curry's."

"All right, all right, keep your hair on. Have a good run. Hope it de-stresses you. Have a good day at work."

Maggie left the house still frowning. She set off at the steady pace down the road, but not before she had double checked for anyone who could be tailing her.

She was sure – certain – that someone had tried to access her computer, and had possibly succeeded. Her password was a secure one, but working in MI5 taught you that spooks could get round most barriers. The big question was: who was it who had targeted her? It could be Schizo and those Internal Security investigators, but it could be someone much worse. The Dong had always cautioned them against paranoia, but this was the real thing.

A threat.

42

MO

"Hello. Is that Internal Security?"

"It is. Who am I speaking to?"

"My name is Maureen Dennis. I work in H11, if you've heard of it."

"Of course. How can I help you, Ms Dennis?"

"I need to speak to Mr Peregrine Webb, urgently, on a matter of internal security."

"Mr Webb is out of the office for the next hour or so. Can I take a message for him?"

"It's very urgent. I need to speak to him personally. I can't talk to my own boss in H11, because… because I can't."

"Where are you now, Ms Dennis?"

"I'm on Doncaster station. I'm about to get the train down to London. I'm on a payphone, because I know GCHQ can listen in to my mobile, and I… don't know if I can trust anyone. I need to speak to Mr Webb personally."

"Can you tell me what it's about?"

"It's something I've remembered, worked out. My mind was jogged by a news item. It's very important, maybe national importance."

"Can you let me know the outline details? You're talking to Miss Parmenter, Mr Webb's Personal Assistant."

"I need to talk to him face to face – it's too important for anyone else. I know how phone calls can be intercepted. My train is about to leave – I have to get on."

"Don't worry, Ms Dennis. I will tell Mr Webb, and we will send a team from the service to pick you up from your train when it arrives. Which station?"

"King's Cross, at 3.40. These trains are very fast. How will I recognise our people?"

"We'll recognise you, Ms Dennis, don't you worry. You have a nice relaxing journey down, and we'll do all the rest."

"You're very kind, Miss Parmenter."

"Not at all. We'll see you in no time. Goodbye."

"Bye then."

When she alighted at King's Cross, Mo told herself to stay brave. That nice Miss Parmenter said a team from the service would be here to meet her; a whole team – it suggested they were taking her seriously. All she needed to do was to tell Mr Webb what she remembered about that day when she had the incinerator training, and they would take it from there. Once the secret was out, she would be in no danger. She could go back with Rajah to her house in Penge and put her feet up.

As if he was replying, she felt Rajah shift his weight in his wicker basket, and give a growl.

"Nearly, there, darling," she said as she walked down the platform. She kept her eye out for the team sent to meet her. There was a bustle of travellers, echoing announcements and some giggling Asian girls looking for Harry Potter's platform, but no sign of MI5 on platform 5.

"Ms Dennis?" A tall man in a baseball cap had stepped out from behind one of the brick arches. He looked tense and shifty; Mo didn't like his unshaven chin and a musty smell of tobacco.

"Oh, you gave me a start! Are you from the service, come to meet me?"

"That's right." The man's accent was a lot smarter than his appearance, she thought. It was a shame that standards had slipped in the service over the last few years.

"Well show me your card, then. I'm not getting in a car with any old person. I have been trained, you know."

The man seemed reluctant, but he slid his service card from a pocket in his waxed Barbour jacket.

"Hmm – Special Ops, eh? Why haven't they sent Internal Security?"

"You said it was important. We can't hang around. My colleague is waiting with the car."

Mo didn't think it was a very satisfactory answer, but she didn't push it. "Okay. Well, if you carry my case please, Mr. Longford, I'll carry my cat." She handed him her small blue Marks and Spencer suitcase, and continued walking.

"Isn't this place magnificent?" she breathed as they emerged into the huge vaulted concourse, the webbed ceiling stretching out towards the street. She saw the Pret A Manger outlet; normally she would have stopped and bought a sandwich, but right now she had an acid feeling in the pit of her stomach. This was all so horrible – she felt the same as when she'd seen Vindi in her garden.

The Special Ops man called Longford didn't reply to her. Keeping his head down, he guided her across the concourse, and out to the taxi rank.

"This is us," he said, opening the door to a black cab.

"Oh, is this a service cab? Wasn't there a service car available?"

"Standard taxi, Miss Dennis," Longford said. "So it's best not to say anything confidential, just in case the cabbie can hear." He put the blue suitcase in the car and then helped her into the cab, before walking round and getting in the other side.

As soon as they pulled away, Mo sensed there was something wrong. They joined a queue waiting for the lights at the junction of Pancras Road and Euston Road; she had the urge to open her door and jump out. She clutched the door handle.

She heard the door lock click.

Longford smiled, but it wasn't a warm one. His teeth looked like they hadn't been cleaned in a while. "Security. They all lock automatically when you get going. We'll soon have you with Mr Webb – don't you worry."

Mo took a deep breath. Stop being so silly. Remember you've worked for MI5 for more than two decades.

She bent down and murmured to Rajah, whose face was pressed to the wicker grille of his basket. "You don't like car journeys, do you my love? You've been ever so good – not long now. I'll get you a big treat when you get home." She put her finger through the grille and he licked it. She felt calmer.

She watched the London streets go by as they made their way across the West End, southwards towards Thames House. Mo didn't often go up shopping to the posh shops, so it was fun to see both the smart and the tacky on display on this late afternoon.

But her anxiety gnawed away at her, gradually invading her thoughts. Why was the taxi driver wearing a cap that came right down over his face? Surely he couldn't see properly with that cap. And her escort – he had a baseball cap low over his face. She'd done training once when they'd been taught it was a classic way to avoid CCTV coverage.

"Do you wear that hat to avoid CCTV coverage?" she asked Mr. Longford.

He smiled. "It doesn't do any good to have your face recorded too often in our line of business, Miss Dennis. I'm sure you can appreciate that, what with all your years in the service."

For some unknown reason, a story from her childhood came back to her: Jemima Puddleduck. This man wasn't exactly a gentleman fox with sandy whiskers, but…

The taxi turned off the road, under an arch, and then down a ramp into a NCP car park.

"Where are we going?" She couldn't keep the alarm out of her voice. She didn't want to sound like a silly hysterical woman in front of this colleague but this was an unexpected shock.

"We're changing cars. Mr Webb can't interview you at Thames House, because of the sensitivity of the case. There are certain people in the service who might have an interest in stopping your testimony. I'm sure you understand that." Mr. Longford's voice was calm and soothing, but Mo felt anything but soothed.

The taxi cab made its way down another level.

Mo shook her head. "I've changed my mind. I'm not going to talk to Mr Webb, or anyone from Internal Security. Please let me out right here. I'll make my own way home." She looked the man square in the eye, daring him to obstruct her.

"Miss Dennis, we can't let that happen. Your safety is at risk."

The cabbie parked the taxi in a far corner of the vast car park.

She knew how weak her position was: no one except Miss Parmenter knew she was in London, let alone in this underground place. There seemed to be no members of the public or car park attendants around. She had nothing to defend herself with, and there were two men to overpower her. "Put Mr Webb onto the phone. I won't go anywhere until I've spoken to him."

"Of course." Longford fished inside his jacket pocket. He handed her his phone. "I'll dictate Mr Webb's number."

She held the phone, waiting.

She felt a small scratch on her arm, like that of a rose thorn.

"You've… you've…" She felt outrage, fury, but she couldn't get the words out. "You've…" He'd stuck a needle in her, she knew that, but everything was whirling and…

She slumped forward onto her knees. Her head slammed down onto Rajah's basket.

43

LORD BROOKE

TELEGRAM ENCRYPTED TEXT MESSAGING SERVICE

A ONE OF MY SOURCES HAS TOLD ME THAT YOUR DIRECTOR-GENERAL THINKS HE'S GOT YOU ON TOAST. 'THE NET IS TIGHTENING' – THOSE WERE THE PRECISE WORDS.

B HE'S INSISTING ALL CCTV FROM H11 GOES STRAIGHT TO HIS OFFICE – THAT'S ALL. IT'S NO BIG DEAL. HE'S NOT GOING TO FIND ANYTHING FROM THAT SOURCE. IT WAS ALL SORTED DAYS OR WEEKS AGO, AS I TOLD YOU.

A HE MUST HAVE SOMETHING MORE. HE THINKS YOU'RE A LIABILITY TO OUR CAUSE.

B DID THIS COME FROM YOUR SOURCE?

A YES.

B THEN PERHAPS HE'S PLAYING YOUR SOURCE. PERHAPS YOUR SOURCE IS BLOWN AND HE'S FEEDING YOU A LOAD OF CRAP, JUST TO CREATE DIFFICULTIES BETWEEN US.

A I THINK NOT. MY SOURCE CAME UP WITH SOMETHING ELSE VITAL TODAY – IF HE OR SHE WAS BLOWN, THEY WOULD HAVE NEVER HAVE LET SLIP THIS INFORMATION.

B ARE YOU GOING TO SHARE IT WITH ME?

A NO.

B FAIR ENOUGH, BUT DON'T UNDERESTIMATE ADAM THORNTON.

A I COULD SAY THE SAME TO YOU. THINK ABOUT HOW HE MAY HAVE TIGHTENED THE NET AROUND YOU.

B HE'S DONE IT BY POISONING YOUR MIND AGAINST ME.

A TERMINATES EXCHANGE

44

MADDY

Maddy King slipped the key into the lock of her flat. She was thinking about how she would use this opportunity; she'd had a text from Toby:

Not home tonight. In Zurich. Bank business. I'll try not to enjoy the frauleins too much. Love and snuggles, Tobes xxx.

"Good evening, George."

She whirled round.

Vindi was lounging by the lift. He was dressed in a loose black T-shirt, tight black jeans and expensive trainers. He had a cool grin on his face and a beautiful bouquet of lilies and irises in his hand.

"What the hell are you doing here, Vindi?"

"You can call me Damian if you want. We're off duty." He moved forward, holding out the flowers. "For you, Maddy. Aren't you going to invite me in?"

Maddy stepped back a pace. "How did you… how did you know Toby was away tonight?"

"I'm an intelligence agent – remember?" The smile played round his sensuous lips. She could smell his fragrance over the lilies – Tobacco Rose by Papillon, if she wasn't mistaken. Classy.

"No, seriously – how? Have you been spying on me?" Her heart was galloping.

"I have friends in high places, including Toby's boss. I had him sent to Zurich. He'll have a great time." He licked his lips – a little too theatrically, Maddy thought. "So will we."

She thought about it carefully for, oh, about two seconds.

"Well, that's settled then. You'd better come in." She took the flowers and pushed open the door. "I hope you're not expecting haute cuisine."

"It wasn't what I had in mind."

45

MO

"Mr. Webb can't be with us this evening. He's authorised me to listen to your story, Miss Dennis." The Special Ops man had taken off his baseball cap, revealing a receding hairline.

"Where am I?"

"You're in a service safe house."

Mo looked round the drab undecorated walls, the makeshift blinds and at the peeling paint on the door-frames. "It looks more like a crack den or a student house."

"MI5 budgets aren't limitless, as you well know. As soon as you've told your story, we can take you home to Penge. Your life is at risk until you've done that." She could tell the man was struggling to stay patient.

She was still feeling woozy from the drug, but at least they'd given her a cup of tea. It had come out of a Thermos so it wasn't perfect, but at least it was hot. She was sitting in a moth-eaten brown armchair that smelt of damp and tobacco. The light bulb above her was bare. "Where's Rajah?"

"He's in the next room."

"I want him with me."

The Special Ops man – she remembered that his ID had the name 'Longford' – nodded to the 'cabbie'. "My colleague will get him for you." The 'cabbie' got up and left the room. Mo noted the door wasn't locked. She could hear the sound of traffic in the street outside.

The cabbie returned with the wicker basket. He opened it up, and the large furry bundle that was her adored Burmese cat emerged stiffly from the basket. When Rajah saw her, he immediately leapt into her lap, kneading her thighs.

"He needs feeding."

"All in good time, Miss Dennis. As soon as you've told us your story we can take you home."

"Why did you drug me back in…?" She couldn't recall: was it an underground car park?

"We were being followed by the people you are going to tell us about. They want only harm to you, Miss Dennis. We had to shake them off. Now, what was it you remembered? What memory was it jogged by a news item?"

"Miss Parmenter has briefed you, then?"

She saw them look at each other.

Longford shook his head. "It was Mr. Webb who briefed us. He's authorised us to talk to you."

"Look, I may be half drugged, but I'm not stupid. Unlike you, I've been in the service for over twenty years. There's no way I'm talking to anyone except Mr. Webb. So please get him here now, or I walk out of this shabby place and get myself and Rajah a taxi to Penge." There, that told them!

The cabbie spoke for the first time. "Miss Dennis, with the greatest respect, we value your lengthy service and experience, but time is of the essence. Please tell us your story, or…" He left it hanging.

The threat wasn't lost on Mo. She wasn't actually tied up, but she was their prisoner. They had drugged and abducted her; she was being held at a place unknown, being menaced for the information she held. She noticed both men were wearing gloves.

"You're not a real cabbie, are you? I'd like to see your service ID, please." She kept her chin up, and fixed him with her eyes.

The cabbie didn't blink. "Just tell us what you were going to tell Mr Webb, please."

"I'm saying nothing until Mr. Webb gets here. And don't think you can fob me off with someone masquerading as him – I've met him before." That last bit was made up, but it made her feel better.

The cabbie shook his head. "Look, Miss Dennis, Mr. Webb has authorised us to use drugs on you if you fail to co-operate. So if you don't want…"

"Now why would he do something like that? He knows I've come to co-operate with him. There's no way that Mr. Webb would threaten me like that. There's no way loyal members of the service would threaten me with drugs. If you won't let me ring Mr. Webb, I'm going to get a taxi, go home and phone him." Her voice was quavering; she hoped they'd think it was rage, but there was mounting terror, too. "And I shall report you two for gross discourtesy and threatening me. I've remembered Mr. Longford's name from his card." She was breathing very heavily. Please, please let me go, she silently prayed.

The cabbie nodded to Longford, who got up from the grotty armchair he had been sitting in, and moved towards her.

She shrank back in her chair. "Don't you touch me! Don't you dare!"

Longford moved forward as if he hadn't heard her.

Mo knew it was time to make a last, desperate stand. Making a silent apology to her cat, she hurled Rajah at Longford's face with all the force she could summon. The cat flew through the air with a hideous screech. His claws dug into Longford's face.

"Ow, fuck! Get off!" Longford grappled the cat, but its claws sunk ever deeper.

Mo was up out of the seat, pushing past Longford, making for the door.

The cabbie moved across, behind Longford, barring her way. With a strength born of terror, Mo slammed into him. The cabbie staggered back under the weight of a woman of more than fourteen stone, and for a second Mo thought she might make it. She swung open the door. She could smell the exhaust fumes from the street.

Then an arm was flung around her neck, yanking her back, nearly strangling her.

"Bitch! You're going to pay for this," Longford hissed in her ear. She could see blood on his face. He hauled her back and pushed her down in the chair. He moved behind her, his hands on her shoulders, holding her down.

"Get off me!" Mo summoned up her deepest outrage but she felt no hope. She could see Rajah cowering in the corner of the room, tail bottle-brush. She was so sorry that she had used him in such a way. He hissed, then shot across the room and out of the open door.

The cabbie seemed to have taken command. "Miss Dennis, unless you answer our questions, we will be forced to do something very cruel to your beloved Rajah." He spoke softly and his face remained bland, but there was no mistaking that his threat was real.

Mo had been in the service long enough and had read enough thrillers to know what was going to happen: they were going to kill her. No genuine MI5 men would threaten her cat. She knew Mr. Longford's name and his service number – they wouldn't let her go now.

She screamed. It was a shriek of terror, of defiance and desperation, a cry for help, all rolled into a brief second before

Longford's hand clamped down on her mouth and her head was savagely yanked back.

"Don't piss us about, lady." She could feel his spittle in her ear. "If you want to live you'd better do exactly what we tell you to do." He looked over to the cabbie.

Mo saw the cabbie pull a face and shake his head.

Mo felt a scratch on her neck. Not again!

This time there was blood literally pouring in a wave down her white blouse. It wasn't a scratch. She struggled to understand. There was a bubbling noise and it was coming from somewhere...

She put her hand to her throat; it came away with great gouts of blood on it. She tried desperately to call out, to shriek her anger, her terror and her pain, but no sound came, just the dreadful bubbling noise. She understood now: Longford had cut her throat. No, no, no – she had to fight it!

Her eyes were losing focus and her arms fell limp.

"What are we going to do about the fucking cat?"

Those were the last words Maureen Dennis ever heard.

46

ADAM

"Miss Parmenter hasn't turned up to work today."

Adam had asked Perry to sit, but he was pacing up and down Adam's office carpet, clearly agitated.

"Have you had word from her?"

"She emailed me to say she wasn't feeling well, and that she was taking some holiday; she is currently owed several weeks." Perry stopped behind a chair, and tapped on it.

"Have you phoned her?"

"Yes: no answer. None of this is like her at all; she's always totally reliable."

Adam gave a humourless laugh. "Except when she's passing information over to the Vilnius cabal."

Perry stopped pacing, and leaned over the chair in front of him, his sharp nose thrust aggressively towards Adam. "That's what's caused this – I'm in no doubt at all. It's your responsibility." He glared down at Adam.

"Explain."

"That phone call you made to me: it was too obviously disinformation. The enemy have picked up on it and have realised she's been compromised. So they've either hidden her or they've killed her to cover their tracks."

"What responses have you initiated?"

"I've sent a man round to her place to investigate."

"Good. Keep me informed on any development."

"You're taking this very calmly, I must say." Perry threw his arms about as if to demonstrate that he, at least, wasn't taking anything calmly.

"It doesn't materially alter the crisis. At best, she's taken a few aspirins and gone back to bed to sleep off her illness, and at worst they've killed her and we've lost a conduit for our misinformation."

Perry shook his head. "That's a very dispassionate view I can't share; I've worked closely with her for the last five years."

"And she betrayed your trust. We weren't going to be able to use her extensively, and she was unlikely to be able to tell us anything we didn't know already." Adam paused. "In fact I have already received some much more disturbing news this morning."

"What's that?" Perry stood still at last.

"Lord Brooke has managed to bring the preliminary court hearing on the Vilnius case forward to Wednesday."

"What? Next Wednesday? That's just five days time. The courts don't work that fast."

"They do if Lord Brooke is greasing the wheels. He's got a lot of money and influence behind him."

"So you've got to find the missing evidence by next Wednesday?"

Adam nodded. "I prefer to use the term 'we', Perry, or even 'you': it's a matter of internal security."

"Can't you stall the court case – say there are matters of national security?"

"Not without the backing of the Home Secretary. Effectively, she's the defendant in this case. Obviously I can't brief the Home Secretary about the missing evidence."

"What a mess!"

"Yes. To make things worse, I've just received intelligence of an imminent major terror-related attack. All department heads will be briefed later this morning. At present it's easy for us to forget that the public sees prevention of terrorism as MI5's major role."

"Oh, Christ!" Perry theatrically wheeled away towards the grandfather clock, before turning back.

Adam nodded. "Oh Christ indeed. So you see, Perry, Miss Parmenter not turning up for work this morning is something I'm going to leave in your capable hands."

Perry took a deep breath. "Yes sir. I quite see your point. I'll do my best, and report back to you. And good luck with all the other issues." He marched off to the door, waited a second or two to be buzzed through, and exited.

Adam sat looking at the door for a while after Perry was gone. He felt disquiet, and not just about all these crises arriving at once. Perry was acting out of character. He was normally the most reserved and placid of fellows, on the dull side of dependable, but now he was jittery and excitable. His speech was perhaps slightly slurred. The pressure was obviously getting to him – perhaps Adam had loaded too much onto him, but a section head with over thirty years' experience in the service ought to be able to handle it.

Adam's secure line rang.

"Hello. Who's speaking, please?"

"It's Gerard Bell."

"Hello, Gerard. What can I do for you?"

"Farah – Maureen Dennis, one of my admin assistants in H11 – has disappeared."

"Please explain the circumstances." Adam suppressed an urge to laugh hysterically. He could take one disappearing secretary in a morning, but two…

"I briefed you on the break-in to her house. She was very shaken up, so I sent her to stay with her cousin in Doncaster. I've been phoning daily to check that she's okay. Yesterday morning her cousin said she'd left the house, with her cat and a suitcase. The cousin didn't know where Maureen Dennis was going, but said she was quote 'all of a flutter' unquote. I assumed she'd returned to her house in London, but when I phoned last night, she wasn't there, and she hadn't returned to Doncaster."

"I take it that, given the previous fate of two of her H11 colleagues, there's a good reason to fear for her safety." He left his thoughts unspoken, particularly when you, Gerard, would be the number one suspect for her murder.

"Absolutely. We must do all we can to find her – if it's not already too late."

"I agree, but I am tied up with unrelated crises right now, about which you will hear more later this morning. Perry Webb will give you the resources he can spare and the authorisation to direct the search. However, MI5 resources are about to get stretched critically over the next few days. You know the lady best, so you will know how to target and focus the search effectively."

As if to back up his point about other crises, an orange light on his console started blinking. It was the hotline from Downing Street.

He was about to be summoned.

47

GERARD

"We are meeting in this incident room upstairs due to a grave combination of factors. Nylon is here to help us set everything up for this desperate search." Gerard paused, and looked round what was left of his team.

Maybe looked intense, her glasses gleaming in the computer light. Lydia was fidgeting – she was obviously frustrated not to be searching for the missing files. Nylon was fiddling with a lead in the back of a monitor. Vindi was cool and detached, as always, and George looked like the cat who'd got the cream – she kept glancing across at Vindi and smiling. Gerard drew the obvious conclusion, and hoped it had been pleasure, not business.

"We are here to try to track down our beloved colleague, Farah." Again he paused to check their reactions. Maybe shook her head, Vindi stayed cool, Nylon looked up sharply from behind the monitor screen, George's mouth fell open, while Lydia narrowed her eyes in an accusatory way. "You all know she took some leave after being shocked by a break-in at her house, but yesterday she went missing. She left her cousin's house in Doncaster, taking a suitcase and her cat, and hasn't been seen since. We urgently need to find her. Because we have no internet links to the outside world in H11, we have to do that up here, in the incident room."

"Do you think she's in danger?" Maybe asked.

"I do indeed."

"Do you think it's linked with the deaths of Double D and Luther?" George was blinking back tears already.

"I fear it's a possibility." Gerard weighed his words carefully. He was aware of Lydia's eyes boring into him. "Let's find her and discount it."

"Why are we doing this work when it should be carried out by Internal Security?" Lydia sounded like a cross-examining lawyer.

"I was coming on to that. This morning our Director-General was called to a meeting of COBRA, where they activated Operation Tamperer. For those of you who aren't acquainted with this, it means the security rating has been raised to critical, that a major terrorist attack is imminent, and that the armed forces have been mobilised to work alongside the security services to combat the threat. The target is believed to be a sporting venue somewhere in London this weekend. All leave is cancelled and all MI5 personnel are directed to work on the threat."

"Except us." Lydia folded her arms.

"That's right. The Director-General (who seems to have become quite a friend of yours, Schizo) has deemed Farah's disappearance to be of sufficient gravity to exempt this small team from working on the national crisis. I am grateful to have the services of two former members of Internal Security, Schizo and Vindi, to help the rest of us novices in this field. Any questions?"

"Can I help you?" Nylon blurted it out. "Farah was – is – special to me."

Gerard nodded. "Special to all of us, I can assure you. If you get clearance from your boss, we'd be pleased to have you."

"Farah's mobile phone – has it been traced?" If Vindi was feeling any guilt for his break-in of Farah's house, Gerard couldn't detect it.

"It hasn't been used since the night before she disappeared, and it's not showing up anywhere now. So where do you suggest we start our search, Schizo?"

"CCTV footage of Doncaster train and bus stations."

"My thoughts exactly. The footage has been sent over from Cheltenham, and is ready for you to go through on these consoles. I suggest we get to it with a will. The life of a colleague may depend on it."

It took them less than forty minutes to come up with the first sighting of Farah. She was spotted by Vindi, lugging her suitcase and a cat basket into Doncaster train station. From the first sighting it was easy to follow her progress to the ticket office, then to a public phone box, and finally to see her get on the fast train to London King's Cross.

Gerard immediately asked GCHQ in Cheltenham to make available the CCTV recordings from the London station.

"Any thoughts, impressions, of what you've seen so far?" He asked his team as they were waiting.

Lydia was first to respond. "The fact she used a public phone box suggests she didn't want anyone listening in to her conversation. GCHQ won't have a record, unless they can get us the record of the calls from that phone box. It suggests she had something important to say – something relevant to the deaths of her colleagues, perhaps. Maybe she had identified the person who broke into her house. Perhaps she was in fear of her life."

Gerard studied Vindi's reaction, but, predictably, there was none. That boy would make a good poker player.

Gerard nodded to Lydia. "I agree. So who did she call from that phone box?"

"If it was someone in this room..." Lydia looked round at each person, "...they're not owning up to it. You'd have expected her to have called you." She looked squarely at Gerard.

Gerard spread his hands. "Which she didn't do. So if she was alarmed by something, who else would she have called?"

Again it was Lydia who answered. "If she wanted to report something about someone in this room, she would have called Internal Security. She would have called Peregrine Webb's office."

Gerard was watching Lydia closely, and a momentary flicker of her eyelids told him all he needed to know. As she was talking, she'd worked it out: Farah's call from Doncaster had come through to Miss Parmenter in Perry's office, and...

What was clear to Gerard was that Lydia knew Parmenter had intercepted the call and had passed it on, not to Perry but to persons unknown. He had been correct: Parmenter had been blown.

He kept cool. "That's your next port of call," he said to Lydia. "Get up to Webb's office and find out what happened to that phone call. Meanwhile, we'll follow Farah's journey."

As Lydia got up and left the incident room, Gerard found himself trying to control tears of rage. He had no doubt about what had happened to Farah once they'd got wind she was going to spill some beans. Those bastards! He'd told Brooke: no more killing, and the first thing they'd done was to kill his dearly beloved admin assistant, the woman who had kept them all comforted with tea and cakes over the years – a lady who had never harmed anyone in her life.

The rest of the investigation was depressingly predictable: the CCTV footage from King's Cross showed Farah walking along platform 5 at Kings Cross, being accosted by a man who materialised from behind a pillar, being guided by the man across the concourse into a taxi. All the way through the station they had walked where the CCTV coverage was at its weakest, and the man in a baseball cap never showed his face. It was clear that Farah was being guided by a professional who'd been trained to avoid surveillance and who knew exactly what surveillance there was in the station. He even appeared to be limping to disguise his normal gait.

They checked on the taxi's number plates and followed it up: the taxi had been stolen earlier in the day. There were no clear views of the driver or the passengers as Gerard's team used street cameras to plot the taxi's route across central London. The taxi had turned into the Marble Arch underground car park at 4.10, and that was where the trail ended.

They contacted the NCP, whose staff were helpful – up to a point. Yes, the CCTV cameras in the Marble Arch car park had been vandalised earlier that afternoon – both the ones in the lower floors, and the ones covering the exit. Yes, a stolen taxi had been found abandoned on the second level. Gerard ordered it to be seized for forensic analysis. He was sure it would yield evidence of Farah and her cat, but no evidence of its other two occupants.

Lydia had returned with the news that Perry Webb had never got a message from Farah, and that Parmenter had not turned up to work this morning, claiming leave to which she was entitled; she had been traced taking a British Airways flight to Berne, Switzerland.

"Conclusions, anyone?" Gerard asked the question of his team, but he was insulting their intelligence.

Ten minutes later, Gerard sat in the toilet cubicle, savagely tapping out a Telegram message:

B I SAID THERE WAS TO BE NO MORE KILLING. WHY DID YOU KILL HER?

A ANYTHING THAT HAS BEEN DONE HAS BEEN TO PROTECT

YOU. YOU'VE BEEN VERY UNTIDY.

B WHO KILLED HER? WHERE'S HER BODY?

A THIS IS NONSENSE.

B IF THERE IS ANY MORE VIOLENCE, I WILL BLOW THIS WHOLE THING.

A YOU HAVE NO EVIDENCE. YOU BURNT IT – REMEMBER? IF WE THOUGHT YOU'D LIED TO US, YOU'D BE JOINING YOUR TEA LADY.

There was nothing else he could do. He turned off his phone, stood up, flushed the lavatory, unlocked the cubicle and pushed the door open.

Perry Webb stood at the basins, staring at himself in the mirror. Their eyes met.

Perry swivelled round to face Gerard, before fixing him with a wild stare. He steadied himself, clutching the towel rail beside him.

"Hello, Gerard." He said it with a slurred voice and an aggressive leer on his face.

"Hello, Perry." Oh Christ, what's all this about? The last time I was in a situation like this was in the school bogs at Winchester with some bully who fancied my arse. Don't tell me Perry is propositioning me.

"So why have you been allowed out of your little hutch in the basement, then?" Perry leaned back against the basin.

Gerard looked round; all the cubicle doors were open. They were alone and Perry was between him and the door. "Look Perry, you're obviously tired and emotional, so why don't you go home and sleep it off like a good chap, eh? I won't say anything to anyone."

"You little shit!" A gob of phlegm spat out of Perry's mouth and landed on the white tiles between them. "You've always thought yourself above everyone, but now we know all about you and your wife: you're just common dirty blackmailers, no better than West End spivs."

What was all this about? Perry had always been the model of restraint, dull, sober and boring. Was he having a breakdown or was he just drunk?

"Perry, those are words you may come to regret. I suggest you drink a lot of water and then go home. I strongly advise you not to repeat any of these wild baseless allegations to anyone else. Now, if you'd kindly step aside, I have important work to do. As you know, we're on 'critical' right now."

Perry moved along the basins to block Gerard's route to the door. "Lydia Twomey – she's a damned good investigator. She showed us where to dig the dirt on your sordid little businesses, Gerard. You and Louisa, you've been blackmailing your so-called literary clients for years, using the filthy secrets you hoard down in your hutch. Well, now your chickens are about to come home to roost."

"How, exactly, will they be roosting? What do you mean?"

"This wretched, treacherous business with Brooke: you've subverted my personal assistant, ruined her life, you've probably got your own personal assistant killed by Miles Mason's Special Ops crew, and you think you're going to walk away scot free, don't you? Well, you're not. I'm going to tell Brooke you've played him false, and he'll get Perma-tan Miles to do the same to you as they've done with the others. And Louisa, that stuck-up bitch, she'll be for it too. It's all coming down around your ears, Gerard, and it couldn't happen to a nicer chap."

Gerard took a step forward. "Are you threatening my wife?"

Perry looked down his aristocratic nose at him. "You've been threatening everyone for years and years. You don't like it when the boot's on the other foot, do you?"

Gerard drove his fist into Perry's stomach. It sank into the softness, and he heard the air exhale from Perry's mouth in a violent grunt. He stepped back.

Perry sank to his knees, gasping for breath.

Gerard bent down to whisper the words in Perry's ear. "It was your negligence that's probably killed Mo Dennis. And don't you ever threaten my wife again."

He stepped over Perry and pushed out of the toilets, into the corridor. Two young women bustled past him, oblivious to the scuffle that had just occurred between two extremely senior members of the British security services.

He walked back towards the incident room where his team was waiting for him. He felt dazed, roughed up, and incredibly depressed.

What now?

48

LYDIA

Lydia thought Gerard had aged ten years in the ten minutes it had taken for him to have a toilet break. His face had extra crumples and his shoulders seemed more stooped. Perhaps he really was affected by the fate of Farah.

"So there you have it: it's likely Farah has been abducted and killed by members of our very own service, and there's nothing we can do about it, except hand the case over to Internal Security. I've just spoken to their director, and I'm not holding out many hopes." His voice croaked, and a spasm seemed to cross his face.

There was a leaden silence.

"So what do we do, Dong?" Maybe asked.

"It's nearly six o'clock. You've put in a full shift today. We all go home. We appreciate our loved ones. We try to rest. We pray for Farah if that's your thing. We report for duty tomorrow to combat the current critical national threat. We are at the mercy of others right now." He sighed. For once Lydia didn't think he was acting. "Goodnight."

George, Vindi and Maybe got up and moved over to their bags, ready to go home, but Lydia quickly went to Gerard. "I'd like your permission to put in a few hours' overtime down in H11 this evening."

"Why?" He looked at her with tired eyes.

"I've got work to do for the Director-General. You know what the work entails."

"You aren't allowed to be down there on your own. I'm going home, and I'm sure the DG has his hands full with the national crisis."

"I was going to ask Vindi to work with me. And I've already got the Director-General's permission, so I was asking you as a courtesy."

"So what do you want me to say?" He turned his back on her and walked away.

Lydia turned to the group preparing to leave. "Vindi."

He turned when she called his name. There was a smile on his face, as if he knew what she was going to ask. "Yes?"

"Will you put in a couple of hours down in H11 with me, please?"

Vindi's eyes flicked towards George, who had stopped packing her bag. He paused, then smiled. "Yeah. Why not?"

Lydia could see the wounded look on George's face as she watched Vindi follow her out of the incident room.

As they travelled down to the basement in the lift, Lydia studied Vindi like a hawk. She was searching for any signs of aggression, discomfort or nerves, but he lounged easily against the wall of the lift, his face a picture of relaxation.

It wasn't until they were inside H11 and seated amidst the artificial flowers in the main office that he asked the obvious question. "What are you looking for? Do you want my help, or do you just need my presence because of the rules? Or..." He paused and smiled slyly. "Have I been inveigled down here for an entirely different reason?" He picked a pink plastic lily out of its vase and held it against his face.

"I haven't got you down here to break poor little George's heart, if that's what you were hoping."

"What do you mean?" He pulled a look of injured innocence, then smiled like a cheeky boy.

"She looked devastated when you agreed to come down here. Poor girl – I hope you won't be too cruel when you let her down."

"I thought she looked angry. Don't underestimate George – her claws are sharp when they're unsheathed. You don't cross her lightly."

"So why did you come down here with me?"

"Because you asked. Because we're both on the same side. Because I want to know what you're up to. What is it you're looking for?"

"I'm looking for the murderer of Martin Froome and Dennis Dunn."

"And you think I did it?" He gave a little laugh, and replaced the lily in its vase.

"Gerard and Mo were here in H11 when Dennis Dunn was murdered. He must have let his killer in, so that suggests it was a work colleague. It leaves only four suspects: Maybe, George, Nylon and…"

"Me." Vindi spread his hands. "Actually, there's a fifth suspect, a work colleague whose movements that afternoon are unknown."

"Who?"

"You."

"I have the advantage of knowing that I didn't murder Dennis."

"So why get me all alone down here now? Surely that's very dangerous if you think I did it; I could kill you to shut you up.

There's no one here to rescue you – we're totally sealed off from the world." He flexed his long fingers.

"I'm sitting under a surveillance camera, the feed of which is streamed straight to the Director-General's office. He could be watching us right now."

Vindi laughed outright. "Ha! Don't flatter yourself. He's managing Operation Tamperer – it's a national crisis. He won't have a moment for us little people. Anyway, I'd heard he was off to Cheltenham in a helicopter." He leaned back in his swivel chair. "So – you've got me intrigued now: what are you looking for down here?"

"The murders were to cover up the loss of some vital H11 materials."

"The ones the DG was searching for the other day."

"Yes. The file boxes for those materials have been filled by old stuff which should have been copied and then incinerated. The logbooks state that this task was carried out by Martin Froome and by Dennis Dunn."

"So they put the vital materials in the incinerator instead of the old copied ones?"

"That's what we're all supposed to think. But I think someone has hidden them, somewhere within H11. The Director-General has given me until Tuesday to find them."

"Who do you think hid the materials?"

"The person who was with Martin Froome and Dennis Dunn when they supposedly burned the copied materials."

"Sounds like the Dong to me. He has to be present every time the incinerator is used."

"Yes. He's signed the log."

"The problem with your theory is that he can't have killed Dennis Dunn."

"Find the materials, and we'll find the murderer. Fail to find the materials before Tuesday and we'll never discover the murderer."

"So where do we start?"

"Bell's office. This is a rare chance to look while he's not around. Come on."

Lights flickered on as they peered into Bell's office. The air was stale and smelt of old books. Lydia felt like a naughty girl pushing into forbidden territory.

"Where do we start?" Vindi asked.

"You start with his desk, I'll start with the bookshelf. He's a clever clogs – his hiding place will have some riddle, some joke, or something he thinks only he can work out."

Vindi sat down behind Bell's desk. "You don't like him, do you?"

"I don't know what to think. Do you like him?"

"Oh, I love him. He's an inspiration. He really cares about his team." Vindi looked up at the camera behind him. "And he'll watch every minute of the CCTV tape of this conversation and search tomorrow morning."

Lydia started with the books at the top left corner, taking each one down and flicking through them. She didn't really expect a hollowed copy of *Das Kapital* or the *Concise Oxford English Dictionary* with the materials neatly nestling within, but maybe there would be a sheet of paper with the location of the materials which would flutter to her feet – just like the sheet of paper she had hidden in her own *Penguin Book of English Poetry*.

The Carthaginian statue of Baal in the recess amongst the books watched her impassively. Its blank eyes seemed to mock her efforts.

She kept going, her back to Vindi.

After she'd completed the top shelf she turned to him. "Found anything?"

He shook his head. "Nothing interesting in his drawers. To be honest, I've been distracted."

"By what?"

"You, stretching up to that top shelf – very nice. I can't help it."

She turned back. She didn't know whether to be disturbed, revolted or excited by him, but she knew she had to remain calm and professional.

Gerard Bell's choice of books in his office was fascinating: poetry, philosophy, politics, reference books, some biographies, arranged in no discernibly logical order. She stood back and tried to work out some secret code or order – by the colour of the spines, the subject matter, and authors' names – but nothing came to mind. Bell would no doubt laugh at her feeble efforts when he came to watch this on the CCTV footage.

She turned back to Vindi, who was now staring at the computer screen on Bell's desk.

"Have you got into his account?"

Vindi nodded. "The outer reaches, at least."

Lydia looked up – and froze. The CCTV camera had a drink coaster jammed in front of its lens.

Vindi followed her eyes. He stood up and came round to the front of the desk, smiling. "We don't want to be disturbed, do we? Come here." His voice was soft.

She could smell his expensive cologne and could see his muscles under his sports vest. He moved towards her.

"No!" She side-stepped him and made for the camera. His fingers trailed across her wrist as she passed him: an electric shock seemed to run up her arm. She tore the coaster from the camera. "Are you insane?"

"I could be." His mouth turned down as if he was sulking.

She clapped her hands and spoke as briskly and confidently as she could. "Let's get back to work, then."

Lydia found it hard to concentrate for the next hour. She could still feel where he had touched her wrist, and she found it hard to turn her back and go through the books on the other shelves. She had a growing feeling that she was getting warmer, closer to cracking some puzzle Bell had set her, but she was still in the dark. She took a turn on Bell's computer, but there were areas of the computer which both she and Vindi couldn't access without a password. She made a note to get Adam Thornton to force the password from Bell next time he had the opportunity.

All the time, Baal watched her with clay eyes from his recess within the bookshelves. Lydia really didn't like him.

When they left, Vindi made a token effort to invite Lydia out – after all, it was Friday night – but Lydia pointed out she was forbidden by no less than the Director-General himself for security reasons to leave Thames House without a security detail. They had all been called up for a long Saturday to deal with this terrorist alert.

It was only when Vindi had left the building and she was preparing for sleep behind the curtains in the dormitory upstairs that it came to her: Vindi hadn't blocked the CCTV so he could seduce her – it was just a diversion. He had done it because he didn't want anyone to see what he might discover sitting at Bell's desk.

49

ENSEMBLE

Easter Saturday, and everything on the edge: Adam had time to sit at his own desk, close his eyes and listen to the sonorous chimes of his grandfather clock.

Five o'clock. All the premier league football matches, bar one, were over. The rugby matches: over. The London mega-fun run – the hardest to protect: complete.

No bombs.

The COBRA meeting had considered postponing all high-profile sporting fixtures in the light of the intelligence that a major sporting event was going to be targeted by the bombers, but had decided it would create too much panic, especially when they didn't know what sport was going to be hit.

Now it looked like the decision had been vindicated.

Maybe the bombings had been called off. Maybe they were just postponed. Either way, now was a moment for Adam to enjoy a brief moment of peace.

Mark Longford fingered the scabs on his face, inflicted by that sodding cat. To add insult to injury, the cat had escaped.

He was so tired and pissed off. They'd been waiting in an unmarked van for four hours, ready to go in hard against a known fundamentalists' base, but the order had been delayed. The balloon hadn't gone up when it had been expected, they'd been on standby with nowhere to have a pee and the van steaming up.

The death of the lady had been upsetting, even for someone as experienced as Mark. The fact she had been a colleague made it much worse. It was easy to draw a knife across a throat, but the clearing up was always endlessly complicated. First there was the cock-up with the cat. Then they had to get into disposable overalls, hairnets and gloves. The body had to be carefully wrapped in plastic. The room had to be mopped and scrubbed extra carefully with a cocktail of unpleasant chemicals. The body had to be conveyed into the van without any possible witnesses, then the van had to be driven to the site they often used – a place in Essex where dodgy meat gets dumped. The hole had to be dug, the body buried and the overalls, hairnets and gloves burned, all in the dead of night.

Mark prided himself on his professional detachment, but slitting the throat of a middle-aged lady colleague was bound to prey on your mind a bit, and he and his mate had both been quiet on the drive back into London.

Mark had returned home at four in the morning, only to get the message that Operation Tamperer was on, a terrorist attack imminent and all leave cancelled. He barely got time for some cereal and toast before he was out again, reporting for duty. His colleagues had laughed at his scratches, speculating on what he'd done to get clawed so badly by his wife, but they'd quickly shut up when he gave them the evil eye.

Mark was not someone to mess with.

Maddy King spent her Easter Saturday in high anxiety. She'd been due to go to her parents in Surrey for the holiday, but this crisis had put paid to that. Worse, Toby had insisted on going to watch Harlequins against Saracens at the Stoop. Knowing about the terrorist threat against a sporting venue but not allowed to tell him, she'd tried to persuade him not to go, but he'd been adamant – all his chums were meeting up and going for a few lagers beforehand. She had sat miserably at the CCTV monitors in Thames House, scanning for possible sightings of the alleged conspirators, wondering whether she'd ever see Toby again.

She thought about Vindi, too, and about what was going on down in H11. What was Schizo up to down there? Was she down there today, digging up something bad? Was Vindi with her? She'd texted him, but he hadn't responded.

At least Toby hadn't been blown up at his rugby match. It had finished safely and he'd texted to say he was 'going on somewhere for a few beers', which sent her into fresh convulsions of worry: what if the bombers had changed their target to pubs? They'd attacked them before.

Maggie Willis was sitting a few monitors down from Maddy. She'd noticed how on edge George had been lately, and it was worse today. Something was up between Vindi and her as well – hopefully it was just a bout of healthy lust. But she needed to keep an eye on them both.

Maggie also speculated on what Vindi had been doing down in H11 with Schizo the previous night – whatever it was, it wasn't healthy. And the Dong had looked completely done in when he'd called a halt to the operation to trace poor Farah. She hoped he wouldn't crack up.

Her own family had not taken it well when she'd said she wasn't able to join them for the trip out to her parents in Chigwell. Dean had threatened not to take the kids – 'they're your parents, not mine' – and Lara had thrown a strop. Dean had suggested she pull a sickie, and Maggie had told him in no uncertain terms that such cheating was never, ever an option.

Now the crisis seemed to be past. With any luck this whole thing would be over in a couple of days. But there again, life often wasn't that neat.

Gerard Bell had been appointed commander of the London surveillance section of the operation. It was tedious and he was tired, having slept very badly. He had little experience or expertise in surveillance. Most of his cobbled-together team had little or no idea who he was. They had been sitting, eyes glued to their screens for a full day now without spotting anyone identified as a terrorist.

He thought about the punch last night: no one had pulled him aside and told him there would be a disciplinary procedure, so he supposed Perry hadn't reported it. Anyway, he doubted he'd get hauled up for something between two adults in private. He was more worried about what Perry might tell Lord Brooke. Brooke wouldn't hesitate to eliminate anyone who presented a threat to his plans.

This whole thing had got so complicated, so out of hand and so ugly. Still, at least it wasn't boring.

Bri Powell had been running around like a blue-arsed fly all day. There were so many people today using hardware and software that they were unfamiliar with, that he and his fellow techies had been racing from one malfunction to another, though in most cases it was human error and silly twittering apologies by the perpetrators. Not that he wanted to be out on the frontline with the soldiers – those Para days were long behind him. In fact his technical expertise made him feel quite important – he liked being in control.

He'd spent a lot of the time trying to locate where Lydia Twomey was stationed today, but he hadn't run into her. He'd been thinking about her quite a bit recently. Once you do a bit of research on a subject it's easy to get a bit carried away. The way she'd looked, her arse up in the air, down in Stack 3 when he caught her scrabbling under the shelf, it had totally rocked his boat. She'd opened those big blue eyes in alarm, and he was in heaven. He'd gone back and found the cassette she was trying to reach. Possessing it had given him a card that he wasn't ready to play yet, but the right moment would come soon.

Lydia had completely taken Bri's mind off Maddy King. He must be so shallow to switch his affections so easily. Out of the frying pan, into the fire.

Lydia was on liaison duty with an army unit outside a premier league football match. The match was over and the crowd were streaming past her. Young men were chanting and waving their scarves, fathers were shepherding their bright-eyed kids, the hot dog stand was doing a brisk business, and in the shadows the soldiers waited with their guns. Lydia shuddered to think what carnage could have been wrought, and thanked every deity she knew (except Baal) that the bombings hadn't happened.

She'd rung her mum in hospital to tell her she wouldn't be able to visit her. Sarah had said they'd withdrawn her guard, and asked if it meant that they no longer held her responsible for the shootings. She also said she was being moved to Frimley later in the day. She said she was feeling much better, and that 'certain things were coming back to her'. Lydia told her not to say any more – she couldn't guarantee that this conversation was not being intercepted. Sarah laughed and said 'what rubbish'.

Lydia tried to contact Adam to ask why her mum's guard had been withdrawn, but the answer was pretty obvious: every able-bodied member of the security services had been drummed into combating this terror threat. Lydia could hardly argue against that. It didn't stop her biting at her fingers – accessible fingernails were a dim memory now.

Perry stared at his bedroom wall and wished the day would end.

He had phoned the DG to say he was violently ill and would be more of a hindrance than a help on such a vital day. The DG had sounded preoccupied (unsurprisingly) and had seemed very understanding – even relieved, as if he knew what had happened. He'd said that Perry's deputies, Andrew Elms and Sophie Hutchings, would do an excellent job – not what Perry had wanted to hear.

Perry's stomach was knotted in pain, and he had passed some blood. He put it down to Gerard's punch, but he knew the little white helpers had finally turned on him and betrayed him grievously in his hour of greatest need. He knew it had to be over between them and him.

As for Gerard Bell and Miles Mason, he was still determined to bring down both smarmy traitors, even if it dragged him down with them. He'd sent an email to Lord Brooke from his home computer in which he carried out the threat he'd made to Gerard: he told Brooke that Gerard and Louisa had double-crossed them all. He didn't give any details because he was ashamed that the DG hadn't let him in on what exactly had been going on, but he was sure the email would stir the pot nicely.

Glenys had hovered anxiously all day but he'd told her to leave him alone. A wave of self-loathing broke over him. He closed his eyes, but sleep wouldn't come.

Damian Curry was on liaison duty with an army unit outside a premier league football match in north London. Unlike all the other matches, this one was an evening kick-off and yet to start, so the tension remained high.

He was enjoying himself: the adrenalin was coursing through his body and the army guys were all high on it too, ready to ping at the slightest disturbance, ready to 'waste any towel-head' who was stupid enough to try to bomb a match the whole country and a worldwide TV audience of hundreds of millions wanted to see.

Vindi knew what was coming – he could feel it. These army guys were gung-ho but they had no real chance of intercepting all four of the suspected bombers in this swirling noisy crowd. It was going to get messy.

He waited, earpiece monitoring all the excited chat, eyes peeled for the first bomber.

Lord Brooke looked out of the window to the lovely early evening light falling across Green Park. His phone was in his pocket but it hadn't rung that afternoon. Like everyone else, he was waiting. Everything was on course and long months of planning were finally moving towards fruition. He had put so much work into this and he knew that attention to detail allied with utterly ruthless execution was a winning formula. He only bet on certainties.

The one blot on an otherwise spotless progress sheet was a crazed email he'd received from that idiot, Perry Webb, trying to wind him up about Gerard. As if he needed to be wound up about that bastard! Brooke wasn't sure whether Perry was playing some game on behalf of Adam Thornton, who was almost certainly desperate by this point, or whether Perry was just lashing out because he'd found that his PA had done a runner.

That reminded him: Parmenter had gone off the radar in Switzerland; she needed to be located. She was a canny old bird, and probably thought it wise to hide out somewhere away from both friend and foe for a while. She was correct.

Either way, Lord Brooke knew he held all the aces. All he had to do now was to wait.

Adam Thornton opened his eyes.

He jabbed the button on the console to activate the hotline.

"Yes? Home Secretary speaking."

"This is Adam Thornton. Ma'am, I strongly recommend that we call off the last premier league match, immediately, before it starts."

"Why? Have you new intelligence?"

"No, but as you know we had very firm intelligence that a major sporting event today would be targeted. I understand your reasons for not wanting to postpone all the matches in the land, but this is the only one left to play now. It would be far less radical to postpone a single match, citing specific intelligence."

"But most of the crowd are already at the stadium. There's a huge international audience for the live coverage."

"That's why I think they've chosen this match. There's more: Lord Brooke in his press conference was careful to criticise what he termed 'the weak indulgent approach to the current terror threats' and he promised a crackdown if his clients were restored to power. This is playing into his hands."

A pause.

"I'm sorry – it's too late. You should have put this to COBRA yesterday. Giving me this advice so late is just unhelpful. Any abandonment now would present as panic and weakness. Tell our chaps on the ground to be extra vigilant. The game goes ahead."

The first tentative report to Adam suggested that there had been some problem with the physical structure of a set of stairs, but the second report was clear: a bomb had gone off inside the stadium, somewhere under the new north stand, twenty-one minutes into the game, at 17.51 hours.

Adam made his way to the incident room on the floor above his office. The place was hushed. Hands were over mouths. Then the reports started flooding in and the place became a gabble of voices.

Adam gave the order that the teams outside the stadium should stand by. They should not go into the stadium. He was sure that the bombers would be outside, ready to strike the fleeing crowds.

He was proved correct. The evacuation appeared to be progressing in an orderly fashion when reports were received of disturbances outside the ground. After some initial confusion, it became clear that these disturbances were attacks by three suicide bombers. The promised attack was on.

Two hours later, Adam left the incident room and returned to his office to give the Home Secretary as full a briefing as he could. The line to be given to the media was that the security forces had done a brilliant job to keep casualties to a minimum. The bomb inside the stadium was probably planted somewhere deep inside the structure of the new stand. It had blown away a length of wall and had caused a stairway to collapse. At this point, there had only been two confirmed fatalities and an unspecified number of injuries inside the stadium. In the second wave, the security forces had intercepted and shot dead three suicide bombers before they were able to get to the heart of the crowds issuing from the stadium, but at least one bomb had been set off and to date there were three confirmed fatalities outside the stadium, in addition to the three bombers. The headline figure for the news media was eight fatalities, over fifty injured.

The Home Secretary was incandescent that the game had not been called off, but Adam didn't remind her of the conversation they had shortly before kick-off. As with all such conversations, it was recorded but would never be used in the inevitable ensuing inquiry.

In addition, but not for release to the media, Adam informed the Home Secretary that their intelligence had suggested four bombers; so far only three had been identified and killed, so it was likely a fourth was still at large. He had ordered a hunt and had sent forces into all the known haunts of the three terrorists and their contacts.

There was another serious matter he wanted to raise with the minister about the bomb detonated inside the stadium: it had not been mentioned in any of the intelligence. From the reports in so far, it appeared to have been buried inside the newly built structure. That suggested a plot hatched before the building of the stadium and the bomb buried during the construction work – something way beyond the capabilities of the supposedly unsupported group of four fundamentalist bombers who carried home-made bombs. It echoed the IRA bombing of Margaret Thatcher's Brighton hotel, when the bomb had been planted nearly a month before it was detonated.

Adam couldn't be sure at this early juncture, but he suspected a bigger plot behind this terrible incident.

Lord Brooke was seething. He'd fired off a Telegram message with the words:

FIND HIM AND KILL HIM. DO NOT ALLOW HIM TO BE CAPTURED ALIVE.

Almost everything else had gone very well: the bomb inside the stadium, the bombers outside the stadium – multiple fatalities (although they'd hoped for more). There was plenty of material with which to attack the Home Secretary and to distract the Security Services in the days before the crucial court case. Then the news came in that one of the idiot bombers hadn't showed up at the stadium, hadn't blown himself up. You could plan everything down to the last detail but you had to rely on humans, and humans could always let you down.

He thought about the protests of bleeding-heart liberals like Gerard Bell about the number of deaths, but they obviously weren't students of history. In most revolutions, deaths ran into the thousands, and in the case of the Communist revolutions in Russia, China, Cambodia and others, millions had died. History would judge this revolution as one of the most bloodless ever.

Not that the deaths were over yet. Now was the time, while MI5 and the police were paralysed by the terror attack, to clear the decks of all those who could lay stumbling blocks to the new revolution.

50

LYDIA

On the day after the bombing, it took Lydia fifteen seconds to get through to the busiest man in England, but another ten minutes to convince Adam she needed to visit her mother in Frimley Park Hospital. He had picked up Lydia's call to his personal phone immediately, but he'd vetoed her visit; she was needed down in H11 searching for the vital materials, and given the current emergency he couldn't spare an armed driver to escort her to Frimley. Every able-bodied man licensed to carry a firearm was needed to capture the fourth bomber, who was still at large. Lydia pointed out that her mother was becoming lucid again, and might have in her head the knowledge that could cripple Adam's enemies. Eventually he'd given in.

On the way down to Surrey, Dylan, her driver/guard, had expressed his opinion on the mission. "When I signed in this morning I didn't expect to be taking a girl to visit her mum, stopping at a supermarket on the way to buy flowers." He was a big man with shag spots and a bad haircut.

Lydia didn't bother to reply.

Dylan tried again. "I thought I'd be out tracking down the terrorists who are threatening our country, not taking in the scenery in Surrey."

Lydia bit this time. "Let's be clear about this, Dylan: I am on a mission sanctioned personally by the Director-General, and we are both in considerable danger from assassins who pose far more threat to our country than this fugitive bomber does. You need to be on full alert at all times."

"Yeah, whatever." Dylan's eyes were hidden by his dark glasses, but his lip was curled into a sneer.

Lydia wanted to start 'If I was a man…' but instead she pressed her lips together and scanned the road ahead.

It was nearly eleven o'clock when they finally arrived at the hospital, half an hour into public visiting times, so the car park was already clogged. It was Easter Sunday – not the best day for finding a parking space; they drove round for several minutes before finding one. They got out, Lydia picked up the chrysanthemums (all the supermarket had left) from the back seat, Dylan locked the black Mercedes and they made their way under the multi-storey section of the car park towards the main entrance.

Lydia had already spotted the two men standing on the corner of the new building under the helipad. They wore white coats denoting them as hospital staff, but they had followed with interest Dylan's attempts to find somewhere to park.

As Dylan and Lydia crossed the road to them, one of the men, a thin sallow man, stepped forward, hand outstretched. "Miss Twomey, is it?"

She nodded.

"I'm Doctor Khoury and this is Mr. Aziz. We are here to take you to your mother." He held out his hospital trust lanyard for her inspection. "Because of security issues, we are not using the main entrance. This way, please." He waved her along the side of the building, away from the ER and main entrances.

Lydia looked carefully at Dr Khoury as he walked beside her, while Dylan and Mr. Aziz walked behind them. Dr Khoury had an authentic-looking lanyard, but something didn't feel right about him. He didn't smell of antiseptics, his shoes looked smart rather than comfortable and he was walking faster than she would have expected. Maybe this was just her paranoia, but she'd been trained to be suspicious. She hoped that Dylan behind her was in the same mode.

"Where are you originally from, Dr. Khoury?" she asked.

"Lebanon."

"What would the NHS do without people like you?" She knew she was burbling stupidly, but she was desperately trying to think of some question that would trip up an assassin. "How is my mother?"

"Not so good. That's what we need to talk about before you get to see her." They had turned the corner of the building, and were now in a secluded area between two buildings. Khoury gestured ahead. "We are entering through Entrance B that you see in front of you – through the Eye Treatment Centre. It is closed today."

Entrance B was labelled with huge letters on a wall of blue ceramic tiles, but it was a small door, obviously not normally used by the public. Mounted on the wall above it was a CCTV camera, but… Lydia could see the wire from the back of the camera was loose, disconnected.

It was enough for her.

"Excuse me, I've got something in my eye," she said as casually as she could. "Would you please hold these for a second?" She handed Dr Khoury her flowers. I might be just about to make a complete arse of myself, she thought.

He took the flowers, startled by the suddenness.

She fumbled for her Beretta in its shoulder holster. "Dylan!" She shouted his name, shrill with alarm. There could be no doubt as to what she was telling him.

A gun went off, shockingly near her. She could feel the heat through her jeans. She wondered if she'd been hit.

Miraculously, she found she was holding her gun, the safety catch off. Oh my God, oh my God, oh my God.

Another gunshot behind her – she prayed it was Dylan firing.

She whirled round: Dylan had sunk to his knees and Aziz had moved in for the kill, his gun against Dylan's shaven temple. Another gunshot: Dylan's head jerked sideways, a spurt of blood burst from his temple; his body subsided onto itself, rolling over on the concrete like a half crushed slug.

Lydia raised her gun and fired. It was pure instinct, maybe training. Certainly there was no rational thought in her head. She saw Aziz stagger backwards, a deep frown on his face, and then he was wracked by a spasm and a barking cough which sent blood spewing down his white coat. He turned away from her, staggering towards the car park.

I did that? No way.

She turned to Khoury.

He had dropped her mum's flowers and had his hand inside his white coat. He was pulling his gun out, she was sure. Rules of engagement: she was allowed to shoot him. But perhaps… just do it, for Christ's sakes!

She saw his eyes widen with fear – he knew he was about to die.

She squeezed the trigger. Her gun kicked in her hand. She flinched at the sharp report so close to her.

Khoury's eyes closed as he anticipated the agony of a bullet ripping into him. Then he opened his eyes.

Somehow, she had missed.

She fired again. Again her eyes closed.

She opened her eyes, expecting another body in front of her. She was wrong.

Khoury had his gun in his hand. She'd missed again. How could she possibly miss from two yards? This was like a nightmare – irrational and unfair. She had fired first so she should have won.

She launched herself at Khoury, slamming into his chest. She heard his grunt as the wind was punched out of him. He wasn't a large man, and he staggered backwards. She grabbed his wrist, yanking his gun away from her body. He was stronger than her, and slowly his arm forced the gun back round towards her head.

She swung her foot and kicked away one of his legs. Locked together like dancers, they both collapsed onto the concrete path, him on top. The breath was driven from her.

Inexorably his weight and muscle overpowered her – inch by inch his gun was turned towards her. Her own gun – where was it? She must have dropped it.

She could feel her strength failing. She tried to kick him in the balls, but he was wedged too firmly on top of her. He smiled – a savage gold-tooth victory celebration. He was actually enjoying this.

Blind panic took her, and she lunged towards the smile with her own mouth. Her teeth clamped onto his cheek, then sank into his flesh. She felt bristles from his moustache against her gums. She yanked her head backwards, tearing at his flesh. His scream, just few millimetres from her ear, deafened her, and a gust of his dyspeptic breath washed over her.

Now she sank her teeth into the wrist holding the gun.

"Bitch! Bitch! I'll kill you!"

In her mind she screamed a reply. "Of course you'll kill me, you fucking moron – that's what your gun is for." She kept her teeth fixed in his wrist. She could taste his blood in her mouth. She wanted to vomit.

He'd dropped the gun and she released the grip her teeth had on his wrist. Now he was concentrating on getting both his hands around her neck. His rage had taken over and he was going to throttle her. Blood was pouring from his ripped cheek, spattering her face.

"Whore! Bitch! *Surtuk*! *Fahişe*!" He spat the words into her face. His spittle mixed with his blood.

He was too strong for her; his hands were round her throat, pressing. This won't take long, she thought. My only hope is that someone comes to the rescue.

No, I have no hope.

Her hand scrabbled on the concrete beside her. She felt the shape of a gun. She grasped it just as she began to lose consciousness. She raised the gun to the side of Koury's face. Through grey-bordered fading vision, she saw Khoury's livid face still concentrating on squeezing the life out of her. He had no idea of what was about to happen..

She squeezed the trigger. The muzzle flash and report were shockingly close to her face.

She felt the pressure release on her throat. She saw Khoury's face go slack, blood seeping from his eyes into the wound on his lower cheek. Then the lifeless face crashed down on top of her in a hideous embrace, his bad breath and sticky blood enveloping her. His moustache scratched her cheek.

"Get the fuck off me!" she yelled, even though she knew he was dead.

Franticly, she heaved at his carcase. He refused to move. She felt too exhausted to make the effort – maybe she could lie here until someone found her and took her round the corner to A & E.

Out of all the anguish and terror, a single thought struck her with total clarity: these men – they had been here to kill her mother.

She pushed with renewed energy at the unresponsive weight on top of her.

It flopped away from her.

She got to her knees. Her throat was on fire. She could feel it swell up, and for a moment she worried she might suffocate. Then she was gasping, sucking in great gulps of air, her stomach heaving.

She used a handrail by the hospital entrance to haul herself to her feet and then to steady herself as a wave of giddiness and nausea swept through her.

Two men dressed in the blue overalls of hospital porters were standing silently by the edge of the new building. They were uncertain, ready to retreat round the corner of the building.

Lydia staggered over to where Dylan lay in a heap. She tried to call out to the porters that they should get this one to A & E immediately, but nothing came out of her bruised throat. She felt for a pulse on Dylan's neck, but she couldn't find one.

It was time to find her mother. She turned and made for Entrance B.

She'd expected it to be locked, but obviously Khoury and Aziz had sorted it out, because she was able to push through. She lurched into an empty corridor, past some floor-washing signs and gear, through another door to a corridor with a service counter on the right-hand side. There was a woman sitting behind the glass screen. Lydia propped herself against the counter and tried to control her breathing.

"I'm sorry; the pharmacy is closed at this time on Easter Day." The woman said it without looking up.

"Hi. I'm looking for Brunel Ward." She had to whisper it – she had no voice.

The woman looked up. "Are you all right? Do you need A & E?"

"I need Brunel Ward – very urgently. Please!" Her whisper rose to an impassioned croak.

At this moment an alarm went off in the corridor – a strident klaxon. The woman looked doubtfully at Lydia.

"Please!" Lydia whispered urgently. "I may be able to save the life of one of your patients."

The woman hesitated. "Along Grey Street here, take the stairs on your left up to the first floor, straight along from the stairs along Grey Street, turn left onto Green Street, Brunel is second on your left before you get to the Maternity Suites."

"Thank you, thank you."

Lydia noticed the woman pick up the phone as she turned away, but she ignored it and crashed off down the corridor with the grey stripe on its side, turned left through some doors, hauled herself up the stairs, and pushed through another door. Before she knew it she was standing in front of a nurse who barred her way into a ward with the name Brunel above the doorway. All the while the klaxon sawed its way into her head.

"I've come to see Sarah Twomey. Is she all right?"

The nurse appeared to be shaking. Lydia had no idea whether this was laughter, fear, or some ailment. She was starting to lose a grip on reality herself. The klaxon was still sounding but there seemed to be sirens coming from outside, too.

The nurse closed her eyes. "I'm afraid Mrs Twomey passed away early this morning."

Suddenly all that had been holding Lydia up drained away. She sank to her knees. Her head felt like a giant ball of heavy cotton wool and the clamour of the klaxon was fading. She knew she was losing consciousness but she didn't care.

Her mother was dead.

51

LYDIA

The next minutes (or were they hours?) passed in utter confusion. She wasn't sure if she was conscious, or if she was dreaming, delirious or drugged. Someone asked her if she gave consent to be sedated, and she had no idea what her answer was. At one point she was on her back, watching the lights in the roof of the corridor slipping by like the lines on a road. She knew people were doing things to her and that she cried out in physical pain and emotional anguish. Someone told her everything was going to be all right, but she knew it could never be all right, ever again; her mother was dead and she was the cause. She had led her mother into danger and had failed to save her.

"You're all right now, darling Lyds. You're safe now." The voice was kind, familiar. There was a hand on her arm.

Lydia opened her eyes.

Her mother was sitting in a chair beside the hospital bed. Sarah's left arm was in a sling and she wore a white hospital dressing gown, but she was sitting up, smiling.

Alive.

"Mum." Lydia closed her eyes, then opened them again. This was so confusing. She looked around: she was lying in a hospital bed in a small white room with the light streaming in from a large window. She didn't believe in Heaven.

"They told me you were dead."

Sarah nodded. "I'm sorry about that – I asked them to say it." Seeing her daughter's utter bewilderment, she continued. "When I was moved here to Frimley Park, I had no guards. They told me when they left me that they were all needed for some terrible bombing that's happened up in London. So I arranged to be moved upstairs to this private suite and told the nurses that if anyone asked for me downstairs in the ward they were to say I was dead."

"Why?"

"If people had come to kill me, they'd think I was dead already and they'd go away." Her mother gave a grim laugh. "And that's exactly what happened less than an hour before you arrived. Those two men who were killed outside: Sister Benitez told me they came asking for me. They were dressed as doctors and had security passes, but they went away when sister Benitez told them I was dead. So until all this blows over, if anyone comes asking, I am officially dead."

"Clever old you. You saved yourself, even without the soldiers to guard you." Lydia could feel emotions welling up.

"And clever old you, too. You fought off those assassins. They're both dead, you know. How do you feel?"

"Woozy. Confused. My throat hurts."

"You sound husky – deep, dark and sexy."

"I certainly don't feel sexy."

"The doctor told me the bruising round your neck is nasty, but nothing is permanently damaged. You've been very lucky." Her mother brushed a tear from her eye.

"What about Dylan – my driver?"

"He's dead. I'm very sorry for him and his loved ones. They took him with the two assassins to intensive care, but Sister Benitez said they were all dead on arrival. I'm sorry – it must have been awful for you, my darling." She squeezed Lydia's arm. "And now you must get some rest. I'm in the next room, and there are armed Surrey police guarding the stairs, so you've nothing to worry about."

Lydia shook her head. "I can't rest, Mum. I've got stuff that's urgent. First off, I need to interview you, now you're getting better."

"What, now?"

Lydia nodded. "Yes please. Can you remember any more about the day when you got your injury?"

Sarah closed her eyes. "More and more is coming back to me, and none of it good. When the police came up here an hour ago to check on you, I nearly had palpitations. I was afraid they were coming to interview me about what I did."

"You needn't worry about any of that. The authorities know it was an attempt to kill you, just like it was today. What I need you to remember was what you found out on your computer that made them want to silence you."

Her mother's face clouded over. "It's really silly: I can remember some of it totally clearly, but I know there's more."

Lydia sat up in bed. "Just tell me anything you can remember. Take your time."

"Well, the bit that really got me excited was…" she paused, brow furrowed. "You know you asked me to research some individual names?" Lydia nodded, trying to look patient and encouraging. "I remember their names clearly: Nesrin Cevdet, Ian Forrester and Louisa Bell. Those were the three."

"Spot on, Mum. You see, there's nothing wrong with your memory."

"There is, unfortunately. But I do remember this: I did something a bit wacky. I put all three names together into

Google Search Images, and you know what? I found a picture of all three of them together."

"In the same photograph? Surely not."

Sarah nodded. "I know – it's weird, isn't it? What were the chances of that? It was obviously more than just a coincidence."

"What was the photograph? What was the site they were on?"

"It was a young lad's Facebook page. His name was… oh, I can't remember."

"Take your time."

"He was related to Nesrin Cevdet. I think he was her nephew but his name has gone from my head. He lives in Turkey, and Nesrin was on a visit to Istanbul, where he lives. He posted a picture of his aunt with her friend Ian Forrester."

"Ian Forrester was with Nesrin Cevdet, out in Istanbul?"

"Yes. This lad had tagged him in the photo, as if he knew him. He boasted about all these important people whom he'd driven in his taxi that weekend."

"How do you know that, Mum? You can't read Turkish."

"I'm not stupid, dear. I can use the translation facilities on my laptop. Anyway, I looked more closely at the photos he'd posted, and there in the background to one of them, was none other than Louisa Bell. You can't mistake her. She's very striking."

"So they were all in Istanbul together." Sarah nodded. "When was this picture taken?"

"I can't remember; maybe a year ago, maybe less, I really can't remember."

"Do you know where my clothes are?"

"You're not getting up, Lyds. You're in shock. You need rest, or you'll kill yourself. They said that when you arrived at Brunel Ward you were covered in blood and babbling nonsense. They carted you off to A & E. You were there for ages. I thought you must be dying, like the others."

"I'm not getting up, but I need my phone. What you've just told me is very important. You found something that a whole team of my colleagues failed to find when I gave them exactly the same task to do. You're very clever and you may have just played a vital part in solving this crisis. Now please find me my phone."

Her mother's eyes shone at the praise. "Well, I must say it's been very exciting. It's just awful that people have to be killed. And I know there's something more I need to tell you. I think I've remembered it once, but it's gone out of my head again, somehow."

"Mum. Phone, please, or I'll have to get up to find it."

"Oh yes, of course, dear."

"And while you're finding it, try to remember the name of Nesrin Cevdet's nephew."

Sarah didn't hesitate or blink. "It's Kemal. Kemal Cevdet. Didn't they used to have a leader of their country called Kemal something?"

"Yes they did: Kemal Ataturk. Thank you, Mum. You're wonderful. One day they'll give you a medal for this."

"Ha! More likely a hospital bill. Wait there – don't move. I'll go and ask for your phone."

Two minutes later Lydia was talking on her phone to Adam Thornton.

Adam sounded as if he was in a corridor – voices faded in and out. "I'm so relieved to hear that you and your mother are safe. I was just about to contact you. I was briefed just ten minutes ago on what happened. I must apologise profusely to both of you for the removal of your mother's guard – it wasn't done on my order, but things have rather preoccupied me. A new guard detail is on their way by helicopter to the hospital as we speak."

"My mother has remembered the vital details from her internet research: she found a photo which placed Nesrin Cevdet in Istanbul with both Ian Forrester and Louisa Bell. It was on a Facebook page of an Istanbul taxi driver called Kemal Cevdet. I haven't followed it up yet because the Facebook account will have been deleted and I don't have the facilities here to resurrect it. Besides, I'm lying in a hospital bed."

"That sounds very interesting. Please thank your mother." Adam's lack of excitement disappointed Lydia. "We'll follow it up. How are you feeling now?"

"A bit out of it, drugged up, bruised round the neck, but okay. Thank you for asking."

"Good. I need you to return to London on the helicopter that brings your mother's new guard detail. The hours are ticking down to Wednesday's deadline, and you're still the best hope of finding what needs to be found."

"Yes sir. I'll get someone to find my clothes. They were rather blood-spattered when I was last wearing them. I'll be with you as soon as possible, just as soon as I've recovered from nearly being throttled and as long as I'm released by the hospital – and by my mother."

"Splendid. Report straight to me when you arrive."

Was Adam autistic or just too busy to express concern, she wondered, as she struggled out of bed in her hospital gown?

52

MARK

Easter Sunday had been a very long tedious day, following an unpleasant Good Friday and a long tiring Easter Saturday. When Mark Longford and Darren Holmes were finally stood down at 9pm all they wanted to do was to go home and sleep. They'd spent a pointless day being moved round London by their MI5 commanders, searching for the fourth bomber in places they knew would prove fruitless, but now it was time to deliver: they had to carry out the orders from their 'shadow commander' – go in and 'disappear' the bastard.

They knew where they would find Ahmed Fazouli. That was the easy bit: they themselves had set the bombers up with the safe house in the first place. The problem was getting in there quietly and extracting him without witnesses. Fazouli would have an active bomb and a twitchy finger, Mark and Darren were shattered, and the whole city was on tenterhooks, looking for terrorists out of their back windows. Once they'd got Fazouli to a lay-by on the A127, there was the business of garrotting him without him kicking out their windscreen. Finally, there was digging him a grave next to the one they'd dug on Friday for the MI5 lady. It was going to be another knackering night at best, with plenty of scope for a cock-up.

Their target was in a third-floor flat off Joyce Avenue, Edmonton. It had been chosen because the CCTV in the area was crap and because there was no community cohesion – no one noticed anything that happened in this neck of the woods in north London, and even if they did, they'd be too scared or too hostile to report it to any authorities. It was Cevdet territory, in walking distance from the football stadium where the bombing took place. Everything had been fine until this twat had bottled it at the stadium.

Mark and Darren parked their Citroen Berlingo at the foot of the flats on a double yellow line but it wouldn't attract any attention in this area. They took the lift up to the third floor; it smelt of piss and weed, but at least it was empty. The safe flat was just two doors along from the lift.

Darren knocked on the door; Mark hung back, gun concealed behind his back.

There was no response.

Darren nodded to Mark, who stepped forward and slid a single sheet of paper under the door. Written on it were the words:

IT IS YOUR FRIENDS COME TO TAKE YOU TO A BOAT IN FELIXSTOWE. GOLDEN HORN.

The last two words were the password they'd used in communication with the bombers before, so they were hopeful Ahmed would open the door without a fuss.

Still no response. They had a Plan B: blow the door off its hinges, go in and shoot the bastard, but it would be messy.

Darren nodded to Mark again.

Darren took a set of keys from his pocket, found the right one, and inserted it into the keyhole of the heavy door lock. He opened the door a few inches, but as they'd predicted, the chain on the door prevented it being opened any further.

Mark stepped forward. He leant against the door and kept his voice to a whisper. "Ahmed, we know you're in there. We've come to help you – get you out of the country. We've got a new passport for you – everything you need."

There was no reply, but Mark knew they had their man – he could hear breathing the other side of the door, and he could smell food.

"Come on, Ahmed. We can't stay here all night. If you don't open up now, we're off to tell our boss that you refused our help."

"Why do you want to help me?" Fazouli sounded on the verge of tears.

Mark and Daren exchanged smiles.

"Our boss ordered it. He promised you all the help you needed – remember?"

"My bomb did not go off. It wasn't my fault. Allah did not favour me."

"Yeah, yeah. We're not blaming you for anything, Ahmed. We're here to get you on a boat out of Felixstowe. We don't care what you've done or not done, mate. But if you leave us out here much longer someone is going to come along and then things will get very ugly, so just open the door – all right?"

"I don't deserve to be saved."

Darren mouthed the words 'we're going in', and stood poised.

The explosion was like a punch to Mark's stomach, driving the wind from his lungs. It threw him backwards, slamming him into the wall on the opposite side of the corridor. The mangled door sagged off its hinges, and a cloud of ugly smoke was billowing down the corridor. There was a nasty bloodstained mess of flesh and fabric plastered to its inside.

"Shit! The twat's blown himself up." Darren was hauling Mark upright. "Let's get the fuck out of here."

Mark hardly heard his mate – his ears seemed to be a whirl of feedback. He stuffed his gun back into his jacket pocket and ran, following Darren along the corridor, towards the lifts. Darren didn't stop to get the lift, but carried on, down the stairs.

They took the stairs three at a time, slowing to a walk on each of the two landings. Mark could feel the adrenalin coursing, but he stayed cool. He was a veteran of this sort of thing.

They got to the Berlingo without hearing any shouts and without seeing any potential witnesses. Darren started it up and they swung away from the double yellow lines; they were off the estate within sixty seconds.

"Let's hope the note you posted him got burnt in the blast," Darren said.

"It won't tell anyone anything." Mark wasn't bothered. "The important thing is we get a decent night's sleep after all."

53

ADAM

It wasn't an ordinary Monday morning at work, just as it hadn't been an ordinary weekend. It was Easter Bank Holiday, but Thames House was firing on all cylinders, all leave cancelled. Even though they'd found the fourth bomber, Ahmed Fazouli, and intelligence suggested that there were no more immediate threats, there were post-mortems to be done, forensic examinations of the flat where he'd apparently blown himself up, examination of the extremely fragmentary CCTV coverage in the area, together with trails to be followed on who had hired the flat, where they had got their bomb-making equipment, who had given the bombers logistical and technical support, who had radicalised them, and much, much more. Parliament was in recess for its Easter holiday, but the Home Secretary needed all the answers by yesterday.

Adam was pretty sure the investigations would lead to dead ends. There were reports from the neighbours who said they heard voices in the corridor just before the bomb blast that killed Fazouli, but there were no CCTV images and no visual witnesses. There were fragments of a note that suggested accomplices, but the door had been chained from the inside, so he'd blown himself up without any assistance. The people behind this attack were just too professional and co-ordinated – it would take some extraordinary stroke of luck to connect Lord Brooke and the Vilnius cabal to this atrocity. Adam didn't believe in luck.

He took a sip of his coffee. He'd been living on coffee for the last few days – it was better than Benzedrine. He synchronised his breathing to his grandfather clock.

He thought back to his meeting with Lydia Twomey the night before. It had been very uncomfortable: the bruises round her neck were an ugly reminder that he'd failed to protect her or her mother from Brooke's assassins; his hauling her out of a hospital bed to return to work at Thames House was brutal, maybe inhuman, but he felt he'd had no alternative: the court case was just two days away and if the Vilnius evidence hadn't been found by then, the coup d'etat would succeed. Yes, the picture of Cevdets with Louisa Bell and Ian Forrester was useful, but it didn't tie Vilnius or Brooke to the case, and it didn't provide the key to finding the lost evidence. Lydia needed to go back to searching. She would be safer from assassination in Thames House, he assured her.

At least the picture discovered by Sarah Twomey and retrieved by the technicians from Kemal Cevdet's deleted Facebook account had opened up one last avenue of hope, one that he was about to try and open up.

"Come in, Gerard."

Gerard entered Adam's office, and padded across the thick carpet in his open-toed sandals. He was wearing his usual white linen suit and a jazzy Nelson Mandela shirt.

"Do sit." Adam indicated the armchair next to his own.

Gerard sat down, crossed his legs and smiled at Adam. "This is cosy. I'm very flattered that you should spend some of your precious time on such a crucial day to have a chat with me."

"I've asked to see you because I want to appeal to your decency, your sense of justice, and to your political conscience." Adam paused, but Gerard didn't react. "We both know you have hidden rather than destroyed a set of evidence held in H11 that could convict a ring of politicians of a right-wing hue of certain serious sexual misdemeanours."

"That was an awkward mouthful."

"I studied law, not literature." Adam continued. "These documents are due to be used in a court case in two days time. I need you to hand them over to me this morning. If you don't do so, the Home Secretary and several people in this service will be forced to resign and this government will fall to a far-right coup. Power will be in the hands of those who wish to end democracy. Is that what you want?"

Gerard's craggy features remained impassive. "Last time I looked, there were materials in the relevant file boxes. If they prove to be fakes, it won't have been me who falsified the materials."

"Gerard, we both know what has gone on. I am appealing to your sense of..." Adam struggled for the correct word. "Look, I know you hate Brooke and all those hard right bastards. Why are you facilitating or maybe even supporting their coup?"

"I don't know what you're talking about, Adam."

Adam sighed. "I hadn't wanted to bring this up, but it looks as if I will be forced to."

"Ah, at last you've got to the point." Gerard sat back.

"As you know, your friends killed Lydia Twomey's mother yesterday to shut her up. I hope you're ashamed of that."

No response from Gerard. His face remained set like a Lucien Freud painting.

Adam continued. "Before she died, she had led us to a picture taken in Istanbul last year which shows together in the same frame the Cevdets, Ian Forrester (the man known to have stalked Dennis Dunn and is suspected of killing him and Martin Froome) and your wife, Louisa. Add to that the fact that Lord Brooke was in Istanbul on the exact date of the photograph, and you can see we have strong evidence to link Louisa to conspiracy to murder, as well as conspiracy to overthrow the legal government."

"Extremely weak evidence, I'd say." Gerard blinked several times, and examined his hands.

Encouraged by Gerard's obvious dismay, Adam ploughed on. "We are willing to offer Louisa and yourself an amnesty if you hand over the lost materials. If you hang onto them you have absolutely nothing to gain except a rabidly right-wing government, and you endanger both yourself and your wife."

"An amnesty!" Gerard barked a laugh. "Oh, thank you so much! I have a permanent amnesty already."

"What do you mean?"

"You can never prosecute me or Louisa for conspiring in a plot that can never officially exist. If you prosecute me you'll have to admit to the Home Secretary that you lied to her about the missing documents and that you covered it up with falsified documents smuggled by you into H11. I am bomb-proof and you know it. I need no amnesty from you."

Adam paused. This wasn't going well. He needed to try another tack. "Do you think you're really doing the best thing for Louisa? We will be handing over the photo to the police who are investigating the murder of Lydia's mother."

Gerard shook his head. "Adam, you've played your last card desperately and very badly. You have threatened my wife. You've offered an amnesty which could be rescinded at any time in the future when you want to betray us. You've given me the best incentive possible not to co-operate with you – that is, of course, if I had indeed hidden these materials, which of course I deny categorically. As for loyalty to the cause, it's your cause, not mine. It's your job on the line, not mine. Do you think I'm going to be swayed by the promise to keep my dead-end job in your deepest basement?"

"Let's forget about self-interest, then. Let's ignore the threat to your wife's well-being. Let's concentrate on doing what is right."

Gerard threw his head back. His eyes were shining. "Some years ago I stood up for what was right: you'll remember I blew the whistle on another serious sex scandal involving politicians, murders and paedophilia in Northern Ireland. The result was that an innocent officer formerly in our service served decades in prison, I was sent to the outer reaches and then to H11, while the politicians and the MI5 officers involved in cover-up, including the precious Peregrine Webb, went scot free."

"It was regrettable, but it was some years ago, before my time in charge."

"And this vital evidence on these right-wing politicians that you say has gone missing: if it could convict them of serious sexual misdemeanours, why hasn't it already been used to do exactly that? Could it be that you're part of a cover-up?" Gerard got to his feet. "I'm sorry, Adam, but you're defending a rotten corrupt state by threatening me and my wife. Hang your head in shame."

He turned on his heels and strode off to the door.

Hmm, thought Adam: that could have gone better. "Think it over," he called.

The door had already shut.

54

PERRY

Peregrine Webb felt like shit warmed up but he'd made it into work on a Bank Holiday Monday. Every bone in his body ached. Every pore in his skin was sweating. He craved a little white helper but he'd flushed them all away last night. In the middle of briefing his top officers, Andrew Elms and Sophie Hutchings, he'd broken off to rush to the lavatory where he'd puked piteously, but he'd come back and finished directing them to their tasks for the day: Andrew's team was to track down Maureen Dennis, or identify her killers, and Sophie's team was tasked with identifying the two killers shot dead at Frimley Park Hospital. The honour of the service was at stake: one officer – Dylan Smith – as well as Lydia Twomey's mother had been killed, and Maureen Dennis was presumed killed. It was time to fight back – put these bastards on the defensive. He didn't say it but it was uppermost in his mind: if he could nail Perma-tan Miles Mason and Special Ops, then it would all be worth it.

As soon as Andrew and Sophie had left his office, Perry examined his hands: they were shaking uncontrollably. It was as if he had the DTs. But he was made of stern stuff – he came from a proud family – and he wasn't going to blot the family escutcheon. He wondered if Andrew, Sophie or his temporary PA had noticed his problems. Really, it didn't matter. All that counted was getting back at these swine who'd been killing with impunity.

It was Andrew who called in with the first good news.

"We've found Maureen Dennis's cat, sir."

He rolled his eyes and he looked up at the portrait of the Queen above his desk. "What's the significance of this?"

"She had it with her when she went missing."

"Where did you find it?"

"Some waste ground in Edmonton. Apparently it's a very valuable Burmese cat, so the cat lovers who rescued it took good care of it. It was very hungry and let them feed it. It had a microchip implant, so they were able to trace the owner. They tried to contact Maureen Dennis to return it. That's how we got contacted."

"Where's the cat now?"

"Downstairs, with Reception Security. The people who found it came all the way over from Edmonton."

"We must arrange a handsome reward for them. Andrew, get the cat taken to forensics. I want every inch of that cat examined and any traces of human DNA collected and identified. And this is strictly hush-hush – I don't want anyone except the people directly involved in the forensics knowing anything about it."

"Of course, sir."

Perry put the phone down. He felt better already.

55

GERARD

Gerard closed his eyes and sat back. The rattan chair creaked. It'll soon be over, he told himself – at least this phase will be.

He opened his eyes. His Carthaginian god stared back at him from the bookshelf. Baal had never let him down, and wouldn't do so today.

He turned to watch Lydia tapping away furiously at the keyboard on his desk. He had to admire her perseverance, even if he was slightly disappointed by her lack of intellectual inspiration. Hacking away with a terrible cough, she had spent the entire day searching, her bruised neck swathed in a scarf; she hadn't come near to finding the wretched missing evidence. He'd thought about dropping a clue, just to make his day a tiny bit more interesting, but that would be irresponsible.

She'd made one correct assumption: she'd looked him in the face and said "I'm presuming the hiding place is bound up with some intellectual puzzle you've set."

"I don't know what you're talking about," he'd replied. "There are no missing materials – the Home Secretary herself checked the file boxes in question, in the presence of our revered Director-General, and declared the materials all present."

She wasn't put off. "You will have set some puzzle you think only you can solve because you really do believe that you're cleverer than everyone else."

"I think you'll find that 'more clever' is the correct grammar." He went back to his *Times* crossword.

He couldn't settle to it. Normally he could sail through it in less than twenty minutes, but today the clues by one of his favourite setters might as well have been in Hottentot clicks.

His conversation with Adam was still buzzing round his head. Most of what Adam had said was true: Gerard did hate Brooke and his fascist backers, and it would satisfy him greatly to dump them in the proverbial shit. But first he needed to dump the present blandly rotten establishment in it. Clods like Perry and nonentities like Adam didn't deserve to be saved if they couldn't save themselves.

Lydia Twomey was another matter altogether. He studied her furrowed brow – she was lost in ferocious focus on her task. He followed her big blue eyes scanning the screen as she pressed the scroll bar. She was cute, clever and honest; she didn't deserve the failure that was now almost certain. She certainly hadn't deserved to have lost her mother, and she didn't deserve to have been brutally assaulted and nearly killed herself. He marvelled she still had such energy after the trauma of Easter Day. He'd have liked her to defeat Brooke, but that wasn't how the world worked.

And there was another thing: Reza Hamid had insisted on meeting him this evening. It was never bland or boring with Reza, but he was feeling much too tired. He thought about standing her up, but a bit of TLC and acting the vulnerable old roué would probably smooth whatever had ruffled her feathers. It might even perk him up, too.

Lydia looked up from his computer. "There are areas of your computer I can't access. It's demanding a password."

"So?"

"We're not allowed to have any areas of any computer down here that can't be accessed by all staff."

"Thank you for informing me."

"Please give me the password."

He was about to tell her to get the Director-General to order him, but he hesitated. She would probably do exactly what he challenged her to do. She deserved a break, and it would relieve the tedium of his day to see if she could find anything worthwhile. He was pretty sure she wouldn't find anything; she still had no idea what she was looking for.

"hesperus7. All lower case."

"Thank you."

He'd change the password tomorrow. Anyway, it was almost too late: the court case was less than forty hours away. He turned back to his crossword. 'Moderates get revolutionary to swallow arsenic': the answer was staring him in the face, just as the answer to Lydia's search was now a few keystrokes away, but he just couldn't see it.

Gerard arrived at Reza's flat in Fulham just after eight. He'd taken a taxi and had spent the journey looking out of the back to check he wasn't being tailed. So what if someone did follow him, anyway? He knew all the dirt on them, and now it seemed that they too knew all the dirt on him. They were all in the dirt together. Lydia had found nothing on his computer so now all she could do was to wait for more dirt to hit the public domain at Wednesday's court case.

Reza opened her door to him, and stood aside as he walked into the hall. She shut the door. He caught a glimpse of that fiery glance she gave him when she was angry, but he was already committed to sliding his arm around her waist, pulling her to him, and placing his mouth on hers. He felt the moist warmth of her lips. Immediately she pulled away, shoving his chest and shaking her head.

"No, no! I said I needed to talk to you, not to fuck you."

Gerard stepped back. This wasn't entirely unexpected, but it was still disagreeable. "What's the problem, my darling?"

She was wiping her mouth, eyes blazing. "You've just come here for your usual, have you, as if nothing was wrong?"

"I don't know what you're talking about." He'd said that to Adam, then to Lydia, and now to Reza. Each time he knew exactly what they were talking about. He felt like St Peter, thrice denying Jesus before betraying him. "Can we sit down and talk calmly about whatever it is that's upsetting you, please."

She turned, her black hair swirling across her face, and led the way into her small living room. "Sit down." She indicated the armchair.

He obeyed, trying to convey an expression of injured innocence. "What is it, my darling?"

She remained standing, holding onto the door with such ferocity that her knuckles showed up livid white. "Don't call me your darling ever again. If there was once the remotest feeling between us, and I very much doubt that now, it has been replaced by my total and utter contempt for you."

He loved the way her English was so perfect and yet her accent was Middle Eastern. "Have you seen the film 'A Man and a Woman'? Probably not – it was 1966, before you were born. But you should see it for the most beautiful actress, Anouk Aimee."

"What is all this bullshit?" She spat out the words. "Don't think you can deflect me."

"You look just like Anouk Aimee in 1966, standing there at the door like an avenging angel. I am entranced."

"I need to speak to you about the present, and you talk this crap about 1966."

"I only mention Anouk Aimee to pass the time, my darling, while I wait for you to tell me what this is all about."

"Your betrayal."

"Do you mean our betrayal of Louisa? She knows all about us, as you are fully aware."

"One thing you're not is stupid, so don't act as if you are."

"So why don't you sit down on the sofa, take a deep breath, and then calmly tell me all about the betrayal you want to discuss?"

She stood her ground, clutching the door. "You've betrayed the cause – our cause."

"In what way have I betrayed our cause? Who has put this strange notion in your head?" He kept up his injured innocence rather well, he thought, although maybe he'd strayed into a few film-script clichés.

"Don't patronise me!" There was venom and vehemence in her voice. "We had a plan: draw out Brooke and his vile fascist backers into the open with promises that you had destroyed the evidence of their disgusting crimes and then produce the evidence to destroy their reputations and their political ambitions."

"That was the plan. It still is the plan. What's the problem?"

"You're not intending to publish the evidence, are you? I know you're going to keep it all safe and allow the court case to go ahead on Wednesday. You're going to allow them to bring down this government, and you'll sit back and let them set up a right-wing dictatorship."

"Whatever has given you this wild idea?"

"I have found out that you and Louisa have been blackmailing Brooke's friends for years, even decades, using the evidence you keep in that cess-pit archive of yours."

"Who told you this?" Gerard shifted his weight. He felt strangely gaseous all of a sudden.

"Does it matter who told me? It's true."

"Yes, it does matter, because it's a complete fabrication."

"I received convincing evidence of your blackmail activities delivered to this address today by special courier."

"Ah." Gerard sighed. "It came from Brooke. He's trying to drive a wedge between us."

"He's succeeded, Gerard. He's convinced me: you are only interested in making money from blackmail, and in paying back your old enemies in the MI5 establishment. At last I can see you for what you really are: a bitter, greedy old man. You're a lecher who has used me like you've used countless other women before me."

"Oh, come off it, Reza. We used each other. You got a publishing deal out of it, or had you forgotten?" He gave himself a mental slap – retaliation would be counter-productive. Stick to the injured innocence.

"You even wanted me to seduce that lovely young woman, Lydia, just so you could betray her as well. Betrayal is so ingrained in your life that you don't think twice about it – it's become normal. Do you feel any guilt at all?"

Gerard shook his head in a show of sorrow. "Reza, my darling…"

"I'm not your darling."

"You will always be a darling to me, the most lovely, fascinating woman I have met. You said you called me here so we could talk. You've had your say. What you've regurgitated is a tissue of lies concocted by Brooke. I can assure you that I am still fully intending to release the evidence before Wednesday, and to bring down the evil men we vowed together to destroy. I promise you."

Reza looked away, shaking her head. "I don't believe you." She almost whispered it. "I would love to believe you, but I can't."

"So why did you call me here, if nothing I can say will change your mind? You're far too intelligent and sensitive a woman to have called me here just to spit accusations at me. Do you want to see me cry, to suffer? Is that it? I've never put you down as someone who enjoyed a melodrama, a shouting scene. You're better than that, Reza my darling."

"I called you here to kill you, Gerard." She said it calmly, stripped of emotion, as if the fire that had been burning earlier was extinguished.

"I see." Gerard couldn't think what to say or do. He didn't know what to think, except that he had grievously misjudged this woman. Of course he knew that she was fiery and passionate but he really hadn't seen this coming. Was it age that had blinded him? Perhaps he had taken her too much for granted. The incident with Lydia had been ill-judged, he had to admit, but it was hardly motive to kill him.

She continued. "I think that's what Brooke probably wanted me to do, when he sent me the evidence of your betrayal. I think he wants you dead because he's finally convinced that you haven't kept your side of the bargain to destroy the evidence – you're hiding it, ready to blackmail his clients again once they've taken power."

It was on the tip of Gerard's tongue to assure Reza he'd set up a mechanism for exposing the hidden evidence if he died unexpectedly. But he kept his mouth shut – if she knew that, she'd surely kill him to get the evidence out in the open. It would be a lie, anyway – he was intending to set up such a mechanism, just in case Brooke sent his assassins after him, but he was only halfway through organising it.

"So how are you going to kill me, Reza? You know I still love you passionately." His spook training was coming to the fore. She hadn't taken the opportunity to poison him, so she would need to commit an act of violence against him. Was she psychologically capable of such a thing? Definitely – she was very strong willed and had left a country where killings had become routine. So how would she try it? Out of Thames House, he always carried a gun in his pocket, but he couldn't get it into play quickly enough if she was holding a knife in the hand obscured by the door.

"I'm not going to kill you. I can't do it." She rested her head against the door. She sounded tired. "You may have betrayed everyone who ever loved or respected you, but you're not a killer. I know you haven't been responsible for all the deaths that have occurred round this case. I don't have the right to judge and convict you and I'm not going to do Lord Brooke's dirty work for him. I called you here to say goodbye and to explain why I will never see you again. I'm getting a taxi to an airport and then the first flight to anywhere a long way from here. One day, when it's all over, maybe I'll write a book all about betrayal and corruption."

Gerard smiled for the first time that day. "That's my girl. It'll be a bestseller."

"Now you need to go." She didn't return his smile. "Please thank Louisa for all she did for my career."

Gerard struggled to lever himself out of the low armchair, but he managed it, puffing a little. He really was out of shape, and he would have been defenceless if she had attacked him where he was sitting. It was true: he was getting old and careless.

As he passed her by the door, he moved to kiss her one last time.

She stepped back against the wall. "Please go. You make my flesh crawl."

There wasn't anything else to say; as a last line it was pretty conclusive. He let himself out of her front door and closed it without turning back. He stood on the pavement outside, fished in his pocket for his phone then called for a taxi.

He stood leaning against the low wall in front of the house. The taxi would be five minutes, so Reza would have to watch him standing there for a while longer, and then he would be out of her life.

The death threat had been a wake-up call: as soon as he got home, he needed to brief Louisa on how to read the clues to locate the missing evidence files – just in case something happened to him. He'd never thought before that he was in any danger from Brooke, but what Reza had said had rattled him. Was Louisa in danger as well? He needed to warn her – maybe she should pop over to their French bolthole until this all blew over.

A young couple passed him, chattering excitedly about some gig they were going to that night. Gerard smiled at them – what he'd give to be young again.

There was a gangly chap following them. He was limping, and just as he got to Gerard he stumbled, nearly falling onto Gerard. Gerard put out his hand to ward off the man; the man lightly brushed against him, his watch or something metallic catching Gerard's hand.

"Sorry, mate." The man looked away, but Gerard noticed he had some nasty scratches on his face.

The man limped on down the street.

No, maybe he didn't want to be young again. For every nice young couple, there were poor sad cases like the man with the scratched face. And Reza – she might be a strong woman, but he was sure she'd be crying in her flat behind him.

He spotted the cab moving slowly between the rows of cars parked on both sides of the road. He levered himself up from where he had been resting against the low wall, and moved forward to the road, his arm up.

Christ! He felt a sudden pain in his chest – so violent that he gasped like a fish thrashing in the bottom of a boat.

He staggered forward, lurched against the cab door, and pulled it open.

"Where to, sir?" He could see the cabbie eying him suspiciously.

With a desperate effort he managed to keep his voice steady. "Kensington, please. Phillimore Place."

"Right you are, sir."

Gerard slumped in the back seat, and clawed at his Nelson Mandela shirt, undoing the second and third buttons. He was sweating profusely. He could feel his heart racing ridiculously. Stop it, he told himself – this is not the time to have a panic attack. The pain in his chest seemed to be deepening, spreading – it was paralysing him. He wondered if he was having a heart attack.

Christ, what a cock-up if I die now, with the evidence files hidden and no way of telling anyone where they are! No chance to say goodbye to Louisa, to make it all up to her.

This pain is getting worse – it's not a panic attack. I'm not focusing on…

Gerard tried to lean forward, to tell the cabbie he was changing the destination: he needed to divert to an A & E department. But it was as if a stake had been driven through his heart, pinning him to the seat.

This pain, this pain, this pain.

He wouldn't make it to A & E. The word 'pathos' was running round his head. Was it an answer to one of those crossword clues he'd failed to solve?

This is my 'Rosebud' moment, he thought.

The pain in his chest seemed to burst a dam, and his brain refused to take any more.

56

LORD BROOKE

Lord Brooke enjoyed a leisurely breakfast. He tapped out a message on the encrypted service Telegram to a certain unnamed ex-politician, soon to be vindicated and restored to power.

It read:

ALL YOUR DUCKS ARE IN A ROW.

He didn't expect a reply.

As he sipped his coffee and looked out over Green Park, he planned out his day. First there was the press conference, at which he would chastise the Home Secretary and MI5 for their failures to keep Britain safe from terrorism, and for their vilification of patriots. He would promise that sensational details would emerge from tomorrow's court case.

Then he would have a conversation with the grieving widow. He would press his deepest condolences to Louisa Bell and ask her if it had been a heart attack. He presumed that since the balloon hadn't gone up either the evidence had indeed been destroyed or that Gerard hadn't told his wife where to find it.

It was possible that Louisa did know the location of surviving evidence and was sitting on it, but Brooke was confident he could intimidate her successfully. He could intimidate anyone in the country – it was his professional speciality.

He would tell her the Bell Agency's blackmailing days were over, and that all his clients would be cancelling their accounts with her immediately. If she cut up rough, he would threaten her with what had happened to her husband, but in his long experience he'd found that going in hard immediately after a trauma was enough to cow the opposition. Brooke was pretty sure she'd take the hint and retire gracefully to her lovely place on the Dordogne; 'such a shame Gerard won't be there to enjoy it with you'.

The Cevdets had bleated about losing two more of their gang at Frimley Park, but even if they'd failed for a second time to take down the daughter, at least the mother was dead. That meant the Facebook evidence would now stay buried – again a cock-up created by the Cevdets. Brooke had so much more faith in the British professionals – they were properly trained by the best of MI5 – they had a 100% success rate. Miles Mason and his team had earned their imminent promotions.

Then all that remained was tomorrow's court case. My God, he was going to relish his day in the sun! Once Adam Thornton finally admitted to the Home Secretary that the real evidence had actually gone missing and that the stuff she had seen were fakes, the Home Secretary would probably inform the court that the government was not offering any evidence, so ending the case. But the press gallery would be packed and Brooke would be able to let rip to them about the Home Secretary and travesties of justice. She would have to offer a grovelling public apology to the court and also to his clients, and the rest, as they say, would be history.

He would enjoy being Lord Chancellor.

He had an agenda.

57

LYDIA

Lydia knew from Adam's face it was bad news. He had always looked so unflustered, so in control of himself and the situation, but now he looked deflated, defeated. He'd called her in with a message he'd sent at 6am. She'd come straight down from her dormitory bed in Thames House, before she'd washed or had any breakfast.

"Gerard Bell died last night."

She felt as if she'd been punched in the stomach, the breath forced from her lungs. "Oh my God. How?"

"It seems as if he had a heart attack in the back of a taxi. Apparently the taxi had picked him up from outside Reza Hameed's flat. The cabbie took him to A & E but he was dead on arrival."

"Foul play?"

"It's possible. Reza Hameed caught a flight to Mexico early this morning; we've put a warrant out for her arrest. But Gerard was under a lot of stress." Adam took off his glasses and rubbed his eyes. "Correction: I put him under a lot of stress."

"He put himself in that position, Adam."

"Whatever the cause of death, it's the effect I need to discuss with you. Gerard's death removes our last chance of finding the missing evidence. I will speak to Louisa Bell this morning, but I don't hold out any hopes she will be willing or able to help us. After that it's down to you and Damian Curry to have one last search in H11."

"Damian Curry? You trust Vindi?"

Adam looked at her through red-rimmed eyes. "Yes."

"But he's my prime suspect for murdering Martin Froome, Dennis Dunn and Maureen Dennis. He's boasted of his skills at evading surveillance."

"Look, I have a confession to make." Adam rubbed his eyes again then put his glasses on. "He's been working personally for me, all along, just as you have."

"But you told me…"

"I thought two approaches were better than one. I needed to maximise our chances."

"What's he been doing behind my back?"

"Much the same as you. He's also hacked computers and planted bugs in the homes of all the suspects – he was working for me when unfortunately he scared Maureen Dennis in her home."

"And what has he come up with? What have his bugs – or should I say your bugs – uncovered?" She couldn't keep the outrage out of her voice.

"Nothing significant, I'm afraid."

"Perhaps that should be a warning to you. In taking him into your confidence, you've probably forewarned him about everything I've been trying to do."

"I trust him. I trust you, too, Lydia."

"So was it him – or you – who bugged my flat as well?"

"No. Not that I know of."

"Not that you know of – hardly a reassuring answer. You're asking me to work alone down there in H11 with a man who I think may have murdered three of our colleagues."

"Trust me on this, Lydia. Just for today. I need you."

"Like I've trusted you so far. Like my mother trusted your security arrangements." She wasn't addressing her boss the Director-General, she was telling this tired-eyed man called Adam how she felt. He looked like a guilty boy, stripped of authority. "Anyway, what does it matter now? You're telling me we've already lost."

"Something may come up. You may get a flash of inspiration. Maybe sharing notes with Damian will trigger something."

"Most likely trigger a knife in my guts." She tried to repress her emotion but it was hard. Adam had created a personal bond between them, and now came the realisation that there had always been three in the relationship. "May I remind you that I was sent down to H11 to investigate the murder of Martin Froome, not to cover anything up? I am still dedicated to finding the murderer, and if it's your precious Damian Curry, I shan't hold back."

"If you don't find the hidden evidence, Lydia, the resulting regime change at MI5 will ensure the murderer gets off scot-free, and I won't be around to listen to your vituperations."

They left it there.

As she was leaving the Director-General's suite, Lydia felt her feet dragging. She really didn't want to go down to H11 for another soul-crushing day of searching, with Gerard dead and the murderer still down there. Gerard hadn't been a good man, but she couldn't help but feel sad for him: he'd had charm and style, and she couldn't believe he had orchestrated the murders.

Adam's PA looked up from her desk. "Ms Twomey, I've had a message to say there's someone waiting to see you in reception. Because of your status as being at risk of assassination, you need to go to the observation booth to identify the member of the public before you meet them."

"Has this person given us a name?"

"Angel Ngidi. I don't know if that's male or female."

Lydia made her way down to the observation booth. The African woman sitting in the lobby was certainly the nursing sister from the Central Middlesex Hospital. Lydia phoned through to the duty officer on the front desk to admit Sister Ngidi to the interview room.

Lydia met her at the door and shook her hand.

Sister Ngidi shook her head sorrowfully. "I'm so sorry about your mother. It's so sad to hear about what happened. I only heard last night."

Lydia nodded, and ushered Sister Ngidi to a chair. What was this all about?

"You know, your mother had a premonition something bad was going to happen to her. And then it did happen. It's shocking."

Lydia twigged: Sister Ngidi had heard the false story that Sarah Twomey had died in Frimley Park Hospital. Surely this woman hadn't come all this way just to offer her condolences?

"Yes," Lydia said. For her mother's security, she couldn't tell the truth. "I'm heartbroken. Thank you for coming in to offer your condolences."

"I'm surprised you're still working, what with the trauma."

A brief flicker of suspicion wormed into Lydia's mind. Was Sister Ngidi an agent sent by the enemy to find out if Sarah Twomey really was dead? Lydia's finger hovered near the alarm button. If she pressed it, the office would be locked down and the alarms would ring out, with an armed response unit springing into action.

Lydia manufactured a brave smile. "Work keeps my mind off it all."

"I understand." Sister Ngidi put her hand into the breast of her jacket.

Lydia readied herself to react to the sight of a gun in Sister Ngidi's hand. Her finger was a millimetre from the alarm button.

"Your mother left you this." Sister Ngidi held out an envelope. "As I said: she had a premonition. I would have brought it earlier, but we've only just had your sad news."

Lydia took the envelope. On it, written in her mother's handwriting, were the words: 'To Lydia, in case something happens to me'. She tore open the envelope, took out a piece of Central Middlesex Hospital notepaper, and read the message.

Saturday morning.

My dearest darling Lyds, I am giving this letter to Sister Ngidi to give to you in the event of something happening to me. She has looked after me very well, and right now I feel great. But I am to be moved to Telletubbyland in Surrey somewhere, and for some reason my very nice guards are being withdrawn. They say there's some sort of emergency on. So I am worried those people who tried to kill me may try again.

I want you to know that I love you very, very much. You have been my rock in the eight years since your dad died. You mustn't blame yourself for anything that has happened to me. I chose to help you and I have enjoyed it more than anything I've done since I got ill. I wouldn't have missed it for anything.

I have remembered the important points of the research I did for you. First of all, look at someone called Kemal Cevdet's Facebook profile. I found a picture from Istanbul last year, tagged to show together not just two of the people you asked me to research, but all three! Nesrin Cevdet and Ian Forrester were tagged, and I recognised Louisa Bell in the background. How clever is that?!!

Secondly, take a look on Louisa Bell's Literary Agency website. There's something very fishy about a puzzles corner they have. Why would a literary agent have a puzzle corner? The

location of the week was much too hard for me. Can you work it out? It was 'From the pink, to 3,500 steps.' What's that all about? Are you impressed I remembered how many steps? I must love you and leave you. They're packing me up to take me away to Telletubbyland. I love you so much.
Your mum xxx

Lydia looked up with tears misting her eyes. Sister Ngidi was dabbing her eyes, too. "Thank you, Sister Ngidi. This letter will always be very important, very precious to me. You've done a very good thing."

"It was the least I could do. She was a lovely woman, your mother."

"She was. Thank you again."

After she had seen Sister Ngidi to the door of Thames House, hugged her and said goodbye, Lydia turned back. She was going upstairs to Internal Security, not down to H11. She had a lead to work on.

She passed a man in the lobby; he looked at her a bit too closely and held his eyes on her just a little too long, before hastily looking away. He had scratches on his face and he looked wired, as if his eyes were burning on a diet of cocaine and strong coffee.

Lydia felt a chill run through her. Instinctively her hand went up to feel her bruised neck.

The man was wearing a service lanyard and he looked as if he knew his way around, moving briskly and confidently to the lifts behind her without a backward glance. His face was familiar. There was no reason to suggest he wasn't a bona fide member of the service.

Paranoia, she thought. Gerard Bell had warned her it came with the territory in H11. But it was magnified hugely when they'd already tried to kill her twice.

She waited for the next lift.

58

MARK

Mark Longford was running on empty. He'd always prided himself on being an action man, but the last few days had taken their toll. Even for him, three terminations in five days was going it some, especially as two of them had been MI5 colleagues. He had to admit, he'd found the terminations exciting (did it make him a psychopath or just a cool professional?) but they still drained him. Either way, he was psychologically and physically knackered.

For a moment he'd been taken aback when confronted by the girl in the lobby. It was the Twomey girl, the one whose flat he'd searched and bugged and who the Turks were meant to have terminated. Was she waiting for him? Was she about to challenge him? He'd held his nerve and walked right past her to the lifts, so no damage had been done.

As he rode the lift up, he fingered the scratches on his face. He'd found himself picking his scabs, and a couple of them had got infected. That fucking cat! But now it was nearly over and there were no more terminations in the pipeline – just the prospects of rewards for a series of jobs well done. He was expecting some uplifting praise from Miles Mason in the next half hour, even if the main message would still be 'steady as she goes'.

He stepped out of the lift when it opened on the fifth floor. A female colleague called Daisy stepped out beside him, and walked on up the corridor, but Mark's way was blocked by a middle-aged bloke whom he recognised from the third floor.

"Mark Longford, is it?" the man asked. He had an aquiline nose and an accent from a major public school.

Mark instinctively assessed the situation. The man with the beak wasn't alone. Standing casually by the window to the left was a flabby pale figure – probably a senior manager who'd never left his office seat in the last twenty years, and behind him, by the lift door, was a much younger man, twitching and swallowing, obviously nervous as hell.

"Yeah, I'm Mark Longford. Who wants to know?" Mark nodded, holding out his lanyard for inspection. He managed a smile.

"I'm Peregrine Webb, Head of Internal Security, and these are my colleagues, Andrew Elms and Jon Small." Webb held out his lanyard.

Mark called on his training and relaxed all his muscles. "What can I do for such an august body of colleagues?" They shouldn't forget: he'd been to public school, too, even if it was only a minor one.

"We'd just like to borrow you for twenty minutes down on the third floor, if it's all right, Mark." Peregrine Webb spoke so nicely, Mark half expected him to bow.

"I'm afraid it will have to wait, gentlemen. I've got an urgent meeting with my boss, Miles Mason." Mark emphasised the name – Miles Mason wasn't a man to cross. He moved to resume his way along the corridor.

Webb stepped across to bar his way. "He's been informed that you will be late."

All Mark could do was smile. "Well, what foresight! Lead on, then."

They took the stairs. As he descended with the three men, his mind was racing. What was all this about? Surely they could have nothing on him? Had they got to Darren? Had the note to Fazouli been analysed? Had he been picked up by some security cameras somewhere in the last few days? Surely not – they'd been so careful. And Darren wasn't the sort to dob his colleague in. No, as long as he stood cool and firm, there was no danger.

He was taken to Webb's office and invited to sit in a very comfortable armchair. He looked up at a portrait of the Queen in her younger days. The three men sat round in a semi-circle in front of him. It wasn't going to be a torture session, but neither was it likely to be a gentleman's chat.

"Do you mind if I just give my boss a quick call?" Mark took out his phone.

"Yes, I do rather mind," Webb said, and held out his hand for the phone.

Mark gave it to him. Maybe it was going to be a proper interrogation after all. What could they possibly have on him?

Webb took a sheet of paper off his desk and handed it to Mark. "This sheet contains a number of time periods over the last week. Could you tell us where you were on each of these dates and times, please?"

"Am I under caution, or something?"

Peregrine Webb smiled, but there was no humour in it. "Of course not. We're not the police. We're just investigating some internal security issues."

Webb's reply had given Mark time to look carefully at the times on the sheet. They confirmed his worst fears: all the times when he'd been off on his 'black ops' duty dealing with Maureen Dennis, Ahmed Fazouli and Gerard Bell, were listed.

He tapped the piece of paper. "Well, as you know, I've been a very busy man over the last week, as I'm sure you all have been. We've had the national emergency to deal with."

"We have your duty sheets. They're impressive. You've been working hard, as we all have, but the times on this list are outside your logged official hours."

"In that case I can say confidently that I was sleeping at home. Because it's all I've been doing for the last few weeks: working and sleeping."

"Have you been in North London – Edmonton, maybe – in your off-duty hours at any time in the last week?"

This was turning nasty. The cat lady had met her end in Edmonton, and so had Ahmed Fazouli. Did they have something from a camera? Mark was always so careful not to be recognisable to CCTV, but maybe he'd slipped up. Even so, it wasn't evidence of a murder.

"No, I haven't been to Edmonton this week. What's all this about?"

"How did you get the scratches on your face?" Webb sat back in his chair and almost drawled the question, as if he was enjoying himself. The other two just sat there with unmoving pudding faces.

"Brambles."

"Where?"

"On service business. Surveillance. It's classified information."

"Would you like to think of an alternative explanation?"

Webb was playing with him; Mark wasn't going to give him any more satisfaction. "No, I wouldn't."

"I would strongly advise you to tell the truth."

"Unless you tell me what this is all about, I can't help you any further." He folded his arms.

Webb took his time. "A colleague of both of ours, named Maureen Dennis, was met by two men on King's Cross Station last Friday at 3.42pm. The CCTV footage from the station shows you were one of the two men who met her."

"It can't be me. Your analysts have that wrong." Mark was confident he couldn't be clearly identified by any CCTV at King's

Cross. They were guessing, but it was disconcerting that they were on the right line.

Webb ignored him and continued. "The two men drove off in a taxi with Maureen Dennis and her cat. This taxi drove to an underground car park near Marble Arch. Maureen Denis was never seen alive again."

"Why, has she been seen dead?" Surely not, Mark thought; she was six feet deep in Essex clay.

"Her cat was found alive on waste ground in Edmonton. DNA analysis of blood on the cat's claws is a direct match with your DNA, Mr Longford. I thought you would like to share your thoughts with us before I hand over the evidence to the police. It might help you to have our support and understanding when you are interviewed under caution by the police."

That fucking cat!

Mark tried to compose his face. "I can't comment on this, except to say your forensic analysts have obviously made a mistake."

"There is no mistake, I can assure you. There is enough cast-iron evidence to convict you of conspiracy to murder."

Mark doubted that claim, but the situation was far from ideal. He sat there, unmoving.

Webb continued. "However, we are willing to make a deal with you. I have the Director-General's authorisation to offer you total immunity if you are prepared to disclose who ordered the death of Maureen Dennis. We'd need some proof, of course."

Mark wanted to threaten this supercilious git with action from his own boss, the feared Miles Mason, but that was a non-starter now; Mason would cut him adrift to save his own skin – he may have already done so.

Mark made a motion to signify his lips were zipped, refolded his arms and composed his mind for the long haul.

"Don't think your silence is loyal, professional or noble." Webb stayed patient. "And don't think your controller will protect you. He will probably have you killed to ensure your eternal silence."

'Eternal silence'! This man had been reading too many thrillers.

Webb shook his head. "Still unconvinced? Think about what happened to Ian Forrester. Maybe remember what you yourself did to Ian Forrester. He was on your side, but they needed his silence. Gerard Bell – he was on your side as well."

All true, Mark acknowledged to himself: he knew exactly what had happened to Forrester and Bell, of course. But the crucial point was that after tomorrow it would be a different world, one where the likes of Webb and his Director-General would be powerless has-beens while Miles Mason, Mark and his crew would rule the world.

Up yours, Peregrine Webb.

59

LYDIA

Five minutes after Lydia had arrived in Internal Security, there had been a stir. Through the glass wall of the open-plan office she'd seen Webb, Jon Small and Andrew Elms leading the man with the scratched face who'd stared at her in the lobby. Webb had looked pumped up, a spring in his step. They'd disappeared along the corridor. She'd resisted the urge to go and find out what was afoot – she had her own urgent work.

She set to work solving Gerard's puzzle. She went on the Bell Agency website, and sure enough, she found the puzzle corner tucked away at the foot of the 'news' page. But the location question had changed from the one her mother had reported in her letter: it was now 'From the waterwheels, blinded by the light'.

Lydia set to work, solving the clues. It was quite fun but it seemed frivolous, considering the clock was ticking down to the court case and the murderer was still out there somewhere.

In the left corner of her vision she saw a bulky man hovering by the photocopier. It was Brian Powell. What did he want up here?

Her fists clenched so hard that she broke the pencil she had been fiddling with.

She tried to ignore him, but it was impossible. His presence, even on the other side of a large open-plan office with three colleagues between, was freaking her out. She got up out of her seat. She had to confront him.

As she walked over she saw that he was contemplating turning tail and leaving, but he stood his ground. His hand stopped twiddling his beard and was raised in a little wave.

"Hi, Lydia."

She kept her voice firm and tone brisk. "Hi Bri. What are you doing up here? Has something broken down, or have you something to tell me about the case?"

Nnnrrrnnggg. "I got a call to fix this photocopier, but when I got here it seems fine."

"Who called you?"

"I don't know who it was. Some woman."

"We normally email your department if we have a problem."

"Not if it's urgent. Well, it's all right anyway, so I'll be on my way back down." His fingers were back in his beard. He turned to go.

Lydia was torn between getting to the bottom of why he was there and the blessed relief of Brian leaving. She chose the latter – she needed to work on Gerard's clues.

"Bye, then. Thanks for coming up."

"Bye." He was already halfway to the door.

As she walked back to her desk a girl called Lindsey looked up from another work station. "Has that weirdo got the hots for you, Lydia?"

"No. Why do you say that?"

"Oh, he's been hanging around here lots of times in the last few days, asking when you're going to be in, that sort of thing. I think you've got a secret admirer."

"I hope not!" She laughed as she said it, but it was a hollow laugh.

She walked back and sat at her desk. She closed her eyes and took a deep breath. There was no time for anything else – she had to work on Gerard's clues. Block everything else out.

She cracked the clue given to her by her mother in less than fifteen minutes: 'in the pink' referred to the pink city of Jaipur in Rajahstan, while the 3,500 steps were of the step well at Abhaneri, near Fatehpur Sikri.

Okay – so what? Was this just a fun puzzle for the clients of the Bell Agency? Was this Gerard Bell playing mind games, laying false trails, or simply demonstrating how clever he was? How could it possibly have anything to do with finding the missing evidence?

She was just starting on the second clue when Adam Thornton walked into the office. Lindsey and two office juniors, the only other people in the office, sat and watched their Director-General with mouths hanging open.

"Hello," she said. "What brings you here?" She was aware she didn't sound too welcoming.

"I thought I'd find you in H11. Damian Curry is waiting for you down there. As you know, he's not allowed to be in H11 on his own."

She flushed at the implied criticism."I've been handed an important lead, which I am working on. I need access to the internet, so I can't follow it up down in H11."

"Where did this lead come from? What is it?"

"My mother left a letter. It's..." She hesitated. She didn't want to admit she was enjoying Gerard's recreational puzzles. "It's a set of clues Gerard Bell posted on his wife's website. We think they may tell us the location of the missing evidence."

"Well, you can personally ask his wife about them, because you're coming with me to visit her now."

"And what will Damian be doing in the meantime?" She couldn't resist it.

"I'll order one of your colleagues into H11 to substitute for you. Come on." Adam turned away.

Lydia logged off and shut down her computer, grabbing her jacket and following Adam out of the office.

In the bullet-proof official car, they sat jammed into opposite corners of the back seat, as far apart as they could get. Adam briefed Lydia on what was going to happen when they met Louisa Bell. "You are there because you've met her and you knew Gerard Bell and this case. I want you to closely observe her reactions and to give me your impressions afterwards. As a woman, you can be a shoulder to cry on, should the opportunity arise."

"It won't arise – Louisa's not like that."

"You're probably correct but we'll see. You can ask her about the clues on her website – are you sure she didn't set them herself?"

"They are absolutely Gerard's style."

"Good. Oh, by the way, Perry Webb has caught the killer of Maureen Dennis. He's one of our own, working for Special Ops."

"I'm glad. Have they found her body, then?"

"Not yet."

"Was it the man with the scratched face?"

Adam looked at her sharply. "That's the one. How did you know him?"

"I didn't. I just saw him in the lobby."

"Of course he's unlikely to incriminate anyone else and of course we're not allowed to torture him, but Perry's hoping we can identify him as the killer of Martin Froome and of Dennis Dunn as well."

Lydia shook her head. "He didn't kill Dennis Dunn. Dennis would never have opened his door to a stranger."

"In which case, we may have to conclude that Dunn did indeed commit suicide."

"The killer is still down in H11." She said it with total conviction.

They turned into Phillimore Place, passing the corner where Lydia and Reza had been attacked. Lydia closed her eyes and tried to erase it from her mind.

What had Gerard been doing at Reza's flat last night? Why might Reza want Gerard dead? There was so little time to think about it all.

The driver stopped the car outside Gerard's house; he got out and scanned the street before opening the door for Adam. Across the road another chauffeur stood, leaning against a gleaming Bentley.

Adam rang the doorbell; they stood and waited. The door stayed closed.

"Louisa said she would see us," Adam muttered.

The door opened. A tall bald man in a suit very like Adam's stood in the doorway, regarding them with an amused look on his fleshy lips.

"Adam Thornton – I thought I might see you here. Come to pay your respects to the widow?"

Adam pursed his lips. "Brooke. What a pleasure."

"Well, I must hurry along. The early bird catches the worm, as they say. I'll probably see you tomorrow at the Old Bailey. Court number 3, I think it is." Lord Brooke smirked as he turned and strolled over to his Bentley.

The housekeeper showed Adam and Lydia up to the drawing room on the first floor.

Louisa Bell wore an immaculate dark Burgundy wool suit and sat regally in the centre of a powder blue sofa. Her black hair was perfect, but she wore dark glasses.

"Please be seated." She indicated two armchairs but did not rise herself. Lydia guessed she was deeply shaken but was determined to put on a good show.

Adam and Lydia sat.

Adam held his hand out to Lydia. "This is Lydia Twomey, whom I believe you've met already. Her mother was killed this weekend by associates of the Cevdets, who we believe may have been involved with Gerard's death."

Louisa nodded towards Lydia, but said nothing. Her face gave nothing away.

Adam leaned forward. "Louisa, we've come here to offer the service's deepest condolences to you at what must be a terrible time. And may I add my own personal condolences? Gerard was a good man, much loved by his colleagues. If there's anything we can do to help you in this hour of need, just let us know."

"Thank you for the speech." Louisa's voice was clear and steady. "Now, would you like to cut to the business?"

"We met Lord Brooke on your doorstep. I presume he was here to threaten you – or as he would put it, to advise you. He needs your silence. I am here to put the other side of the argument: I would ask you in the memory of your husband to tell us all you know about the conspiracy."

Louisa's back straightened and her nose tilted upwards. "What conspiracy? Please don't play spiteful games at this time."

"Gerard was ready to tell us all. He was going to expose Lord Brooke and his conspirators on the eve of the upcoming court case, but they killed him before he could tell us. He hated them, Louisa – he was going to ruin them. He didn't die of a heart attack; he was murdered on the orders of someone you've met very recently. They will do the same to you if they feel threatened."

"My husband died after overexerting himself with his mistress. He had nothing to do with any conspiracy."

Lydia gave herself a mental slap – Gerard and Reza were lovers! Why had she failed to see it, or even guess the possibility? This was a world of betrayal and she was hopelessly naive.

Adam kept his voice soft and patient. "Gerard may have been a good man, but he was involved in the conspiracy. So were you." He let the words sink in.

Louisa's sunglasses never wavered. "That is actionable slander, Mr Thornton."

"Mrs Bell, we have a picture of you in Istanbul with proven conspirators Ian Forrester (now deceased) and Nesrin Cevdet, who was arrested this morning; you were with them in front of a hotel where Lord Brooke was staying. If Lord Brooke was here just now to assure you that you're safe from prosecution, he has misled you grievously: we are actively considering your arrest. In contrast to Brooke, I can offer you guaranteed immunity if you respect what Gerard was about to do and help us expose this conspiracy. We can give you full protection."

Her lip curled. "Just like you fully protected Gerard, you mean? You and your clique have kept the most brilliant mind in all MI5 cooped up in that dismal oubliette in Thames House for years and years while you've promoted mediocrities and arse-lickers. I don't expect to see any of you at the funeral. I shall be retiring to France as soon as it's over. I think we've said all we need to say. Goodbye."

Lydia raised her hand, as if she was back in a classroom. "Just one more thing, please. Can you help me with the puzzles on your agency's website news page: did you or Gerard set the location clues?"

The sunglasses masked any emotion, but Louisa's head went back in surprise. "What an extraordinary question to ask at this time! What's this all about?"

"I think Gerard set the questions, and I think they were his message to you." This was pure guesswork; Lydia prayed Louisa wouldn't ask why she had this hunch.

Louisa paused. Lydia could see she was weighing things up. "He set them."

"Do you know the significance of the locations? He changed them several times in the last few months. I think they were something he shared with you."

"You may be right." She almost whispered the words. Then she seemed to gather herself, because her voice steadied. "But I have no idea about any deeper significance. I'm afraid I can't help you."

Lydia smiled. Something had cleared for her. "Thank you very much, Louisa. I think you have helped me."

"I can't think how. My housekeeper will show you to the door."

She didn't get up, but they shook her hand anyway.

On the way back to Thames House in the car, Adam was gloomy. "Brooke had obviously got to her – threatened her; that's why she's giving up her agency and retiring to France. She was our last hope."

Lydia was still smiling. "I think she may have just helped us massively."

"How?"

"I've worked out the significance of the locations. I think Gerard fully intended to share the significance of them with Louisa – I don't know why he never got round to it, or maybe he did and she's refusing to tell us."

"Are you going to explain it to me?"

"If I gave you this clue, where would I be located: 'From the waterwheels, blinded by the light'?"

"Hmm." Adam pondered. He'd never jumped to answers, and now he was typically slow. "'Blinded by the Light' was a song by Bruce Springsteen, covered by Manfred Mann's Earthband."

"I'd never put you down as a rocker."

Adam sighed. "This job ages one. In my younger days I was very different. I was a prog rocker, actually. I played keyboards in a band at Cambridge. Have I helped you crack the clue?"

"Possibly."

"Forgive me for asking, Lydia, but how are these clues relevant to our predicament?"

"I can't be certain." She found it hard to repress the excitement in her voice. "However, I think all the locations in the clues are places of significance in his life with Louisa, places they visited together. They are places he would have photographed."

"So?"

"On his computer down in H11 he has a huge file of his photos from all round the world. He uses them as a screen saver for the plasma screen in his office. I wasn't able to access those files because they needed a password, but yesterday I threatened him with you, and he gave me the password. I think he's been moving the missing evidence around H11 from file box to file box, and he's been recording each new location on his computer, hiding that record in his photo library, a different location each time. So the location for the missing evidence was hidden between photos of Jaipur and Abhaneri, but has been moved to a file between a picture of waterwheels and a picture of somewhere where someone was blinded by the light."

"Maybe he's got some music files on his computer and the location is hidden between a track by Bruce Springsteen and a song about a waterwheel."

"Thanks, Adam. I never heard Gerard playing rock music, but maybe I just missed it."

Adam smiled. "Sorry – I confess to a moment of levity, quite inappropriate for a person in my position in a situation as grave as this."

"You don't think I'm on the right track, do you? What I know for certain is that Gerard was playing games constantly to pass the time down in H11, and this is just the sort of game he'd play."

"It's worth a try, Lydia. Anything's worth a try now. This time tomorrow it will all be over."

60

LYDIA

When Adam's car delivered them back at Thames House, Lydia took the lift straight down to H11. She was a woman on a mission.

Vindi buzzed her through to the cloakroom, and then through to the office. It was only when she was standing in front of him that she felt terror – it hit her like a blow to her solar plexus. He was standing by the artificial flowers covering Farah's old desk, dressed in skimpy shorts and athletic singlet, sandals on his bare brown feet, looking totally at ease, while she braced herself, willing her legs not to give way.

She had just locked herself into a basement, alone with a killer.

She could feel the fear in her bowels. She wondered if he could hear her stomach rumble. She resisted the urge to run to the toilet and lock herself in.

"So how's it going?" he asked, stroking his clipped brown beard, a little smile playing on his lips.

"We're down to our last hours." She swallowed. "I'm going to have one last look on Gerard Bell's computer – see if anything comes up."

"It's a shame he's dead. He was a strange old bastard, but I liked him. Do you think he was murdered?" He was standing close to the door. If she was going to get to Gerard's office, she would have to almost brush by him. She wasn't sure if she could do it.

"I don't know. He was under a lot of pressure."

"Did Adam Thornton tell you about him and me?" Still the smile.

"What? That you're having an affair? I never guessed you were gay." She made a feeble attempt at a laugh, but it came out quavering.

"You know what I meant. Did it upset you to find out you weren't his only one?"

"I've got to get on. Every minute might be vital."

"Now you're aware we're both working personally to Adam, perhaps we should pool our information. It's something you suggested when we first met."

"Sure – fine by me. I haven't got anything to share right now. As soon as I do, I'll let you know. If I keep something back from you then I'm sure Adam will pass on to you anything I tell him."

"Ooooh!" He threw his head back and laughed.

"I get your message, Vindi: we're on the same side. Now let's get on."

"You can call me Damian now. The nicknames were Gerard's and Farah's – Mo's. Now they're dead it seems wrong to keep using them."

"We don't yet know for sure Mo is dead. Then again, maybe you know more than me."

"You're right – perhaps she's still alive."

He was enjoying this. He could see her fear and he was blocking her way to the door, relishing his power over her.

"Damian, if you could move out of the way, I'd be grateful. I'm going to Gerard Bell's office now." She kept her voice level and looked him in the eye.

For a long moment, he stood there, but then, still smiling, he stepped aside. "You know – I think you're onto something that you're not telling me about. You've got a wild look in your eyes. Call me when you've cracked it. I promise I won't claim all the credit."

She walked past him, through the door, took the left turn, walked the few steps along the corridor and opened the door to Gerard's office. The lights flickered on automatically. She shut the door behind her and leant against it, breathing heavily. She'd made it in. Would she ever make it out again?

To think that she had once, only days ago, found this man sexy – it made her shudder now. There was just a thin door between them, and no lock on any door in H11 except the toilet, but there were massive steel doors and security screens between her and safety, four floors up.

Concentrate on the task in hand, she told herself fiercely. The wild look in her eyes was terror, but Vindi was right: she was nearly there.

She waited for the computer to boot up. From the other end of the room Baal watched her inscrutably from his recess. She wondered if the word 'baleful' derived from Baal.

"Well, you didn't protect him very well yesterday, did you?"

Baal didn't grace her with an answer.

She sat down to navigate her way to Gerard's photo files. She remembered the password – hesperus7 – and she was into Gerard's personal files. One more click and she was into the photos. She entered Abhaneri into the search box, and up came several pictures of an extraordinary sunken palace with a well and 3,500 steps. And sure enough, the photo before the step well was of Jaipur, the pink city.

She hoped there would be some file between the two photos, but there was none. It was only to be expected: Gerard had changed the location clue to 'From the waterwheels, blinded by the light'. She typed the clue into the search box, but she got no result – Gerard was going to make her work for this.

She closed her eyes, and concentrated with every cell of her brain. 'From the waterwheels, blinded by the light'. 'From the waterwheels, blinded by the light'. 'From the waterwheels, blinded by the light'. Gerard had once said he thought she would crack it – that was probably why he'd asked her to join his conspiracy. So it wasn't impossible.

She opened her eyes – and looked straight into the desk light. In the moment it blinded her, she had the answer.

Damascus.

Saul had been blinded on the road to Damascus. It led to his conversion to Christianity, his new name Paul, and eventually his sainthood.

She tapped Damascus into the search box.

On the screen was a row of icons for photos of Damascus. The jpeg file before Damascus in the full sequence was of Hama. She clicked on it: a picture of waterwheels. So the unnamed image between Hama and Damascus was…

The screen went black.

The lights cut out.

The computer fan stopped.

Total darkness – she couldn't see her hand in front of her face.

Total silence. The deep black of a sealed basement four storeys below ground level, where there is no power of any sort.

Like the inside of a buried coffin.

She wanted to scream but she sat still, waiting for the emergency generator to come on.

Nothing changed.

Her mobile phone was in her jacket in the locked cloakroom. She felt for the landline receiver on the desk and picked it up.

It was dead.

It had to be sabotage: an electrical fault might interrupt the power supply, but the back-up generators were on a completely different circuit. For both to fail simultaneously it would take someone with detailed knowledge of the system down here to deliberately destroy both. That person would have to be inside H11 at this moment.

Damian Curry had sabotaged the power and cut the phone line. There could be only one explanation as to why he would do such a thing.

He was going to kill her.

She sat perfectly still in Gerard's desk chair, controlling her breathing so she made almost no sound. Her stomach rumbled.

She assessed the situation. When George had shown her round, she'd said H11 was a fortress, designed to withstand a siege from above. The emergency grilles would now be down and the blast-proof doors would be locked. It would take any rescuers at least half an hour to get through – plenty of time for Damian Curry to kill her.

He would be armed. The sensors at H11's entrance would prevent him from smuggling in a gun or knife or even a spray can, but there were kitchen utensils and he would have had years in H11 to manufacture and then hide some home-made lethal weapon.

He would know intimately the layout of H11 in total darkness, whereas she was new to this place. He would have a plan: if he was going to kill her, he would have to make it look like self-defence, because there was no escape from this place after the deed was done. He would strike quickly and then pose her corpse to make it look like she'd been the attacker.

For a moment fear paralysed her. She'd been trained to root out secrets on phones and computers, interview tricky suspects, trawl social media accounts – not kill someone in hand-to-hand combat in a blacked-out basement. If this was a nightmare, she wanted to wake up now, please.

She took a deep breath. She'd already killed two men – shot one of them in the head – at point blank range just two days ago. She could do it. Stay ahead of him, out-think him, do the unexpected.

She needed a weapon and a plan of her own. She ran her fingers over Gerard's desk, but came up with nothing better than a fountain pen. She'd seen a film where some woman had stabbed her attacker in the eye and killed him, but in this blackness it would need a miracle to achieve that. In the top drawer she grasped a pair of scissors with pointed ends. She slid her fingers through the handles. They would have to do. She could plunge them into his neck. There was a Hitchcock film where a woman did that, too.

Grasping her scissors, she got down on her knees and crawled to the door. The only lethal substance she could think of within H11 was the possibly radioactive gunk they painted onto the files. If she could get a spray can of the stuff she might have a chance. Damian would expect her to be in Gerard's office, so she would find a corner to hide in the file stacks. He would expect her to walk or even run, so she would crawl. If he had a torch, so much the better; it would tell her where he was holding it. If they bumped into each other in the corridor, he would be standing above her, so she would be able to stab upwards with her scissors – stab him in the prick that he seemed so proud of.

The door opened almost silently, but the faint swish it made on the carpet sounded like an avalanche to Lydia.

She stopped to listen: silence. There was a faint smell of cologne; she could smell her would-be killer – he was somewhere close. Maybe he was standing, stock still, just a few feet down the corridor, waiting for her.

Like a tortoise, she put one hand out in front of her then brought it down gently on the carpet. Then the same with a knee, another hand, another knee.

She stopped to listen. Nothing.

She resumed her slow journey. Of course he would be waiting somewhere for her, but he wouldn't wait long. Time was not on his side. In thirty minutes or so the security doors would be breached and the lights and CCTV would come back on.

She passed where the door to the main office was on her right. She could see nothing of it, but the slightest movement of air told her of the space. If Damian was waiting for her in the doorway, now was the moment he would pounce.

She stopped, listening for his breathing: no sound, but she could smell his cologne more strongly now. Her mouth was dry and her heart was pounding.

He was somewhere close.

There was some other smell – one she couldn't identify. Was it some leftover plate of food in the office, some residual aroma from…

She froze.

Her hand, instead of coming down on the corridor carpet, had alighted on… what? No, that couldn't be right…

Human skin.

It was somebody's arm, unmoving on the corridor floor. She had crawled onto a person. Why wasn't this person moving?

It had to be a corpse.

With her left hand she followed the arm up to the shoulder, across a shoulder strap to the neck.

The neck felt wet, maybe sticky. Lydia knew without seeing that it was blood on her hand. Whose blood?

Her hand followed up to the victim's chin. Short bristles prickled her hand. The victim had a beard.

Damian Curry was lying dead in this corridor.

Lydia gasped, but suppressed her scream. She stayed rooted as thoughts cascaded chaotically through her brain: who killed him? It must be someone Vindi had let into H11 after she'd come down. Who would he let in? It could only be Adam Thornton. Surely Vindi wouldn't let anyone else into H11. But why would Adam want to kill Vindi, or kill her? It made no sense.

She felt a swirl of air behind her. Someone was behind her!

She turned, but of course she could see nothing. She listened, but there was no sound – maybe she'd imagined it. But there was just a faint smell of… what?

She got to her feet, turned and ran the few steps back to Gerard's office. She knew she was panicking, but she had to do one thing – maybe what she should have done straight away.

She shut the door, felt across to Gerard's desk, went round to the other side of it, and gave it an almighty heave. Please budge, please budge, she implored it.

It moved. Straining every sinew, she moved it inch by inch across the floor towards the door. She knew she probably only had seconds before the door would open and her killer would sweep in.

The desk moved so slowly! With no Wi-Fi in H11, there were wires connected to the desk that were now trailing, almost tripping her up. The phone crashed to the floor off to her left. The killer would have heard her flight to the office, and would be with her in a matter of seconds. The scissors in her right hand dug into her flesh as she pressed against the desk.

The desk refused to move any further. She went round and felt the other side. It was resting against the wall. Now all she had to do was to push it round straight and it would be barricading the door to the corridor. It was a significant obstacle but she knew a determined attacker would be able to smash the upper part of the door and climb over the desk. But she'd be able to hear the killer coming and it would buy her some time, maybe not enough for the rescuers to break into H11 from above but at least…

She had done it. She stood by the desk for a moment, breathing heavily. Now she needed to get her brain back in gear. She had panicked, and panic could lead to bad moves.

Behind her, the rattan chair creaked.

"Hello, Lydia."

61

LYDIA

Lydia literally jumped – both feet left the floor. Her breath caught in her lungs, stabbing through her chest.

"What..."

"Hello, Lydia." It was a female voice. "I could call you Schizo, but I always thought the name was rather unfair."

Of course! Damian Curry wasn't alone when Lydia had come down to H11 – he had to be accompanied by a colleague at all times in H11. Lydia had rushed into Gerard's office to crack the clues without thinking about who else was already down there.

"How... how did you get into this room?"

"I was waiting by Vindi, standing behind you in the doorway to the main office."

"It's Maybe, isn't it?" Lydia said. "Mrs Willis."

"Maggie would be fine."

"Maggie it is, then." Lydia battled with herself to regain her composure. She wanted to beg for mercy, but she steeled herself to fight for her life. "Tell me, Maggie, why haven't you killed me already? You didn't hold back on Vindi, and you didn't show Dennis Dunn, Martin Froome or Gerard Bell any mercy, either."

"I didn't kill Gerard Bell."

Keep her talking – that was her only hope. Lydia was a trained negotiator and interrogator – she needed to use those skills to save her life. "I take it from your reply that you're guilty of the other two murders."

"There's no guilt."

"So why haven't you killed me? You could have done it when I was by Vindi's body, or when I was barricading the door."

"We need to make a deal."

"What deal?"

"I need you to tell me where Gerard Bell hid the evidence."

"What makes you think I know?"

"Damian Curry told me less than ten minutes ago that you'd cracked it."

"So you killed him."

"Careless talk costs lives."

"And what do I get from this deal?"

"You get to live. If you fail to give me the location of the evidence you die now in this room."

Lydia shook her head, even though she knew Maggie couldn't see her. "How does that work? If I give you the location of the evidence, you won't need me anymore and so you'll kill me. Even if you let me live, there's still Damian's body to explain. You still get done for murder."

"It works like this: you give me the location of the evidence. Together we destroy the evidence. With no electricity available, we will have to burn it with some matches I have thoughtfully brought with me." Maggie Willis spoke slowly and without emotion. "When they finally break down the doors and restore the power, we say we caught Damian Curry trying to destroy some evidence with matches and that he tried to kill us, but we managed to kill him in self-defence. I keep you alive because I need your testimony to back up my story."

"No inquiry would buy that, not if Forensics do their job properly."

"You forget, Lydia: after the court case tomorrow, as long as we can destroy this evidence, there will be a regime change in MI5, and the new controllers will see that we are exonerated."

Keep the conversation flowing. "We haven't got time to find the evidence and destroy it before they break through the security doors and restore the power. They'll be here in less than thirty minutes."

Maggie gave a little laugh. "Who told you that? George? That girl knows nothing. It will take them at least three hours to get through H11's defences. Believe me, we have all the time in the world for this."

"What if I haven't yet found the location of this evidence?"

"Then I have nothing to worry about – the evidence will stay safely hidden until after the court case. I don't need you, so I can kill you straight away, giving me a full three hours to arrange yours and Damian's bodies in such a way to suggest that you killed each other. So – are you telling me that you haven't found the location?"

Lydia paused. This needed a careful answer. "I've found it, all right. What's more, I shared the clues with the Director-General before I came down here, so you're correct: you do need to make a deal with me. Otherwise once they break into this place, they'll step over my dead body and go straight to the evidence." Lydia could feel the confidence returning. It was true: she had given Adam the clue.

"Okay, Lydia, so I need to destroy the evidence before they get through to us. Where did the Dong hide it?"

Lydia felt she could hear the faintest of cracks in Maggie's calm. She still had a chance. "It's not that easy. We need to talk first."

"Why?" Now Maggie sounded openly irritated.

"If I'm getting into this conspiracy with you then I need to know more about you and why we're doing it. Why did you get tangled up in all this, Maggie? What's in it for you and your family? Why kill your decent colleagues for those rich bastards who pull your strings? Do you think they care at all about your concerns?"

Silence.

For the first time, Lydia felt a twinge of hope. She seemed to have hit a raw nerve. She pressed home her advantage. "Do your kids and husband know you're a killer?"

"You really don't want to know this stuff."

"If you don't tell me what I'm getting into, there's no deal between us. Why on earth did a good citizen like you get involved with these people?"

Maggie sighed, then started in a low voice. "Gerard Bell. He needed someone to cover his tracks when he was blackmailing these people. I signed things off for him and he paid me well. My family needed the money – a taxi-driver doesn't earn much, not enough to live decently in London. Gerard Bell has paid my kids' school fees."

"So he recruited you for this conspiracy?"

"It's not a conspiracy. It's decent people taking back power from the weak liberals who've allowed this country to go to the dogs. MI5 has served the permissive society and has allowed illegal immigration, terrorism, drugs and organised crime. I thought you'd be able to see that, Lydia. You and I, we're from the working class in this posh boys' playground. We understand the real issues. My husband doesn't feel safe in his taxi and my kids see gang warfare killing children from our own neighbourhood. Something has to change, and these people who will take power once this court case has happened are the people who will create a decent Britain."

"I don't think Gerard Bell had the same view of these people."

"That's why he betrayed us and hid the evidence he said he'd destroyed. He was just interested in blackmailing people he despised. He was good to me but he was what my father would have called a degenerate."

"You killed Martin Froome."

"I was trained to do that sort of thing. I haven't always been a good little secretary like Mo Dennis, you know. Before I was transferred to H11 I worked in Special Ops. I'm surprised you never made a thing of it – you must have read my file."

"So you killed Martin to keep up your skill levels, eh? Just a spot of practice?"

"Martin Froome was an idiot. We knew he was compiling a list of file numbers, so we assumed he was doing it to unmask us. It turned out from the list of numbers that we recovered from your flat that he was working on his own little blackmail scam – the numbers had nothing to do with our case."

"And Dennis Dunn: he seemed a lovely bloke, the sort who wouldn't hurt anyone. Why did you kill him?"

"He was going to spill the beans to you. He'd caught Mr Bell fiddling the incinerator records once, inserting Double D's name in it. Mr Bell persuaded him it was just a silly error and that nothing dodgy had actually happened, and Dennis had seemed quite happy about it. But he must have realised it was significant when you started asking questions. He would have led you to the truth. He'd already written a long screed ready to hand over to you. It would have sunk our enterprise."

"How could you butcher someone you worked with?"

"We'd tried to intimidate him into keeping his mouth shut, but it didn't work. After he contacted you, we had to act. I was as gentle as possible. He didn't suffer. I persuaded him to do it himself, to save his partner. I didn't actually kill him." Her voice hardened. "But don't think I can't do it again. I will kill you like a rat if you don't do as I ask. We've done enough talking. The clock is ticking. We'll have a lot to do in the next three hours. You need to tell me where the evidence is hidden."

"Well, there's a problem." Lydia's spirits sank. She wasn't going to be able to talk her way out of this – not for three hours, anyway.

"Explain."

"The location is on Gerard's computer. I had it displayed on his plasma wall screen. You've cut the power, so the plasma screen is dead."

Silence. Maggie was obviously weighing up her answer.

The rattan chair creaked. Had Maggie got to her feet?

"So what do you say, Maggie?" Lydia couldn't keep the rising panic from her voice.

There was no reply.

Lydia understood: Maggie had got as much information as she could and had now decided to kill Lydia. She was moving forward silently, towards the place Lydia's voice had been coming from. She was probably brandishing a knife – Vindi had his throat slit.

Maggie was moving in for the kill.

Lydia held her breath. If she stayed still she was a sitting duck, but if she tried to move she'd make a sound which would give her location away. She was backed up against this desk, with wires from the computer and printer trailing all around her.

What do I do? Please, what do I do?

Lydia held her scissors out in front of her. It was a forlorn hope that Maggie would walk right into them and impale her eye on them, but it was all she could think of.

She waited for the imminent stab or slash and the intense pain of her flesh being sliced. It would come without warning from the dark.

Silence.

Lydia strained to catch any sound of her attacker moving or breathing, but she could hear nothing. It was as if she had just imagined Maggie's presence and had played out the conversation in her head. But she knew Maggie was there, maybe a few inches away, maybe circling to the side to slash at her throat as she'd done with Vindi.

Suddenly a sound – a faint click just inches from her.

Lydia started; volt of fear shot through her. Her hair felt electrified. She raised her hands instinctively to protect herself.

There was a rustle of wires, something crashed off the desk, the wires snagged round her ankles, there was grunt from a mouth somewhere just inches to her right and Lydia felt an exhalation of air brush her face.

Screaming, she lashed out with her scissors, felt them dig into something, and then they were ripped from her grasp. She leapt forward, but the computer wires round her ankles had tightened, and she crashed face first to the floor, away from the desk.

She got to her knees, wires still round her ankles; she dragged herself forward but her shins smashed into something – it was the low coffee table with the silk lilies. She crashed over it, landing on her face. She dragged herself up on her knees, kicking wildly at the wires around her ankles. She crawled to the far end of the office, under the bookshelf.

Why hadn't Maggie come after her, finished her off?

Her head hit the bookcase at the far end of the room.

She heard groaning and gasping coming from the desk end of the office. Perhaps there was hope.

The groaning came closer. Maggie was approaching again; this time Lydia had no scissors, no weapon at all.

She felt behind her. She grasped a book – anything to shield herself. It was a paperback – no use at all. She threw it in Maggie's direction.

Maggie was close. She'd stopped groaning, but Lydia could hear her ragged breathing.

Lydia's scrabbling hand reached up, grasping something heavier and harder than a book. It was Gerard's beloved statuette of Baal. She hefted it in her hand. What had Gerard called it? A protective spirit.

Here's to the Gods of Carthage.

Even though she had braced herself for it, the shock was overwhelming as Maggie's knife sliced into her side. It robbed her of her breath and her wits. Instinctively she swung her hand holding the statuette toward where she imagined Maggie was kneeling. Her hand crashed into flesh and bone, and she felt Baal shatter on impact; she was left holding crumbling shards of pottery.

Stillness.

Just her own panting, gasping for breath. Pain spreading now, as if her body would only gradually admit what had happened to it.

What had happened to Maggie? Was she dead? How? There was no sound coming from her attacker.

Lydia explored with her hands the floor around her.

Hair.

She was touching Maggie's head. It was resting on the floor, sticky with something that could only be blood.

Was Maggie dead or just stunned by the blow with the statuette? Would she suddenly recover and leap up with her knife, screaming like something from a horror movie?

Lydia's fingers sought out Maggie's throat; it was slick with blood. She pressed with both hands, desperately trying to throttle the life out of this monster. She kept on applying the pressure with a grim determination – she had no idea how long she had to do it to kill someone. She knew it was murder, but she couldn't bear the thought of Maggie regaining consciousness. Did the MI5 rules of engagement say anything about squeezing the life out of a colleague?

She kept pressing, her eyes screwed shut in the blackness.

62

ADAM

It had taken over three hours to break into H11; even when they had broken through and restored the power, progress was agonisingly slow. The complicated protocols meant that only Adam himself and Perry Webb were permitted to go in and secure the place. Because they had no idea who would be left alive, if anyone, they had to proceed cautiously. It felt very strange to be carrying a gun again and Adam could tell that Perry was even more jittery – he kept waving his gun at the shadows.

First they searched and secured the cloakroom and the main office. They found Damian Curry's body first, throat slit, in the corridor outside the main office. It was an ominous start, and Adam felt real anguish – Damian had been so pleased to work directly for Adam, and had expressed his hopes about earning his ticket out of H11.

Not this way.

Their next job, as per protocol, was to search and then secure the archive stacks, so any rescuers couldn't accidentally get access to the sensitive information. Adam breathed a sigh of relief that there were no bodies in the stacks. There was no one in the toilet or the galley, so that left just Gerard's office.

Adam had studied the CCTV footage streamed from H11 before the power failure, so he knew they should expect Lydia Twomey and Maggie Willis to be in the office. He prayed that Lydia would be found alive – his feelings of guilt were high enough already without some ghastly bloodbath tragedy. He couldn't believe they were both in there, healthy and holding hands.

The door was jammed, so he and Perry had to get a crew in to cut away the top half of the door. The fact that there was no audible response from inside the room was not a good sign.

Adam poked his head through the hole in the door.

"Lydia? Are you there?"

The room looked as if an elephant had gone beserk in it: the desk was across the door, the chairs were overturned, books had been torn from the shelves, wires snaked across the floor and blood was spattered on the walls. Silk lilies were strewn over the overturned coffee table. Stretched out in the middle of the floor, legs tangled in wires and smashed head resting in an ugly cushion of dark crimson, was the body of Maggie Willis.

"Lydia?"Adam called out, desperation rising.

She was sitting hunched in the corner behind the desk, knees up in front of her chin. She appeared to be shivering. Her face and hair were soaked in blood and Adam could see more blood seeping down her side onto the carpet.

"Lydia! Are you all right?"

Her eyelids drooped, as if she was forcing herself to stay conscious. "I've found the location of the evidence."

Christ, how slowly everything worked! Even once Lydia had told him how to find the location description on Gerard's computer, the 'crime scene' had to be secured and everything recorded before he could replug in the computer and get it booted up. The forensic team suggested Maggie Willis had tripped on the wires, had fallen, stabbing herself and also getting a pair of scissors embedded in her chest, before getting up and attacking Lydia Twomey on the far side of the room, where she had stabbed Lydia before being hit on the head by what seemed to be some sort of pottery. She had finally died through strangulation, but Adam suggested to the forensic team that they conclude that she was probably already dead by then.

While the forensic team worked on the crime scene, a couple of medics attended to Lydia where she lay in the corner of the room. She insisted they shouldn't move her until Adam had found the correct file on the computer, but she had lost a lot of blood from a flesh wound to her side; her voice slurred the words and she drifted into and out of coherence.

She kept muttering 'hesperus7', and 'Hama to Damascus' as if these words might slip from her memory.

Finally, Adam got the computer working and negotiated the passwords given to him by Lydia. He found the evidence location file, a jpeg hidden between images of Hama and Damascus: there it was, emblazoned on the huge plasma screen, the answer to his prayers, a series of file numbers that might look dull, but which meant so much.

He heard Lydia starting to cry softly. To his utter amazement, Adam felt a lump in his own throat, and then he, too, was fighting back the tears.

If Tuesday night had been a living horror, Wednesday morning was pure bliss: the puzzled look on Brooke's face when Adam arrived in Court number 3 with a fat file under his arm gave Adam enough joy to last a lifetime. When Adam proceeded to lodge the evidence with the judges, the look of panic on Brooke's face was priceless. Brooke stammered a request for a brief recess and rushed outside to phone his clients. Adam assumed he was asking them for instructions – did they want to gamble that this was all a bluff from Adam?

Brooke returned to court with a sick grin, like man trying to look brave about going to the scaffold. His clients had rolled the dice and instructed him to continue with the case. It was all about to come out into the open.

Of course, the details never reached the public domain. The panel of three judges, having scrutinised the evidence, ruled that it could not be published. They dismissed Lord Brooke's clients' case and awarded costs against them.

Afterwards, the Home Secretary beamed to the media; she trumpeted it as a vindication of her government's stance and called on the litigants to publicly apologise, which they did, after a fashion. She said the recent football stadium terrorist attack had been contained and all the conspirators had been detained or killed. Britain was 'healthy and immensely strong' in the hands of the present government.

Privately, she praised Adam and told him that his turn would come for some high honour, but she did confess to some misgivings: hadn't there been an 'incident' down in H11 the night before the court case? Weren't there rumours that Adam had been sailing rather too close to the wind on this one? Weren't all the deaths of H11 staff rather an unfortunate coincidence?

"All's well that ends well," had been Adam's gnomic response.

The Home Secretary nodded. "We're all in the results business."

63

ENSEMBLE

Sarah Twomey was awarded an MBE in the Queen's Birthday Honours for services to the Crown and for her community work. Adam Thornton presented her with a new high specification laptop.

Miles Mason left MI5 to work for a well-known merchant bank where he quadrupled his salary (before bonuses).

Reza Hamid took a post teaching creative writing at the University of Hawaii.

Peregrine Webb retired from MI5 and was knighted in the New Year's Honours list. He was elected Seniors Captain of his golf club. His wife Glenys was delighted to become Lady Webb, but was secretly disappointed that her husband didn't get a peerage.

Maddy King, as the only surviving member of H11, was given the task of training up a completely new team in H11, with the promise of a transfer as soon as things were restored to normal 'down there'.

Brian Powell's career was unaffected. He remained on the technical staff at Thames House.

Mark Longford was charged with the murder of Maureen Dennis, but the CPS decided there wasn't enough evidence to prosecute and the case never came to court. He was dismissed from MI5 and found employment with an international security firm.

Nesrin Cevdet was charged with conspiracy to murder, but she broke her bail to abscond to Turkey, from where she was not extradited.

The historic charges against the ex-politician code-named Vilnius were not pursued as it was judged to be 'not in the national interest'. Vilnius retired to his estate in South Africa, and several of his associates followed him abroad.

Lord Brooke moved to a corporate law practice in Singapore.

Adam Thornton continued as Director-General of MI5. He regained his sense of anonymity.

Lydia Twomey spent a week in hospital and another week with her mother before returning to her desk in MI5's Internal Security Section, where she resumed her task vetting new graduate recruits to MI5. She received an internal commendation. She still has a horror of the dark and always sleeps with the lights on.

IF YOU'VE ENJOYED 'SHADOW OF A SHADOW'

STORM FORECAST

"*Line of Duty* meets *Spooks*, John le Carré meets Agatha Christie. A political thriller loaded with haunting menace".

Has Lydia Twomey of MI5 Internal Security found love, or is she entangled with a lethal psychopath?

Fact: in autumn 2018 the handling of security threats from right-wing extremists was transferred from Counter Terrorism [SO15] to MI5. There were 'teething troubles'.

When an informant in a right-wing group is killed and others are threatened, MI5 and SO15 blame each other. Lydia is caught in the middle, not knowing whether the charismatic SO15 officer Giles Mortimer is working with her or scheming to kill her. Her bosses repeatedly ignore her warning of a catastrophic 'storm' planned for Christmas.

Lydia and Giles face a deadly showdown on the icy Essex marshes.

Available as a paperback or Kindle ebook coming soon.

Read on for an extract.

1

BAZ TOMKINS

"your dead Baz. I always wanted to write that & now i can. twat"

"WTF r u talking about"

"your walking dead Baz mate thats the word"

"whos word"

"youll no soon"

"whos word"

Lion has logged out.

Baz slapped his thigh in frustration. "Talk to me, you bastard coward!"

There was no response on the screen – just the image of a fat bulldog in front of a Union Jack.

Baz logged off and sat back in his leather-padded desk chair, puffing out his cheeks. What was all that about? Who was Lion, anyway? Obviously one of the chosen few, otherwise he wouldn't be on the forum, but he (assuming it was a 'he') couldn't be one of the inner circle – Baz would have recognised his style. But Lion knew Baz – and hated him.

Nah, it was probably just one of his many victims, someone he'd trolled in the past, who wanted to put the wind up him and had hacked into the forum. Jesus, Baz had trolled enough snowflakes, bleeding heart liberals, Pakis and gays in his time; he must have racked up several thousand enemies who'd wish him dead. It came with the territory, and he accepted it. It was part of the cross he was happy to bear. He couldn't afford to give a flying toss for what his victims thought or felt. Hate was just a word, part of the game.

But…

He eased himself out of his chair. He couldn't sit there stewing over anonymous trolling from some moron. He had things to do. He hadn't fed his beautiful Paraguayan Rainbow Constrictor, Victor, for nearly a week. It was time for the show.

Baz wheezed as he walked across his room. He had to admit, for a thirty-five-year-old he wasn't in great shape: he hadn't shaved for a few days but his stubble definitely wasn't designer, his dark hair was long and straggly; his belly peeped out from under his Iron Maiden T-shirt. Too long sitting at computers – that was the reason – but what the hell, he was an important part of the political debate of a whole nation.

He took a pair of gardening gloves from the side, put them on and opened up the lid of a small vivarium; he thrust his hand in. He loved the warm light that flooded upwards from each vivarium and he was reassured by the warm air, musty with animal scent that flowed with it. There was no central light in the room, just the illuminated worlds of each reptile environment and the kaleidoscope of computer screens, each displaying their own world.

The rats were tightly packed, so his glove easily closed round a squirming squeaking body. As he lifted it up out of the vivarium, the little bastard started to pee. He resisted the impulse to smash its head on the counter, but instead walked over to the three-foot long vivarium in the corner of the room, opened the top hatch, and popped the struggling rat through the opening.

The rat plopped down on the floor of bark chips, bounced, then scuttled to a corner. Victor was curled up in his hide of branches and leaves at the far end, but Baz could see that he was awake – his chocolate brown and caramel striped head emerged from the cover. Victor was watching the rat panting, just three feet away.

This was the bit that Baz loved. He owned four beautiful snakes and a variety of weird and wonderful lizards, but feeding time always provided endless fascination. Some of the lizards would go into instant action when their prey was dropped into their vivarium, but Victor the Boa was patient, even lazy. He would savour the smell of the rat's fear for a good while before making his leisurely but inevitable move.

But…

Baz found his gaze being torn away from his prized snake back to his central computer screen. He had a range of screens and no less than four computers softly whirring, a bank of blue, green and red lights blinking, as befitted a major online player, a political journalist and blogger – the voice of the right and scourge of lefties, the sword of the righteous, as he tagged himself.

Why had Lion freaked him so badly?

Because… because other little warning signs had been subtly winking at him for the last few days. There was a chat room that no longer accepted his logon, a phone number that was now unavailable – both connected to the inner circle. If he was paranoid, he'd say that he was being frozen out.

And now the death threat.

Nah – it was twattery from some young punk who envied Baz's standing in the online community. When he himself had been a thrusting youngster in the English Defence League, he'd handed out death threats like confetti – he hadn't thought twice about it.

But… Baz knew that in his genre of writing, it paid to be paranoid.

He tore himself away from Victor's meal and walked over to his desk. He opened the third drawer down, rummaged through a selection of phones, and pulled out the one he wanted.

It held only one number. He pressed 'call'.

"The number you have dialled is no longer available. Please dial 07598878946 and ask to speak to Sam."

Baz had been told about this change weeks ago, but he'd put it to the back of his mind. He'd even thought the change might be a good thing – that the new people would just forget about him and leave him alone. He'd hoped against hope that the old blackmailers hadn't handed over all the shit they had on him, and that he was free of the whole shitshow.

But now he needed them.

He redialled, wrote the new number down, and then dialled it using the same phone.

"Hello. Who's speaking please?" The voice was male. Posh accent.

"Is that Sam?"

"Sam speaking. How can I help you, Baz?"

"I think they're onto me."

"Why do you think that?"

"I've had a death threat."

"Who from?"

"Someone tagged as Lion on a chat room."

"What makes you think it's a genuine threat?" This Sam didn't seem concerned.

"I just know." Baz injected just a little urgency into his voice. "I've been in the business long enough. And there are other things, subtle things…"

"Such as?"

"You don't believe me, do you? Listen pal, you don't know me. I don't bullshit."

"I read your blog and I follow your tweets. It's serialised bullshit." Sam chuckled at what passed as his own wit. "So what do you want us to do about it?"

Baz didn't laugh along. "Find out who this Lion is. Protect me!"

"You'll need to give me more details, Baz, like about the chat room and how to access it." Baz could hear him yawn.

"You don't sound like you could give a stuff about my welfare. I've risked my life for you lot."

"Shall we meet up and talk about it, Baz?"

"You don't get it, do you?" Baz could feel his temper rising; this Sam was an idiot. "I can't meet you – I'd be signing my death warrant."

"I think you're exaggerating…"

"You've just inherited me and you don't give a shit about me, do you?"

"Just calm down, Baz…"

Baz hung up on the bastard.

When he got back to Victor, there was no sign of the rat, and Victor was covered by leaves in his hide. The show was over and Baz had missed it.

2

NICHOLAS MASTERS

Nicholas Masters took the reins of his bay gelding Kitchener from his groom Moxon, and raised his left leg, ready for a leg-up from the servant.

He swung up into the saddle, and looked back down. "So Moxon, do you know the connection between a fat slag and a concrete patio?"

Moxon's weather-beaten face remained blank. "No, sir."

"They've both been laid by Poles."

"Good one, sir." Moxon smiled, but Nicholas felt that his man could have laughed or at least smiled more broadly.

Nicholas flicked the reins and applied his heels to Kitchener; the magnificent four-year-old trotted out of the stable yard. Nicholas then turned Kitchener left, onto the gallop round the north field. He wanted to check that there were no tyre tracks round the copses nearest the Gedding road. Just recently there had been a lot of talk about poachers coming up in vans from London to Suffolk, shooting the deer on the estates and selling it back in London. Last night he'd looked out across the fields from their bedroom window and he thought he'd seen a light. By the time he'd dragged Rowena out of bed to confirm it, the light had disappeared.

Kitchener settled into a nice rolling canter; Nicholas relaxed. It was good to be alive on such a beautiful crisp autumn morning, riding a magnificent beast, surveying the well-kept farmland, all of which he (and the bank) owned. He was in the prime of life, fifty-two years old, healthy and quite handsome, an elected County Councillor to boot. People looked up to him. It made him proud to be English.

However, there were clouds on the horizon that couldn't be ignored. The poachers were the least of his worries. The bank was run by Jews who wanted to screw him for every penny and to ruin his businesses, but he and his accountants knew how to get round them; likewise the faceless taxmen and the Communist idiots in Westminster.

No, it was the other political stuff that worried him – it was all getting very heavy. It had been exciting at first and he thought he'd been quite clever playing both sides, but the balancing act was getting much more complicated now that the nice friendly police had been withdrawn. He'd detected some questioning glances between his associates and he'd been rattled yesterday when that chap had turned up to sort out their electrics; Rowena swore she hadn't reported a problem, and when he'd phoned the electric company they denied all knowledge. Nicholas reckoned his house was now bugged, but he didn't know by which side.

He slowed Kitchener to a walk. They were close to the Gedding road and there was a patch of mud ahead. If there were tyre tracks to be found, this is where they would be.

No – there were no tyre tracks. The light he'd seen last night must have been on the road.

But…

There were fresh boot marks. None of his men had been up this end of the estate for at least two days, he was sure. Of course, it could be some errant rambler who'd ignored all the threats to trespassers that Nicholas had placed all round the estate perimeter, but that was unlikely.

A sudden glint in the trees of the copse a hundred and fifty yards to his left caught his eye. He turned in his saddle.

He could see nothing but he felt dread like a sudden dose of acid running through his guts. That glint – he'd seen it so many times when he'd been out on shoots. It was a gun. He knew it instantly.

Viciously, he dug his heels into Kitchener's flanks. The startled horse surged forward, nearly throwing him from the saddle. He kicked again, and Kitchener set off in a wild gallop back along the edge of the field towards the manor house.

There was some sort of pop somewhere behind them; Kitchener stiffened then violently leaped sideways, sending Nicholas into the air. Purely by luck, he landed back in the saddle.

Kitchener was now careering along, totally out of control, maddened by something. Nicholas hung on, his heart hammering, his lips mouthing profanities.

Half a mile on, Kitchener began to slow, his gait oddly awkward, as if he'd gone lame.

"Come on boy, keep going!" Nicholas kicked hard but it had no effect. His horse was slowing to a walk when there might be an assassin closing in on them. He had to get Kitchener going – there was still nearly half a mile to the safety of the house.

He looked back. There was blood streaming down Kitchener's hind left leg.

Kitchener stopped completely, his blood-streaked leg off the ground.

Nicholas kicked for all he was worth.

Kitchener didn't move.

He swung down from the saddle and tried to look at the wound on Kitchener's leg, but the stupid horse shied away, causing him to drop the reins he held. He looked back, but there was no sign of any pursuit. When he tried to grab Kitchener's bridle, the horse awkwardly hobbled back, eyes dilated and teeth showing.

"Bugger you, then," Nicholas muttered, and he started to run to the house, leaving the horse standing at the edge of the field.

Nicholas was reasonably fit from his riding, tennis and squash, and his panic lent him new impetus, so he made good time, until he tripped up and crashed into the hawthorn hedge. The thorns ripped into his face and hands. He loosed profanities into the crisp air. He tried to disentangle himself, but the bloody thorns were hooked into his jacket, causing him to topple forwards again – more ripping of his skin and yet more profanities.

"Damn! Damn!"

Eventually, he was able to crawl out backwards, the thorns scratching across his scalp. All the while he was sure he could hear the assassin approaching, gun trained on his arse. He got to his feet, but there was no one to witness his humiliation with the hedge. As he started to run again, he realised that his pants were moist. Good God, I've pissed myself with fear. How dare somebody do this to me on my own estate!

He had slowed to a walk when he reached the stable yard; he was met by Moxon. "Are you all right, sir?"

"Of course I'm not! Do I look like I'm all right?" He was just about to say that there was a madman out there shooting at him, but instead he strode straight past, to the house.

He burst into the kitchen where the new woman was at the sink. He couldn't remember her name so he just ran on into the corridor, where he stumbled over some Wellington boots that had been left lying out of place. He swore, grabbed at a waxed jacket that was hanging up to steady himself, before crashing into the sitting room.

The golden retriever, Molly, jumped up barking, and Rowena rose from the sofa, throwing down a magazine.

"Good God, Nick, what's happened to you? You look like you've been through a hedge backwards. Have you had a fall?" Her immaculately sculpted blonde hair looked unmoved, but her perfectly made-up face was creased with anxiety.

"I've been shot at. Kitchener's been hit! Get me my phone!"

She picked up the phone from the coffee table.

"No, not that one!"

He stumbled over to the door to his study and pushed through. He took a key from a pewter mug sitting on a bookshelf, unlocked and opened the bottom draw of his oak desk, rooted through some old bank statements and came up with a phone. It held only one number. He pressed 'call'.

"The number you have dialled is no longer available. Please dial 07598878946 and ask to speak to Sam."

"Damnation!"

Nicholas threw the phone down and blundered back into the sitting room. "Give me my phone."

Rowena, eyes as wide as side plates, held it out to him.

He phoned 999. He got an answer almost instantly, but they took him through all the rigmarole of asking him what service he required and then assessed the severity of the crisis, asking the questions with agonisingly slow clarity.

"Someone has shot at me and winged my fucking horse. Is that severe enough?"

When he got through to the police he demanded to talk to James Jones.

"There's no one of that name in our force, sir."

"He's Counter Terrorism – SO15. Get him to phone me – now!"

"We will send a response vehicle to you as soon as we can, sir, with appropriately equipped personnel. It may take a short while for them to arrive at such a rural location, but in the meantime…"

"Get James Jones here."

Nicholas rang off.

Rowena stood across the room, in front of the magnificent arrangement of dahlias.

"Darling, what have you got yourself into now?"